My Past

Versus

My Future

Dollie James Jamerson

JamerSun Publishing, LLC

My Past Versus My Future

Copyright © 2022 Dollie James Jamerson

ISBN-13: 978-1-7370816-2-3

Library of Congress Control Number: 2022909057

JamerSun Publishing, LLC
Canton, Michigan

Printed in the United States of America

My Past

Versus

My Future

Chapter 1

DING, DONG! DING, DONG!

The sound of my doorbell awakened me. I got up, put on my robe and house shoes, then peered at the clock. It was 9:15 in the morning. "Who can it be this early in the morning?" I thought aloud as I walked downstairs. "The yard man was here on Wednesday, and Mrs. Riddle isn't due until next week." As I peeked out the living room window, I saw the UPS truck parked out front. I had forgotten the mirror I ordered from eBay was scheduled for delivery that day.

I opened the door to two men who stood holding a large box. After greeting them, I held the door open so they could push the box inside. "Can you stand it against this wall?" I asked, pointing to my right.

"Yes, ma'am," one of the men said. "This thing is heavy! What is it?"

"A mirror," I replied.

He glanced around the room quickly before heading out the door behind his partner. "Nice house!" he said.

"Thank you!" I said as I closed the door behind him. I then ran upstairs to brush my teeth and wash my face. I don't know why, but I felt the need to tend to those tasks before opening the mirror to finally see what it looked like.

I hurried back downstairs, grabbed a pair of scissors, and prepared to cut open the box. They didn't work, though. I had to get my pliers to pull out the big staples that held the box together. Once that task was accomplished, I was faced with rigid Styrofoam that protected the mirror and plastic that had to be removed. I pulled the plastic away and was in awe at how beautiful it was and how it matched the table perfectly!

After taking the trash to the garage, I stopped in the kitchen to turn on the coffeemaker. I then returned to the family room, sat in my cream-colored chair, and admired the mirror. "I love it!" I thought to myself. I got up, put my hair into a ponytail, and headed back into the kitchen to pour a cup of coffee.

It was about time for my morning devotion and Bible study, which I did on my computer daily—except for Saturdays, when I prepared for the Sunday school lesson, just in case the teacher didn't come, and I would be asked to take her place.

"When I finish my studies, I'm going back to bed to relax and watch TV. I'm not going anywhere today, so I'm keeping on my PJs all day," I said aloud to the room.

I grabbed my coffee—made expertly just the way I liked it, with one teaspoon of sugar and two of cream—and toast, turned on the radio, and listened to the Nashville Gospels while enjoying my morning routine. I fondly reminisced on the times my mom and I would sit and listen to the radio on Saturday mornings, singing along with the songs. I missed her so much and knew she would have loved the mirror because she loved beautiful things.

Two days prior, I had dropped my laptop. The battery case fell out and broke, and the screen was cracked in three places. I threw it in the trash. Troy—one of my coworker's sons—typically worked on my computer whenever I had a problem, but he had moved out of town. I would have to buy a new laptop soon, but the desktop worked well…until now. I went into my office and pushed the power button on my computer, but it didn't come on. I couldn't figure out what was wrong because the keyboard was locked. "Well, I guess this has to go, too!" I thought to myself.

Before setting my mind on trashing it, I got on my cellphone and Googled a technician to come out and work on it. Ferguson's Computer Company's ad drew my attention: "For a fee, I will come out. If parts are needed, there will be an additional charge." I called the company and was told the owner, Mr. Ferguson, was out on a call. "Do you know if he's on-call near Highway 23 and the Riverside subdivision?" I asked.

"I don't know," the young lady replied.

"I really need someone to look at my computer today," I said with desperation.

"I'll call him to see if he's in that area. Can you give me your number so I can call you back?" she asked. I gave her my number and waited for the return call. After about ten minutes, she called back and said, "He said he could be there around 11:30. What's your address?"

"I live on Riverside Drive. I'm next to the last house at the end of the street on the right. It's a large brick house with brown trim, a long driveway, and a two-car garage attached to the house. He can't miss it." We said our goodbyes before ending the call.

Chapter 2

I returned to the breakfast room to finish my coffee as I flipped through a Good Housekeeping magazine. Minutes later, the doorbell rang. "Is it 11:30 already?" I asked myself. When I looked at the clock, it was only 10:45. I hurried to the door and asked, "Who is it?"

The deep voice on the other side said, "Mr. Ferguson, the computer man." I opened the door to a black man in his early 60s at the most, with curly salt-and-pepper hair. He was neatly dressed and drove a navy-blue double-cab Ford Ranger truck with "Ferguson's Computer Company" printed on its side. He looked at me and said, "Good morning. Are you the one with the computer problem?"

"Yes, sir. Come in."

He didn't move. He just stood there looking at me. "What's your name?" he asked.

"Lexie Harris."

"Ms. Harris, it would be nice if you got dressed before I come in."

I was astonished at what he said. "Yes, sir." I closed the door, went to my room, and slipped on a pair of jeans and a sweatshirt, all while feeling embarrassed. I wondered if he could see my nakedness through my PJs. While getting dressed, I thought, "I wonder if he's the man who lives down by the highway?"

Once fully dressed, I returned downstairs, opened the door, and invited him in again. As he entered, he looked around and stated, "You have a beautiful home."

"Thank you." I led him to my office.

"I didn't know this house was down here. I live in the second house off the highway on the same side," he commented.

"I have been here a little over seven years now."

As he fished through his toolkit, he said, "This is really a lovely place."

I stood there, feeling like a fool. A total stranger had to tell me to get dressed. I was sure I wasn't showing any skin except for my arms. I suppose it wasn't a good look for a man to come and work on my computer, and I was still in my PJs. I should have known better. I thought of the scripture, "He doesn't want his good to be evil spoken of" (Romans 14:16).

While working on my computer, Mr. Ferguson drummed up a conversation. "My son is here from the Army for a week. He's outside waiting for me in the truck. He is going to Iraq when he leaves, but today, he's taking his old Pop out for lunch." He paused and then laughed before saying, "He thinks I work too much."

"That's wonderful!" I replied. "I was in the Air Force for eight years."

He stopped what he was doing, looked at me, and exclaimed, "You don't look old enough to go into the Air Force!"

"Yes, sir." I let out a soft giggle. "I went in right out of high school."

"My son is retiring from the Army when he returns from Iraq. He will have served five years."

"Is he your only son?" I inquired.

"Yes, I have one boy and two girls." When he finished working on my computer and gathering his tools, he said, "If you need any other work done on your computer, call my shop and make another appointment. I'll be happy to come by."

"Yes, sir. I will."

"The cost for today's service is $75.00: $60.00 for labor and $15.00 for me coming out," he stated.

I thought it would have been much more. I handed him $80.00 at the same time he gave me the receipt and thanked him for coming. He paused when he looked at the money. Before he could say another word, I said, "Thanks for coming out on such short notice."

He smiled and replied, "Thank you."

"No, thank you for coming out so soon," I said as I escorted him to the door. I saw a man sitting in the truck, smiling at Mr. Ferguson as he climbed in and closed the door. I wondered if he would tell his son about me coming to the door in my PJs. "What a nice man," I thought to myself as I took a seat at my computer. I wondered if he was strict on his girls like he was stern when he told me to get dressed. I thought of my daddy at that moment. He didn't like me wearing pants—loose or tight. As a matter of fact, he preferred I wore dresses and skirts…and no

8

lowcut tops. Daddy would say, "Ain't no child of mine going to be walking around showing her body!"

He also didn't want me or anybody else walking around the house without shoes.

I recall one Sunday, after returning home from church, Mama was cooking dinner. She had scalloped potatoes in a glass dish in the oven. When it was time to remove them, Mama asked me to take them out for her. I grabbed a wet dish towel off the sink, pulled the food out of the oven, and it fell to the floor. The dish broke, and glass went everywhere. The steaming hot scalloped potatoes landed on one of my feet. I screamed so loud, Mama and Daddy ran into the kitchen quickly.

"Let's take her to the emergency room!" Mama screamed with panic in her voice.

"Rose, calm down," Daddy said. "She is going to be alright."

Mama called for my brother Leon to clean up the glass and potatoes.

Daddy was so attentive to me. I saw the compassion and love he had for me while trying to make me feel better. Mama was crying. "Lexie, you are never to put a wet towel on a glass dish that's hot," Daddy said. He then turned to Leon and instructed him to break off a piece of Mama's Aloe Vera plant and bring it to him. He squeezed the gel out of the plant onto the burn on my foot. The gel took the heat away and made the pain subside. I could see the concern for me on my Daddy's face. When he saw I felt better, he said, "Do you see now why I told you to wear shoes in the house?"

I also remember Leon being angry at me because he had to do my chores for a couple of days.

Chapter 3

I sat staring at the computer screen, thinking of my family. My Daddy was hit and killed by a drunk driver when I was in middle school. He was crossing the street on his way to work at the time. My brother Leon was killed in a drive-by shooting when I was in the Air Force. He was walking out of the store, and someone passing by shot him and another man. I didn't make it home until a day after his funeral. When I got home, Mama was devastated and cried all the time. Mama didn't want me to leave her when it was time for me to return to Germany, but I had to go.

I was back in Germany about six months and was attacked, raped, and left to die. That's a time I wish I could forget, but it often popped up its ugly head, causing me to remember the fear I went through on that day all over again. After I retired from the Air Force and returned home, my Mama had a heart attack and died. All my close family was gone.

I sometimes found myself feeling lonely. I had no close family or friends. I had a couple of cousins, but I didn't see them or even know where they were. Yes, I talked to people at my job and in the church, but they weren't people with whom I bonded, visited, or hung out.

My Mama's oldest and only sister lived in Michigan. Her name was Ida, and she had two sons. Aunt Ida was on her way home from work one day, hit by an 18-wheeler, and was killed. My aunt's passing was really hard on my Mama. I remember we would go to Ypsilanti for Thanksgiving, and my Aunt Ida's family would come to our house for Christmas. (Mama told me Aunt Ida's husband died when I was two years old.)

During the summer one year, we went to Ypsilanti to Aunt Ida's son David's high school graduation open house. She had made a punch bowl cake that I recall looked so pretty and tasted good, too. I took pictures of it, and Aunt Ida gave me the recipe so I could make it when I got home. I remember her saying, "All you have to do is layer it. No cooking at all!" She also showed me how to make a tie blanket. "It is so simple to make," she said. "All you have to do is cut and tie it!" I liked the way she simplified everything. Each time we went to Aunt Ida's house, Mama would say I was so spoiled because I was the only girl. Aunt Ida gave me the tie blanket she showed me how to make because the material had cars on it. "You can give it to your son when you have one," she said. I remember telling her I was never getting married, to which she replied, "As pretty as you are, some

10

smooth-talking guy will come along and sweep you right off your feet. Before you know it, you will be married and have a house full of children!" I thought of how funny she was and always had me laughing. Mama would laugh at her, too.

Aunt Ida's youngest son, David, went to Michigan State University, and Carl, the oldest son, worked in the truck plant. Mama said that after Aunt Ida died, the insurance company paid them a lot of money. "Hmm… I haven't seen them since Mama died," I thought to myself.

My Daddy's brother, Andy, had three children: a boy named Matthew and two girls, Kathy and Liz. Uncle Andy was killed during the Desert Storm war. Mathew was ten, Kathy was eight, and Liz was four at the time. As I thought about them, I decided I needed to look for them. I didn't know if they were still in the city or perhaps married with their own families.

Chapter 4

The ringing of my phone brought me back to reality. Mr. Ferguson called to ask if he had left his receipt book behind. I looked around and saw it sitting on the table by the door. "Yes, sir. It's here."

"I'll be there to pick it up in about 15 minutes," he responded.

While waiting for his arrival, I sat in my cream-colored chair near the table where his receipt book was and looked lovingly at my mirror. "I'm going to love that mirror on that wall," I said aloud. "I'm going to get a green plant to set beside it and two big butterflies to place on the wall over the plant."

I looked out the window just as Mr. Ferguson walked up to the door. I opened it and handed him the receipt book. "Thank you," he said. "When you start getting older, it's easy to lay things down and forget where they are."

"No, you are not old. I think you were just excited to go and spend time with your son."

He laughed and replied, "Maybe so."

"Thanks again for working on my computer, Mr. Ferguson. Have a great day!" I watched as he walked back to his truck and waved at the person sitting in the passenger seat before closing the door.

That day, I worked on my Sunday school lessons until late afternoon.

Chapter 5

After church on Sunday, we had choir rehearsal for our Church Anniversary that was coming up at the end of the month. That Monday, I went for my daily jog after work and passed by Mr. Ferguson's house (his truck was in the driveway). I knew I had seen that man before he visited my home! At that moment, I recalled him telling me I needed to get antivirus protection on my computer and how I thought to myself, "I think I need to buy a new computer!"

That Wednesday, as I prepared for my daily jog, I decided to ride my bike—just in case it started to rain as forecasted. As I approached Mr. Ferguson's house, I noticed a man standing in the yard. I spoke, and he spoke back, adding with a smile, "Your husband lets you ride by yourself?"

"I don't have a husband, so yes, I always either jog or ride my bike by myself," I said as I cruised to a stop.

"So, that means you don't have a man around, right?"

"No, I don't have a man around."

"Well, since you don't, can I jog or ride my bike with you?" By that point, he is laughing at our playful exchange.

"Yes," I replied, "but I have already ridden one mile. Going back to my house will be it for me today."

He slowly approached, eyeing me from head to toe. "I'm Myles."

I knew that name from somewhere. "I'm Lexie." I then remembered where I knew him from: grade school.

"Lexie?"

"Yes, that's me!"

"Where have you been all my life?" he said with a wide grin.

"In 4th grade, you sat behind me in class, pulling my ponytails."

"I did?"

"Yes, you did. You have grown up, but you still look the same, Myles."

He stood in place with a puzzled look on his face as if he were trying to remember me. "Oh, my God! You're the little girl with the ponytails and the thick glasses!"

"Yes, I did wear glasses." I was laughing at how he stood there looking at me in shock.

"Leon Harris is your brother, right?"

"Yes, he was my brother."

"I lost contact with him when your family moved. How is he doing?" Myles asked.

I suppose he didn't hear me correctly when I used the word 'was.' I looked down at the ground, feeling the hurt of my brother's death all over again. That day was the first time someone had asked about him since his death. I took a deep breath and replied, "He was killed in a drive-by shooting four years ago."

"I'm so sorry to hear that," Myles replied with a sad look. "Did they find out who did it?"

"No, they never did."

He shook his head in disbelief and murmured, "I am so sorry to hear that. Are you alright?"

"Yes, I'm okay. It's just that you are the first person to ask about him since he died."

"I'm sorry," he said as he walked over and touched my bike. "I'm so sorry for your loss." The moment was disturbed by someone calling him from inside the house. "Lexie, it was nice seeing you again. So, you live down the road?"

"Yes, down the road next to the last house on the right."

"I was at that house a couple of days ago with my dad. You were the one with the computer problem, right?"

"Yes, that was me." I still wondered if his dad told him I came to the door in my PJs.

"You have a nice house. Maybe I'll get to run or bike ride with you before I leave for Iraq," he said with a smile as he walked back toward the house. "Wait. I feel raindrops. Do you think you can make it home before the rain comes?"

"Yes, the sky is turning dark, but I think I can make it."

"I can take you home if you want me to," he offered.

"No, thank you. I should be home before it rains harder. Bye for now!"

"Okay. Bye!" He then turned and went inside.

As I rode home, I thought, "Did I talk too much to him? Oh, my God! He's tall, has pretty brown skin and beautiful white teeth, and he sure was looking good in that muscle shirt! No doubt, he lifts weights. He reminds me of The Rock and has curly hair like Rick Fox. And those hazel brown eyes? Wow! I don't know what cologne he was wearing, but he smelled good!"

Just as I rode into the garage, the downpour came.

Chapter 6

Friday morning, I opened the garage, preparing to leave for work. As I walked out to get in my car, a motorcycle drove up my driveway. "Who could this be?" I thought. I watched as the rider got off and removed his helmet. "Myles! It's you!"

He laughed and said, "Good morning, Lexie! Yes, it's me. I'm stopping by to let you know I am leaving for Iraq tomorrow, but I see you are on your way out."

"I'm on my way to work. I have a training to do at 11."

"Don't let me hold you up," he replied as he turned to get back on his motorcycle.

"No, no. You are not holding me up. I was going in early to set up a couple of things, so I have a few minutes to talk. Are you ready to leave for Iraq?" I asked as he walked toward me.

"No, I am not. Since I saw you the other day, you have been on my mind. I'm sorry to stop by unannounced, but I didn't get your number when we talked."

I smiled and let out a little laugh before saying, "Ohhhh! The little girl with the ponytails and thick glasses was on your mind?"

He smiled back and said flirtingly, "You are not a little girl anymore. I like what I see."

"Okay, okay. Nice line, Myles. Seriously, though, I'll be praying for you. Be safe over there."

"I'll need all the prayers I can get!" he said with all seriousness. He walked back to his bike, put on his helmet, and finished the conversation by saying, "I look forward to seeing you when I return. Oh! You sure are looking nice, and I like your car." I drove a red Grand Am.

"Thank you. I like your motorcycle, too, but it's nothing I want to ride."

He burst into a fit of laughter as he got on his motorcycle and rode away.

Chapter 7

As I drove to work, I thought about what Myles said: "Since seeing me the other day, I had been on his mind." I then found myself thinking, "Too late now! He's on his way to Iraq. He is handsome and has a beautiful smile. And boy, he smells good!"

Talking to Myles made me think of my brother Leon. He, too, was nice-looking, loved sports, and always talked about getting a motorcycle. He also told me he would fight anyone who messed with me. He was so protective of his little sister. When Leon would get upset with me, he would call me a car because Mama named me after the Lexus brand but spelled my name L-E-X-I-E. I can hear Mama telling him, "Boy, leave that girl alone!" I would laugh, stick out my tongue at him, and go stand by Mama. He would be so angry at me.

When Daddy was killed, he started acting as if he were the man of the house. We all took it hard when Daddy died, but Leon remained strong for our mom and me. He then started calling me "Pretty Girl" because that's what our Daddy always called me.

Leon cried the day I enlisted in the Air Force, saying he didn't want me to go. I told him I would be okay and asked that he take care of Mama. When I came home after Basic Training, he was so happy to see me wearing my uniform. Sadly, before I retired, he was killed. Although the news of his passing truly hurt me, Mama was devastated. I thought she wasn't going to make it another day.

My thoughts then turned to Howard Blair. He was a man I met six months before my retirement. He, too, served in the Air Force for 12 years as a Recruiting Officer and had lived in San Antonio, Texas. His job took him to different cities throughout the United States to recruit young men and women. We talked nearly every day when he was in town but started dating roughly four months before I retired. He was a nice-looking man who stood about 6'2" and was very quiet. When he smiled, the cuteness of the dimple in his chin shined through.

After I retired, Howard flew to Nashville to meet Mama. She enjoyed talking to him, but I could see uncertainty on her face. Once back home from dropping him off at the airport, Mama said, "Howard is a nice-looking man, but he is too quiet for me. He acts as if he's hiding something." The way she said it and how she looked when she said it, I could easily see the question marks in her eyes.

"He is okay, Mama. He is just a private man," I said assuredly. The strange look on her face never dissipated.

Two weeks later, I had to fly back to San Antonio to complete discharge papers for my retirement. I called Howard to let him know I would be in town. He explained he was in Atlanta and wouldn't return until that Sunday afternoon but offered for my mother and me to stay at his apartment until then (the spare key was under the mat by his front door).

Mama and I flew out that Friday morning on Southwest Airlines. Once we arrived, I rented a car and drove to his apartment so that I could change clothes for my 1:00 p.m. appointment. Mama stayed behind while I went to my meeting, saying she wanted to relax after the long flight. After finalizing everything, I picked up Mama, and we went out to dinner to celebrate. We then drove around, looking for a mall. That was one thing I could say about my Mama: She loved to shop and buy beautiful things! By the time we returned to the apartment, we were exhausted. We watched a movie together and then went to bed.

We got up early, loaded the car, and went out for breakfast on Saturday morning. We then went sightseeing at the San Antonio Riverwalk and The Alamo. After lunch, we headed for the airport. Along the way, I got on the wrong highway and had to drive out of the way until we could exit. I remember how Mama had me laughing. She was sitting in the passenger seat, praying:

"Lord, help us! Lord, we will miss our flight, and this girl doesn't know where she's going. Help us, Lord! We need Your help!" She concluded by telling God she wasn't going anywhere else with me.

"Mama, we are on the right highway now. See? The sign right there says 'To the Airport.'"

"Thank you, Jesus!" she exclaimed. I laughed at her while she fanned herself with her hands. We arrived in time to make our flight and landed back in Nashville at 6:30 p.m.

The following weekend, on that Saturday morning, Howard had a layover in Nashville on his return trip from Washington, D.C. I picked him up from the airport and drove to Mama's house, where she had prepared lunch for us. I then took him back so that he could fly out at 5:40 p.m. A baby's pacifier fell out as he pulled the ticket out of his pocket to see which gate he would be flying out of. He had an astonished look on his face and said, "Oh, my God! The baby's pacifier! I know Kathy is looking everywhere for this!"

"Who is Kathy?!" I asked, confused.

He didn't answer me directly but said, "I picked up my sister the other day. She flew in from Dallas for a job interview and is at my apartment."

"I can tell the baby is a girl. Pink pacifier…" My voice trailed off.

He smiled and said, "Yes, she is nearly three years old." He looked down at his ticket, noticing the time. "They are boarding now. I can't wait to see you next weekend. Call me!" He gave me a quick kiss before turning to board the plane.

While driving home, I thought, "He never told me he had a sister with a baby."

Chapter 8

The weekend I was scheduled to fly to visit Howard, I had a workshop at my job that conflicted with my plans. I called to let him know I wasn't coming, only to have a woman answer his phone. "This must be his sister," I thought. "Hi. I'm Lexie—a friend of Howard. Is he there?"

"Yes, he is. And why are you calling for my husband?" the woman said venomously.

A sense of fear overcame me when she said 'my husband.' "I met your husband when I was stationed at Lackland Air Force Base. I was calling to see how he's doing," came my response.

"He is doing great. Your name is Lexie?"

"Yes."

"Well, I'll tell him you called." Before I could say another word, she ended the call.

Nervousness overtook me. I cried as I thought about Howard and I dating for four months, and he never told me he was married. When I got home from work and told Mama what happened, she said, "I thought there was something strange about that man. I don't think he even lives in that apartment he let us stay in."

"Mama, why do you say that?!"

"It didn't smell like a man's apartment. I didn't see any clothes in his closet, no toothbrush, no socks or underwear. Nothing that made it look lived in."

"Mama! You went through his stuff?!"

"Yes, I sure did!"

I had to laugh, but I was hurting. I really liked him. Six weeks passed, and I hadn't heard a peep from Howard…until one Friday evening. Mama and I were eating dinner when my house phone rang. I answered. "Hello?"

"Hi, Lexie! How are you doing?" It was him on the other end, sounding cheerful as if nothing had happened.

"Why are you calling? I think you have the wrong number. Bye!"

"Lexie! Don't hang up! I need to see you."

"Oh? You do?" I asked with dripping sarcasm.

"Yes, I'm in Kentucky. Can you drive down?"

"For what, Howard? I don't date married men and would very much appreciate you not calling me anymore."

As I spoke, he was trying to cut me off. "Wait! It wasn't' supposed to turn out like that. Please don't hang up on me!" I stood there holding the phone while he tried to explain why he did what he did. "When I met you, yes, I was married but had been separated over four months. I moved out and into the apartment where you and your Mama stayed. Later, I found out Kathy was five months pregnant with a boy. I was so happy to hear she was pregnant with my son. I moved back in with her but kept the apartment until the lease was up. Then, I met and fell in love with you. Lexie, I didn't know how to let you go."

"Tell your wife to drive down to see you. Like I said, I don't date married men. Bye, Howard." At that, I hung up the phone. I wanted to tell him to go to hell, but Mama was looking at me.

She came over and hugged me, saying, "Lexie, you handled that well."

As the months passed, I never heard from Howard again.

Chapter 9

Two years later, Mama had a heart attack and died. That was a devastating time for me. I took six weeks off from work, trying to get myself together. Arriving at work, I sat in my car and thought about my Mama, Howard, and Myles. For some reason, when I saw Myles, he reminded me of Howard. They were both tall and handsome, but, in my opinion, Myles was better-looking than Howard. I headed into my office to prepare for the workshop. I thought to myself, "This is going to be a long afternoon. I will be glad when this day is over."

On my drive home, I was grateful the day had come to an end—although I did enjoy the food they served during the workshop. Once home, I stopped at the mailbox to grab the mail. As I turned into the driveway, I reflected on the two years Mama lived with me after the house was built. When I got home from work, she would be waiting for me with dinner ready. Since her passing, I realized just how much I missed her. I pulled into the garage, turned off the car, and remained in my seat for a few minutes longer. "This house is too large for me. Should I sell it and move into an apartment? Lord, what should I do?" I thought.

I finally got out of the car, went inside, and set my purse on the island in the kitchen. I then proceeded to the wall where I had photos of all my family members. Tears began to fall. I went upstairs to my room and prayed, telling God how lonely and broken I was and asking Him to help me. A week later, I was shopping at Walmart and met a woman named Mrs. Riddle. She talked to and prayed with me right there in the store. I knew then that God heard my prayer and sent her to me.

Chapter 10

I had been attending Morning Star Church all my life with my family in the suburbs of Nashville. Since they were all gone, I didn't like driving to the suburbs alone, so I started going to church where two of my coworkers attended. It wasn't close to my house, but it was closer than driving to the suburbs. The church's minister had planned a trip to The Mall of America for the youth and single people in the congregation. We had a meeting to discuss who would be chaperoning the trip and the sleeping arrangements. They chose me as one of the chaperones, saying I acted more mature than any of the other young people who were going. In addition to me, there were two married couples, the bus driver, and his wife.

Two weeks before the trip, Pastor Montgomery's son, Keith, and another boy were in a car accident. Keith's leg was broken, and he had a couple of bruised ribs. The other boy wasn't hurt. The trip was canceled. I never had a conversation with Keith other than speaking to him after church was over. Since he wasn't coming to church because of his leg, I started calling to check on him, cheer him up, and to see if there was anything he needed (he was a year older than I was and acted shy).

When Keith first started coming back to church after the accident, he rode with his dad. After service, he and I would talk while his dad greeted the parishioners after the service. When he started driving again, he would come by my house after church. I enjoyed talking to him, and we grew to be close friends. No "benefits." Nothing romantic. He always talked about his job, the churches and places he traveled with his parents, and the things he used to do when he was younger. I enjoyed his company. He made me laugh, which helped remove the loneliness I often felt when alone. I loved him but wasn't in love with him. He was simply someone I could talk to comfortably. We would have dinner at my house or go to the movies. Sometimes, we would watch a movie in my theater room. We laughed and joked with each other and played board games. He reminded me of my brother, although they didn't look at all alike (Keith looked like Eddie Murphy and was 5'6" tall with a light brown complexion). Keith did many of the same things as my brother. I guess that's why I enjoyed his company.

Six months or more had passed, and our friendship continued to grow. One Saturday, Keith stopped by just as I was putting a shelving unit together to put my

CDs on in the theater room. He worked on the shelf with me and out of nowhere said, "Lexie, everybody at the church is talking about how much time we spend together. They think we are involved with each other. My dad thinks we are spending a lot of time together, too."

"Does your dad think we are sleeping together?! I hope you told him we are friends and that nothing is happening here!"

He started laughing and replied, "What if we get married to hush up the gainsayers?"

I started laughing then. "Are you crazy? You are my friend! I love you, but I'm not in love with you. I repeat: You are my friend."

"You can marry your friend, can't you? I know we don't love each other. I know we are friends. And I know we like being around each other."

I thought of what he said. If I married the pastor's son, that would be awesome! I would have prestige because the Montgomerys are known throughout Nashville, and I would be well-known if I married the son of the Pastor of New Harvest Church. I replied with excitement, "Yes! Let's get married! Who knows? We can grow together and fall in love with one another."

Keith was thrilled! He immediately called his dad to tell him the news. In response, Pastor Montgomery was so happy, he announced our engagement in church that Sunday.

I was so caught up in the moment that we set a date and married that same year on September 20th. We had a big wedding. All the members of the church helped with the decorations and reception. It was truly a beautiful ceremony, and everyone was happy for us. Our honeymoon was spent at my house, watching movies and talking like we did before marriage. Keith fell asleep on the couch that night, and I retired to my bedroom.

The next day, Pastor Montgomery was rushed to the hospital. Keith stayed there with him, and when he was released, he stayed at his daddy's house.

Two weeks after the wedding, reality set in. "What have I done? I married Keith for his company and the prestige I could get. I shouldn't have married him. I had never kissed him outside of the peck on the lips when the pastor said, 'You may kiss your bride.' I couldn't kiss him romantically! He is my friend! Oh, my God! What have I done?" I cried out aloud.

Chapter 11

I tried hard to be a wife to Keith without loving him. Soon, he started acting as if something was on his mind. I think he felt the same way I did but didn't want to initiate the conversation. We slept in different bedrooms and didn't consummate our marriage until after Thanksgiving.

One day, after work, I stopped by to check on Keith's dad. When I arrived, he was in bed, saying he wasn't feeling well. I stayed with him, waiting for Keith to get off work. I got sleepy and went to lie down in one of the bedrooms, slowly drifting off to sleep. When I woke up, Keith was in bed with me. I knew he didn't want to sleep in a different room in his daddy's house because we were "married." That was the night we consummated our marriage. It was funny when it happened because it was ridiculous. It wasn't romantic at all. As a matter of fact, we couldn't stop laughing at each other because I just didn't seem right, even though we were "married."

On the last day of November, Pastor Montgomery was rushed back to the hospital with high blood sugar. At the time, Keith was out of town visiting a friend in Little Rock. When the pastor was released from the hospital, I took him home and stayed with him until Keith returned that night. We slept in the same bed at his dad's house again because we didn't want Keith's dad to know we were having problems.

One of the sisters from the church was his dad's caregiver. She would come to the house on Tuesday every week for two hours. As for me, I started going by every other day after work to cook his food and do his laundry if the caregiver didn't get to do it.

When Keith came home, he acted as if something was on his mind. He stayed upstairs in the theater room or would be in the sitting room reading his Bible. Most of the time, he was on the phone talking to his friend. I wouldn't say much of anything to him because I knew he was more concerned about his father than our "marriage."

In February the following year, I learned I was pregnant. We both wondered how it happened, especially since we had only been together twice.

"Are you sure it's my baby?" Keith asked.

"Why would you say something like that?" I yelled.

"I know that man named Daniel from your job has been here."

"Keith, I cannot believe you would imply something happened between Daniel and me. That man stopped by here to bring my driver's license that he found on the sidewalk in front of my job!"

"Well, how did he know where you lived? And you sure did talk to him for a long time when he was here."

"Keith! Helloooo! My address is on my license! Oh, my God! You are crazy!" I hollered as I walked away from him. I couldn't believe he was questioning the paternity of his child already!

I often suffered from morning sickness and didn't attend church as I did in the past. In March, I told Pastor Montgomery I was pregnant. He was happy and said he would be glad to be a granddaddy. He told me Keith was a mama's boy and mentioned how his wife spoiled him since he was her only son and baby boy. He mentioned they also had two daughters who lived in Chicago. Keith had told me about his two sisters when we got married, although neither came to the wedding because one of them was in the hospital.

The last week in April, Pastor Montgomery was rushed to the hospital again with high blood sugar. Once they got that under control and he was preparing to be discharged, his blood pressure went up so high, he had a stroke and died.

I was at work when Keith called and told me. I was in a total state of shock. I was just getting to know him as a father. He was a good man and a superb pastor. I felt sorry that he died before his first grandchild was born. Needless to say, Keith was devastated when his daddy died. He stayed at the church all day and at his dad's house at night. After the funeral, he remained at his dad's house with his two sisters, cleaning the house to prepare it for renting.

After the house was rented, Keith's sisters returned to Chicago, and Keith disappeared. I had no idea where he went. I thought he was with his sisters. Three days later, he came back and said he was visiting a friend before going into his bedroom in my house. He seemed different. I thought it was because of his dad's passing, but when I tried to talk to him, he wouldn't say anything one way or another.

Chapter 12

Three months after Pastor Montgomery died, the church appointed Keith to be their new Pastor. I became the First Lady and loved the attention I received when we went to other churches in the district. A couple of times, I spoke at prayer breakfasts. Keith was a good pastor who knew the scriptures. More people joined the church, and he started a New Members' Class and a Recovering Drug Addict Class. In two of the classrooms, he converted them into a daycare center.

I went on maternity leave and started working from home. My doctor recommended I stay off my feet because they kept swelling, and I continued to have high blood pressure. Plus, my back hurt something awful.

The night of August 24th, I went into labor. Sister Owens drove me to the hospital because Keith was out of town at a Church Leadership Conference. Keith Junior (KJ) was born on August 25th. He was a beautiful baby, weighing in at seven pounds. When Keith got back into town, he drove me home from the hospital. He said he was happy that I was doing well, but he didn't seem excited about the baby. Everyone said KJ looked like me but had Keith's eyes and lips.

Keith didn't spend much time with the baby because he was busy doing church work. He quit his job and devoted all his time to the church. I worked out of my office at home, and when KJ turned three months old, I started going back to church regularly. I also returned to my job in the Human Resources Department for the city of Nashville. I worked every day, but on Fridays, I worked half-days. While I was working, I put KJ in the daycare at the church.

On Wednesday nights, I taught a class at church from 6-7 p.m. with young girls ages 12 to 16. Sister Owens was my assistant. We taught the girls how to carry themselves as they become young ladies in the Lord. One week out of the month, they made tie blankets for the nursing home and local children's hospital.

Five months or so had passed, and I began to take notice of a woman named Brenda Lee, who had been attending services for about six months and was in the New Members' Class. I would sometimes see her exiting the Pastor's (Keith's) office. She smiled when she saw me, but we never had a conversation. She reminded me of Diana Ross' daughter, who had a role in one of the soap operas, but she was taller and had a pretty smile. I noticed Keith's whole attitude changed when Brenda joined the church.

One day, while we were home, I asked Keith, "Did you know Brenda before she started coming to church?"

"Yes, I knew her before she went away to college," he replied while playing with KJ. He finally looked up at me and asked, "Why do you ask?"

"Well, it doesn't look good for her to be coming out of your office every time I get there."

"She's working on Mother Stone's birthday surprise!"

"That's my job, Keith. And Mother Stone's birthday is two months away," I said accusingly.

"You didn't say anything about it, so I told her yes when she asked if she could do it," he answered sharply.

"She's in the New Members' Class. How did she know anything about Mother Stone's birthday?

"Look. She's doing it now, and that's that," he answered with a condescending attitude.

"I'm available if she needs my help," I offered. I picked up the baby and headed upstairs.

He called out, "We have everything together. We'll let you know when it's time for the decorations and food."

I stopped, turned around, and stated, "You are acting as if she's the First Lady instead of me." He didn't respond. He just walked past me up the stairs, eating an apple. I knew he didn't love me, but the difference in his attitude toward me ever since Brenda showed up on the scene was outrageous and demeaning.

Chapter 13

Keith was already gone when I got up the following morning. On my way to work, I dropped off KJ at the church's daycare, wondering why his daddy didn't take him with him. After picking up KJ from daycare, I went to Keith's office. His door was closed. I tried to open it, but it was locked. I knocked on the door and wondered where he could be? After all, his car was in the parking lot. As I turned to walk away, he opened the door with papers in his hand. He looked genuinely surprised to see me. "Oh! You're off work early today?" he asked.

"I have always worked half a day on Friday. Plus, I'm tired. I have a meeting tonight at work, so you need to be home by 5:00 to get the baby. Why was your door locked?"

"I didn't know it was locked. I'll keep KJ here and bring him home with me since you're tired."

"No, I'll take him home with me now. You look like you are busy yourself. Let me sit down and take off these heels. I need to put on my flat shoes. This boy is heavy." I passed KJ off to his daddy and entered the office. There sat Brenda by his desk with papers in her hand, giving the impression that they were busy doing paperwork. She looked surprised to see me. I thought to myself, "What type of paperwork are they working on for a birthday party that's five weeks away?" I spoke to her as I took a seat and pulled the flat shoes out of my bag. She spoke back with a shy-looking grin on her face. Keith remained standing, holding KJ and looking at me as if to say, "Hurry up!" "I see you two are busy working on the birthday party," I said as I put on my shoes. "Remember: I need you home by 5:00. Don't forget." I took KJ out of his arms, leaving Keith standing there looking silly.

I had KJ in bed with me when Keith got home. He came into my room and asked, "How are you feeling?"

"Rested since taking a nap."

"Good," he replied before heading into his bedroom.

In reality, I wasn't upset with Keith for having Brenda in his office. It was just the principle of it. I was trying to make it work between the two of us, but I felt like it wasn't working out how I envisioned.

I got dressed, put KJ in his crib in his room, and told Keith I was leaving for my meeting.

Chapter 14

Three weeks later, I stopped by the daycare to pick up KJ and then headed to Keith's office to remind him of KJ's upcoming appointment. When I turned the corner, he was standing in the hallway talking to Brenda. They were in such a deep conversation, I was nearly on top of them before they saw me coming. When Brenda saw me, she said, "Hi, First Lady! You are looking nice today!"

"Thank you."

She had this suspicious smile when she said, "I stopped by to let Pastor know things are going good for Mother Stone's birthday."

"Why did you have to stop by?" I asked. "What's wrong with the telephone? Couldn't you have called to tell him that?"

Brenda looked at Keith before responding. "I was passing by, so I just stopped in to let Pastor know."

"I thought you lived on Baldwin Street on the Southside of town. You drove all the way over here just to tell him that?"

Keith must've felt the tension in me rising. "She was coming from work," he interjected.

"I thought she worked at the school down the street from her house," I said, eyeing Brenda carefully.

"Pastor, I will see you on Sunday," she said before walking away.

"Keith, what is going on here? And why don't you answer your phone when I call? And why is Brenda always in your office?!"

"Like I said, she just stopped by to tell me how things are going with the party."

"She drove all the way across town to tell you that when the phone is right there?" I pointed at the phone sitting on his office desk.

He took KJ from my arms and started playing with him. "Why are you here anyway?"

"I tried to call you first, but you didn't answer your phone. I stopped by to remind you of KJ's appointment tomorrow morning at 10:00. It's always late when you get home, and I'm already asleep. I don't get to see you before you leave in the morning, so you need to answer your phone when I call." He stood there looking as if something was on his mind. "Keith, do you hear me talking to you?"

"I think I have a business meeting tomorrow at 11:00."

"When were you going to tell me?" I asked.

"I forgot about KJ's appointment." I noticed he didn't apologize.

"Okay. I'll just call and let my supervisor know I'll be in late. I wish you would have let me know before now. After the appointment, I'll drop him off at daycare, but you will have to pick him up because it will be late when I get off work."

"Okay," he replied.

I took KJ from his arms and left. In my gut, I knew something was going on between Keith and Brenda. For the next couple of weeks, I barely spoke a word to him. He would always come home late and go directly to his room, the theater room, or be on his phone.

After service one Sunday, as I was coming out of the daycare, Mother Hamilton met me outside of my office and said, "First Lady, can I talk to you?"

"Yes, come in. This boy is heavy." She chuckled. When we got into my office, I asked her to have a seat.

She sat there looking at me for a moment before she started talking. "I don't want to start anything, but it doesn't look good for Brenda Lee to be in the Pastor's office all the time by herself. When she goes in, you need to be in there, too."

"Yes, ma'am. You are right. Pastor said they are working on Mother Stone's birthday party, though." In the back of my mind, I thought, "I know something is going on. It doesn't take all this time to plan an 80-year-old's birthday party."

Mother Hamilton continued. "Some of the other members are saying the same thing. It just doesn't look good for her to be in his office all the time without you."

"Thanks for your concern, Mother. I have been feeling the same way, too. Maybe after the party, she won't be spending time in his office."

She sat there rubbing her hands together, looking at me. I could see tears in her eyes. "Are y'all having problems at home?"

I tried to think of the right words to say. "Mother, we started having problems a couple of weeks after getting married."

"For real, First Lady? What's going on? You two are such a nice-looking couple," she replied with a puzzled look.

"Mother, we may be a nice-looking couple, but we are not in love. And a baby doesn't make a marriage. I know I married for the wrong reasons. I wanted to be popular and well-known, so I married the Pastor's son. I guess he married me because he missed his mother. I don't know. We loved each other as friends. We shouldn't have gotten married, though. I did think that once we exchanged vows, our love would grow because we enjoyed each other's company so much. Now that we are married, things are different. I am trying my best to make it work— not for me but for our child. No one else knows this, but we sleep in separate bedrooms. I'm okay with that, but I never thought Keith would be disrespecting me like he is, having that lady coming out of his office all the time—and right in the church, too! I am not talking against him as the Pastor. He is good in the Word of God, and I know he loves the church. Like I said, maybe after the birthday dinner, things will change. Who knows?"

Mother Hamilton sat there looking at me in shock and with tears in her eyes as she listened to what I said. "I hope things will change when this surprise party is over, dear. I'll pray that everything works out for the best."

"I'm glad you stopped to talk to me, although I did most of the talking. Thank you, Mother." She smiled as we walked out together.

Chapter 15

Valentine's Day fell on a Saturday that year. I was in the exercise room, doing my workout, when the doorbell rang. I ran to the door to see who it was, but they had already gone. Keith stood in the doorway with a dozen red roses and a box of Valentine's chocolate in his hands. He was looking down, reading the card that had been attached to the flowers. When he saw me coming toward him, he said, "Happy Valentine's Day!" as he handed me the flowers and candy. He then tore up the card and dropped it in the trash can before going upstairs.

"Thank you! Oh! It is Valentine's Day, huh?" I said gleefully as I went into the kitchen to set the flowers on the island. On my way upstairs to talk to him, I saw a small piece of the card he ripped up on the floor. I picked it up to put it in the trash can but paused when I saw what was written on it:

"I love you. S."

"Who is 'S'?" I pondered as I ascended the stairs.

I found Keith in the theater room on his phone. I heard him say, "We got to talk. Yes, I got them."

"Keith, who are you talking to?" I asked.

Without answering my question, he hung up the phone and said to me, "When you open the candy, I want a couple of pieces of it."

"Okay. But who were you talking to?" I asked again.

He didn't answer—again. Instead, he got up and looked through the DVDs as if he were looking for a movie to watch. KJ started to cry, so I walked out of the room to tend to him, all while thinking, "The flowers and candy weren't even for me! Somebody actually sent that to him! That's why he tore up the card." I thought he was sorry for the way he had been treating me. When I handed him the candy, he ate all but three pieces. Meanwhile, I was thinking, "Who is 'S'? Brenda's last name is Lee."

Sunday morning, as I prepared for church, I noticed Keith had already left. He doesn't like being late, but he left earlier than usual. It was okay because we never

34

rode together anyway. I was surprised by a call from Brenda. "How are you doing, First Lady?"

"I'm blessed, Sister. How are you?" I replied suspiciously.

"I'm good. I was calling to see if you can call a meeting after church today so that we can get someone designated to decorate the hall and get a menu together for Mother's surprise party?"

"I'm glad you called. Everything is already taken care of. Three ladies are doing the decorations, and the other ladies know what foods to bring. I'm bringing the silverware, cups, and napkins, two of the brothers are responsible for the drinks, Mother's daughter is bringing the birthday cake, and the Assistant Pastor will pick up Mother in time to be at the church by 3:00. We all know to be at the church and done by 2:45."

In a faint voice, she asked, "Is there anything you want me to bring?"

"No, you and Pastor have done enough. We got it from here."

"Hmm…" she said before hanging up the phone. She didn't even say goodbye.

After that call, I thought, "I know she wasn't trying to tell me what to do! Heck, it's already done!"

I know she had gotten to Keith before I could because when I made it to church that morning, he asked, "You didn't want me to pick up Mother?"

"No, it's all taken care of—and it didn't take two months to get it done," I replied sarcastically.

Chapter 16

On the day of the birthday dinner, I arrived at the church early to ensure everything was ready and to help set up the food as it came in. On the cake table, we had balloons with 80 on them. There was also a separate table just for gifts. Everything looked fabulous, and there was plenty of food for everyone.

When Mother Stone got there at 3:00 on the dot, she was wearing the same colors we had decorated the hall with. She was genuinely surprised! She said she thought we were throwing a party for the pastor. I went out of my way to invite some of her relatives she hadn't seen in a long time.

While everyone was gathering and chatting, I stopped to think, "I don't know what Brenda and Keith did. I invited the family, the ladies at the church did the decorating and brought the food. Brenda and Keith did nothing."

It was so obvious something was going on between the two of them. Wherever Keith was, she was right there, touching him on his arm like she was the First Lady—and he acted as if he enjoyed every minute of it. I thought about the Valentine's Day flowers and candy, still wondering who 'S' was.

My thoughts were interrupted when one of the ladies said, "First Lady, go and sit down. You've been on your feet ever since you got here. Some of the younger sisters can serve the food."

She was right. I took a seat at the table with Mother Stone, Mother Hamilton, and some of the other Mothers. I could feel them looking at me as I sat there trying to look happy while feeling embarrassed. Eventually, I excused myself and told them I was going to check on KJ.

When I made it to the daycare, KJ was asleep and the only child there. I told the young lady who was sitting with him that I would stay so that she could go to the dinner. When she left, I sat there thinking, "This is so embarrassing. Lord, what shall I do?" I remained in the daycare for about 30 minutes before waking KJ and returning to the festivities. I turned off the lights and exited the room. That's when I saw Keith and Brenda standing in his office door. The lights were on, so I stood there looking at them. They couldn't see me because the hallway was dark where I was standing.

I began walking towards them before he turned off the light in his office and embraced her. When they turned to walk away, I was standing right there. They both jumped, obviously startled by my sudden appearance. "Hey! What are you two up to?" I asked with a smile.

"Where did you come from?" Keith asked.

"Umm… You see our child in my arms, don't you?" I stormed away. I wanted him to know I saw them without saying a word.

When I returned to the dining room, someone had taken my place at the Mothers' table. There was a table in the back where two ladies were sitting. When I approached, they got up, getting ready to leave. "I hope I'm not running you off," I stated.

One of the ladies replied, "No, you're not. We have another birthday party to attend at our church for our pastor's wife. Mrs. Stone's daughter invited us. We grew up on the same street she lives on, but we are going to say bye to her before we go."

I smiled and said, "Thanks for coming."

They turned to leave and walked toward Mother Stone's table.

Chapter 17

I sat in the back of the room, listening to different people talk about Mother Stone. Keith walked up and said, "Why are you sitting back here? I have been looking for you." He acted as if nothing had happened.

I looked up and noticed a smirky look on his face. I also saw a trace of lipstick on his lips. "Do you want a baby wipe?" I asked.

"For what?"

"You have your woman's lipstick on your lips. By the way, where is she? She's been behind you all this evening."

"Do I have lipstick on me for real?" He said it like he didn't believe me.

"Yes, you have lipstick on you." He stood right in front of me, grabbed a napkin from the table, and began wiping his face.

He looked at me and said, "We need to talk when I get home."

"Yes, I agree. We do need to talk. It doesn't look good for you, walking around with that lady following you. You are an embarrassment to this church."

"She is not following behind me. She just knows some of the same people I do." He looked toward the door and said, "There's Brother Clark. Let me go and talk to him." At that, he walked away.

At the table in front of me, I heard some ladies talking. My back was to them, but I heard them clearly. "Why is Brenda standing there in Pastor's face?" one asked. I turned to see what they were talking about, and sure enough, Keith was talking, and Brenda, Brother Clark, and two other people were huddled together, laughing.

Another lady said, "Where is First Lady?"

"I don't know," another replied. "When we were in line getting our food, I thought I saw her going out. She's probably in the daycare with her baby."

"She's at the table right behind us, feeding her son. Lower your voices," yet another said.

I could still hear them.

"Did you know Pastor and Brenda dated before she went off to college? Maybe they are picking up where they left off," one said.

"He can't do that! He's a married man with a baby and has a church!" another exclaimed.

A different lady commented, "You know he has a baby by Brenda, right?"

At that point, I strained my ears to hear the entirety of the ongoing conversation.

"Wow! For real?" one of them asked.

"Yes, for real. I heard Pastor really loved her. He wanted to go to college with her, but his mother was sick, and his dad wanted him to stay here to help take care of her," one of them explained.

"So, you're telling me he has a baby by her?" another asked, surprised.

"Yes! You know, there was a rumor going around…"

Right then, KJ started to cry. I tried quieting him down while feeling in his diaper bag for a bottle. I could no longer hear any of what the ladies were saying over his crying. When I got him quiet, I heard one of them say, "I heard that, too, but a couple of months later, we saw Brenda with a big stomach. That child should be about eight or nine years old by now."

"That could be a front. After his mother caught him, he hooked up with Brenda. I think his mother got sick behind that. She was so crazy about him. You know some men do stuff like that," one commented.

What in the world were they talking about? What did Keith do to his mother?

One lady said, "I wonder if that's what killed Mother Montgomery? Bless her sweet soul."

"Pastor [Keith] took his mother's death hard. If I remember correctly, he left home for a couple of months," another said.

"Brenda's been back in town for almost a year now. She teaches at the elementary school on Baldwin Street—the same one where I teach," one of them said. That voice sounded younger than the other voices at the table.

"I wonder why he's treating First Lady like that. She's a beautiful woman. Have you all seen where she lives? I drove by her house when I heard where she lived, and that house looked like a mansion! Did you know she works for the city?" one of them inquired.

"Oh, my God! They are talking about me now!" I said to myself.

"Where is the house?" one asked.

"It's in a subdivision off Highway 23 on Riverside Drive. You turn off 23 onto Riverside, go around the lake, and you will see a long circle driveway that leads to a mansion with a two-car garage. I heard she had it built from the ground up. It's not like she married Pastor for the money. I heard she was already well-off. Plus, she served in and retired from the Air Force," the youngest voice said. "You can tell she has money. Just look at how she dresses."

I sat there listening to them talk about me. I wish I could see who they were. After all, they knew all my business. Just then, KJ started to cry again. He was fussy and sleepy because I woke him from his nap. His diaper probably needed to be changed, too. I picked up his diaper bag, preparing to take him home. I looked around for Keith to let him know I was leaving and saw him and Brenda talking to another group of people. I walked toward them just as he looked up and saw me carrying KJ. He stopped talking and looked at me with a curious look on his face. I spoke to everyone with a smile and said, "Pastor, I'm taking our child home. It's past his bedtime. You continue to enjoy yourself. I'll see you at home."

"Is KJ okay?" he asked.

"Yes, he's fine. He's just sleepy. I'll see you later." I firmly grabbed Brenda by the arm, pulling her away from the group. She didn't say anything; she just went along with me and walked with a puzzled look on her face. I stopped out of earshot of everyone and said to her, "You have disrespected me all this afternoon. You are following behind my husband, and now I see you standing there with your hand on his arm, looking cheap."

"I'm not following him. We just know the same people," she replied.

I looked her dead in her face, smiled, and said, "I'm doing the talking. You listen. You have been seen by everyone here at this dinner. You need to go somewhere and sit down." She just stood there looking at me. I gave her my friendliest smile, side-hugged her, and walked away. I found myself thinking if I really loved Keith, I would have scratched her eyeballs out. Either way, I didn't want her to think what she was doing was okay.

As I walked away from Brenda, I began to think that maybe Keith told her we were just together because of KJ. As I exited the party, I felt everyone watching me. I put a big smile on my face as I approached the Mothers' table. Mother Hamilton was the first to notice me with KJ and the diaper bag and asked, "Are you leaving?"

"Yes, ma'am. It's getting late. I am going to take KJ home. It's past his bedtime."

"I am praying for you," she said quietly.

I hugged her and said, "Thank you."

Mother Stone spoke up. "Thank you, First Lady. Everything was so nice."

"You're welcome, Mother, and Happy Birthday again!" I hugged her and said goodbye to the other Mothers at the table. As I walked out, I looked toward the table where the ladies had been discussing Keith and me. I recognized two of them as members of the church. The others, I did not know.

Chapter 18

During my drive home, I reflected on the night's events. I wasn't jealous about anything Keith did. It was more about how he disrespected me in front of all those people. Thanks to the conversation near me, I finally saw the real connection between him and Brenda. For as long as I have known Keith, he never mentioned Brenda or a son to me. Once home, I fed and bathed KJ, then put him down for the night.

I waited for Keith to come home, which didn't happen until after midnight. I was sitting in the family room when he came in. He didn't say anything to me, though. He headed straight upstairs. I called out, "Keith, you said you wanted to talk to me when you got home." He stood about midway up the stairs and stared at me. I continued. "You know, you embarrassed me big time tonight. I saw you with Brenda in the hallway, and then you came over to me with her lipstick on your face. You must have been kissing her to have her lipstick on you. She was following behind you like she was the First Lady of the church all night. Why didn't you tell me you dated Brenda and had a child together?" He remained stoic and refused to speak. "What did you do to your mom to make her cry?"

At the mention of his mother, his expression changed. He raised his voice and said, "What are you talking about? Where did you hear all of that from anyway?"

"Is it true?" I asked. "Do you have a past with her?"

Once again, he avoided answering me directly. "I don't think I had to discuss my past with you. Our time together was before you and I even met. Brenda has helped me through a challenging time in my life, which has nothing to do with you. She's my friend, and I am grateful for her being here for me."

"So, you're kissing your friends now, huh?" He fell silent again. "Keith, you are a preacher who teaches God's Word, yet you are not living it yourself. All the saints at church see what you are doing, and I know God is not pleased with you."

"Okay, okay. Yes, we dated. Yes, she has a child. What are you griping about? It has nothing to do with you. Let me ask you something…"

"What do you want to ask me, Keith. After all, you did say we needed to talk when you got home. I'm waiting."

He remained on the stairs and looked around the house before saying, "I thought our relationship would have grown by now, but it hasn't. It's nothing that you have done. I love you, but not enough for us to stay together. Things are not working out for us. I think it would be best if we go our separate ways." He paused and then stated, "I want a divorce." Now, that stung when he said that. All he said was true: things weren't working out for us, but I thought I would be the first to ask for a divorce. Before I could answer him, he then said, "And I want this house." He left me in a state of shock.

"You want what?!"

"I want this house and my son."

"You are not getting this house or my baby!!!" I hollered. He walked down the stairs toward me with a serious look on his face. "I don't know what you and Brenda have been talking about or what plans you have made, but you are not getting my house or my baby. Now, get out of my face!"

"Leave her out of this!" he demanded. He pointed his finger in my face and said, "I am telling you what I want."

I pointed my finger back at him and said, "And I'm telling you that's not going to happen. You will never bring another woman into my house! The only thing you brought into this house was your clothes, and that's what you're leaving with! Now, Mr. Keith Allen Montgomery, I'll be happy to give you a divorce, but you are not—I repeat—not getting my house or baby! Think about what you are going to tell the saints at church tomorrow. I will not be going. You can tell Sister Owens to take over the class with the girls. She knows what to do." He stood there looking at me. "Oh, yes, Mr. Montgomery. When you leave out of my house, you are not welcome back. You can see KJ when you want, but not at my house. I'll keep him in the church daycare until I can find a daycare closer to my house."

He finally walked away and headed back to the stairs. He turned and said, "I'll file for the divorce. You pay half, and I'll pay half."

"That will be fine with me," I responded. He rolled his eyes at me and went upstairs. I sat there thinking about what had just happened.

A few minutes later, he came down with his luggage and a suit bag. He looked at me and said, "I'll see you in court."

"Leave my keys and garage door opener on your way out."

He threw the house keys onto the couch beside me and then went out to retrieve the garage door opener out of his car, which he placed on the island in the kitchen. "When the divorce is final, I will get those things back, and you will be out of here!" He slammed the door when he left, leaving me to think just how crazy he was.

I sat on the couch and cried—not because he wanted a divorce but because he wanted my house and my baby. Well, that was not going to happen!

Chapter 19

As expected, I didn't go to church that Sunday. I stayed home and packed the rest of Keith's things, just in case he came back for them after service. On Monday morning, I went by the daycare to drop off KJ on my way to work. I saw Keith's car in the parking lot and figured he must be staying in the church since his dad's house was rented out. As I walked into the daycare, I was greeted by the caregiver. "First Lady, are you alright?" She was looking at me with a sad look on her face. The other caregiver was cleaning the toys, but I could see her peeking over at me.

"I'm good! How are you?" I asked in a cheerful voice.

"I am sorry about you and Pastor," she replied.

Not knowing what he told the church, I quickly changed the conversation. "KJ was a little fussy this morning. Call me if he is acting sick." I placed his pampers and change of clothes in his cube and his food in the refrigerator.

The caregiver walked behind me and said, "Pastor told the church yesterday that you asked for a divorce. He said that you stated things are difficult for you as the First Lady."

"That's not true. I didn't ask for a divorce; he asked me for one. And it had nothing to do with me being First Lady. This is all him."

"I am sorry," she repeated.

"It's for the best. I'll see you this afternoon. I'll call to check on him during my break," I said before kissing KJ and leaving out of the door. As I drove away, I didn't feel bad about what the caregiver said. I actually felt a sense of relief, although Keith lied and placed all the blame on me. I thought back to the chain of events that led us to this point: I loved Keith as a friend, married him, and had a baby. Now, he wanted my house and child all to himself.

When I got to work, time seemed to fly by. I had so much work to do with what seemed like little time to do it. On my lunch break, I called to check on KJ. The caregiver said, "He cried a little after you dropped him off, but he is fine now. His dad is with him."

During that week, a couple of the Mothers from the church called to see how I was doing and said they missed me. Mother Hamilton called and said I shouldn't give up on my marriage so soon. I explained to her it wasn't me giving up; it was Keith. I told her the truth: He asked me for a divorce and wanted my house and child.

She sounded shocked when she replied, "For real? Oh, my God!"

"Mother, this is for the best. I'm happy, and I want him to be happy, too."

Chapter 20

Three uneventful weeks passed until I went by the daycare to pick up KJ one day. When the caregiver saw me walking up, she met me at the door. "He's not here, Mrs. Montgomery. Pastor picked him up two hours ago and told me he'll be the one dropping him off and picking KJ up from now on."

"He said what?!"

"I thought he had talked to you about this," she replied.

"No, I haven't heard from him." I pulled my phone out of my purse to see if I had any missed calls from him. Nothing. I walked to my car, got in, and thought back to his demands. He said he wanted my baby and my house. Now, he has my baby. I wonder if he told his lawyer he has been the one taking care of KJ so that he can get his dirty claws on my house. I started to panic. I called Keith's cell phone, but he didn't answer. "Oh, my God! I need to talk to someone. Should I call the police? No, because I know what they'll say. 'That's his son, and we can't do anything because you're still married.'"

I thought to call Mrs. Riddle. She always gave me good advice when I needed it, but she was out of town. I couldn't think clearly. Keith had my baby! I looked around the church's parking lot but didn't see his car. I then drove by his daddy's house, the barbershop, and other places I thought he would be to see if I saw his car. I grew increasingly nervous by the minute. All of my thoughts were crashing around in my mind. I started to cry when I thought about what he told the caregiver. I was crying so hard, I had to pull into the Kroger store's parking lot to pray and pull myself together so that I could make it home. All the while, the loudest thought that ran through my mind was, "Keith took my baby!!!"

As I turned into my subdivision, I thought about Keith's love for the church and knew he wouldn't walk away from it. He was probably in a business meeting somewhere and took KJ with him. But why did he tell the caregiver what he did? As I passed by the lake and went around the curve, I saw a black car by my mailbox. I approached my house and saw it was Keith's car! As I got closer, I saw him and a lady standing outside. It was Brenda—and she was holding my son! I stopped my car, got out, and took my baby from her arms. "Keith, why are you here?!"

"I was showing Brenda our house," he said with glee.

"'Our house'? Negro, you haven't paid a penny on my house. If you don't get your broke tail off my property, I'm going to call the police!"

"Once the divorce is final, I will get the keys back that I left here, and you will be gone," he said while laughing.

"So, you filed for the divorce? Good! The sooner, the better!" I replied.

"No, I haven't filed yet, but I will," he said, still laughing. He remained standing in place, looking at my house and back at Brenda with pride. She stood there looking at me with a smirk on her face. "Do you like what you see?" Before she could answer, I said to her, "You will never set foot in my house!" I pointed at my house as I spoke. "My advice to you is to keep your teaching job because this negro has nothing but his daddy's house and that church." I then directed my next comment to Keith. "If you think you can use my baby as a shield to get my house, I want you to know it won't work! Now, both of you get off my property!!!"

He laughed in my face, put his arm around Brenda, and they left.

Chapter 21

I stood in the driveway, hugging my baby. I was so upset at Keith but happy to have my baby back. I watched as they drove away, thinking he must be crazy if he thought he would get my house. I put KJ in my car and drove into my garage.

When I got inside, I got a wet towel and wiped his face. I knew Brenda had been kissing on him. I thanked God for my baby. He was all I had, and no one was going to take him away from me! Once he fell asleep, I laid him in my bedroom. Ever since my Mama died, I hadn't slept in my suite, so I decided to move back down there. As I looked around, I thought, "Tomorrow would be a good day to move back into my bedroom suite and bring KJ's crib down here with me."

On the way to my office, I stopped at the picture wall leading to my living room. I stood there and looked at the pictures of my Daddy, Mama, brother, and all the awards, certificates, and ribbons I had received through the years. On the table under the pictures was one of me when I was the second runner-up for a beauty pageant when I was stationed in Germany.

I then thought about how I was raped, beaten, and left for dead in a park. It was the scariest day of my life. The man threw me to the ground, covered my mouth with his hand, and forced himself into my woman part. I can still hear his whispers as he told me he had been watching me for a long time. That night, I thought I was going to die. Fortunately, a woman passing by saw a man running towards a car near where she was walking and heard me yelling out for help. She remembered the license plate and said it had a sticker with two red birds. She drove me to the hospital.

The police were called. I told them I didn't know who the man was, but I had scratched him on the right side of his neck. The lady who drove me to the hospital got the assailant's license plate number and the color of his car: black. Two days later, the police picked up a man who was driving drunk. He was driving a black car. After running his license plate, they learned it was the same as my rapist's—with the bird sticker. They brought the man to the hospital so that I could positively identify him. When I said it was him, he lied, said it wasn't him, and told the police he was in another town when they said the assault happened. When they saw the scratches on the right side of his neck, he then said we had consensual sex. The forensic team got the skin from under my fingernails, which matched the skin from his neck. I heard them say to the man, "If it was consensual, why did you beat this lady like that? And why did she scratch you?" Those questions were asked as they escorted him out of the room in handcuffs.

A court date was scheduled for my case against him because he kept saying it wasn't him, but before we went to court, I found out the man was a high-ranking officer with 18 years of military service. He was a resident of Germany and married with three children. As for me, I was a black woman from the States who accused that man of raping me. Although he was guilty, they closed the case and settled it out of court. I was awarded "hush money"—$450,000.00 and an additional $1,000.00 a month for the rest of my life. The military didn't want that news to get out of Germany, so my orders were changed, and they transferred me back to the States.

My eyes were then drawn to the picture of Gina. She was the lady who saved me that night. She often came by the hospital to check on me during my stay, and when I was released, she visited me at home to make sure I was alright. I cannot express how grateful to God I am for Gina being there that dreadful night. Because of her, that man was caught. After I received the settlement money, I looked her up and gave her $10,000.00 to show my appreciation for the unconditional love she gave me. In exchange, she gave me a photo of her. I fondly recall her saying, "I didn't know your name. I just called you 'The Pretty Lady from the States.'"

When I called home to tell Mama what happened to me, she was distraught and cried her heart out. "Baby, you need to come home. I already lost my son. I don't want to lose you, too." I explained I would be transferred from Germany in two weeks, home for a week, and then stationed at Lackland Air Force Base in Texas until I retired. "Thank you, Jesus! My baby will be back in the States!"

As I remained looking at the picture wall, I remembered coming home, purchasing the land, and providing an exact blueprint of how I wanted my house to be built. Tears began to fall as I thought about the fear and pain I endured that provided the funding for my dream home, only to have Keith believe he would take it from me. The nerve he had to show another woman my house and say he wanted my child, too! That night, I went to bed with the horrific memories of what that man did to me in Germany and cried myself to sleep.

Chapter 22

Tuesday morning, I called into work and told my supervisor I was going through something with my family and would be working from home for the remainder of the week. She asked if I was okay and if I had any appointments scheduled, and I replied, "No, I just have to do transfers."

"Okay. See you next week."

I spent the rest of that morning moving all my things from the upstairs bedroom to my downstairs suite. I also took KJ's crib apart, took it downstairs piece-by-piece, then reassembled it in my room.

Around 11:00 a.m., I called the lawyer that worked in the same building as me and made an appointment to speak with him about the divorce. I knew Keith's broke behind didn't have any money, and I was ready to get our marriage over with. "If he wants a divorce, I will give it to him. He just has to pay his half, as we agreed," I thought to myself.

That afternoon, I worked in my home office for the rest of the day.

On Wednesday morning, bright and early, KJ and I started looking for a new daycare center. Each was either filled, or he was too young.

On Thursday at 2:00 p.m., KJ and I sat in the lawyer's office. I was told how much it would cost and was informed that as long as Keith didn't contest the divorce, it could be done in six months or less. I told the lawyer, "Keith won't contest it because he was the one who asked for the divorce, my child, and my house."

He laughed and asked, "What did you do to that man?"

"Nothing but put up with his mess!" We both shared a good laugh at that one.

"Okay, Lexie. Tell me: What assets do you have together?"

"None, Mr. McKinney. We have been married a little over a year. He came to my house with nothing but his clothes. Everything is mine. He never bought food or paid any bills. He didn't even clean up behind himself because I have a housekeeper who does that."

After paying my half of his fee, he said, "Okay. I'll start the paperwork immediately. Does Mr. Montgomery have a lawyer?"

"No, he doesn't have any money. If he doesn't pay his half, I will. I just want him out of my life. Can you believe he already brought his new woman over to look at my house?!" Mr. McKinney laughed so hard, tears actually came out of his eyes!

When I got home and retrieved my voicemails, one of them was from Keith asking why I wasn't bringing KJ to the daycare. I didn't respond to his message.

When Friday came, I ended up dropping KJ off at the daycare at the church and went on the hunt again for a new daycare center. I prayed, "Lord, please let me find a daycare before this month is over."

Keith was there when I returned to pick up KJ. I told him I started the divorce paperwork, how much it cost, and that he needed to have his half of the money when everything was final. He stood there looking like a foolish, penniless man but said, "Okay."

Chapter 23

Three months later, Keith and I met at my lawyer's office. Keith told Mr. McKinney he wanted me to pay him spousal support and that he wanted the house and our child, to which my lawyer asked, "Are you being represented by a lawyer?"

Keith replied, "Since she already had one, I didn't think I needed representation of my own."

"Well, Mr. Montgomery, you do need a lawyer if you are going to fight her for spousal support, the child, and her house. I'm her lawyer. I can't help you." Keith sat there looking dumb. "Mr. Montgomery, what assets do you have together?"

Keith looked at the walls, the floor, and anything else he could, trying to think of something. I spoke up and said, "He brought nothing into the marriage. I had everything when I married his broke behind." Mr. McKinney turned away towards the window behind him and let out a small chuckle.

When he composed himself, he turned to face Keith and said, "Mr. Montgomery, I'm sorry to say, but you get nothing. You will, however, have to pay her child support." Keith had the funniest expression on his face when he was told he would have to pay me child support. I struggled to keep from busting out laughing at him. My lawyer continued. "I need an account of your finances. You can mail or bring them to me. I can then determine the amount of child support you will have to pay. The other option is for you to obtain your own lawyer and go to court for a hearing. All of those fees will be on you, including the court cost."

Keith finally found his voice. "Mr. McKinney, Lexie has a lot of money. She doesn't need me to pay her child support."

"Mr. Montgomery, is it her money?"

"Yes, sir."

"And whose child is it?"

Angrily, Keith said, "He's my baby!"

"Well, you must pay her child support," Mr. McKinney stated. Case closed.

I looked over at Keith's face and saw how enraged he was getting. He was no longer smiling like he was when we first arrived. I stood and said, "Thank you, Mr. McKinney," as we shook hands. Keith laid his part of the payment in a check on my lawyer's desk and walked out without saying a word to either of us. He was obviously too angry to shake my lawyer's hand. I followed him out the door with a smile on my face.

As we walked out of the building, Keith said, "That was a setup. That's why you got that lawyer. You know you don't need money for child support."

"Remember, Keith: You asked for the divorce, and I'm glad you did." He didn't say anything more. He got into his car, trying to leave in a hurry, but a man in a red car driving slowly through the parking lot slowed his departure.

Chapter 24

A couple of weeks passed, and I found it challenging to get up early, drive across town to drop KJ off at the daycare at Keith's church, and still make it to work on time. I prayed the Lord would bless me with finding a daycare center closer to my house—and He did!

As I passed my street on the way to the supply store in the strip mall, there was a red sign with an arrow pointing toward a church that sat on a side street. The sign read:

"Looking for a daycare? We're here for you! Check us out!"

I had never even noticed that street or sign with the arrow pointing toward that church, and I'd been to that strip mall plenty of times!

After leaving the store, I turned onto the street, and sure enough, there was a daycare named The Bright Star Christian Community Daycare Center in big, bold red letters. The Bright Star Christian Church was attached to it. I went in to get information about their hours and to see if KJ could get enrolled. The young lady in the front office asked me a couple of questions, such as why I was there and my name, and then asked me to have a seat while she went to get the Director. From where I sat, I could see various rooms and some of the children toward the rear of the building. The Director came in to introduce herself. She looked familiar to me.

"Hello. I'm Mrs. Watkins, the Director here," she said while shaking my hand.

"Hi. I'm Lexie Harris. I am looking for childcare for my son. He's 18 months old."

She looked at me and cocked her head to the side slightly. "Is your mother's name Rose?"

"Yes, ma'am."

"I know your mother. You look so much like her," she said with a smile. "When do you want to start your son in the daycare?"

"Immediately, if possible."

"And how is Ms. Harris doing?" Her smile never wavered.

"Mama passed away four years ago."

That was when her smile faded. "Oh, my God. I am so sorry to hear that. She was a beautiful lady, inside and out."

"Thank you."

Mrs. Watkins sat down in the chair beside the clerk, obviously trying to get over the shock of learning about my mother's passing. She cleared her throat, regained her composure, and asked the clerk to get the information needed to enroll KJ in daycare. While the clerk tended to that duty, Mrs. Watkins escorted me throughout the facility. She showed me where the children spent their days. There was a room for the babies, a toddlers' room up to age three, a four-year-olds' room, and a larger room for the five and six-year-old after-school children. In each room, I was introduced to the caregivers. I thanked her for the walkthrough, told her I liked the way everything was arranged, and that she would see me the next day with the completed paperwork.

As I left the daycare center, I praised and thanked God for showing me the sign that directed me there. I then called Keith at his church. He didn't answer, so I called his cell phone. When he picked up, I told him the divorce was final and that I would drop off the papers and the rest of the things he had left at my house when I picked up KJ. "KJ's not at the daycare right now. My oldest son came into town, so I took KJ to meet him. I'll keep him tonight, and you can pick him up from the daycare center tomorrow. Or, if you'd like, I can bring him to your house late tonight, maybe around 11:30."

I thought about those options (knowing I didn't want him at my house ever again) and said, "You keep him for the night. I'll pick him up tomorrow from the daycare when I get off work."

Once home, I sifted through the mail. Someone from Arkansas had sent Keith a card. The return address had an 'S' for the person's first name. It looked very similar to the 'S' on the Valentine's Day card Keith tore up. I put the card with his other mail and the things he had left at my house.

The next day, I took the papers to enroll KJ into his new daycare to Mrs. Watkins. She greeted me and said, "You know, you look so much like your mother. She and I worked at the same school for years. She was a good teacher."

I laughed and replied, "I thought Mama was a good teacher, too. I was in her fifth-grade class. It was hard for me to call her Mrs. Harris. I would often forget to do

56

so and called her Mama!" We shared a laugh. "I was so happy when I passed to sixth grade. I needed to get out of her class—but I still had to be on my best behavior. If I got into trouble at school, she got me good when I got home. On the other hand, my brother Leon was always in trouble."

Mrs. Watkins laughed and said, "Yes, I know. He was in my class. How is he doing?"

That question took my breath away. I paused and inhaled deeply before replying. "Mrs. Watkins, Leon was killed in a drive-by shooting."

Once again, she took a seat with an obvious state of shock written on her face. "I'm so sorry. I didn't know that." When she got herself back together, she said, "Now that I'll have your son in my daycare, we will get a chance to talk more often."

"Thank you, Mrs. Watkins, for accepting KJ into your daycare. I am truly blessed." A parent came in, ending our conversation. I hugged her and said, "See you on Monday!" I felt good about leaving my baby in a daycare with someone who knew my mother.

Chapter 25

I hadn't seen my baby since Wednesday when I dropped him off. I called Keith to let him know I was on my way to pick up KJ from the church's daycare. When I arrived, I called Keith again and told him to come to get his things out of my car, along with his copy of the divorce papers. While waiting for him to come, I told the caregiver I enrolled KJ in a new center near my home and that he wouldn't be coming back unless his daddy brought him in.

"Do you need any paperwork from me?" she asked.

"No, I had copies of all his records at home."

"I'm sad he's leaving, but I understand. I'm going to miss him," she replied sadly.

Just then, Keith walked in. As we walked to my car, I could tell he was angry. I opened the trunk and waited for him to grab his things, mail…and the divorce papers. He secured KJ in his car seat, then turned to me and said, "You now have me paying childcare over at a new daycare center when he could remain here for free."

"I'm not asking you to pay additional for his childcare. I can use the money you pay me for his daycare. As a matter of fact, I'm not asking you for anything other than to stay out of my life. The divorce papers outline when you can have visitation with KJ."

"Lexie, you're the reason our marriage didn't work. You never gave me a chance to show how much I cared for you."

"Keith, let's be real here. You didn't love me. You're the one who asked for the divorce, and it was the best thing for both of us."

He looked at me from head to toe and then said, "I saw you coming out of your job with that man the other day." I sensed he was angry about it.

"I can come out of work with anyone I please! Wait. So, you are stalking me now? You are a sick man."

"Yeah. Whatever. You thought you were looking good, standing there grinning in that man's face."

"I know how I look, Keith. I also know whatever I wear, I make it look good on me. Just look at me!" I threw my arms in the air, spun around, and said, "Remember the table in my house with my picture from when I was second runner-up in a beauty pageant out of 50 women? You do not need to tell me what I already know. I know I look good. I think it's time for you to go home to Brenda. I heard she is with child, and you got married so that you won't be living in sin while trying to preach." He just stood there looking at me.

Before I drove off, we agreed on a drop-off and pick-up spot for KJ every two weeks: Saturday at noon at the McDonald's on 5th and Main Streets. I didn't want him at my house for any reason whatsoever.

Chapter 26

KJ had been at his new daycare for eight months and loved it. One Sunday morning, I decided to visit the church. When I entered, I was greeted by Mr. Ferguson. He remembered me and asked, "I see you never called for that protection I recommended for your computer. How's it holding up?" I could tell he didn't remember my name, but he did recognize my face.

"No, I didn't call. I bought a new one. The one you worked on was outdated." He smiled then left to greet some of the other saints coming in. I walked to a pew and sat down, all while thinking, "If he remembers me after three years, I know he remembers telling me to get dressed." I learned Mr. Ferguson was one of the head Deacons at the church. He returned to me, played with KJ's hand, and told me about the nursery during service. "Thank you. I'll keep him with me today. He is already enrolled in the daycare here at the church."

"Oh, so you already know about the daycare program. Great! Well, welcome to the church!" he said with a smile. "I hope you enjoy the service today."

"Thank you."

As it turned out, I did enjoy the service. I enjoyed the word the pastor spoke and the songs the choir sang. KJ and I were there every Sunday from that Sunday forward, and Mrs. Watkins would sometimes sit with us. Everyone was friendly, and the location was nice and close to my home.

A year and some months had passed since I had joined the church. Since then, KJ turned four years old, so I started letting him go to the nursery with the other children his age. He liked when Mr. Ferguson walked him there because he would give him a bag of fruit snacks.

One Sunday, Mr. Ferguson wasn't at the door to greet us, so I kept KJ with me. I was enjoying the service, and KJ was playing with his alphabet game beside me. Someone behind me pulled my hair. I thought it might have been a lady sitting behind me pulling a piece of lint or something out of my hair, so I didn't look back. Then came another pull. I turned to see who was doing the tugging. It was Myles! He had a smile on his face and used his hands to make the shape of a heart over his own. I was genuinely surprised to see him and glad to know he safely made it back from Iraq.

After church was over, Myles hugged me and said, "I told you I would see you when I got back. Why are you at this church? I heard you were married to a preacher. He lets you visit other churches on Sunday mornings?"

"Myles, I have been divorced for two-and-a-half years now and have been coming to this church for over a year."

He smiled and said, "Well, I know you have met my dad. He's a Deacon here."

"Yes, I've met him. He's my son's best friend. He always walks KJ to the nursery and slips him a bag of fruit snacks, thinking I don't know," I replied with laughter.

"That's my dad for you! So, this must be KJ?"

"Yes, he's my son." We stood in the parking lot talking for a while more until KJ said he was hungry.

Myles asked, "Will I see you again?"

I lovingly rubbed KJ on the head before responding. "I don't see any reason why I can't." Myles smiled, opened the rear car door, and helped me secure KJ in his car seat. He then opened my door, waited for me to get in, gently closed it, and waved bye to us as I drove away. I found myself thinking, "Oh, my God! He looks good! That smile on his face is so pleasant to look at, and he smells good, too. Oh, my God! He wants to see me again! Bye-bye past and hello, future!"

When I got home from church, I rummaged through a box in the storage room to find the crystal vase from my mom to put my fresh-cut flowers in. I found it wrapped in the tie blanket my Aunt Ida gave me. I gave the blanket to KJ, and he loved it! He carried it around everywhere he went in the house.

One day, while we were sitting watching TV, he asked, "Mama, how did you know I would like a blanket with cars on it?"

"I didn't know. Your great-aunt Ida showed me how to make it when I was little. She told me to give it to my little boy whenever I had one, and you are my little boy!" I started to tickle and kiss him, and he tried to cover himself with the blanket. That was so funny to him.

As time passed, Myles would ride his motorcycle to my house to visit us twice a week. KJ was genuinely fascinated with Myles' mode of transportation. He would put his helmet on KJ's head and ride him down the long driveway and back. It was a beautiful red and black Harley-Davidson motorcycle with a matching helmet. Myles kept it clean and shiny, calling it his "toy."

I liked the attention Myles showed KJ and me, and KJ loved him. The Lord blessed me to feel free from my rollercoaster past. I was living my life dedicated to raising my son—and I loved every moment of it!

Chapter 27

My past mistakes kept haunting me and showing up in my future, namely Keith Allen Montgomery. I would see him when I didn't want to, and he was watching my house (for what, I do not know). It couldn't have been because he wanted KJ. After all, he had his designated times to spend with him. He wasn't after me because he had remarried. Why did he keep driving by my house?

I remember the night I was checking on KJ in his room, and when I looked out the window, I saw Keith's car parked by my mailbox. A couple of weeks later, I picked up KJ after his weekend visit with his daddy, and during our ride home, he said, "Mama, me, and daddy were sitting in his car looking at the house, and we saw you looking out the kitchen window."

I was shocked! "When did you see mommy looking out the window?"

"The other night," he replied.

"You did? I was probably cleaning the windowsill. Why were you sitting looking at the house?" I asked.

"I don't know, I guess daddy wanted to see his house."

"KJ, it's not your daddy's house. I already had my house when your daddy and I met." He didn't say anything more about it. He just sat there looking as if he were in deep thought. That innocent conversation with my son confirmed what I already knew: Keith was stalking me.

Chapter 28

As the months passed, Myles and I became good friends. He was funny yet serious and always smiling that dazzling smile of his. I observed how much KJ and Myles enjoyed each other's company, which was essential. Myles often came to his dad's house and then jogged with me in the afternoon when I got home from work.

If KJ wasn't at his dad's house, Myles sometimes took him fishing in the lake near my home. I went with them a couple of times but soon realized fishing wasn't for me.

When I started hosting Bible study in my home on Friday evenings from 6-7 p.m. twice a month, Myles attended. There was a group of eight people from our cell group at church: the cell minister, his wife, two men, two ladies, and Myles and me. The minister taught from a two-year lesson plan book our pastor had written that accompanied the Bible. At the end of the two years, if we finished the class, we would receive a certificate signed by the pastor. Myles really enjoyed coming and said he was studying hard to catch up since he started the class late. He insisted on getting his certificate at the same time each of us received ours.

I learned to appreciate KJ spending time with his father because it gave me some alone time. However, I began to feel uneasy when KJ came home and told me, "Daddy is asking questions about you, mommy."

"What kind of questions?" I asked.

"Like what I do when I'm home, who comes over to his house, if I have friends sleeping over, and if any of his stuff is still in his room."

While KJ ran through the list of questions, I thought, "Why is that man asking our son questions about me? I gave him everything he owned when we divorced." I had to pray to keep from telling KJ to tell his daddy to stay out of my business. After all, he was married to Brenda, and they have a son of their own. Why be in my business at all?

I recall the weekend KJ came home upset after visiting his dad. He said, "Mama Brenda always has me babysitting Brandon."

I tried to be empathetic. "Well, you are the big brother. Maybe Mama Brenda is tired of running after two boys all day." He just looked at me and frowned. When he turned away, I laughed at the expression on his face.

Chapter 29

Myles' father became ill, so most of his time was spent alongside his father at the computer shop. As a result, I didn't get to see Myles often, but he did call me twice a day while I was at work and when I got home in the afternoon.

I believed he was in love with me by how he acted when he was around me and what he said when we talked on the phone. I had been praying that the Lord would bless me with a man who loved my son and me, and I felt like Myles was that man.

We had been friends for over a year, often going places together. For example, one Saturday, I had Human Resources Training to do in Indianapolis, Indiana. Myles offered to drive, and since it was my weekend to keep KJ, he came with us. Myles said KJ would be his company while I was at my workshop. We left Nashville on Friday and arrived in Indianapolis later that evening. The hotel was The Marriott—the same one where the workshop was being held. The company I worked for paid for the room, which had two beds and a pull-out bed in the living room. I told Myles there was no reason for him to pay for a room when he could stay in mine. He slept on the pull-out bed, and KJ and I slept on the others. Saturday morning, I was up by 8:00, dressed, and downstairs to get everything set up by 9:00. They were still asleep when I left.

I was so glad when the workshop was over. By the time I made it back to the room, Myles and KJ were gone. Myles called to see if my meeting was over and when I told him it was, he asked that I come downstairs so we could go out to dinner. We walked to Outback Steakhouse since it was close to the hotel. After dinner, I checked out of the hotel, and we headed home. "My next workshop will be in Memphis, Tennessee," I said to Myles.

He laughed and replied, "Can I come?"

"I don't know right now. Once I get the schedule, I will see. But I think they are going to fly a team of us down there."

"Well, I enjoyed myself today."

"Me, too!" yelled KJ from the backseat.

"What did you guys get into?"

Myles was the first to speak up. "We went sightseeing and to the Fashion Mall that was connected by two buildings. We stood on the archway glass and looked down at the traffic below. KJ was so excited about seeing the cars below us. Then, we went to the Soldiers and Sailors' Monument. That was exciting, too."

"I'm glad the two of you enjoyed yourselves while I trained all day!" We both laughed.

KJ was in the backseat playing with his game. He paused and said, "Mama, a man asked Myles for a cigarette, didn't he, Myles?"

"Yes, he did."

"Mama, Myles told him he didn't smoke and that smoking was bad for his health. Didn't you tell him that, Myles?"

"Yes, I sure did, KJ! Smoking is bad for your health."

KJ was quiet for a while and then said, "Myles, tell Mama about the two ladies who talked to you."

Myles let out a laugh and asked him, "What ladies?"

"Remember that lady who said she liked the way you smell?"

"Yes, I remember. She wanted to know the name of the cologne I was wearing."

KJ wouldn't let up. "She was looking at you and smiling at you, too!"

I had to laugh then. "KJ, what did he say to her?"

"He said he didn't know the name of the cologne because it was a gift to him. And that other lady said she was lost. Myles told her to find a policeman because we were here for a conference and didn't know anything about the city. Mama, that lady followed us for a long time. I think she liked Myles."

Myles laughed so hard at KJ's account of the day with the ladies. "Boy, that lady didn't like me!"

"Well, she did follow us for a long time."

"You call yourself telling on me. Tell your Mama about the little girl who kept looking and smiling at you at the mall!"

KJ took the bait. "She was looking at me because I'm a little boy, but that lady followed you because you are a man. And that other lady said I was handsome like my daddy. She thought you were my daddy, didn't she?"

"What lady?" asked Myles.

"That lady with the red top on when we were eating breakfast. She dropped her napkin, and you picked it up for her. She said thank you and that your little boy is handsome."

"Wow, KJ! You remember all of that?" Myles seemed impressed.

"Yes! I remember everything!" KJ said amid a yawn.

Myles and I laughed at all KJ said, and when I looked back, he was fast asleep. I told Myles KJ was taking notes on him, which brought on a fit of laughter between us.

By the time we made it back to Nashville, it was late, and KJ was in a deep sleep. Myles carried him into the house for me and laid him on the couch. He jokingly said, "I should have woken him up and made him walk, telling you all that stuff about me!" He pulled me to him and said, "I enjoyed my trip. Thanks for letting me tag along with you."

"Thank you for driving us."

"How about we thank God for a safe trip there and back?" Myles suggested as he hugged me. "Did I tell you how beautiful you are?"

"No, you didn't, but thank you."

Myles grew serious. "I'm going to be heading out of town for a few days. I'm driving my dad, uncle, and aunt to Oklahoma for a funeral. One of our cousins died, and they are having a memorial service on Wednesday."

"I'm sorry to hear that. I will be praying for your family."

"Thank you, Lexie." He kissed me on my forehead before leaving and said, "I'll be calling you while I'm away."

Chapter 30

The following Saturday, I was in my exercise room doing my morning workout when the doorbell rang. It was around 11:30. As I walked to the door, I thought I would be greeted by the mailman. I had ordered a set of books off eBay for KJ's 7th birthday and was expecting them to arrive that day. I planned to pick him up after his visit with his dad, take him to Chuck E Cheese's, and then give him the books as his gift.

Before opening the door, I looked out the window and was surprised to see it was Myles—and he was holding something behind his back. I opened the door, and he walked in and kissed me. He had never done that before. "Myles! I'm all sweaty and in my workout clothes!" I was wearing a tank top and some Daisy Duke shorts. I felt embarrassed about him seeing me like that but was glad to have him over.

"I love you in your workout clothes and your sweats, too!" he said, laughing. He had never approached me like that before, let alone used the word love in any of our conversations.

I stood in place, looking at him while trying to think of what to say next. I pushed my sweat-soaked hair away from my face, still feeling uncomfortable about what I wore. Myles then brought a bouquet of flowers from behind his back. "Aww! Are you bringing me flowers?"

"Yes, I am." His words were followed by another light kiss on my sweaty forehead.

"Thank you. They are beautiful."

"Beautiful flowers for a beautiful lady," he replied.

"Are you in a hurry?" I asked as he followed me into the kitchen. I needed to put the flowers into a vase.

"No, I'm not in a hurry, but I do have to stop by my dad's house when I leave here."

"Have a seat. Let me shower, and I'll be right back." I hurried to take a shower and put on fresh clothes.

When I returned, Myles was looking at the pictures on the wall. He turned, walked toward me, and said, "You smell good—and you are looking good, too!" He pulled me close to him and smelled my freshly washed hair. "Where is KJ?"

"At his dad's. I made taco salad before I exercised. I'm hungry. Would you like something to eat?"

"Yes, make me a bowl, please."

We sat in the breakfast room, eating and talking. I served lemonade and a slice of cheesecake afterward. When he finished eating, he got up and walked to the window. "Your mailman is here."

"Did you see if he put a package in the mailbox?"

"No, I just saw mail pieces."

"Hmm… I'm expecting a package. I ordered some books for KJ for his birthday. I thought they would be here today."

Suddenly, he turned and pulled me up from the table into an embrace. He looked me deep in the eyes as he gently pushed my hair back from my face.

"Where did all this come from?" I asked shyly.

"I've wanted to do this for a long time now and ask you: Will you marry me?"

I thought he was being funny, but I could see he was serious when I looked into his eyes. "Myles, are you sure you want to marry me?"

"Yes, I'm sure. I love you, Lexie. There's a saying: 'To love is to share one's happiness in another person's heart.' I want to share my happiness with you."

"Wow, that's so poetic. Before I give you an answer, let me think about it."

He held my face in his hands, kissed me on the tip of my nose, and asked, "What is there to think about? I love you, Lexie. Do you love me?"

I blushed. "I think I do. When you are here, I don't want you to leave. When you're not here, I think of you all the time."

"I feel the same way." He tightened his embrace. I felt his heart beating against my chest and I could smell the scent of his cologne. "When I was in Iraq, I vowed to the Lord that I would keep myself until I got married if He brought me home alive. I knew I wanted to marry you. When we were in Indianapolis, that night was torture for me. I laid on that couch thinking about how much I wanted to hold you. You are making it hard for me right now."

I laughed at his playful accusation. "What did I do?!" I knew what he was trying to say. As I laid in my bed that night, I thought the same thing about him.

"Nothing. Just being close to you, I never want to leave." He held me even tighter and gave me a passionate kiss. "Would you like me to help with the dishes?" he asked after nearly taking my breath away.

"No, thank you. I can put everything in the dishwasher."

"Well, Ms. Lexie Harris, I hate to eat and leave, but…"

I cut him off. "Are you leaving because I didn't give you an answer to your proposal? There's so much going on in my head right now. I need to pray about my decision because when I marry again, I want it to be forever." I looked deep into his hazel brown eyes, not wanting him to leave.

"No, that's not why I'm leaving. I understand your position and appreciate your honesty. I need to go and check on dad. He came home early from work yesterday, saying he didn't feel well. I didn't like how he sounded when I called him this morning. I'll call you when I get back to my apartment." He hugged me tightly, kissed my forehead, and left. Just when I thought he was gone, my doorbell rang. I opened the door, he handed me my mail, and said, "I love you." He then got on his motorcycle and drove away.

I retreated to my exercise room, sat down, and began reading my mail. My thoughts interrupted the moment. "What is wrong with me? I should have yelled as loud as I could, 'YES! I WANT TO MARRY YOU! I LOVE YOU, TOO!'" I laid back on my exercise bench. The sun shone through the window as my thoughts continued to wander. "Myles has all the qualities I'm looking for in a man. He's respectable, he supports me, he's never made any out-of-the-way advances toward me, and he is a saved man who just told me he loves me. I can see he cares for KJ, too. Was Myles God's answer to my prayer? Oh, my God! What's wrong with me? I love that man!"

I was scheduled to attend a woman's retreat that weekend. I'll tell Myles I want to marry him when I return home.

Chapter 31

My phone rang, and Keith's name showed up on the caller ID. "What does he want now?" I said aloud. When I answered the call, it was KJ on the other end. "Hi, Mama! What are you doing?"

"Nothing."

"Can you come and pick me up?"

"Pick you up? Why do you want me to do that?"

"I just want to come home."

"KJ, what have you done? Let me speak to your dad."

"Mama, I didn't do anything. Promise. I just want to come home."

"Honey, you can't come home right now. I will be going out of town this weekend, and there's no one to keep you."

"Can I go with you?" he asked excitedly.

"I'm sorry, but no. I'm going to a retreat just for women."

"Well, Myles can keep me while you're gone!"

"No, he can't. Myles has to work."

"Oooo! I know! You can drop me off at Mrs. Riddle's. I want to see her anyway."

"No, KJ. You are staying at your dad's house. When I get back, you can come home. Okay?"

I heard his dad say something to him in the background. "Okay. Bye, Mama. I love you."

"I love you, too, baby."

As I hung up the phone, I thought about how strange that call was. He never called home for me to pick him up early before.

Chapter 32

I saw Myles at church on Sunday, but he left before the service ended. Apparently, his dad got sick, so Myles took him home. On Monday, he called to let me know how his dad was doing and complimented me on the blue outfit I wore to church. Before hanging up, he told me he loved me. I could tell in his voice that he was concerned about his father's bad heart.

We talked every day that week. On Thursday, Myles came to my job and took me out to lunch. He said it was my "going away lunch" before I left for the retreat on Friday. While taking me back to work, I told him that I would have an answer for him when I got back from the retreat.

"I hope it's the answer I want to hear," he said with a giggle.

The moment turned serious again when I said, "Myles, KJ called and asked me if you could keep him while I'm away on my trip. I told him no because you have to work."

He smiled as he squeezed my hand and replied, "I can keep him if you want me to. He can come to work with me."

"Nope, he's staying with his dad. He will be okay." I could see the concern on his face about his dad being sick. Plus, he talked a lot about him during lunch. The last thing he needed was a child with additional demands on his time.

When we pulled into the parking lot at my job, he got out first and then came around to open my door for me. We stood there, embracing one another. He ran his finger through my hair, kissed me, and said, "I'm going to miss you when you're gone."

"I'm only going to be gone for three days, Myles."

"I'm still going to miss you. Enjoy your trip. I love you, Lexie Harris." The kiss that followed was divine!

He remained standing by his car, watching as I entered the building. I turned to wave goodbye to him—and that's when I saw Keith sitting in his car across the street, looking in my direction. I acted as if I didn't see him and wondered if he was, indeed, stalking me. I thought of the day he followed me to the police station.

Just as I walked into my office, my phone was ringing. My secretary was on the other end. "Ms. Harris, you have an important call on line one." I wondered if Myles was calling, but I suspected it wasn't him because he always called on my cell phone.

I picked up the call, only to hear Keith laughing. "Keith, is KJ alright?" I asked, although I knew I had just seen him across the street.

"Yeah, he's good."

"Then why are you calling me?"

"I just wanted to say I saw you getting out of that gray Charger. Was that your new man?"

I felt myself becoming enraged. "Pastor Montgomery, you need to be somewhere praying. I thought you were bigger than that—calling me at my place of work with this mess. You are a sick man. Don't call me anymore unless it's about KJ!" His laughter grew louder. I slammed down the phone, walked to my window, and saw a man getting into Keith's car before he drove off. "That man is crazy!" I said quietly.

My first thought after that interaction was to call KJ before Keith got home to make sure he was okay. That last conversation I had with my son wanting me to come pick him up disturbed my spirit. I called, and KJ answered. "Hi, baby! How are you doing?"

"Good."

"What are you doing?" I could tell he was doing something.

"Just playing with my remote-control car."

"Okay, I just wanted to call and let you know I will be leaving tomorrow on my weekend retreat and that I will see you next weekend."

"Mama, I want to go with you."

"Remember I told you it's a women's retreat? No men allowed."

He busted out laughing. "Okay. I love you, Mama."

"I love you, too. Bye!" As I hung up the phone, I knew I would miss my baby.

Chapter 33

Friday at noon, I left for my retreat to a remote area in the mountains of Nashville. I was so excited about going for the first time. When I arrived at the campground, there were three cabins in a row that were made from logs, a lake that sat behind them, and a big white log cabin with a porch. The sign on the building said it was the Fellowship Hall. From the schedule, I knew that would be the place where classes were going to be held. It was a beautiful scene.

Once inside, I was amazed. The interior did not look like a log cabin. There were beautiful, knotted pine walls and hardwood floors. In the cabin's center was an open space that looked like a living room. It has two couches, a table, and two oversized chairs. Each cabin slept 40 women. There were 20 bedrooms—two ladies in each room. I shared the room with my pastor's wife. The rooms had twin beds placed against opposite walls, a table with four chairs, and a bathroom with a shower.

The check-in time was between 4 and 6 p.m., and the get acquainted hour was from 7-8 p.m. in the Fellowship Hall. There was plenty of food to go around for everyone. I met many wonderful, saved women from other churches around the state. We had to be in our rooms by 9:30. There was no TV, and they didn't want us on our phones unless it was an emergency. Fortunately, I enjoyed my pastor's wife's company. We talked until around 1:00 a.m. the next morning. I thought to myself, "She reminds me of Mrs. Riddle."

Saturday morning, we were up at 7:00 for breakfast and at prayer at 9:00. While in prayer, I prayed about me marrying Myles. There were also things I had been carrying around for a long time that I needed to release once and for all. As I laid my prayers at the feet of God, I felt Him lifting those things from me. I finally felt delivered and free!

In the Fellowship Hall, teaching sessions were ongoing. We were able to choose the class we wanted to attend. I chose three different ones. Each was two hours long in various rooms throughout the building. One teacher taught on Growing in the Grace of God from 9-11 a.m. The next taught how the Fruit of the Spirit should be in our lives as we become women of God from 11:30-1:30 p.m. The last instructor taught "How to Study God's Word with a Purpose" from 2-4 p.m.

A time was designated for questions and answers in each class after the teaching session. Each teacher provided Bible verses to back up their responses.

I enjoyed all three sessions. I learned a lot of things that would help me with my daily walk with God. Questions I needed answers to were answered with scriptures. I thanked God for allowing me to attend the retreat. I needed that time to be alone with Him. Along the way, I got to know my pastor's wife. She was deep into God's Word and was a woman of great faith and wisdom.

After class, I went shopping with one of the ladies who drove her van to the retreat, along with three other ladies. Once back at the retreat, all the attendees came together in the Fellowship Hall for a fun time. We ate, played games, talked, and exchanged phone numbers. I met women who were lawyers, teachers, nurses, and business owners. There was a mixture of women of various races from around the state. We all had one purpose for being there: to get a closer walk with God while seeking His purpose and direction.

On Sunday morning, everyone joined together for devotions, breakfast, and to say our goodbyes. At noon, we headed home on the bus that brought us there. The chatter on the ride home was all about the wonderful time we experienced and how we all looked forward to returning the following year.

It was raining by the time we made it back to Nashville around 4:00 p.m. I was glad I had left my car at the church. The church van driver took some of the ladies home, and I dropped off two who lived in the same direction I was headed so that they didn't have to wait in the rain for someone to pick them up.

Chapter 34

I couldn't wait to tell Myles what a great time I had on the retreat. I stopped by Starlite Restaurant to get a Chef Salad on the way home. While eating, I felt an urge to pray and thank God for a safe trip and for giving me clarity on the things that were troubling me. I called Myles' house phone to let him know I was home but didn't get an answer. I left a message for him to call me. I then called his cell phone. He didn't answer that either. I decided to put my clothes away and await his return call. I thought back to our conversation about him visiting his family. Perhaps that's where he went…but why wasn't he answering his cell phone? When 7:30 p.m. came, and he hadn't returned my call, I tried his cell phone again. I suppose the battery was dead at that point because it went straight to his voicemail.

I thought about my ride home and realized I didn't see his car at his dad's house on my way in, but his dad's truck was there. I called his dad's house, and his niece answered. I told her who I was and asked if she had seen or talked to Myles. "Yes," she said, obviously distraught. "He's at the hospital with granddaddy. Granddaddy isn't doing well."

"What hospital is he in?" I asked. After she told me, I thanked her and immediately prayed for Myles' dad. I knew Myles needed someone to be with him, so I decided to go to the hospital to be by his side. As I drove through the rain, I thought about Myles' love for his dad. I knew he was hurting deeply as he watched his father suffer.

When I made it to the hospital and learned where Mr. Ferguson was, I located Myles first. He was sitting in the waiting room with a man I'd never seen before. He looked up, saw me walking toward him, and said, "I just tried to call your house to see if you were back. My phone is dead." Before I could say anything, he said, "Lexie, it doesn't look good. It doesn't look good at all." I could see he had been crying. I didn't know what to say, so I just hugged him close. He stepped back from me and introduced me to his uncle. "Lexie, this is my Uncle Eddie, my dad's brother."

"Hi. It's nice to meet you, sir," I said as we shook hands.

"Nice to meet you, too," he replied. Worry was written all over his face.

Myles and I sat down as he held my hand. "How did you know I was here?"

"I called your dad's house, and your niece told me you were at the hospital with your dad."

"When did you get back from the retreat?"

"A little after 4:00 this afternoon."

"You didn't have to come here. You just got back into town, and the weather is bad."

"Yes, I did have to come. I wanted to be here with you."

He hugged me and said, "I'm glad you are here. Pray with me, Lexie." I held his hand, he grabbed his uncle's, and we prayed. He was so broken, the tears streamed down his face.

Almost immediately after our prayer, Myles' sister came into the room with us. She was crying and asked Myles, "Why didn't you call me to let me know daddy was here?"

He stood and said, "Mae, I did call. I was told you were in surgery with a doctor. When I called again, they told me you were at lunch. How did you know daddy was here?"

"I called home, and Trina told me you took daddy to the hospital. Myles, what are the doctors saying?"

"It's his heart. It will be a miracle if he lives through the night," he replied sadly. Those words struck a chord in me because my own Mama died from a bad heart.

Mae started crying uncontrollably. She sat by her Uncle Eddie, holding his hand. "Mae, this is Lexie." She looked up with tears running down her face and managed to say, "Hi."

"Hi, Mae. It's nice to meet you. I'm sorry about your dad." With her face buried in her hands, she murmured a faint thank you.

Myles grabbed both my hands in his and said, "Lexie, I know you are tired from your trip. Go home. I will call and let you know what's going on. Thank you for praying with us."

"Are you sure you want me to leave?"

"Yes, I'm sure. I'll call you later."

"Okay." I turned to face his family. "It was nice meeting you, Mr. Eddie and Mae. I'll be praying for Mr. Ferguson."

Myles walked me to the door, kissed me, and said, "Thanks for coming. I love you."

When I got home, I prayed for Myles' dad and went to bed.

Chapter 35

Monday morning, as I prepared for work, the doorbell rang. I looked out the window and saw Myles standing on the other side. I quickly opened the door and immediately noticed the tears in his eyes. Without saying a word, he drew me into an embrace. I had a feeling his dad had passed away.

"Come in and sit down," I coaxed gently.

"He left us around 4:00 this morning. My dad is gone, Lexie." I hugged him and cried, feeling his pain. "My dad is gone. My dad is gone. My…dad…is…gone!" he said through his heavy sobs.

The only thing I could think of to say was, "He's gone to a better place. He's not sick anymore. He's with the Lord."

"I know he's with the Lord, but he left me too soon."

I had no other words to say to take his hurt away, so I just stood by his side and rubbed his back. I remembered what it felt like when my mom died, with the difference being that I had no one except the Lord to comfort me. When He blessed me with Mrs. Riddle, she talked to me and helped me through the pain of my loss. I wanted to be the one there for Myles in his time of need.

"I know you're getting ready for work. Can I stay here for a while? Right now, I want to be by myself to think. There are so many people at dad's house."

"Yes, you can stay here as long as you need to." I planted a soft kiss on his forehead. "Are you sure you are going to be alright? I can call in and take the day off to be here with you."

"No, no. You go to work. I'll be okay. I just need some time alone." I hugged him close and walked away to finish getting prepared for the day ahead.

At work, time seemed to creep by. "Should I have stayed home with Myles?" I kept asking myself. When I arrived home that afternoon, he was already gone.

On Tuesday, Myles called and said, "Thank you for coming to the hospital and praying with us. I really appreciated you letting me stay at your house for a while."

"That's what I was supposed to do. Is there anything I can do to help things go a little easier for you?" I asked.

"No, I am closing everything down for the week at the shop. I'll hopefully see you tomorrow. I love you."

Wednesday afternoon, Myles stopped by to tell me they were flying his dad's body back to Myrtle Beach, South Carolina, where his oldest sister lived. He was to be buried in the family cemetery. He went on to explain that he, Mae and her family, Uncle Eddie, and a couple of our cousins would be leaving early Thursday morning. Our pastor would fly in on Saturday morning for the funeral that was scheduled to begin at 10:00 a.m. and return home that same evening.

"Do you want me to come with you?" I asked.

"I do, but no. I will be riding with Mae and her family, and we are going to stay a couple of days after the funeral to handle some business with my other sister Sharon."

I felt so sorry for him. He was so sad and broken. I knew how much he truly loved his dad.

Chapter 36

During Friday night's Bible study, our group prayed for Myles and his family. Our study ended early that evening. By 6:45, they were all gone. I thought about Myles and wondered how he was doing on the eve of burying his father. I know how I felt when my mom passed away, mainly because I was the only one taking care of her final arrangements and everything else that went along with tending to her affairs.

I laid in my bed, thinking about my mom and Myles' dad. I thought back to when I first started going to the church where Mr. Ferguson was one of the greeters. He made KJ and me feel welcome and made sure to speak to us every Sunday. KJ seemed to enjoy having Mr. Ferguson rub him on his head when we entered the church and when he was slipped a pack of fruit snacks as they walked to the church's nursery.

I recall the Sunday Mr. Ferguson wasn't at the door to greet us, and KJ didn't want to go to the nursery because his "escort" wasn't there to walk with him. The next Sunday, while driving to church, KJ said, "I hope Pawpaw is at church today."

"Who is Pawpaw?" I asked.

"The man at the door is my Pawpaw, and I'm his little man. He always rubs me on my head and gives me a pack of fruit snacks!"

"Did he tell you to call him Pawpaw?"

"Yep, and I'm his little man," he repeated. That day, Mr. Ferguson was standing at the door, making KJ so happy because I was sure he got his fruit snacks again.

Mr. Ferguson was a good man who would have made a fantastic granddaddy for KJ. I was definitely going to miss him greeting us every Sunday at the door. A sad reality hit me suddenly. "Oh, no. How am I going to tell KJ his Pawpaw died?!"

I wonder if Mr. Ferguson knew Myles and I were a couple. There was one Sunday in particular that I remember that let me know he might have had a clue. He met me at the door and said, "Myles will be a little late for service today. His car had a flat."

I smiled and replied, "Okay. Thank you." He then took hold of KJ's hand and led him away to the nursery. Did Myles ask his father to tell me he would be late? I was sure he noticed Myles and me sitting together during the service. I also wonder if Myles told him he wanted to marry me.

I laid there and cried, thinking about Mr. Ferguson, Myles, and their family having to bury their loved one the following day. Eventually, I drifted off to sleep.

On Saturday morning, I stayed in bed until 11:30. KJ was at his dad's, so there was no reason for me to get up any earlier. When I finally got up, I ate a late breakfast, got dressed, and went to work to catch up on a couple of things I didn't finish before leaving for the retreat. I worked until late that afternoon. I stopped by Subway to pick up a sandwich, chips, and a drink for dinner on my way home.

I pulled into my garage, got out of the car, and heard the phone ringing. Just as I walked through the door, it stopped. I checked the caller ID and saw Myles called twice, and Keith called once. I called Keith first since KJ was with him. Before he could even finish saying hello, I cut him off. "Is KJ alright?"

"He's good. I'm the one who needs to talk to you. Have you found any more of my belongings at your house?"

"Didn't I tell you before there is nothing else at my house that belongs to you?"

"You make me do what I'm doing," he replied.

"What? What are you talking about? You were the one sneaking around with Brenda while married to me. Are you doing the same thing to her that you did to me?"

"No, but you made me change back to the way I used to be."

"What do you mean? Don't you dare blame your insecurities on me! You didn't love me, and I didn't love you. We've been divorced for six years, and it was the best thing for me. I pray you'll be happy with Brenda because I am happy with who I'm with. I gotta go. I have another call to make. Bye."

"No, don't hang up. I need to talk to you."

"Keith, are you drunk or something? Go talk to God and your wife. Stop calling me with your foolishness. I can't help you." I then hung up the phone. I sat on the couch and thought to myself, "What did he mean about me making him go back to the way he used to be? He sounded confused. Maybe the Lord is dealing with him about something."

When I returned Myles' call, he answered on the first ring. "Where have you been all day? I tried calling your cell phone and the house, but you were nowhere to be found."

"Do I detect a hint of jealousy?" I asked with a giggle. He laughed, but I also heard the sadness in his voice. "I went to work to catch up on some of the things I didn't get done before going to the retreat."

"Why didn't you work out of your home office?"

"Because I wanted to get out of the house. You're not here, and KJ is at his dad's. I felt lonely when I got up this morning, so I went to work. It wasn't until I made it all the way there that I realized I had left my cell phone at home."

He let out an audible sigh. "I just wanted to hear your voice."

"How are you doing?" I asked.

"It was hard, but I am better now after hearing your voice."

"Myles, how is Mae doing?"

"Better than my sister Sharon." He sounded as if he were going to start crying again.

"I'm praying for you and the family. I know it's hard right now, Myles, but everything will be alright. God will never leave you, and you know I'm here for you whenever you need me." The other end of the line was pin-drop silent. In a whisper, I said, "I love you."

He laughed and asked, "What did you just say?"

"I just wanted to see if you were listening to me."

"Yes, Lexie. I heard everything you said." His laughter continued. "I can't wait for my answer from you when I get home. My dad told me not to let you get away."

"You told your dad about us?"

"I talked to my dad about everything. He was my best friend."

"Yes, he was a good man. Did you know KJ called him Pawpaw? He always walked KJ to the nursery at church and slipped him a package of fruit snacks, as if I didn't know."

Myles let out a hearty laugh. I enjoyed hearing him laughing after sounding so sad. "For real? He called dad Pawpaw?"

"Yes, and KJ said he was your dad's little man."

"Oh, my God! That's what he called KJ? That's the same nickname he called me until I went to junior high school. I had to tell my dad to stop calling me that because all my friends were laughing at me." By that point, he was laughing so hard at the memory. "I can't believe my dad called KJ little man, too. My dad was something else. I'm going to miss him."

"I know you will. We'll miss him, too."

"Well, I have to go now. They are calling for me. I'll call you on Monday. We are having a family meeting tomorrow. Pray that all goes well."

"I will."

"I love you, Lexie. Bye." Before I could respond, he ended the call.

I enjoyed my conversation with him. The weekend seemed a lot longer with both him and KJ not around. The next call I made was to Mrs. Riddle. Her talks were always right on time and just what I needed at that moment.

Chapter 37

Sadness overcame me when I walked into the church on Sunday morning, and Mr. Ferguson wasn't at his post to greet me. The pastor made it back from the funeral safely and preached an excellent message about the importance of depending totally on God. The choir sang beautifully as well. After service, I spoke with the pastor and his wife briefly before going home.

That night, as I ate my dinner, I thought about my dad, mom, brother, and Mr. Ferguson. Each was a great loss. I cried myself to sleep but was awakened by the phone ringing. It was Keith again. As I decided whether or not to pick up the phone, I couldn't help but wonder why he wouldn't just leave me alone. I let the call go to voicemail. About an hour later, the phone rang again, but it was someone who had dialed the wrong number.

I went to work on Monday, and after getting home, Myles called to report that the meeting went well. "We will be leaving here on Wednesday morning. I miss you, girl."

"I miss you, too." If only he knew just how much…

Myles and Mae's family returned home that Wednesday evening. He called to let me know they made it back and that Mae had dropped him off at his apartment. "I'll see you at Bible study on Friday," he said.

The group gathered as usual for our Friday night Bible study. Myles came in late. I was so happy to see him again. He looked at me, mouthed the words, "I've missed you," and made a heart with his hands over his heart. I smiled at the gesture.

The teaching that night was right on time: death and grief. When the study was over, Myles told me he really enjoyed the lesson and that it was what he needed to hear. I commented on how it helped me, too.

After everyone left, Myles hugged and kissed me passionately. "Lexie, I am so happy to be home. I've missed you so much."

"I'm glad you're home, too."

"So, tell me, Lexie: What's your answer?"

I loved the way he said my name. I looked at him as if I didn't know what he was talking about. "What's the question?" I asked with a knowing smile.

He got down on one knee and proposed. "Will you marry me?"

I didn't have to think about my answer. "Yes, I want to marry you."

He stood, picked me up, spun me around, and said, "I need you to fill this hole in my heart. I wish my dad were here to witness our exchange of vows." He kissed me again and then placed a beautiful ring on my finger.

"Myles! It's gorgeous!"

"I'm glad you like it. Now that you have said yes, let's go out to dinner to celebrate our engagement. I'm hungry!" He scooped me up and carried me to his car. My goodness, he was so strong! We kissed all the way to his car, with bits of laughter in between.

He took me to his favorite restaurant: Cracker Barrel. He said the food tasted like home-cooked meals. I liked eating there, too. After dinner, he drove back to my house, where he picked me up again, carried me to my front door, kissed me, and said, "I love you. Thanks for agreeing to marry me. You won't be sorry."

"Do you want to come in?"

"No, I must keep my vow I made to the Lord," he said while laughing. He kissed me and then left.

I thought to myself, "Oh, my God! I can't wait to marry him!"

Once he arrived back at his apartment, he called to let me know he had arrived safely. "Goodnight, Lexie. Thank you for wanting to marry me. I love you." He hung up before I could reply.

Chapter 38

Early Saturday morning, Keith called and asked if I could meet him at 10:00 to get KJ because he had a conference to attend at another church. We met promptly at our regular meeting spot, and I picked up my son. On our way home, I told KJ about Mr. Ferguson.

"Are you talking about my Pawpaw?" he asked.

"Yes, he has gone to be with the Lord."

"He's dead?!"

"Yes, KJ, Pawpaw is dead."

"You mean I won't see him at church anymore?"

"No, baby. You won't see him at church anymore."

He was quiet for a while. "Mama, I'm going to miss Pawpaw." He then started to cry. I didn't say anything; I just let him grieve the loss of a great man. His tears didn't stop until I pulled into the garage. Before getting out of the car, I told him Myles was sad about his daddy, too, and that he needed to be strong for him when he saw him. "Mama, I don't want Myles to cry." KJ was so sympathetic and such a big boy.

"I have some good news to tell you, though."

"What, Mama?"

"I'm going to marry Myles!"

He smiled widely and said, "I'll have two daddies! I already have two mommies."

"Do you like having two mommies?" I asked.

"Sometimes," came his reply.

When we finally made it into the house, I began preparing a late breakfast. I called Myles to see if he wanted to join us. "Yes, I would very much like to come over for breakfast. I was just getting ready to leave for the shop. See you in a few!" By the time he arrived, the food was ready. He and KJ were so happy to see one another. We sat in the breakfast room and ate together. I enjoyed watching the two of them interact with one another.

"Myles, you're going to be my daddy?" KJ asked.

"Yes, but only if you want me to."

"I do! Then, I will have two daddies!" KJ paused before saying, "Mama said Pawpaw has gone to be with the Lord."

Myles looked at me and confirmed what I had told my son. "Yes, he's with the Lord now."

"I won't see him anymore?"

"No, you won't see him anymore," Myles responded. Deciding to change the conversation, he asked KJ, "Would you like to come to the shop with me today?"

"Yes! Can I go, Mama?" He was so excited.

"But you just got home!"

"Mama, please? Can I go?"

I gave in. "Yes, you can go—after you both finish your breakfast." I don't remember ever seeing KJ eat so fast.

On their way out the door, Myles kissed me on my forehead and said, "I enjoyed breakfast. Thank you for inviting me. We should be back around four."

When they left, I cleared the table, put the dishes in the dishwasher, and then spotted Myles' cap sitting on the table near the door. "He can get it when they get back. I'll make sure to have dinner ready when they return," I thought to myself. I looked through the cabinet and refrigerator, trying to find something to cook for dinner. I chose to make a meatloaf, mashed potatoes, peas, and peach cobbler for dessert.

When my doorbell rang, I thought it was Myles coming back for his cap, so I didn't even look out the window before opening the door. It was Keith. My heart nearly jumped into my mouth. "Did KJ leave something in your car?"

"No, I wanted to see you."

"See me about what, Keith?"

"Lexie, you are looking good. I see you are letting your hair grow out now," he said, smiling.

"Thanks. But why are you here?" I asked.

"I think about you all the time." The grin on his face disgusted me.

"Why are you thinking about me, Keith? Think about your wife! Go home."

"You're not going to ask me in?"

"No! For what? This visit of yours is not about KJ, so you can leave." He just stood there looking at me. "Pastor Montgomery, go home to your wife. I have things to do." When I placed my hand on the knob to close the door, he saw the ring on my finger.

"Oh! Are you engaged?"

"Yes, I am. Go home, Pastor Montgomery." He looked shocked. The grin on his face changed to an angry frown. I stepped back and closed the door in his face. I peeked out the window and saw him still standing at the door. After what seemed like forever, he turned around, went back to his car, got inside, and just sat there. I couldn't believe he had the audacity to show up at my home unannounced and uninvited! I hoped he would be gone before Myles and KJ returned.

My mind went back to when KJ said his daddy was asking questions about me. I hoped that whatever it was that he was going through, he would get through it soon. The next time I looked out of the window, he was gone.

As I prepared dinner, I thought about Myles' proposal and knew he would want to set a wedding date. When the meal was complete, I remained sitting in the kitchen, waiting for KJ and him to return.

Imagine my surprise when Myles and KJ returned with McDonald's bags in their hands! When they walked in, I asked, "I made dinner for you guys, and you stopped at McDonald's?"

"I didn't know," Myles said. "Why didn't you call me?"

"I wanted to surprise you!"

"I'm sorry, KJ told me you liked the Southwest salad, fish sandwich, and apple pie and that he liked the kid's meal. I ordered a Big Mac meal for myself. I wish I'd known you prepared dinner for us."

"It's my fault. I knew I should have called you."

When Myles saw the meal laid out on the table, he exclaimed, "Oh, my! I love meatloaf and peach cobbler! How about we eat McDonald's today and the meatloaf dinner tomorrow? Do you want me to come over for dinner tomorrow after church? I wouldn't want to miss out on your meatloaf and peach cobbler for nothing!"

"Okay. It's a dinner date after church tomorrow."

After KJ finished his food, he went upstairs to his room.

"I have a surprise for KJ, but he can't get it until six weeks from now," Myles said.

"KJ doesn't need any more toys, Myles."

"It's not a toy."

"Well, what is it?"

"You'll have to wait until then to see it." He was such a tease.

"Okay. Fine," I said with a pout. We both laughed. "On a more serious note, what day do you want to get married?"

"Tomorrow, and we can have what you cooked for dinner tonight for our reception," he said, laughing.

"You are so silly!"

He sat there thinking and replied, "My sister is coming in from Myrtle Beach next weekend to pick up some things from my dad's house. Would it be too soon to get married then? I would like her to be here, if that's okay with you."

"That would be great! It doesn't have to be a big wedding. I'm just ready to marry you."

"Well, next weekend it is!" he said while planting a kiss on my cheek. "I can't wait to hold and love you like I have wanted to for a long time now. Let me get out of here. I have two computers to work on. I told both customers they could pick up their computers before 8:00 tonight."

"You're going back to the shop?"

"It's 5:00 now, so I should be finished around 7:00. I already started on one of them," he replied.

"Okay. Call me when you get back to your apartment. Will I see you at church tomorrow?"

"Yes, I will be there and then be here for dinner." As he hugged me goodbye, he whispered in my ear, 'I really don't want to leave."

"I don't want you to leave, either. But remember: computers." We laughed, kissed, and said our goodbyes.

Chapter 39

I began thinking about the wedding and all I had to do to prepare for the big day. I then thought about the surprise Myles said he had for KJ. I wondered if it was the iPad I heard KJ talking to him about. I spent some time meditating about God before my time was interrupted by a phone call. I looked at the caller ID and saw it was Keith calling. "What do you want this time?" I asked.

"Don't hang up. I want to ask you something."

"What do you want to ask me, Pastor Montgomery?"

"Are you going to marry that guy?"

"What guy?"

"That guy named Myles."

"Yes, I'm going to marry him. Why is it your business?" I could no longer hold back the irritation in my voice.

"I saw him when he left my house a little while ago."

"It's not your house. Wait. Are you saying you are watching my house?"

"All I can say is I saw him leaving."

"Fine. You saw him leaving. Stop calling my house about anything except KJ. You know, you are a sick man, Pastor Montgomery."

"You can call me Keith."

"I know your name, but to me, you are Pastor Montgomery and my son's daddy. Nothing more." I slammed the phone in his ear. A few minutes later, Keith called again. I didn't answer. He repeatedly called until KJ answered it upstairs. I heard him talking. "I went to work with Myles. (pause) Mama's friend. (pause). Nothing. Oh! We stopped by McDonald's. (pause) Daddy, guess what? Myles is going to take me fishing. (pause) Mama made us meatloaf and peach cobbler. We are going to eat it tomorrow after church. (pause) Yes, he's coming over for dinner. Do you want some peach cobbler, too? I will ask Mama to give you some."

I thought to myself, "He is telling his daddy too much. I better say something."

"KJ, who are you talking to?" (As if I didn't already know.)

"I'm talking to daddy. Do you want to talk to him?"

"Tell your daddy you gotta go so that you can start getting ready for church tomorrow."

I heard him say, "I gotta go. Bye, daddy." At that moment, I was glad he was in his room when Myles and I discussed the wedding date.

After church on Sunday, Myles came over for dinner as planned. He complimented me on the meal and dessert and said, "If you cook like this when we get married, we are going to have to start running in the morning and afternoon!"

Chapter 40

With the wedding fastly approaching, I realized that was the week KJ was scheduled to go to his daddy's house. I needed to call Keith to tell him to pick up KJ on Sunday at 3:00 instead of Saturday. I figured Myles could go with me that Sunday afternoon to drop off KJ, and Keith wouldn't have anything crazy to say to me. I hoped he would stop harassing me once he found out I was married. I could imagine the conversation that would be had when KJ informed his father that Myles was his new daddy.

The week of the wedding, I learned Myles had already spoken with our pastor, who agreed to perform the ceremony. I asked for two weeks off of work for my honeymoon. I invited some people from my job, Mrs. Riddle, and her family to our wedding on Saturday, May 5th, at 2:00 p.m. Myles' sister Mae offered to decorate the church and reception hall. All she needed to know was the colors. I also placed calls and ordered the catering and cake. It was a busy week.

When I got off work one day, I pulled into the garage, got out of my car, and heard the phone ringing. I thought it was Myles because he always called around that time. I walked inside, looked at the caller ID, and saw it was Keith. I didn't answer. I noticed he called earlier and had left two messages. The first message was:

"I believe the Lord is punishing me. I didn't do you right, Lexie. I am sorry. Call me. I'm at the church." I deleted the message. The second message was:

"You are on my mind all the time. I didn't know how I felt about you until KJ told me you were having Bible study in my house and that the man named Myles was coming there all the time. That's the house we lived in. Call me." I heard the anger in his voice and deleted that message, too. He truly must be crazy. His house? He didn't pay a dime towards its construction! He was taking things too far.

I waited on Myles to call me when my doorbell rang. Without looking out the window, I opened the door to Myles standing on the other side with a smile on his face. "I didn't know you were coming over today," I said with surprise.

"I was down the street visiting my sister and figured I would stop in to see you." He sensed something was different and asked, "What's wrong? Did I come by at the wrong time?"

"No, that's not it. Come in and have a seat." I sat down beside him. "I just have a couple of things on my mind right now."

"Would you like to put whatever's on your mind on mine?" he offered while hugging me.

"No, I'll take care of it." We sat and talked for a while. I wanted to tell Myles about Keith. I just knew that he would stop it with the nonsense once I got married.

"Where's KJ?" he asked.

"He's upstairs taking a nap."

"I want to thank you again for that wonderful dinner on Sunday." He leaned over and kissed me.

"I'm glad you enjoyed it."

"I can't stay long. I was at Mae's and thought I'd stop in to see you before heading back home. I'm working on a laptop at my apartment that I need to get fixed by tonight so that I can take it back to the shop. The customer will be picking it up first thing in the morning." As he stood to leave, I stood as well and hugged him. "Oh, my goodness. You smell so good. I can't wait until we get married. Let me get out of here so I can get that laptop done."

When we get married, you can't bring your work home. I'll need all your attention," I said, obviously flirting with him.

He ran his fingers through my hair, kissed me on the tip of my nose, and replied, "I promise I will leave all my work at the job when we are married."

"It's raining hard outside," I commented as I looked out the window.

"Wow. It sure is. Do you have an umbrella I can use?"

"Yes, let me get it. It's in my office."

When I returned, he stood with his arms outstretched. "Give me a hug. I really don't want to leave you like this."

"Myles, we will be married in a few days, and you won't have to leave."

"No, it's not that. I can tell something is going on in that pretty little head of yours." He pulled me into a warm embrace.

"I am alright. You go and tend to that laptop. I'm okay. Really."

"Thanks for the use of the umbrella. I'll bring it back. Promise."

"No, you can have it. I have another one in the garage. Once we get married, you won't need an umbrella because you can park your car in the garage."

"Why, thank you, future Mrs. Myles Ferguson!" he said before popping open the umbrella and walking out the door.

After Myles left, I sat on the patio, watching the falling rain. A fleeting thought passed through my mind. "I pray Keith will stop harassing me." That was not to be the case.

I heard the phone ring twice and then stop. "Mama! Telephone!"

"Who is it?"

"Dad." He handed me the phone and walked into the kitchen.

"Hello, Pastor Montgomery. Why are you calling me now?!"

"So, that Myles guy has been in my house?" I couldn't say what I wanted to because KJ was within earshot. I gripped the phone tighter and wondered why that man spoke as if he were nearby. "I saw him leaving. I know he's been there."

My angry response came in a harsh whisper. "You have resorted to watching my house? You are a sick man. But, since I have you on the phone [speaking louder], will you meet me on Sunday at 3:00 instead of Saturday to get KJ? I have something to do, and I need KJ with me."

"What do you have to do that you can't do without him?" I didn't reply

"Will you meet me on Sunday? Yes? No?" It was obvious I demanded an answer.

"I'll be there at 3:00 on Sunday."

Before he could say anything else to disturb my mood further, I hung up the phone. I couldn't figure out why he was crazily obsessed with my house. "Maybe I should tell Myles what Keith has been up to," I whispered to the falling rain.

KJ came out of the kitchen to join me on the patio. I knew he heard me talking to his dad. "Mama, is daddy angry at you?"

I avoided telling him his dad was, indeed, angry by saying, "I want him to pick you up on Sunday instead of Saturday. Do you want to play a game of Connect 4 with me? I'm ready to beat your socks off!"

"Yes! Let's play! But I'm going to beat you, Mama. Look! I don't have on socks!" he said, laughing. We played multiple board games until he got sleepy. We prayed, and then he went upstairs to bed.

Chapter 41

During my lunch break at work on Tuesday, I called Myles. "What are you up to?"

"Sitting here thinking about you," he replied in his sexiest voice.

"That's so sweet of you to be thinking of me. I was thinking about you, too, which is why I called."

He laughed and said, "I spoke to my sister Sharon a few minutes ago about the wedding. She said there will be 15 people coming from Myrtle Beach."

"That's awesome!" I yelled.

"Wow! I see someone is excited!"

"Yes, Myles! I am! They can stay at my house. I have plenty of room. Why should they have to get a hotel room?"

"Are you sure you have enough room for 15 people?"

"I have three extra bedrooms upstairs. KJ can bunk with me or sleep in my office on the couch. Plus, I have a pull-out bed in my bedroom."

"That's too many people to be at your house. I know Sharon and her family will be staying with Mae. That's four. My two aunts and their husbands always stay with my Uncle Eddie when they come into town. That's eight. There are seven of my cousins coming—four women and three men—who are around our age. The three men can stay with me."

"Myles, you only have one bedroom. They can all stay here. Really. I have plenty of room."

"Lexie, I appreciate you more than you know, but you don't know these people. They're strangers!"

"This is what I do know: You. They are your family, and I have room for them," I said with finality.

He laughed and said, "Okay. You win. I will let them know before they book their hotel rooms."

Noticing the time, I replied, "Myles, my lunch break is over. I gotta go now."

"Did you eat?" he asked with obvious concern.

"Yes, I ate while we were talking. You didn't hear me munching in your ear?" I said, laughing.

He laughed along with me. "You were slick with that one! Okay. See you at the church on Saturday."

"No, you will see me Friday for rehearsal," I reminded him. I heard him laughing as he hung up the phone. I wanted to tell Myles about Keith during our call, but he was so happy about the wedding. I couldn't bring myself to say anything. Keith would probably stop his nonsense once I remarried anyway…at least that's what I hoped and prayed for.

Chapter 42

Friday, I didn't go to work. I had Myles' family coming in at 9:00 p.m. and had a lot of things to do before their arrival. I had to pick up my dress and shoes, get my hair done at 3:00, and the rehearsal was scheduled for 6:00 that evening. KJ and I were all over the place, trying to get the house in order before our guests arrived.

After rehearsal that evening, Mae told me to leave because she and a couple of other ladies needed to decorate the church and reception hall. She added, "I don't want you to see it until tomorrow."

Not long after KJ and I got home, he said he was sleepy. I prepared him for bed. He excitedly chose to sleep in my office on the couch. "Mama, I need my car blanket." I retrieved his blanket, and it seemed no sooner than he laid down that he was asleep.

"My poor baby. Mama tired him out today," I thought.

About 30 minutes later, the doorbell rang. It was Myles bringing over my houseguests. He introduced me to everyone: Eric, Davis, Corey, Lynn, Donna, Shelia, and Paula. Paula looked to be in her late teens and was a friend of the family. After the introductions, Myles hurried out to go and set the alarm at the shop. As the group stood looking around, I heard Paula say, "It's beautiful in here."

Lynn spoke directly to me and said, "I love your house."

"House? This place is a mansion!" Eric exclaimed.

I smiled and thanked them for the compliment. "Let me show you guys where you will be sleeping. You can all come back down to get something to eat if you'd like. Bring up your luggage with you."

Once upstairs, Donna said, "It's beautiful up here, too! Did you do your own decorating?"

"No, I had an interior designer do it, but I added a few things myself."

Someone behind me said, "She had an interior designer do this? She must be rich!"

Someone else said, "She must be, to have a house like this!"

They didn't think I could hear them. I just smiled and showed them their rooms. "Okay. Here is the hallway bathroom," pointing as I walked. "Here's a bedroom. Here is another. There's also one at the end of the hall. This is my son KJ's room. He's asleep in my office downstairs, so someone is welcome to sleep in his room. This is the theater room. You guys can watch a movie if you'd like."

One of the young men said, "A theater room? Wow!"

"This is the master suite with its own bathroom and a sitting room. If there's not enough room, someone can sleep in here. The couch lets out to a bed. There are sheets, pillowcases, and blankets in the hallway closet." I directed everyone's eyes to the closet.

One of the ladies commented, "You have a whole house up here plus a theater room!"

"Yes, I actually designed the upstairs living space for my mom. I wanted her to have her own living quarters."

"I love the way you coordinated your colors. It's beautiful up here," Sheila commented.

"Now, I'm not going to tell you all which room to get. That's on the seven of you," I said with a smile. "The towels and washcloths are in the closet with the bedding." I giggled as they playfully fought over the rooms. "When you get settled, please come back downstairs. If you're hungry, I made a taco salad."

After choosing their rooms, the group came back down, went into the hallway washroom to wash their hands, and then grabbed a plate. As they ate, they talked about their trip. Our chatter was interrupted by the doorbell ringing. My heart leaped into my throat. "Who in the world could be coming to my door this time of night? Lord, please don't let it be Keith. I know he's watching my house, seeing who comes and goes," I thought to myself. The doorbell rang again.

I walked to the door and asked, "Who is it?" (Please, don't say Keith. Please don't say Keith.)

The male voice said, "I am the man who's getting married tomorrow to the most beautiful woman in the world!"

I flung open the door and said, "Myles! You're not supposed to see me until tomorrow!" He reached out and handed me bags filled with KFC. "I already have food for everybody."

"This food is my excuse to come by and see you," he said as he kissed me on the forehead. "I can't wait to marry you tomorrow." He came inside and went into the kitchen. "Hi, family! Y'all be good! I'll see you at the church. Don't be late! Bye!" He kissed me and then left.

"Here's some chicken if you want it!" Everyone laughed and asked if I wanted some. "No, thank you. You all can stay up as long as you'd like. I'm going to bed now. After all, I'm marrying the most handsome man in the world tomorrow!"

They laughed and said, "Good night. Thank you for having us here."

I went into my bedroom, prayed about my wedding, and went fast asleep.

Chapter 43

Saturday morning, I woke up early. I did my morning devotion, prepared breakfast for everyone, and then stepped outside onto the patio, leaving the door open. It was around 9:30. I heard two of the ladies talking. It sounded like Lynn and Shelia were in the family room. I assumed they were looking at the picture wall.

One of them said, "Lexie is a pretty lady. It's nice of her to let us stay here. Look! She served in the Air Force. Here are her picture and discharge papers. Girl, she looks like a model!"

The other voice said, "Here is a picture of her in a gown. She must have been in a beauty pageant or something. She favors Halle Berry. Did you see how she walks? She walks like Sondra from that show '227.'" Both started laughing.

I assumed one of them mimicked my walk because one of them said, "She don't walk like that!" They laughed about that for a long time.

As they had their fun, I thought about my Mama. She used to tell me I walked around like a proud peacock. I remember telling her, "Daddy said that's what drew him to you. The way you walk is the way I walk." We laughed.

Mama replied, "Like mother, like daughter! Two proud peacocks!" I recall how funny it looked when she mocked my walking style. My memories faded away when I heard the two ladies inside resume their conversation.

"Look, here is her graduation picture. It seems she's always been pretty," one said.

The other one commented, "This must be her mother. She looks like that lady who plays on The Heat of the Night—the one who's married to the black detective. This must be her father and brother. Wow! He looks like Billy Dee Williams! Just look at his hair!"

The other one agreed. "Umm-hmm! He sure does!"

"The son looks just like his daddy. Man, he looks good! I wonder if we will see him tomorrow. I need to meet him!" one said.

"Girl, you are crazy!" the other said, laughing. "Look. Here's a picture of Myles when he was in the Army, and here's one of Lexie and Myles coming out of

Cracker Barrel. They look good together. Look at how her pretty hair is blowing in the wind."

Listening in on their chatter sure was entertaining!

The other two ladies came downstairs. "What are y'all doing?" one asked.

"We're looking at all these pictures on this wall," one replied.

"Hey, we didn't see this room last night," one of them said.

I assumed she was looking at the living room. That door was always closed.

One of them commented, "Boy, it's beautiful in here!"

I could still hear them talking as they made their way into the living room, but I couldn't clearly understand what they were saying until they exited the room.

"She said her little boy was asleep in her office. That little boy is a cutie. I wonder what type of job she has," one stated.

"Well, Myles is about to marry a woman who looks like she obviously has money," another said.

"Myles has money, too, you know." They all laughed. "Let's ask her what type of work she does from home."

I chose that moment to go back inside. I walked into the family room just as the three men came downstairs. "Good morning, sleepyheads." By the look on the ladies' faces, I could tell that they wondered if I heard what they said.

"Good morning! Lexie, do you work out of your house?" Lynn asked. I could tell she was the one who talked more than the others.

"Yes and no. I'm a Training and Development Specialist. I work in Human Resources for the city of Nashville. Sometimes, I work out of my home office on programs I didn't complete while at work. During tax season, I do income taxes."

"Good. I might want you to do my taxes," Donna said. They all started laughing.

Eric chimed in and directed his comment at Donna. "Girl, with the little bit of work you do, you can do your own taxes on the short form by yourself!" That caused a wave of laughter to roar among us all.

"Well, if you want me to do your taxes, I will do them," I replied while still laughing.

Chapter 44

"You guys, breakfast is ready," I called out to my houseguests. As they gathered in the kitchen, I told them, "There's eggs, bacon, toast in the microwave, and grits on the stove. The orange juice, milk, and jelly are in the refrigerator." I sat at the island while they got their food.

Lynn asked, "How long have you known Myles?"

"I've known him since elementary school, but we lost touch when I moved and started going to a different school. We met again when he was on his way to Iraq. When he returned, we finally connected when I saw him at the church. So, here we are, getting married today! Are you married?" I asked Lynn.

"Married and divorced. No children. We still see each other, though. Tyrone and I were married for three years. When he started using drugs, I divorced him. He went to rehab and has been clean for 15 months. Now, he wants me to remarry him."

"Do you think you're going to?" Donna asked.

"I don't know. What I went through those two years was hard."

Donna shed some light on his "why." "He didn't start using until his parents and two sisters died in that house fire. That was a hard time for him."

"Yes, it was. But it was hard on all of us. Before I knew he was doing drugs, I thought he was losing his mind. Now, don't get me wrong: I still love him. I just don't want to marry him right now," Lynn answered honestly.

"You two act like you are still married," Eric said.

I listened to them continue to talk and learned Lynn owned a daycare center, and Paula worked with her. Donna was an elderly care supervisor, and Shelia was a teacher.

The chatter shifted direction when Eric asked, "Did I tell you Angie told Lorie I had a lady pregnant who worked in Walmart?"

"Why in the world would she think that?" Donna asked.

"Because she walked into the store one day when a pregnant employee was checking my receipt on the way out of the store. Do you know Lorie went to Walmart looking for that lady?!" Everyone busted out laughing.

"Are you talking about my Angie?" Corey asked.

"Yes, your Angie," Eric replied with a laugh.

"That's why we're separated now. She had serious trust issues. Every woman she saw, she swore I liked them."

Davis laughed. "When you see Corey and Angie together, he walks with his head down so he won't be accused of looking at other ladies." The group laughed so hard at what he said. I managed to sneak in an unnoticed chuckle.

"I love her, but she is a bit crazy," Corey said as he continued to laugh.

"Well, in a couple of hours, I will be marrying the man who said he couldn't get me out of his mind for over three years," I said before leaving the room to wake KJ so he could eat breakfast. As I walked away, I yelled back and said, "You guys can eat all the food because KJ's breakfast is Frosted Flakes, a banana, and milk. When I returned with KJ, all the guests spoke to him. He spoke back while I helped him prepare his bowl of cereal and cut his banana. "Everyone, this is Keith Junior. We call him KJ for short."

"When did all of them get here, Mama?" KJ asked.

"They are Myles' cousins. They came in late last night for the wedding. Remember I told you we had guests coming? You were asleep when they got here."

"Ohhhh!" The look on his face let me know he did recall our conversation.

Donna said, "Lexie, he is handsome. He looks like you."

"Thank you." I excused myself and went to my bedroom to answer the phone. The caller ID said it was Myles. "You are not supposed to talk to me until after the wedding!"

"Noooo… I am not supposed to see you until the wedding. How are you doing?"

"I'm good. I can't wait to marry you!"

He laughed and asked, "How are your houseguests?"

"We're all doing great. They are polite and very professional. I'm enjoying their company."

"May I speak to Lynn? And can you ask Eric to get on the other phone?"

"Sure!" I headed back into the kitchen. "Lynn, Myles wants to speak to you and Eric," I said as I handed Lynn the phone. Eric picked up the phone on the kitchen wall. I heard Lynn say, "Okay. I can do that," and Eric say, "Okay. We will see you at the church." Lynn handed me back my phone, and Eric placed the other back into its cradle on the wall. "Are you still there?" I asked Myles while walking back to my room.

"Yes, I am. Do you love me?"

"Yes, I love you. Where are we going on our honeymoon?"

"I can't tell you. It's a surprise. You're going to love it, though. See you at the church!"

Lynn came into my room and said, "Girl, Myles loves himself some Lexie!" She said it in such a comedic way, I had to laugh.

"And I love myself some Myles!" I replied happily.

Chapter 45

A bit later, I let everyone know the church isn't far, but that they are working on the highway. "We'll have to take a detour around town to get on the right highway that will take us back to the church. We need to be dressed and on our way around noon."

Eric responded, "Lexie, Myles said he wants you and KJ to ride with us to the church."

"Okay. I will be ready. I can't be late on my wedding day!"

Around 10:30, everyone had finished eating and socializing. I placed the dishes in the dishwasher and went upstairs to grab KJ's suit and get dressed. I was going to carry my wedding dress and shoes to get dressed at the church.

"I am in love with your theater room," Corey said.

"I'm glad you like it. You are welcome back anytime to watch movies."

"You shouldn't say that," he said with a smile. "You and Myles would have a houseguest every weekend!" Davis said. "Corey didn't go to bed last night. He was up all night watching movies."

"Man, I was looking at Predator. When it went off, I slept in the seat. It was so comfortable, it was like sleeping in a bed!" We all laughed.

After everyone was dressed and ready to go, we left for the church a little after noon. On our way, we got caught in a bumper-to-bumper traffic jam. When we got near what was slowing down the traffic, we saw it was a bad accident. People were outside of their cars, standing around and looking at the scene.

We finally made it to the church at 1:30. When we pulled into the parking lot, I didn't see Myles' car. I thought, "Where is he?" I started to get nervous, thinking about the accident we had passed. KJ and I got out at the church's side door that led to the women's dressing room and choir room. Everyone else went into the main sanctuary. As I walked down the hall, I remember seeing a gray car similar to Myles'. By the time I made it to the dressing room, I was a nervous wreck. I had to sit and pray that Myles was okay. "Junior, go into the choir room, okay? Chyna will help you get ready."

"Okay, Mama."

Mae came into the room. "Is Myles here?" I asked.

"Yes, Lexie. He's here."

"Thank You, Jesus!" I exhaled deeply.

"Girl, you're not dressed! It's going on 2:00. Let me help you. Your dress is amazing!"

"Thank you," I replied. "I like yours, too."

Mae was my Maid of Honor, and her husband Derrick was Myles' Best Man. Their daughter Chyna was my flower girl. She was seven years old—the same age as KJ. KJ was the one who would give me away.

While helping me get dressed, Mae said, "I would always see you jogging by my house all the time. I told my husband I needed to join you, and he said, 'Go for it. You could stand to lose a couple of pounds.'" she said while laughing.

"You are not out of shape, Mae. You are a nice size."

"Tell that to my husband. He always calls me fat. Is that how you keep your weight down? By jogging?"

"Jogging, exercising, and watching what I eat," I answered.

"You know, I never got a good look at you until that night at the hospital. You are a beautiful woman. This dress makes you look like you just stepped out of a magazine!" she said, smiling. "I wonder what Myles will say when he sees you walking down the aisle in this dress."

"Whatever it is, I hope he likes what he sees!" I replied.

The usher knocked on the door. Mae answered. "It's 2:00. Are y'all ready?"

"Yes," I answered. "Please bring in KJ and Chyna."

We heard the pastor's wife singing the Lord's Prayer. Afterward, soft music began to play. My Maid of Honor slowly walked in. She looked amazing in her cream-colored dress with a gold bow across the back. She carried gold and black flowers. The flower girl then walked in wearing a beautiful cream-colored dress, carrying a basket and dropping cream, black, and gold flower petals.

KJ looked up at me and said, "Mama, you look pretty."

"Thank you, baby." I was wearing a long, cream-colored fitted dress with a bow across the back. It was simple but elegant. I must say: I looked good! "Son, you are looking handsome, too!" He smiled at the compliment. He was wearing a cream-colored suit with matching shoes. "KJ, we are next to go in. Remember: When the pastor asks, 'Who gives this lady to be married...'"

He cut me off. "Mama, I know. You told me last night!"

"Okay, baby. Let's go."

Chapter 46

When we walked in, everyone stood. That was my first time seeing the way the church had been decorated for the occasion. There were gold and black ribbons draped on each pew, and the arch had a black ribbon and gold flowers wrapped around it. Lynn and Eric sang "Oh, How I Love You" by Zacardi Cortez as we walked. I thought to myself, "Oh, no he didn't! I heard that song when Myles took me to dinner and fell in love with it. Now, he has Eric and Lynn singing it just for me."

Step by step, I got closer to Myles and could see the broad smile on his face. He, too, was wearing a cream-colored suit with matching shoes. I always thought he was a handsome man, but he looked better than handsome as he stood under the arch. His hazel brown eyes seemed to pierce my soul. Beside him stood his Best Man/brother-in-law Derrick. He looked good in his cream-colored suit, too. Once standing beside Myles at the altar under the arch, Myles whispered, "You look beautiful."

The pastor prayed for us and then asked, "Who gives this woman to be married to this man?"

"I do," KJ shouted with pride. Everyone in the church laughed. I thought to myself, "That's Mama's little man giving his Mama away." He then stepped away and stood by the Best Man.

As we exchanged our vows, tears streamed from my eyes. Myles used his hand to wipe them away while smiling at me lovingly. That was a happy day for me. I married the man I loved. After our vows, the pastor prayed over our rings before we placed them on each other's ring fingers, after which the pastor said, "Myles, you may kiss your bride." It was a lovely, gentle kiss. "Ladies and gentlemen, I present to you Mr. and Mrs. Myles Lee Ferguson!"

One of the Deacons placed the broom on the floor in front of us, and we jumped the broom together. To me, jumping the broom represented jumping out of my past into my future. Someone in the building put on the instrumental version of Bebe Winans' "When I Found You, I Found Love," and Myles sang to me right there in the middle of the church. He stared into my eyes the entire time and wiped away my tears of joy. His singing a solo surprised me. I knew he had a nice voice, but he sounded just like Bebe was in the building somewhere, and he was just lip singing. Eric and Lynn joined in as his backup singers. Everyone in the church stood and clapped their hands as we walked out hand-in-hand, with him still singing to me.

We then went into the reception hall. Mae and the ladies had decorated it in black and gold. There were black and gold tablecloths with tall vases filled with gold and cream flowers and a black ribbon. Everything was simply amazing!

We took pictures with our family and friends inside and outside of the church. The food was delicious. We had cornbread dressing wrapped with sliced turkey, mashed potatoes, green beans almondine, steamed carrots, rolls, cranberry sauce, and punch. The cake I chose stood tall and looked dazzling, too. I couldn't have asked for a better wedding.

I thanked Lynn and Eric for singing that song for me.

"That's what that call at your house was about. He wanted to make sure we were coming and asked us to sing that song," Lynn said.

"Thank you. It was beautiful. I didn't know Myles was going to sing to me either."

They both laughed. "We enjoyed being his backup singers," Eric said as he did a quick two-step dance.

That day, I met Myles' family that lived in town, and his family met my cousin. Myles had a couple of his cousins he hadn't seen in five years drive in from Oklahoma. His Uncle Eddie was the one who told them Myles was getting married. The cousins were all happy to see one another again.

After the wedding, we were scheduled to meet at Mae's house. Myles told me not to ask any questions about our honeymoon, as he had it all taken care of. I waited patiently to see what he had planned.

As we prepared to leave the church, I said, "Myles, I didn't see your car when we drove up. How are we getting to Mae's house?"

"Your ride is out there," he answered.

"I didn't see it."

"It's out there. Open the door."

When I did, I was ecstatic! A pearl white 2017 Cadillac Escalade with gold trim was parked in front of the church. The license plate on the front read "My Lady."

"You rented that just for us to ride to Mae's house?" I asked.

"No, I didn't rent it," he replied with a huge grin. "It's yours."

"For real?! It's mine?! You bought that for me?!"

"Yes, my love. You deserve it."

I walked around the SUV, admiring every inch. "Myles, this is mine? Don't play with me!"

"Yes! It's really yours. Do you see what the license plate says? Look at it. Read it aloud."

"My Lady." My heart felt as if it were going to burst.

He pulled me to him and said, "You are KJ's mom, and now, my lady." After we kissed again, he said, "I love you, Lexie," and then he helped me into the passenger's side of the vehicle.

"Thank you, Myles. I love this!" I couldn't hold back my tears. He wiped them away.

"You're so beautiful, Lexie. And you looked amazing in that dress! Now, my lady, your next surprise is… I have booked a room for tonight at the biggest hotel downtown."

"Wait. We're not going to Mae's house?"

"No! It's our wedding night. They're not looking for us," he responded.

A sense of fear overcame me. "Myles, where is KJ?"

"He's taken care of. He's at Mae's house, so you don't have to worry about him."

As we rode to the hotel, I said, "Myles, I didn't get a gift for you."

"Yes, you did."

"What?"

"You, Lexie. You are my gift." That pleasant sentiment was followed by him singing "When I Found You, I Found Love" again.

"Myles! Lookout!" I yelled.

He slammed on the brakes, barely missing the car that came barreling through the red light. "Jesus! Oh, my God!" He was so shaken up that he had to pull into the McDonald's parking lot. He pulled me close to him and held me so tight, I could feel his heart beating fast. I knew he could feel mine racing, too. As he held me, he repeatedly said, "Thank You, Jesus! Thank You, Jesus!" When his heartbeat slowed down, he managed to say, "Thank you. I didn't even see that car running the red light. It looked like they were going over 80 miles per hour. Thank God they didn't hit us on our wedding night!"

"Thank God it didn't hit my new vehicle."

Myles laughed and corrected me. "We should thank God they didn't hit us in your new vehicle."

After checking into the hotel, Myles picked me up, carried me into the room, and sat me on the bed. The room had red rose petals leading from the bed to the bathroom door and a beautiful red wrapped box on the bed. "Myles, who did all of this?"

"I did. I slept here last night. I pictured in my mind the way I wanted our wedding night to be—minus the near-miss accident." Smiling, he handed me the box. "Open it."

Inside was a red negligée. A girlish giggle escaped my lips. "Myles…"

"Put it on, my lady. I want to see you in it," he coaxed.

I stepped into the bathroom to change. When I walked back into the room, Myles had the lights turned down low and soft music playing in the background. There was a lone red candle lit on the bedside table.

"You are stunning, my lady. I love everything about you." He kissed me and ran his hands through my hair. "Lord, I thank You for helping me keep the vow I made to You back in Iraq. I can now find pleasure in my wife."

That night, we consummated our marriage. He was so gentle with me and whispered how much he loved me and had waited so long for that night to come. We fell asleep wrapped in each other's arms.

On Sunday morning, I woke up to a lovely breakfast from room service. As we ate, he told me how much he loved me and couldn't wait to tell me about the next surprise.

"Are you moving in with me tomorrow?" I asked.

"No."

"What are you going to do?" I pressed.

"I am going to Myrtle Beach."

"You are?!" I asked in disbelief. "We just got married, and you're running off to Myrtle Beach?!"

"Yes, I am." He continued eating his food without making eye contact with me.

I wondered if there was something I said or did wrong. "Myles, for real. You're going to Myrtle Beach?"

"Yes, for real."

"When are you leaving?" I couldn't hide the sadness in my voice.

"This afternoon." He sat there eating a piece of toast with a smirky look. I didn't say anything else. I just sat there and ate my food, thinking about what he said. When he finished eating, he finally looked up at me. "Why are you so quiet?"

"I don't have anything to say."

"Well, I do."

My curiosity was piqued. "What?"

"The surprise is that you are going with me! Did you think this hotel stay was our honeymoon?" He tossed me onto the bed, kissed me all over my face, and said, "Your change of clothes is in the closet."

"You bought me a change of clothes?"

"Yep!" He flashed his beautiful smile my way.

"How did you know what size I wore?"

"I took your picture to the store and asked the sales clerk what size she thought you were. By the way, she said you are cute and that you favored Halle Berry."

"I hear that all the time, especially when I was in the Air Force."

"Well, to me, you look better than her." We embraced, and he kissed me passionately.

"Thank you," I said, blushing.

"When we check out of here, we're going to swing by your house so that you can throw a few things in your luggage. What you don't grab, we will buy when we get to our destination. Okay, my ladybug?"

"Okay, but what about your clothes?"

"Mine are packed and already in the back of Pearl."

"Who is Pearl?"

"Your new ride! I named her Pearl." He laughed so hard at the expression on my face.

"You sure are full of surprises, Myles! Thanks for choosing to marry me."

"I love you, Mrs. Ferguson. Thank you for saying yes."

"We need to get out of here before they charge you for another day. Plus, I have to get KJ ready to meet his daddy."

"Money is no problem. If I must pay for another day, it would be worth it just to be here with you. We won't be late dropping him off. We have a lot of time before check-out," he replied while kissing me seductively. I had to insist that we leave. I didn't want to pile on any issues with Keith and his bad attitude.

As we stepped outside, Myles handed me the keys to Pearl and let me drive my new ride. As I drove, he stared at me. "You look amazing driving Pearl, and that outfit fits you to a 'T'."

"I love my vehicle and my outfit. Thank you for buying them for me."

Chapter 47

We made a quick stop at Mae's house and were told my houseguests were all at my house. When I made it home, I saw them scattered about. Some were on the patio, while others were in the backyard. The young men were playing kickball with KJ. When he saw us coming, he ran to me and said, "Mama, I'm having fun! Hi, Myles!" He then returned to playing with the big boys.

"KJ, it's time for you to get your things ready to go and meet your dad," I called out to him.

"Mama, do I have to go?"

"Yes, you do."

"Will they be here when I get back?" he asked.

"No, baby. They are going home soon."

"But Mama, I'm having fun with Eric, Corey, and Davis!" he whined.

"You know all their names?"

"Yes," he answered proudly.

I thanked everyone for keeping an eye on KJ and then instructed him again to get his things ready to go to his dad's house. I heard Myles tell his cousins to pack their things as well because we were getting ready to head out of town. While they talked, I grabbed a few things and some toiletries to add to my luggage.

Once settled in Pearl, KJ asked, "Is this your new vehicle, Myles?"

"No, it's your mom's. I bought it for her."

"Wow!" KJ exclaimed. "It's pretty!"

Myles, KJ, my houseguests, and I met at Mae's house, where everyone else was waiting for us. Myles said to his brother-in-law, "When we get back, we'll be ready to go." We said our goodbyes and then left to drop off KJ with his dad.

Keith wasn't there when we arrived at McDonald's to drop off KJ. After about 15 minutes, he drove up. I could see he was driving slowly through the parking lot, looking for my car. KJ got out of the Escalade, turned, and waved. "Bye, Mama! Bye, Myles!"

"Bye, baby! We'll see you in two weeks," I yelled as he ran to his dad's car. As we drove away, I saw Keith looking toward us. I knew KJ was in for a lengthy question-and-answer period.

On our way back to meet up with the others, Myles said, "I have a timeshare in Myrtle Beach, and we are staying in a suite on the beach. Have you ever been to Myrtle Beach?"

"No, but I've heard it's a beautiful place."

"It is. I know you're going to like it. You will also get a chance to meet my other relatives who were unable to attend the wedding."

We made it back to Mae's house, and everyone was ready to leave. I heard Myles tell his sister Sharon we would be stopping along the way and would see them when we arrived in Myrtle Beach.

Myles and I left Nashville at 5:00 p.m. Myrtle Beach, South Carolina, was a nine-to ten-hour drive. I enjoyed riding and talking to Myles and listening to him sing to me. He was very comical, and I loved seeing that different side of him. He also seemed very relaxed. When we pulled into a hotel in Augusta, Georgia, I asked, "Why are we stopping here? We only have five hours to go."

He looked over at me and said with a funny grin, "Remember: We are on our honeymoon." He had already made a reservation for us at the hotel, which was why he told Sharon we would see them in Myrtle Beach. My husband was full of surprises!

Once settled in our room, Myles asked me to give him a massage, explaining he was tense from the ride. I had fun massaging my husband's back before lying next to him, talking and kissing until around 9:00 p.m. We got dressed and went across the street to Applebee's. We had a lovely steak meal and strawberry shortcake for dessert before heading back to our room.

"I have to get something out of the truck. Stay right here," Myles instructed. I stood there wondering what he was up to. When he got back, he had a medium-size box in his hand.

I started to laugh and asked, "Is that for me?"

"Yes, it is. Open it."

I opened the box, only to see there was a smaller box inside. He laughed at me as I tore into the second box. When I opened it, he saw the confused expression on my face and said, "Put it on. I want to see you in it tonight. We are going swimming." Inside the second box was a two-piece bikini bathing suit. He continued laughing at my expression. "The pool is all ours tonight."

I enjoyed spending time alone in the pool with Myles. I could tell he thought I didn't know how to swim because of the way he kept trying to protect me. As it turned out, there were two other couples in the pool with us. They, too, were on their honeymoon. We decided to play water basketball together. The night was truly memorable.

The next morning, I was awakened by Myles kissing me on my neck. "How long have you been up?" I asked.

"For a while now. I've just been lying here looking at you sleep." He kissed me again and said, "Come on. Get up and get dressed so we can get out of here."

As we left the hotel, I said, "Myles, you are going the wrong way."

"No, I'm not. This is the right way."

"That sign says we're headed toward the airport."

"I know."

"Why are we going to the airport?" He reached into the armrest and handed me two tickets to Orlando, Florida. "Why are we going to Orlando? I thought we were going to Myrtle Beach!"

"You will see when we get there," he teased. "Remember: We are on our honeymoon!" he reminded me again while laughing.

Upon our arrival at the Orlando Airport, a transporter was waiting for us. When we got into the man's van, Myles gave me boarding passes for a three-day, two-night cruise to the Bahamas. I was surprised and thrilled! I kissed him and asked, "When did you do this?"

He laughed slyly and replied, "I have connections." He then planted a sweet kiss on my cheek.

The driver took us to Port Canaveral, Florida, where we boarded a Royal Caribbean ship. It was massive and amazing! The first day, we visited Coco Cay Island. They were hosting a big picnic with so much food and different things to see and do. On the second day, we went to Nassau, Bahamas. We got a tour guide and went to see the Atlantic. That place was so large, we didn't get a chance to see it all. On the ship, there was food available 24 hours a day, allowing guests to eat anytime they wanted. All throughout, there were different things to do. Myles and I squeezed in as many activities as we could during the trip.

On Friday morning, we arrived back at Port Canaveral. The same transporter was there to take us back to the Orlando Airport. One of my fondest memories about the trip is how much Myles and I laughed every day. We left Orlando and flew back to Augusta to pick up our vehicle and continue our journey to Myrtle Beach, finally arriving in the early evening hours. As Myles drove, I admired the sunset reflecting on the water. It was truly breathtaking. The beachfront was stunning! I could see why people loved to visit.

We checked into our suite. Just like Myles said, it was beautiful. Everything we needed was included in the room. We put our things away and then took a walk on the boardwalk. For dinner, we ate at one of the diners not too far from our suite. On Saturday, we stayed in bed until late afternoon, at which time we got dressed and went to Red Lobster for dinner. After dinner, we took a barefoot walk on the beach while holding hands with the sand going through our toes. We reminisced about the cruise and how the honeymoon was going. Myles stated he wanted to make sure his woman was truly happy.

Once back in our suite, we laid in the bed watching the news on TV until we both fell asleep.

Chapter 48

On Sunday morning, we got up early, did our morning devotion, and then got dressed. We then ate breakfast and went for a morning walk on the beach. I listened intently as Myles told me about his time in Myrtle Beach. He said that two years after his mother died, he and his siblings visited his Uncle Eddie and Aunt Ruby for a week in Nashville and ended up staying. At the time, he was nine, Sharon was 11, and Mae was six years old. He went on to explain that they stayed with his uncle and aunt for two years while his daddy worked in the computer shop. Six months after his time there, the owner sold the shop to his dad.

They moved into the house by the highway where Mae lived, but Mae stayed with Aunt Ruby and Uncle Eddie most of the time. Myles said he went back to Myrtle Beach at least two times a year. When Sharon graduated from high school, she returned to Myrtle Beach to go to college, living with one of his mom's sisters named Gail. His dad had rented their home in Myrtle Beach, but the man who lived there relocated to Mississippi. His dad then gave the house to Sharon after she graduated from college with her master's degree. Later, she married Isaac, and they were still living in the house with their two sons. "I'll take you by there to see the house and visit with Sharon," he said.

After graduating from high school in Nashville, he returned to Myrtle Beach and lived with Sharon. He enrolled in college and met a girl, but their relationship didn't last long because her father got a job working in a truck plant in Flint, Michigan. When they moved away, he joined the Army. The way he said that made me laugh. "The girl moved away, so you immediately joined the Army?"

"No, I didn't drop out of college! I stayed until that semester ended…and then I decided to join."

"So, you really loved that girl?"

"Well, I think it was more like puppy love. She was the first girl who talked to me and showed me around campus."

"What was her name?"

"I don't remember. Mary Jones," he said while laughing.

"Myles, stop it! That wasn't her name!"

"You're right. I'm busted. Her name was Emma. But enough about her. I am here on my honeymoon, and you are trying to make me recall a girl I knew for all of two months."

"You brought her up first," I said accusingly with a smile.

"Oh, no. Are we having our first argument over something that happened when I was 18?" He laughed, picked me up in his strong arms, and said, "I love you, Lexie Rose Harris Ferguson. You are my present and future." He turned serious and asked, "So, why did you join the Air Force?"

"Well, my best friend and I went down to the recruitment office, took the test, and passed. When it was time to take our physicals, I went, but she was a no-show. I told Mama I had passed the physical, and she said that since I hadn't made up my mind about college, the Air Force would be the best thing for me. It turns out it was! I flew to many different places and was stationed at Lackland Air Force Base in San Antonio, Texas, where I worked in Human Resources before being transferred to Fort Bragg in North Carolina. I also served in Hawaii for two years and Wanstor, Germany, for three years. That is a time I wish I could forget. I came back stateside to Lackland and retired from there—and before you ask, it has nothing to do with a boy."

"Umm-hmm. You can tell me anything, and I'll believe you," he said with a roaring laugh.

We returned to our suite, and he made a quick trip to the store. He returned with two Subway salads, chips, a 2-liter orange soda, some mixed fruit, and a box of chocolate-covered strawberries. "Did you miss me?" he asked.

"You weren't gone long."

"Well, I missed you, my lady. What have you been up to?"

"I took a shower and climbed into bed."

"Let's take advantage of the rest of our honeymoon, then," he said while feeding me the strawberries.

Chapter 49

Monday was a rainy day, but we still went sightseeing after breakfast. Myles showed me around, taking me to the family church, the cemetery where his mother and father were buried, and the college he attended where Sharon teaches. I saw different historic sites in the older part of the town and visited the areas where the city's mansions were located. As expected, they were enormous and incredible. Myrtle Beach was truly a beautiful place.

"Do you remember when I first saw you—not counting grade school?" Myles asked.

"It was when you were preparing to leave for Iraq."

"You know, after seeing you that day, I couldn't get you out of my mind. When I was overseas, you were the one who kept me going and determined to make it back home alive. I was in love with you, and you didn't even know it." He gently squeezed my hand. "I kept thinking of you and what I would say to you when I got home. I wondered if you were married or had a man in your life. As a matter of fact, I was home for three months before I approached you. I drove past your house three or four times but didn't have the nerve to stop because a man might have answered the door after I rang the doorbell.

"While visiting dad and Mae one day, I asked if they had seen the lady down the street who runs or rides her bike, and Mae said, 'Yes, I see her often. I heard she was married to a preacher, and they have a child.' When I heard that, something struck me in my heart."

"For real, Myles?"

"Yes, for real. But when I walked into the church that Sunday and sat behind you, I thought to myself, 'Why is she here and not at her husband's church?' I decided right then and there to make my move and give your hair a little tug. You have no idea how happy I was when we talked after church, and you said you had been divorced for two and a half years. I thought, 'God led me to church today.'" I noticed as he spoke, the rain came to a stop, and the sun came out.

As we rode around the city, we passed a movie theater. "Turn around, Myles. Let's see what's playing at the movies. I want some popcorn, anyway."

He turned the truck around and pulled up to the front door. "This is the theater I used to come to with my cousins." We parked, got out, and looked at the list of movies. "Black Panther" was on that list. "I've been waiting to see this movie!" he said excitedly. He paid for our tickets, a large popcorn, and two cokes. Once seated, he said, "We made it just in time." I could tell he enjoyed the movie because he didn't talk at all. He just ate popcorn and sipped on his coke, staring straight ahead. When I would say something to him, he simply replied, "Umm-hmm." He didn't hear a word I said.

Walking out of the movie, I asked, "Did you enjoy yourself?"

"Yes! I loved it! If it's playing at home, I'll take KJ to see it."

"Right. You just want to see it again."

"That, too," he said with a smile while kissing me on my forehead.

As we walked toward our vehicle, we saw a man approaching us who wore ragged clothes, had an out-of-control beard, and a hat pulled down so people could barely see his eyes. Myles moved me to the back of him as we got closer to the man.

"Hey, mister," the man said. "Can you spare some change? I am hungry and homeless."

"How long have you been homeless?" Myles asked. We never stopped walking.

"Since I got home from Operation Desert Storm," the man replied.

We quickly made it to our truck. Myles told me to get in and lock the doors. He stood just out of earshot talking to the man, then they turned and walked away, heading down the street. I watched as they turned into Subway. When Myles exited after about 15 minutes, the man was no longer with him.

Myles got into the vehicle and sat still for a while before speaking. "I'm sorry for having you sit here for so long, but it's hard to feed a man and not tell him about God. That man fought in Desert Storm, got hurt, and came home to nothing. I thought about how the Lord spared my life and kept me safe while in Iraq. Lexie, you don't understand. We were surrounded by enemy fire the entire time. My buddy Tyrone and two other men were killed in one day, but the Lord let me live." I saw tears form in the corners of his eyes before he wiped them away. "I'm so blessed. The Lord let me live. I had to share my testimonies with that man and let him know that if he accepts the Lord in his life, the Lord will also bless him. I noticed the server behind the counter was listening to us talk, so I asked the man if he had applied for a job anywhere. 'Won't nobody hire me,' he answered. The server behind the counter chimed in, 'I'm looking for help.' So, I asked him, 'If this man cleans himself up, you'll hire him?' and the man said, 'Maybe. He will have to take a drug test, get fingerprinted, and pass a criminal background check.' The homeless guy responded, 'I don't do drugs, and I have never been in trouble with the law. I'm just down on my luck right now.' The server gave him an application to fill out and told him to be clean and clean-shaven when he brought it back. 'If everything comes back clean on you, you got the job.' I gave the homeless guy $50.00 to purchase an outfit and get cleaned up. I also bought him a Subway sandwich combo." He smiled to himself before looking at me and continuing. "Lexie, that man is very intelligent and holds a degree in Marketing. I told him that I would look him up when I came back to town. I see God's hand in this thing. The Lord spared my life to be a witness of His goodness to me—and to marry you." He gave my hand another gentle squeeze.

It was late by the time we made it back to our suite. We snacked on some watermelon and watched the news. "What are we doing tomorrow?" I asked.

"Well, tomorrow is visitation day!" he replied.

Chapter 50

The following morning, we woke up around 10:30. We read our devotion, got dressed, and ate mixed fruit for breakfast. Myles then called his relatives to let them know we would start our visiting rounds around noon.

At everyone's house we visited—his mom's sisters, his dad's brother, and his dad's two sisters—food was prepared for us, and we ate each time. By the time we made it to Eric and Lorie's house, Eric was leaving for work, and Lorie had an appointment at their son's school with the teacher. Davis and his wife April lived two blocks away with their six-week-old baby girl. When April heard we were coming by, she cooked dinner for us, too. We didn't want to say no, so we ate a little bit there. I enjoyed my time there, talking to her and holding her baby. Not that it mattered at all to me, but Davis and Eric's wives were white.

Myles had a friend who lived in Myrtle Beach named Ed. He was white, and his wife was black. The men kept in touch with each other after getting out of the Army. When we made it to their house, his wife Faye had food waiting for us, too! We explained we had already eaten but would gladly have a slice of cake to take with us. I also enjoyed talking to Faye. She worked for the Myrtle Beach Water Department and had three children: an eight-year-old boy and two girls ages six and four. Ed worked for UPS as a driver. The two men were happy to see each other and chatted about old Army times. When it was time to leave, Myles invited them to come and visit us.

Ed replied, "Man, I'll be happy to come! I'll call and let you guys know when to make room for us."

Faye smiled and added, "We are coming right now!" The four of us shared a laugh.

When we left, Myles drove slowly, giving Sharon time to get in from work. "I don't want to see any more food today!" he said.

"Me, neither!" We were definitely stuffed.

We made it to Sharon's house around 6:00 p.m., and she was just finishing up dinner. The first thing she said was, "Y'all are just in time for dinner," as she hugged us both. "Lexie, grab a plate for you and Myles. I made his favorite dish." Myles laughed and held his stomach. "What's wrong with you?" she asked.

"Sis, please fix us a doggie bag or carryout plate to go. We are so full and can't eat another bite. With the way I feel right now, I don't want any food tomorrow, either! Every house we visited today, they fed us. We didn't want to say no, especially since they took the time to prepare the food just for us, so we ate each time." We laughed so hard at what he said and how he looked while saying it.

Sharon seemed to understand. "Okay. I'll fix you something to go."

We sat and talked. Her husband, Isaac the Fireman, was at work. They had two sons: Isaac Jr., who was a sophomore in college, and Aaron, who was a senior in high school. "I enjoyed your wedding, especially the part when your son gave you away. And Myles, I had no idea you could sing like that! That was beautiful." As she shared stories about Myles, she had me cracking up! "When Myles was in fourth grade, this little girl in his class liked him. He came home and told me what the little girl said to him and asked me, 'What should I do?' I told him, 'Go and tell the little girl your daddy is a Deacon in the church and doesn't want me to like girls now because I'm my daddy's little boy.' I didn't think he would tell her what I said, but he did! When he came home that day, he said, 'Sharon, I told her what you said, and she said she didn't care if daddy was a Deacon. She still liked me because I'm cute and have curly hair.'" I thought that was hilarious!

Myles kept asking his sister, "Sharon, did I really say that?" She was laughing so hard, it took a while to reply.

"Yes, you sure enough did. You always had little girls calling our house looking for you because you had curly hair and pretty eyes." She turned her attention to me. "Lexie, when Myles was in high school and played football, I got so tired of the girls calling our house looking for him!"

"Stop telling my wife all my business!" He kissed me on my cheek, laughing.

I just had to know the answer to one question. "Sharon, did Myles go into the Army because his girlfriend moved away?"

She laughed so hard at that, she had a hard time catching her breath. "That girl didn't like Myles! I was the one who asked her to help him make his way around campus because he was new. Lexie, when he first got on campus, he thought he was all that and a bag of chips, walking around acting as if he were rich. He wore shades and had his hair slicked back in a ponytail, just like he is wearing it now."

Myles laughed hard as he reflected on those days. "Stop it, Sharon! Stop it! I wasn't acting like that!"

"Yes, you were! On Myles' first day of classes, he came to my office wearing his shades and asked me, 'Where's the McCarty Science building?' I told him, 'Maybe you could see it if you take off those shades!' Girl, he was wearing shades, and it was cloudy and raining outside!" Our laughter continued, to the point that all of our faces and stomachs hurt.

"Sharon, you remember all of that?!" Myles asked in disbelief.

"Yes! I remember you trying to be Mr. Cool."

"What was that girl's name you asked to show me around?"

"Barbara."

"Are you sure her name wasn't Emma?" he asked.

"That must have been another girl because the girl who showed you to your classes was named Barbara Johnson. She was on work-study in my office. She was a sweet young lady who had a boyfriend named Raymond. She talked about him all the time. You were never the topic of her conversations," Sharon stated.

We laughed at him as he shrugged his shoulder and said, "I thought her name was Emma. Now that I think about it, I never even used her name," he replied. "Wait. Sharon, you are sitting there talking about me, but you're not telling how you and Mae always got me into trouble. Y'all had boys coming to our house, telling daddy they were my friends, and he would get upset at me for having boys in the house all the time! The year you left for college, there was one day when Mae and I got off the bus, and this boy followed her home. They were standing outside talking, and then Mae let him come inside to use the bathroom. As soon as they walked inside, daddy pulled up. Mae didn't know what to do! She said, 'Myles, do something! Tell daddy he is your friend!' I told her, 'Nope!' and went to make a peanut butter and jelly sandwich. She was freaking out. 'Myles, don't let daddy come inside!' I asked her, 'How am I supposed to stop him from coming into his own house?' She kept repeating, 'What am I going to do?'

"About that time, daddy came in through the side door. He walked into the kitchen and said, 'Hey, you're making a sandwich, I see. Where's Mae?' I told him she was in the bathroom or bedroom. From where I was standing, I could see Mae in the hallway mirror. She was in the hallway looking scared out of her mind with her thumb in her mouth. To get daddy out of the house, I asked him, 'Where is the bike pump?' He told me it was in the tool house. 'I looked for it in there and didn't see it,' I replied. Sure enough, daddy walked out the patio door toward the tool house, saying, 'I know I put it in there.' I was walking behind him.

"No sooner than we made it to the tool house, Mae popped her head inside and said, 'Hey, daddy! You're home already?' 'Yes, baby girl. How was your day at school?' he asked. 'Good.' Apparently, she had let the boy out through the front door while we were in the back. Meanwhile, daddy looked in the tool house and found the pump. I said to him, 'I must have looked over it.' He laughed and said, 'Boy, if it was a snake, it would have bitten you!' I had to do something to protect both Mae and me because I didn't know what daddy would have done if he caught that boy in the house."

Sharon was laughing so hard, she fell to the floor on her knees, trying to gather her composure. "For real, Myles? Mae never told me that story!"

"I know she didn't. She was embarrassed because she didn't know that boy's name. I didn't know it either." Our laughter was constant.

I got up from my seat to look at the pictures Sharon had on the shelf beside the fireplace. My eyes were immediately drawn to Myles' adorable baby picture and a family photo. Sharon said that picture was taken a year before their mother died. There was also one with Myles, Sharon, and Mae, and a wedding picture of their parents. I asked Sharon if I could snap a picture of all the photos to add to my picture wall. Without hesitation, she replied, "Girl, yes."

As we continued discussing the photos, Sharon's phone rang. Her sons were calling to let her know they were ready to be picked up from the barbershop. She shared with us that Isaac Jr. came home from college for a visit and that the starter when out on his car, so it was in the shop. "I told Isaac, Sr. we are not getting Aaron a car until he graduates from high school. That boy is girl-crazy!" She spoke those words while looking at Myles.

"Why are you looking at me like that? I got my wife!" he said before planting a kiss on my cheek.

"Well, he acts just like you—before you got your wife." Laughter entered the room again. "Let me get out of here to get my boys."

"Okay. Pray for us, Sis. We leave Tuesday morning," Myles said.

"Thanks for stopping by. I really enjoyed going down memory lane with you guys." Sharon hugged us and handed over our two carry-out plates along with two small plates with foil covering them.

It was around 8:30 p.m. when we left Sharon's house. On our ride back to the suite, Myles said, "I could have sworn that girl's name was Emma." We laughed hard about that during our short trip.

Chapter 51

Once settled in our suite, Myles said, "If we lived down here and ate all that food every day, we would be two fat people! I don't want to see any food tonight, my lady. We'll eat what Sharon gave us tomorrow—late in the day!" Both of us laughed as we rubbed our rounded stomachs.

We showered and then climbed into bed to watch the news.

"You know, I enjoyed growing up with my sisters, but Sharon and Mae always got me into some kind of trouble. Daddy expected me to watch out for them, but both were fast behinds and boy-crazy!"

"You didn't sound slow yourself!" I replied. He laughed and pulled me atop him, kissing me. As we settled back down, I laid next to him and said, "Myles, tell me two things about you that no one else knows."

"Well...let me think." He paused while thinking back. "When I was in Iraq, we were in heavy combat, and I peed on myself." We both laughed.

"I bet a lot of troops did that."

"If they did, they didn't tell it. Neither did I."

He turned to face me and asked, "What's one thing about you that nobody knows?"

I knew he would ask, so I was ready to answer. "When I was in the beauty pageant in Germany, I put socks in my bra to make me have bigger boobs."

He laughed so hard, tears fell down his face. "Now, that is hilarious! Okay. What's your next one?"

"When I was 12 or 13, Leon had this handheld game he told me not to touch. One day, when he was outside playing with his friends, I went into his room and played with it. It fell to the floor and broke. I was so afraid of what he would do to me, I threw it in the trash in the kitchen. When he asked if I had seen it, I lied and told him no. He looked everywhere for it. I never told him or anybody else I broke and trashed it."

"Lexie, that was cold-blooded!" he said with a laugh.

"Your turn, Myles. Tell me your last one."

"You already know what mine is."

"No, I don't. What is it?"

"You have known mine ever since we got married."

"You're not being fair!" I slapped him playfully. "Tell me what it is!"

"Okay! Okay! I sleep in the nude." We laughed. "Seriously, though. What I'm about to tell you, only the Lord and I know."

"What is it?"

"You don't know how happy I felt when you said you wanted to marry me. I went home that night and couldn't sleep, thinking of how I wanted to hold you in my arms like this." He was hugging and kissing me while rubbing my side. He felt the scar I got from the assault in Germany. He leaned back and looked at it. "How did you get this?"

I hesitated before answering. "When I was in Germany, I was attacked, raped, beaten, and left for dead."

He sat up in the bed, looked at me, and said, "Oh, my God! Did they find the man?"

"Yes." The memory of that moment caused me to start tearing up.

Myles took me in his arms. He hugged and kissed me while saying, "I'm so sorry. I'm so sorry that happened to you."

I continued. "It was hard for me to talk about, which is why I never told you. When I went on the retreat, I poured out my heart to the Lord and asked Him to help me forget that day and to remove the fear I had of loving someone. I asked Him to give me direction concerning you. I knew I wanted to marry you but didn't want my past to interfere with our marriage. For years, I feared what happened to me over there would happen here. Many nights, I couldn't sleep because I relived the moment in my dreams. I dreamt of that man pushing me to the ground again, putting his hand over my mouth, and ripping off my clothes. It was horrible. In my dreams, I could see his eyes looking at me as he forced himself inside of me. I could even feel his breath." I started to cry uncontrollably.

Myles held me tightly and said, "I'm so sorry, Lexie."

134

I loved being held by him. I gathered myself and told him more of my story. "When I got home from the Air Force, my mom would sometimes sleep with me because I was afraid to sleep alone. After Mama died, I told Mrs. Riddle about my dreams. She advised me to let it go and stop beating myself up over it because what that man did to me wasn't my fault. 'The Lord will deal with that man,' she added. Still, I thought about the assault every time I bathed or showered and felt this scar." I lightly touched it and continued. "I feel a lot better about it now. I now know it wasn't my fault. I was in the wrong place at the wrong time. What happened to me could have happened to any young lady. I thank God that man didn't kill me and for the woman who helped me," I finished sobbing.

Myles hugged me, saying, "Hush. I don't want to hear any more about that." He rocked and kissed me and repeated, "I don't want to hear any more."

We laid in bed, watching CNN news. Eventually, I dozed off but woke up around 5:00 a.m. The TV was still on, and Myles was still sleeping. I turned off the TV and went back to sleep.

Around 10:00 a.m., we got up. He asked if I wanted anything to eat. "No, I'm still full from yesterday."

He pulled me to him and said, "I'm sorry for what happened to you when you were in Germany. I don't want to hear any more about it, okay?" I nodded my head yes. "I love you, Lexie. I love everything about you. I love how you make me feel, your tanned skin, your beautiful brown eyes, and the beautiful shape of your lips. I love the way you do your hair in ponytails and twist them into a knot on your head with a little hair hanging down. I love the way you walk and even love the scar on your side."

"Myles, stop it!"

"I truly love everything about you."

He reached out to touch my hair. "Stop it! You are going to mess up my hair!" Before I realized I had done it, I caught his arm and flipped him on the bed.

He laughed so hard and said, "Oh, my God! How did you do that?!"

"I don't know. I guess my Martial Arts skill kicked in right then." We were cracking up.

Myles pulled me on top of him and gently pushed my hair back from my face. "I will never mess with your hair knot again!" We couldn't stop laughing.

"Honestly, I didn't know I could still do that. Sorry."

"You are good! Do you know how much I weigh? I didn't see that coming. You could have put a hurtin' on me!" He laughed again and kissed me.

I shared with him the story about the day I was coming home from work and stopped by a corner store to get a loaf of bread and some ice cream. "When I walked in, the cashier spoke and said she liked my outfit. Two other men were walking through the store, and another headed to the counter to checkout. I went to the back of the store to get the ice cream and picked up a loaf of bread on my way back to the counter. One of the men came up behind me, stuck something in my back, and said, 'Give me your money.' Before I knew it, I had turned around, hit him with the bread, caught his arm, and flipped him onto the floor. The other man tried to run out the door just as two police officers were coming in. I guess the cashier had pushed a panic button or something because I never saw her on the phone. When the policemen looked at the store's camera, one asked, 'Where did you learn that move from? You need to be on the police force!' The cashier commented that those two men had been in the store for a while, looking suspicious. She said she had pushed the button long before I came into the store. You know, I never told Mama about that night. I knew she would have gotten upset because my brother died when leaving a store."

"For real, Lexie: I will never, ever mess with your knot again!" he said laughing.

I shook my loose hair in his face and said, "You can play with my knot any time you'd like. I love the way you run your hands through my hair. I love the way you call my name. I love the way you look into my eyes and tell me how much you love me. I love everything about you, too." I kissed him and then whispered in his ear, "I love the way you hold me in your strong arms and pull me so close, I can feel your heartbeat. I love the way you make me feel!"

Eventually, we got dressed and went for a run on the beach. It was around 1:45 p.m. when we returned to our suite. By then, we were hungry.

Chapter 52

We looked to see what Sharon had prepared for us to eat. She made smothered pork chops with rice, green beans, and steamed carrots. On the small plates were pieces of German chocolate cake. The food plates were loaded. She really piled the food onto them.

"Oh, my God! She made smothered pork chops and rice! She knows I love me some smothered pork chops!" Myles said excitedly.

I smiled and said, "It does look delicious. There's enough food on one plate for both of us. We can save the other one for later."

As we ate, Myles asked, "During our visits yesterday, did you notice how everyone looked like somebody pumped air into them?" I nodded yes and laughed. "I refuse to be fat." He looked toward the ceiling and prayed, "Lord, please don't let me get fat." I couldn't stop laughing. "They were all round, fat people!"

"Myles, everybody wasn't fat."

"If they keep eating all that food like they were, they will be! Even my friend was fat, and his children were walking around looking like little Roly-Polies!"

"Myles, stop it! Roly-Poly is a bug!"

"They didn't look like bugs, but they sure were round like one!" I laughed so hard, I could hardly catch my breath. "Last night, I dreamt I was fat. KJ and I went on a fishing trip, and I had my pail and fishing rod. I tripped, fell, and went rolling downhill toward the water, calling out for KJ to help me. When I looked back, he was rolling downhill behind me. He was fat, too!" The story had me laughing so hard.

"Did you really dream that?" I asked.

"Yes, I did," he said, laughing.

"Sharon's a nice size. She wasn't fat."

"If she keeps eating all that delicious food like she gave us, she will be a big one, too!" Once we stopped laughing long enough to eat, Myles suggested we go for a walk to help the food settle. We ended up walking to the mall.

Myles shopped for himself and picked out a couple of short outfits for Mae's little girl. For the older two, he bought them a t-shirt with the words Myrtle Beach printed on them. I shopped for KJ and me, getting him some clothes for school and a basketball. I bought Myles a t-shirt that read, "Jesus is the answer," with praying hands on it. I thought it was cute. With his birthday coming in four weeks, I figured I'd give it to him then. I hoped he would like it.

We made it back to our suite around 6:30 p.m. Myles decided to turn in the key since we were leaving very early the next morning. We ate the other plate of food, showered, and went to bed. He turned on the news and said he liked watching so that he'd know what was going on in the world. I watched the news intently and then turned to look at Myles. He was fast asleep. It was my turn to look at him while he slept. I gently ran my fingers through his hair and thanked God for my husband and the love I had for him. He was compassionate, handsome, intelligent, and funny. "Thank You, Lord, for letting him find me," I whispered. I kissed Myles on his forehead, turned off the TV, and fell asleep.

We were up and ready to head back home around 5:00 a.m. As Myles drove, he sang, "Lord, I'm Available to You." We talked about what marriage is and what we wanted in our marriage. He said, "The husband and his wife should honor their marriage by being faithful to God and each other. The husband must go beyond submission to love his wife with the very love God has loved us with." I enjoyed hearing him talk. We had a great discussion, and I could see how dedicated he was to what he believed in.

For breakfast, we stopped at a Cracker Barrel restaurant off the highway. It was around 10:30 by then. After breakfast, we walked through the strip mall next to the restaurant to pick up something for Mae and her husband. I enjoyed our return trip home. At one point, I drove. We talked about the cruise and other memories we made. When Myles started singing again, I said, "Honey, go to sleep."

"Are you saying you don't like my singing?" he asked, faking hurt.

"All I will say is you are more romantic and funnier than you are a singer. I did love it when you sang to me at the wedding, though."

He then started singing, "When I Found You, I Found Love." Suddenly, the song came on the radio.

"Did you plan that?" I asked.

"You will never know. I have magic!" he said, laughing. As we drove along, Myles suddenly shouted out, "Get off at Exit 67!"

"We have plenty of gas. Why are we taking that exit?"

"Just take the exit, Lexie. I have another surprise waiting for you."

I took the exit and noticed we were near the same hotel we stopped at before flying out to Orlando. "I thought you had to be back to work tomorrow."

"Remember, my lady: I'm the boss! Ron and Mrs. Clark can handle it. This is the end of our honeymoon. We must celebrate our last night before heading back to reality."

"You are full of surprises, Mr. Ferguson!"

"You haven't seen anything yet!" he replied while getting out of the vehicle. We stayed the night and remained until checkout time the next morning.

Chapter 53

We pulled into Nashville around 8:00 p.m. and stopped by Mae's house to give her and her family their gifts. While there, we also picked up Myles' car. We then drove to my house, pulled my car out of the garage so that Myles could pull in his car that was loaded with some things from his apartment, and parked Pearl in the space next to his car. I parked my car behind his so that he could drive it to work.

As we walked inside the house, I told Myles I was thinking about selling my car. "Are you sure you want to do that?" he asked.

"We don't need three cars."

"You're right. We don't."

He stood in the family room, looked around, and said, "All the times I have been in here, I have never gone upstairs."

"Well, this is our house now. Come. Let me show you around." We went into the living room to head upstairs.

Once there, he looked around in obvious awe. "Boy, it's big up here!"

"This is KJ's room (I pointed). There are two other bedrooms, a full bathroom, and a theater room." I watched as his mouth fell open. "At the end of the hall is a master bedroom with a full bath. On this side (I pointed) of the hallway is a sitting room with a half-bath and linen closet."

"So strange," he commented.

"What's strange?"

"The house doesn't look this big from the outside," he replied.

"Well, I designed the upstairs just for my mom. I wanted her to have her own space. I pretty much left her alone, other than when I came up here to watch movies with her." I started to tear up.

Myles hugged me and said, "You don't have to talk about it. I know it's hard for you. You built this house for your mother and you, and she is no longer here to enjoy it with you." I nodded my agreement into his chest.

We then went downstairs. "Now, this is my favorite part of the house: the kitchen, my master suite, and the exercise room."

He stood there looking around before asking, "What room did you sleep in when you were married before?"

"He had his room, and I slept upstairs in Mama's suite."

"Well, in that case, the downstairs master suite and exercise room are my favorites, too!" He picked me up and carried me into our bedroom. We were both so tired from the trip, we fell right asleep in each other's arms that night.

I was awakened by him kissing me and saying, "Breakfast is ready. I'll call you later. I love you, my lady!" He then left for work.

I got up, did my devotion, and ate breakfast on the patio. I was grateful for still being off from work and thanked God for such a wonderful husband. I loved hearing him say he loved me.

During his lunch break, Myles called. "I miss you, babe. What are you up to?"

"Sitting here thinking of you," I replied honestly.

"I left computers here that I had to work on, and Mrs. Clark said when she opened the shop yesterday, she took in ten computers that need virus protection added. I still have eight others to work on and three iPads with cracked screens. I'll be home late. Someone is coming in. I gotta go. I love you!"

Around 3:00 p.m., I started thinking about what to make for dinner. I chose meatloaf with spaghetti, salad, garlic bread, and the pieces of cake we got from Sharon. Just as he said, Myles got home late. He ate his dinner and then said, "My lady, dinner was delicious. I am going to shower and head to bed."

I joined him in the bed after taking my shower. I talked to him, thinking he was watching the news, but he was already asleep. Poor guy. He hadn't rested since returning from our honeymoon. Before I got up the next morning, he was already gone to work.

When he had a short break, he called to tell me he would ask Ron if he wanted to work full-time. If not, he would have to hire someone who would because there was too much work to do alone. "I'm thinking about changing the hours from 9:00 a.m. to 3:00 p.m. I don't know how dad did all this work by himself! I'm working on things my dad didn't have a chance to complete. There are computers, iPads, laptops, cell phones, tablets…you name it, they keep coming in. I'll tell Mrs. Clark the new hours. I can't make house calls. Ron or the person I hire can do that if they want to."

"You don't want to make house calls like your dad did?" I asked, laughing.

"No way! When I leave the job, I want to concentrate on you and KJ. Babe, I gotta go now. Mrs. Clark has an unhappy customer coming to pick up her computer, and it's not ready. I'll see you in a couple of hours."

After work, Myles pulled into the garage but didn't come inside. I peeked out the side door and saw he was doing something to his car. I stood in the doorway and asked, "What are you doing?"

He looked over at me and said, "Wow! I've been missing you all day." He stopped what he was doing, approached me, and kissed me passionately.

The next day, I surprised Myles while he was on his lunch break. We ate in the breakroom and, when finished, I got up and started cleaning. "You don't have to do that," he said.

"I know I don't have to; I just want to." I noticed two pictures leaning against the wall and picked up one of them.

Mrs. Clark laughed and stated, "I wanted to hang up those pictures and that mirror over there for a long time now."

When Myles walked out of the room, I whispered to her, "Let's hang them up to see if Myles will notice." We worked together to hang them and stepped back to admire our work.

When Myles returned to give Mrs. Clark some receipts, he smiled. "I like it!"

"Your daddy bought those pictures and mirror over two years ago. I told him I would hang them up, but he kept saying, 'No, you don't have to. I'll do it.' So, I didn't mess with them," Mrs. Clark stated. I heard the sadness in her voice.

"Well, they look nice in here now. I like that mirror hanging on the wall. It makes the room look bigger," Myles said happily. He stood in front of the mirror, rubbing his hair back and looking into his eyes.

"Boy, get out of that mirror before I take it down right now!" Mrs. Clark said.

"Okay. Okay. Don't take it down. I'm moving from in front of it!" Myles replied, laughing.

"Mr. Pinson is on his way to pick up his laptop," Mrs. Clark reported. "Is it ready?"

"Yes, let me get it. I need to show him the problem he was having with it."

Before leaving, I said, "Honey, I'm going home to make room in the closet for the things you have in the car."

"No, don't do that. All that stuff in my car is going to the Salvation Army."

"Oh! Okay! Great! I have a lot of toys, stuffed animals, books, and clothes KJ has outgrown in my storage room already in boxes that can go, too."

"Okay. When I get home, I'll load up your stuff in the Escalade, and we'll drop off everything at once," he replied. We gave each other a peck, expressed our love, and I left.

When I arrived home, I started packing the boxes into the Escalade. I figured by the time Myles got home, we'd be ready to go. As I picked up one of the boxes, I stepped on something. When I looked down, I saw it was the bracelet I had lost that Mama had given to me. I recalled the moment. "Your dad gave this bracelet to me on our 10th wedding anniversary. I'm giving it to you now. It's expensive. Don't lose it!" Mama said. It must have fallen off my arm when I put the boxes in the closet. I recall looking everywhere for it but couldn't find it. "Thank You, Lord! Thank You! I finally found it!" I said aloud. I managed to get as much into Pearl as I could squeeze inside. Two boxes remained that I would drop off one day while Myles was at work. Later that afternoon, when he got home, we dropped the two carloads of boxes off at our local Salvation Army.

On our way back home, we stopped at Bob Evans for dinner. Once home, we did our evening run, relaxed in the sauna, prayed together, and went to bed.

Chapter 54

Three weeks had passed. I was at work thinking about Myles' upcoming birthday that following Friday. I decided to take that day off from the office and work from home. I worked half-days on Fridays anyway. I wondered if he's planning to taking that day off, too.

On Myles' birthday, I woke up early, did my devotion and exercises, and then made breakfast. He was still asleep. I went into the bedroom and sang in his ear, "Today is your birthdaaaay!" I planted a gentle kiss on his cheek.

He pulled me into the bed and said, "I wasn't asleep."

"Yes, you were! Are you going to work today?"

"Yes, I am."

"You're the boss! Why don't you take today off?" I whined.

"That sounds like a good idea, but I have at least 20 computers and laptops to work on. I'm getting calls left and right from people wanting to pick up their equipment."

"Well, I'm not going in today. Any work I have to do, I can do from here."

"Are you alright?" he asked with a curious look.

"Yes, I'm fine. I just have a couple of letters to get out by today. I can do them here. Plus, it's my half-day anyway. I bought your birthday gifts already, but I'll give them to you when you get home from work. Do you want to go out for dinner?"

"No, we have the Bible study group coming over tonight. Remember?" he said, kissing me. "Let me get ready. And have my gifts waiting when I get out of the shower," he teased.

"Nope! You will get them when you get home." He went into the bathroom to shower and get ready for work. I called out, "What kind of cake would you like for your birthday?"

"Let me see. Maybe the punch bowl cake!" he replied, laughing.

"Myles, you have never had a punch bowl cake, have you?"

"No, but I heard you talk about it. It actually sounds good!"

"You are so funny. What if you don't like it?" I asked.

"If you make it, I'll love it!" He kissed me before heading out the door, singing, "It's my birthday! It's my birthday!" as he closed the door behind him.

Once alone, I signed in on my computer and completed the work I had for the day. I then tried to figure out what I could do to make Myles' birthday special. Around 10:00, I put a 'For Sale' sign in my car's window, dropped off the remaining two boxes at the Salvation Army, went to the car wash, and did some light grocery shopping, picking up a cheese and vegetable tray for the Bible study group.

The perfect surprise for Myles popped into my mind. His family had never seen our house. I thought I'd invite them over but didn't have any of their phone numbers. I called Mae to tell her about my plans and asked if she could call her family to let them know.

"Okay. I'll give them a call. If everybody comes, there will be about 20 of us. Do you want me to bring anything?" she asked.

"No, thank you. Just calling them is a huge favor. I really want him to be surprised. Mae, when everyone gets here, have them wait outside until I flicker the kitchen lights at around 7:20."

"Okay. We'll be there! Let me start calling everyone now." She sounded so excited.

When I hung up the phone, excitement overcame me. I found my cousin David's number and explained the reason for my call. He said he was glad to hear from me but was on his way to work, and we would talk later. I then called my pastor and asked him to come and bring his wife.

The next task was figuring out what to feed everyone. I had already made a big taco salad, bought the cheese and vegetable tray, and had punch chilling for the Bible study group. My thoughts were interrupted when Myles called to see how my day was going. "Things are going well. I finished my work, dropped off the remaining boxes at the Salvation Army, washed the car, and went grocery shopping. When I got home, a man called about the car. I told him I'd have you call him when you get in. He left his number."

"Okay. I'll do that when I get there."

"Oh! I made snacks for our Bible study group tonight, too."

"That's awesome! I will see you a little after 4:00. I love you. Remember: It's my birthdaaaaay!" he sang while laughing before hanging up.

No sooner than I hung up the phone, it rang right back. Thinking it was Myles, I didn't bother to look at the caller ID. "Hello, again, birthday boy!" On the other end was Keith laughing. "Oh. Pastor Montgomery. It's you. What do you want? Is KJ alright?"

"KJ is good. I saw you coming out of the store. Lexie, you are looking good! 36, 33, 36—and that walk of yours? My, my, my."

"What are you talking about now?" I asked with obvious irritation.

"Those are your measurements. I remembered them. And I have always told you I like the way you walk." He found the moment humorous. On the other hand, I found the comment appalling.

"Man, get out of my life! By the way, I saw you, too, sitting in a red car with some man. And I see you're growing a beard."

"Why didn't you speak?" he asked.

"You are not important enough for me to speak to you. You're just my son's daddy." His continual laughter got under my skin. "Bye, Pastor Montgomery!"

"Wait! Don't hang up. Can you meet me at noon tomorrow to get KJ?"

"Fine. See you at noon to get my son."

"I heard you got married."

"Yes, you heard right. I'll see you tomorrow at noon." I didn't even bother to repeat my goodbye. I hung up the phone before he could say anything else. I mumbled, "I really don't like him playing with me like that." I immediately fell to my knees and prayed to God that Keith would leave me alone. I even asked God, "Why is Keith acting this way?" before finishing my prayer.

I left the house and went to Dollar Tree to get balloons, birthday plates, cups, plasticware, and napkins. I then hopped across the street to Kroger to pick up cupcakes, the ingredients for the punch bowl cake, potato salad, and two large bags of potato chips. I had already picked up the other food I had in mind to serve when I did my grocery shopping.

After leaving Kroger and heading back home, I looked into my rearview mirror and saw Keith following me in his car. A sense of nervousness entered my space. "Lord, what should I do? I just talked to him 30 minutes ago. Was he sitting, watching me when I left my house? He doesn't live on this side of town. Why is he following me?" I said aloud. I slowed my speed, hoping he would get a hint and pass me. He never did. Then I thought, "Maybe he's not following me. Perhaps he just happens to be going in the same direction." I turned onto an unfamiliar side street to see if the latter thought was accurate. He turned behind me. I stopped at an Ace Hardware store, waiting to see what he would do. When two cars separated our view of each other, I pulled out of the parking lot. As I drove away, my hands were visibly shaking. Just when I thought I had lost him, there he was again. I turned into my subdivision, and he was still following me. I pulled into my driveway and remained inside Pearl as he passed by, looking in my direction.

That was the straw that broke the camel's back. I had to tell Myles about Keith.

Once I was sure Keith was gone, I pulled into the garage and waited for the door to go all the way down before getting out and unloading the SUV. It was time to prepare for Myles' surprise party.

Chapter 55

Around 1:00 p.m., I put the meatballs in the slow cooker and covered them with BBQ sauce. I baked a large can of baked beans and another with lemon pepper chicken wings, leaving them in the oven to stay warm. I then layered the punch bowl cake, which turned out beautifully. I placed the potato salad and punch bowl cake in the refrigerator, and everything else went into my office.

I called Myles to let him know we had to pick up KJ at noon on Saturday.

"Okay. That's fine. I'm getting ready to leave the shop now. What a day! I'll see you in a few minutes."

I wanted to tell Myles about Keith following me but figured I'd wait. I wanted everything to go well for his surprise party. With everything ready for the festivities, I went and sat outside on the patio, reading over some of the Bible study materials while waiting for Myles to get home.

When he arrived, I was never so happy to see my husband. "This has been a long day, my lady. Come. Sit with me. I just want to hold you." We sat in the family room on the couch with his arms around me. "I smell BBQ. Oh. You did say you were serving snacks after Bible study tonight."

"Yes, everything is ready. Would you like a plate now?"

"No, thank you. I can wait. Mrs. Clark brought Ron and me some vegetable soup she made. It was pretty good!"

"Don't get too comfortable. You need to shower before the group gets here in less than two hours," I reminded him.

"Okay. Can you give me the number so I can call the man about the car?" I handed him the number and went into the bedroom. I could tell he was tired. I heard him talking to the man on the phone before calling out to me. "Babe, what time do we pick up KJ tomorrow?"

"At noon."

I then heard him say to the man, "Okay. Tomorrow at noon at McDonald's." When he ended the call, he said, "Thank You, Jesus!" I could tell he had moved from the couch to the big chair by the fireplace. For almost an hour, I didn't hear him moving around.

"Myles! Are you asleep?" I called out.

"I'm getting up now," he replied. Shortly after, I heard the shower water running.

At about that time, the Bible study group started to arrive. As they walked in, I asked if they had any plans after the study and explained I had a surprise planned for Myles' birthday. They all said they could stay. "Great! After Bible study, go outside and join the others who will be waiting for me to flicker the kitchen lights." My excitement continued to grow.

By the time Myles came in, we had already prayed and started our study on "How Faith Works." The lesson was very good. Everyone had an opportunity to share how they used their faith and the Lord blessed them. At 7:00 p.m. sharp, the study was over. We had our closing prayer, and everyone left.

"Babe, I thought you had snacks for everybody after Bible study?" Myles asked.

"Oh, my goodness! Why didn't you remind me? My mind was still on the lesson we had. How did you like it?"

"It was excellent as always," he responded as he straightened up the pillows on the couch.

"Do you want me to stop them and tell them about the food?" I asked.

"No, it's okay. We can eat it tomorrow. Why don't we go upstairs and watch a movie on the big screen tonight? Remember: It's my birthday, and I'm still waiting for my gifts!" he said with a laugh.

"You know what? That's a good idea. Go on up and pick out a movie. I will be up in just a moment." I was hoping he would agree to my idea so that I could bring everyone inside and get everything set up.

He came up behind me, kissed me on my neck, and sang, "Hurry up! It's my birthday! It's my birthday!" His silly song was accompanied by a funny dance as he went upstairs.

When the coast was clear, I quickly put all the food on the countertop, along with the plates, napkins, and plasticware. I then put the punch bowl cake, cupcakes, and birthday balloons on the kitchen island. Once satisfied everything was in place, I flashed the lights, and everyone quietly entered. With the Bible study group, the pastor and his wife, and Myles' family, there were about 30 people in the family room and kitchen. I yelled upstairs, "Myles, can you come here for a minute?"

"Okay. Be right there!" he yelled back. He came down with his shirt unbuttoned and barefooted.

"SURPRISE!" everyone yelled.

He just about fainted. He had to sit on the step and fumbled to button his shirt. It was so funny!

I walked over to him, hugged him, and said, "Happy Birthday, Honey!"

He whispered in my ear, "You caught me just in time. I was getting ready to come down in my birthday suit because I couldn't wait any longer for you to come upstairs!"

"I thank Jesus for keeping your clothes on!" I couldn't stop laughing at the expression on his face when they yelled surprise. He excused himself, went into our bedroom, and put on his house slippers.

Everyone who hadn't seen the house before fell in love with it. There was more than enough food, and the guests seemed to enjoy themselves. Some of the ladies wondered how I made the punch bowl cake and complimented me on how pretty it was. I explained I had gotten the recipe from my aunt in Michigan before she died and that it was the easiest cake to make because there was no baking, only layering. While Myles and the men were spread out between the exercise room and garage, one lady from the Bible study group asked, "How did you manage to keep this secret from Myles?"

"The idea didn't even come to me until today while he was at work," I replied with a giggle.

"Everything turned out so nice, and the food was delicious," she stated.

"Thank you," I replied. "I appreciate all of you agreeing to join in on the fun."

By 10:30 p.m., everybody was gone. I kept teasing Myles about his reaction when everyone yelled out surprise. "Lexie, you did it! I have never had a birthday party in my life. Okay. Where are my gifts?" he asked, much like a spoiled child.

"Aren't you going to open your other gifts first? You have a lot of birthday cards."

"No, I'll open them tomorrow when KJ is here. I want to see what you have for me." I handed him the box containing the t-shirt I bought while in Myrtle Beach and another box with a bottle of cologne I picked up from Macy's. "I love them!" he said with all the sincerity he could muster. He pulled me close and kissed me.

"Go upstairs and get a movie ready. I'll be up in a few minutes. Promise."

"You don't have anyone else coming here to surprise me tonight, do you?" he asked.

"Nope! It's just the two of us for the rest of the night." His concern was justified. I laughed.

He ran upstairs, leaving the t-shirt and cologne behind on the stool in the kitchen. I took them into our bedroom, put on the t-shirt, and went upstairs. When he saw me, he said, "You keep surprising me! Look at you—wearing my birthday present!" he busted out laughing. "Thank you for my party. It was nice seeing everyone." He chose the Will Smith movie "Enemy of the State." Ten minutes or so into the film, I looked over at him, and he was knocked out. I couldn't get the image of him out of my mind from when everyone yelled surprise. I grabbed KJ's blanket, covered him, and let him sleep where he was. I knew he was tired. I slept in one of the spare rooms upstairs.

The following morning, both of us overslept. By the time we finished our morning routine, it was after 10:00. We didn't have time to eat breakfast because we had to clean the car out so that the man could see it in its best condition. I had already driven it through the car wash the day before.

We left the house to pick up KJ around 11:15. I drove Pearl, and Myles drove my car. When we pulled into the McDonald's parking lot, Keith hadn't arrived yet. Myles got into the Escalade with me, and we waited for about 20 minutes before Keith drove up. We got out of the vehicle and started walking toward the door of McDonald's.

When KJ got out of Keith's car, he ran over, hugged me, and then hugged Myles. "Mama, I've missed you!"

"I've missed you, too."

The three of us went inside to place our order. Myles looked out and saw a man standing by the car. He asked me to order his food and then stepped outside. All the while, I watched as Keith remained sitting in his car, looking toward Myles and the man. Finally, he drove away.

I suppose the man wanted to take the car for a test drive, so both men got in and left. I ordered our food, and KJ and I sat down to eat. "So, KJ, how was your visit with your brother?" I asked.

"They weren't there. When I got there, Mama Brenda and Brandon were gone. I had to go to church every day with daddy," he answered.

"Well, when we get back home, I have something for you." About that time, Myles and the man pulled back into the parking lot. KJ and I had already finished eating.

Myles walked in with a big smile on his face. "Jim loved the car. Here is your money."

"Just put it in your pocket for now," I told him.

"He wanted to give me a check, but I told him I needed cash. We made it to the bank just before it closed."

"Thank you so much for doing that for me," I said with a smile.

"There is nothing on this side of Heaven I wouldn't do for the woman I love." He kissed me on the lips with a quick peck, and KJ said, "Yuck!" Myles laughed and rubbed him on his head.

"Myles, I already paid for your food. They are keeping it warm. Do you want to eat it here or get it to go?"

"Let's get it to go."

Once home, Myles handed me the cash. "Thanks again. I will deposit it on Monday. Do you want any of it?"

"No, I am good. It was your car anyway," he said as he hugged me.

I called for KJ to come downstairs and told him to grab the bags out of my office. He came into the living room carrying them with his eyes open wide. "All of these are for me?"

"Yes, all for you. I told you I had something for you when we get home!"

He went through each bag and loved everything he saw. "I like all my clothes. I have five new outfits!"

As KJ went through his bags, Myles opened his birthday cards. "I have over $200.00 here! Happy Birthday to me! Happy Birthday to me!" he sang.

152

"That's a lot of money," KJ stated. When he saw his new basketball, he thanked me for his new clothes and ball. "Can I go outside to play with it?"

"Yes, you can. But stay in the driveway." Myles laughed at KJ's excitement. We sat in the living room so that we could have a better view of KJ playing with his new ball.

"The other day, I was coming home and saw Keith turning off Riverside. Did he come here?" Myles asked.

"No."

"I wonder who else he knows down here," Myles wondered aloud.

I figured that was just the opening I needed to tell him about Keith. "Myles, the day of your party, Keith was following me around town."

He sat up straight on the couch, looked at me, and asked, "He did?"

"He has been harassing me for a long time now."

"Why didn't you tell me, Lexie?"

"I thought I could handle it myself. I was praying that since I'm married, he would leave me alone."

"What do you mean? When did this start?" I could tell Myles was not at all happy about his wife being harassed by her ex-husband.

"Before you and I got married, Keith would sit and watch me come and go from my house and job. We had already been divorced for over a year or more. At work, a male coworker and I would always walk out together. One day, Aston—my coworker—told me that for a week or more, he noticed a black car pull out from the parking lot across the street and that when I left, the car would follow me. He said, 'What I want you to do today is drive to the police station down the street. Let's see if that car follows you or just so happens to be leaving at the same time we do every day.' Well, at the intersection, Aston turned, and I kept going straight. Sure enough, the car followed me. When I made it to the police station, I turned into the parking lot, and the car slowed down. That's when I saw it was Keith." I inhaled deeply before speaking again. "You see, he had a white Ford Focus when we were together. I had no idea it was him."

Myles looked at me with concern the entire time I spoke, surprised to hear all I was telling him.

153

"I would see him sitting in the turnaround at the end of the street in that same black car. One Friday, it was Aston's last day at work before returning to Nigeria to be with his family, so we threw him a going-away party. When it was time for us to leave, the entire team walked out of the building together. Aston embraced each of us as we left. I had to call the police when I got home because Keith was blocking my driveway. He got out of his car screaming at me about hugging that man. I didn't say anything. I just waited for the police to arrive. When they got here, Keith lied and told them I had put him out of his house and wouldn't let him see his son. I called him a lying preacher and told the police we were divorced and that he saw his son every two weeks. I hollered, 'This is not his house! It never was! I want him off my property! Now!' They asked him to leave and told him if they had to come out here again, they would lock him up for stalking."

"Oh, my God!" Myles exclaimed.

"After the police incident, when he would get KJ, he wouldn't say a word to me. You see, he really wanted to take my house from me in the divorce. I started dropping KJ off and picking him up from the daycare to avoid having to see Keith. At some point, he started calling me, saying stupid stuff. Remember that day I invited you to breakfast after you proposed to me, and then you took KJ to the shop with you?"

"Yes, I remember that day well."

"Well, when you left, I saw you had left your cap behind. I didn't bother calling you because I knew I would see you later. When my doorbell rang right after you left, I assumed you were returning for your cap, so I opened the door without looking out first. It was Keith."

"Wait. Are you telling me he came here?"

"Yes, and he asked to come in." Myles stared at me, running his fingers through his hair in frustration. "I told him to leave my house. As I went to close the door, he saw my ring and asked if I was engaged. I told him I was and again told him to leave my house or else I would call the police."

"Lexie, if I hadn't mentioned I saw him, would you have told me all of this?"

"Yes, I was going to tell you. I was just waiting for the right time."

"Do you still love him?" he asked.

Without hesitation, I replied, "No, I do not love him. I wasn't even in love with him when we were together. He was simply my son's daddy." He didn't say anything else, leaving me to wonder what he was thinking. He went outside to play ball with KJ and then came back in, taking a seat at the kitchen island. I thought to myself, "Lord, I should have told him about Keith when the mess first started."

I felt obligated to explain. "Myles, I thought Keith was my problem and that I could handle it. That's why I didn't tell you."

He looked at me and said, "From now on, I'll drop off and pick up KJ to his dad. You won't have to come in contact with him. I know I can't control him watching this house, but I can tell him to keep his distance from you. I will talk to him and tell him how a real man of God should be conducting himself."

"You are going to talk to him for real?!"

"Yes, I am. Sooner than later. Call KJ in so we can pray together. God is in control, not Keith."

Chapter 56

On Friday morning, Myles dropped me off at the airport, where I met up with three other women who were flying to Memphis for our two-day Human Resource Teaching Workshop. We left Nashville at 8:35 a.m. and arrived in Memphis at 10:40 a.m. The first day of the workshop started at 1:00 p.m. that afternoon and ended at 8:00 p.m. The Saturday session started at 9:00 a.m. and ended at 3:00 p.m. Myles and I had discussed him driving down on Saturday after the workshop to go sightseeing that evening and then driving back home on Sunday.

When we landed in Memphis, there was a van waiting to drive us to the Comfort Inn and Suites Airport American Way Hotel. The workshop would be held in the same hotel. I checked into my room and called Myles to let him know I had arrived and to give him my room number. He was with a customer at the time, so I left the message with his secretary.

"Would you like him to call you back?" she asked.

"Just give him the message, please. I'm getting ready for my workshop and won't be in the room." I hung up, got dressed, and hurried to meet the other ladies in the conference room to get everything set up.

After the workshop, the four of us ate in the dining hall at the hotel. One of the ladies had a friend who lived in Memphis. The friend came and picked the other three ladies up to visit Beale Street. I opted out and went back to my room to shower, get my materials together for Saturday's workshop, and then went to bed. Myles called, and we talked until I got sleepy. Early Saturday morning, I got dressed and met the other ladies for breakfast. We made it to the conference room in time to get everything set up for the day and started the workshop at 9:00 am. sharp.

As scheduled, the workshop ended at 3:00 p.m. I was back in my room at 3:30, and Myles wasn't far behind. "Hey, Babe! I've missed you!" he said as he kissed me.

"Myles, I was only away for one night," I said sarcastically.

"Well, I missed you lying beside me. Wow! I like what you're wearing! Is this new?" he asked as he spun me around.

"No, it's not new," I replied with a giggle. I sat on the bed to remove my heels.

"How was your day, my lady?"

"Tiresome. I'm glad it's over. Since I'm the H.R. Regional Supervisor, I'm going to appoint someone else to do some of these meetings, although I will still have to be in attendance. The next meeting will be in Chicago. I'll have to get with the other supervisors in the other states to see what month and day is best to schedule that conference. That meeting is going to be from Thursday through Saturday."

He was lying on the bed, looking at me. "Wherever you go, I will go," he said with a smile. "I enjoyed my ride down here. When I was leaving, Mrs. Riddle was coming in to do the cleaning. I told her I was on my way to Memphis to get my woman. She laughed at me and said, 'Yes, get your woman because you're looking pitiful without her.' I thought that was funny. I let her know her check was on the island. Oh! KJ called last night looking for you. I told him you were out of town. He asked if I could come and get him. I told him no because it was his time to be with his dad, and I couldn't come to get him. I told him we would pick him up Sunday afternoon and that I had something special for him."

"What do you have special for him?" I inquired.

"A bag of hot Cheetos." We laughed so hard at his joke.

"I've noticed he doesn't like staying at his dad's house lately. I wonder why," I thought aloud.

"I don't know," Myles answered. I could tell he wondered the same.

I changed my clothes, and we went sightseeing. Our first stop was the National Civil Rights Museum. We were so impressed with the knowledge we gained about our history. "Myles, why don't we surprise Mae and her family one weekend and bring them to this museum? There is so much they could learn!"

"There's also a Mississippi Civil Rights Museum in Jackson. I heard it's nice. I'll get with Derrick and Mae and see what weekend we can come back here and then drive to Jackson," Myles replied.

We drove by the hotel where MLK was shot and ended up on Beale Street eating BBQ and tasting different kinds of foods while listening to music. It was getting late by the time we headed back to our hotel. On the way, we drove down Elvis Presley Boulevard. I enjoyed riding with my husband, even when we got lost and went the wrong way on one-way streets.

Sunday morning, we met up with the other ladies for breakfast. After eating, they checked out of their rooms and boarded the van to take them back to the airport.

Myles and I returned to my room. I checked out at 12:30 p.m. and made it back to Nashville around 4:00. Before heading home, we met Keith to pick up KJ. KJ was so happy to see us. As he walked to climb into Pearl, he said, "Mama, that was a long two weeks! I wanted you to come and pick me up."

"Well, we got you now," I replied, bringing a smile to his face.

"I have a surprise waiting for you," Myles teased, "but you can't get it until tomorrow."

"What is it?" KJ asked.

"You'll see tomorrow," Myles replied as he rubbed him on his head.

On Monday, since KJ was out of school, he went to the shop with Myles. I was home from work when they got in. Myles came over, kissed me, and asked, "How was your day?"

"I had a good day. Where's KJ?"

"Babe, can we talk?"

"Of course, but where is my son?" He didn't answer. Instead, he picked me up and hugged and kissed me all over my face while laughing. "What in the world is wrong with you? Where is KJ?"

"Calm down, Lexie. He's in the garage."

I walked to the side door, opened it, and a puppy jumped on my leg. I squealed. "Oh, my God! Where did you get it from?"

"That's what I wanted to tell you. Remember I told you I had a surprise for KJ?"

"I do. I also remember you said it was a bag of hot Cheetos."

"Well, I didn't lie. I got him Cheetos, too. He already ate them. But before you say anything, the puppy is trained. I paid a trainer to make sure he was housebroken. He also knows how to sit and listen to instructions."

"Can I keep him, Mama? Please?" KJ begged.

I stood there looking at the puppy and my son. How could I say no? "Yes, you can keep him," I decided.

KJ hugged me, kissed me on the cheek, and said, "Thank you, Mama!" Myles hugged and kissed me, too.

"So, what are you going to name him?" I asked KJ.

"Spot Ferguson," he yelled.

I laughed. "Spot Ferguson? Why that name?"

"That's what the man called him," Myles whispered. Myles bought everything the puppy needed: food, a water and food dish, a cage, and a big, round pillow for the dog to sleep on. The puppy was a white Shih Tzu with black on each ear and a black spot on his back. He was the cutest little thing.

"Myles, what if I would have said KJ couldn't keep the dog?"

"I knew when you saw him, you would say yes."

In short order, I fell in love with Spot. Myles took him to the shop with him every day, and when they got home, KJ would take him outside to play. Myles stated, "When we go out of town, we'll have to put him in a doggy daycare." I agreed.

Chapter 57

As planned, when it was time to drop off KJ to his dad, Myles took him. Keith stopped calling the house, and if he wanted to tell us something concerning KJ, Myles would be the one to talk to him. After dropping KJ off, Myles returned home and asked me, "Is Keith alright?"

"I don't know. I haven't seen or heard from him. Is he sick or something?" I asked.

"He just acted strange today. When we drove up, we didn't see his car. We sat and waited nearly 20 minutes before he got out of a red car. I know he saw us because that same car was sitting in the parking lot when we arrived."

"Maybe he got a new car," I suggested.

"There was a man in the car with him."

"Well, when school starts, you won't have to drop KJ off to him anymore. He will be catching the bus from Mae's house," I replied.

"Yep! You're right!"

I was so thankful for the relationship Myles and I had. I realized how blessed I was to have a husband who loved me. I called him my 'Rock.' He would laugh and say, "So, you're saying I'm handsome?"

"To me, you are better than handsome!" I replied.

He would respond, "I love you. You are the best thing that ever happened to me, other than God."

For a few days, I felt sick in the morning when I got up, but once I ate breakfast, the feeling would go away. I told Myles, and he said, "You're just hungry. That's all." Then, one day while at work, my stomach was upset. Thinking it was something I ate, I asked my secretary to bring me a ginger ale from the vending machine. I ate the crackers I had in my desk and drank the pop. After eating, I again felt better and continued to do my work. When I got home that afternoon, Myles had picked up a chef salad from the Starlight Restaurant. We ate and went for our evening run. Once back home, I worked in my office, doing some work I didn't finish that day at the job. I started feeling dizzy, so I took a shower, laid down for the night, and woke up feeling well the next morning.

A couple of weeks later, after Myles left for work, I felt nauseous and had a headache. I ate breakfast but didn't feel better. I called in and took the day off from work. I called Myles at the shop to tell him I was home because I didn't feel well. I then went to take a nap. When I woke up, I felt better. I worked in my office on some files I had to complete at work.

When Myles got home, I had a big dinner prepared: baked chicken, cabbage, mac-n-cheese, cornbread, and peach cobbler. "Why did you do all this cooking?" he asked. "How are you feeling? Did you go to or call the doctor?" He kissed me and said, "Babe, I think you're doing too much."

"I'm fine. I just needed a little rest. I haven't stopped going since we got married."

"Lexie, that was over 11 months ago. Make an appointment to see the doctor. I'll go with you. I don't like knowing you're not feeling well."

When KJ returned to school, Myles would drop him off at Mae's house to catch the bus with her kids to school. The bus stop was on the highway, two houses from Mae's. In the afternoon, KJ would get off the bus every day except for every other Friday when he went to his dad's house. On Monday evenings, he would get off the bus at Mae's house, and Myles would bring him home. Both of us appreciated not having to meet up with Keith anymore. One evening, Myles told me that KJ said a little girl at school liked him and thought he liked her back. When he told me, I laughed and said, "He's been back in school for a month, and he's talking about a girl liking him? He's only nine years old! Oh, my God!"

"That's what boys do," Myles replied.

"Are you telling me that you were interested in girls when you were nine?"

"At the age of nine, I had kissed a girl and had a crush on my teacher," he said, grinning from ear to ear. I hit him with the paper I had in my hand, and he kissed me once he pinned my hands down.

My doctor's appointment was scheduled for 1:00 p.m. on a Wednesday. Myles met me at the doctor's office. We waited in the waiting room until the nurse called us back. I started feeling dizzy as we walked to the examination room. Myles held me up as we walked down the hall.

When Jessica saw me, she was surprised. "Lexie Harris. How are you doing? The last time I saw you, you were going into the Air Force."

I was surprised to see her, too. We hugged. "Yes, it's been a long time—about 11 years, right? Wow, Jessica Brown! You're a doctor now?"

"Yes, I'm your doctor," she said proudly.

"When I was told Dr. Sharp would be seeing me, I didn't know it was you!"

"Yes, I married James Sharp. We have two boys, ages ten and eight."

"Wow, Jessica! You married James Sharp? I remember you didn't even like him! You married the quietest boy in our class! I know one thing: He did not like Matthew. He said Matthew was arrogant and stuck on himself because he was good at playing basketball and football. What happened to you and Matthew? I remember how in love with him you were."

She smiled at the memory and then said, "Well, that quiet boy is now a teacher at Tennessee State University. And Matthew? Well, that's a long story."

"Jessica, do you remember when James gave you a box of chocolate-covered cherries with a note attached that read, 'I love you. Do you love me?'?"

She was laughing so hard and replied, "Yes, I remember. I told him I loved the candy but not him and then told him to leave me alone."

"Well, what you didn't hear was his reply. As you walked away, he murmured, 'I'm going to make you love me.'"

"Lexie, he said that?!"

"Yes, he did. I guess he accomplished his mission! You married him. I can't believe it! Wow!" I exclaimed.

"I didn't know anything about what you just told me," she said with a curious look. "I'll be sure to tell you about our love story during another visit. Girl, I'm so glad to see you. We must get together soon!"

Myles stood in the background, listening to us talk. "Oh, Jessica. This is my husband, Myles Ferguson."

She looked at him closely and asked, "Doesn't your father own the computer shop on Shelby Drive?"

"I'm the owner now. My dad passed away over a year ago."

"I'm sorry to hear that. He worked on my computer a couple of years ago. Well, I must say you look just like him, only taller," she said with a smile. She returned her attention to me. "So, Lexie, what brings you in today?"

"I have been feeling dizzy and nauseous for a few months now."

"Are you pregnant?" she asked.

"I don't think so…" I hadn't even considered that as an option.

"Let's do a urine test, and we will see what's going on with you." Jessica walked out of the office. Shortly after, a nurse came in to take my vitals. I then filled out paperwork, and she gave me a cup to take the test.

When Jessica returned, I asked, "So, Jessica Brown Sharp, you're my doctor?"

"Yes, unless you want someone else."

"No, I want you. It just seems strange to have my best friend looking at my private parts." I laughed at the expression on her face.

"Remember: You are my best friend and sister. Now, you have the best doctor on this side of Heaven to work on you!" she said, laughing. "We did a lot of stuff together. Those were some good days." She then walked out of the room again.

I took the urine test, and the nurse told me the doctor would be back to talk to me about the results in a moment. Myles and I sat there, waiting for the doctor to return. When Jessica came in, she was smiling from ear to ear. "You guys are pregnant! With the information on your chart and the test results, you are approximately 14 weeks along."

"What?! Are you sure?!" I shouted.

"I'm 100% sure that you are roughly three-and-a-half months pregnant. Please schedule a full examination for next month with the front desk."

Myles was excited. "I knew it!"

Jessica gave me a prescription for prenatal vitamins and iron pills. "Your iron is a little low. I want to see you in a month. That would be on March 9th."

"Jessica, what should I call you?"

"Dr. Jessica will be fine," she said as she walked away.

Dr. Jessica just told me I was with child. I had to get over the shock of that news. Me? Pregnant?

As we went back to our cars, Myles held me up by my arm and said, "Thank You, Jesus! Lexie, I knew you were pregnant."

"How did you know?"

"A couple of months ago, I had a dream. I was working in the back of the shop, and Mrs. Clark called out to me and said there was someone there to see me. I walked out to see who it was, and it was you—and you were pregnant."

"Why didn't you tell me about the dream?"

"It was just a dream, Babe, yet it was so real." He kissed me and said, "I am happy you are having my baby." He opened my car door and helped me climb in. "How are you feeling now?"

"I'm okay, just surprised to learn I'm pregnant. With all the symptoms I had, I never even considered I could be pregnant. I really thought I just needed to rest."

"Well, I'm not surprised." He pecked me on the cheek. "Don't cook anything tonight. We are going out to celebrate. For now, go home and get off your feet. I'm going by the shop to pick up Spot, and then I'll be home. Baby, we gotta pray and thank God for us being pregnant!" His excitement was becoming contagious.

Chapter 58

On Thursday afternoon, after picking up KJ from Mae's house, Myles said, "When I picked up KJ, he told me he was graduating from the Young Children's Learning Class at his daddy's church on Sunday. He wanted to know if I was coming. I asked him if you knew about it, and he replied, 'No, Mama doesn't like daddy anymore. She might get mad if I ask her to come.'"

"He said that, Myles? Oh, no. Where is he?"

"In the garage, playing with Spot."

I called for KJ to come inside and asked, "Do you have anything to tell me?" When he told me about the graduation, I asked, "Why didn't you tell me about it?"

"Because daddy said you were mad at him and don't want to talk to him anymore. I don't want you to be mad at him, Mama."

I thought to myself, "That lying man! Why would he tell our son something like that?" I didn't know how to respond, so I stood there looking at him, dumbfounded.

Myles saw how uncomfortable I was and called out to KJ. "Come here, Peanut. Your Mama loves you. She'll be at your graduation. She's not mad at your daddy. How do you feel about that now, Mr. Keith Jr.?" They started to play wrestle.

"You two better get out of here with all that rough playing," I joked. They went outside and played basketball while the dog ran around playing. I couldn't get past the thought: Why would Keith tell our son something like that?!

On Friday morning, Myles dropped off KJ at Mae's house to catch the bus. It was his weekend to go to his dad's house after school, so it was just Myles and me home for the weekend. I left for work to arrive by 9:00. Around 11:00, Myles called to see how I was feeling and said, "When I dropped KJ off this morning, Chyna said she wants us to pick her up for KJ's graduation on Sunday. You know he told her," he said, laughing.

"That's okay with me. Does anyone else want to come?"

"Not that I know of," he replied. "Well, Babe, I gotta get back to work. Love you!"

When Saturday morning came, Myles went to the shop at 10:00 and said he would be back by 3:00. He didn't usually work on Saturdays, but he was doing inventory with Mr. Ron and Mrs. Clark. I stayed in bed until Mrs. Riddle rang the doorbell at 10:00 to do her bi-weekly cleaning—something she had done faithfully ever since my mom died. I recall the day I called her not long after my mom's death and asked if she could come to take Mama's clothes out of the house because I couldn't do it. The Saturday after that call, she was there with empty boxes in tow. She told me to stay outside on the patio and that she would take care of everything else. Ever since, she has been like a mother to me. When she walked into the house, the dog ran outside. "You got a dog now?" she asked.

"That's KJ and Myles' dog."

"It's such a cute little thing. What's the dog's name?"

"Spot. He's a clean dog. You won't have to clean up behind him. Myles paid a trainer to make sure he was housebroken before he got here." As I spoke, Mrs. Riddle looked at me strangely.

"Lexie, you are glowing! Are you pregnant?"

"Yes, ma'am. Almost four months."

She giggled like a little schoolgirl. "I knew it! If you need a babysitter, I'm here. I knew you were glowing from something! How are you feeling?"

"I feel good, but Myles is acting as if I'm an egg that can be easily broken. He doesn't want me to do anything whatsoever!" She laughed at what I said. "Okay, Mrs. Riddle, I am going to hold you to being my babysitter." Just then, the phone rang. It was Myles.

"A city garbage truck backed into my car," he said.

"Are you alright?" I asked with panic and concern.

"I'm okay. I had just gotten my paperwork out of the car and was opening the door to the shop when it happened. I heard a crashing sound, and then the car alarm went off. Lexie, the truck hit on the driver's side. I turned around just in time to see the airbag deploy. My God! He spared my life again. I know the car is going to be totaled out."

"I am so sorry about the car but glad you are okay. Do you want me to come and pick you up?"

"No, I'll get dad's truck. I'll ask Ron to take me to the storage to pick it up. I'm glad I just paid the insurance on that truck last week." The more he spoke about his dad, the softer his voice became.

"Myles, are you really okay?"

"Yes, I am. I just thought about it. I'll be driving dad's truck for a while." He exhaled deeply. "Okay. I gotta go. My workers are walking in. Mrs. Clark says hi."

"Tell her hi for me." The line went dead. It broke my heart to hear the sadness in his voice. I wondered if he really was okay. I told Mrs. Riddle what Myles said about the car.

"Is he alright?" she asked.

"He said he is."

"Thank You, Jesus! He's okay," she replied. When it was time for her to leave, she said, "Tell my son I am sorry about his car, but I'm glad he's alright." I paid her, hugged her, and then she left. I sat in the living room, waiting for Myles to come home.

Around 4:00, he came home and let the garage door up but didn't pull the truck inside. I waited for him to come in. When he didn't enter right away, I looked outside to see what he was doing. He was drying off the truck while the dog played in the grass. I walked outside. "It looks nice. Are you alright?"

"Yep!" I could see on his face that he had been crying.

"Honey, are you sure you're alright?"

"Yes, Babe. I'm fine. It's just my first time driving dad's truck since he passed away. Ron took it to storage for me and had to take me to pick it up. As I drove home, I thought, 'I would rather have my dad than his truck any day.'" I saw the tears forming in his eyes. He quickly changed the conversation. "How's my fine, pregnant wife doing?" He came over, kissed me, and held me close. "You sure do smell good. Did you miss me?" he asked.

"Looks like we've been missing each other too much already! After all, I'm pregnant!" He laughed.

"Can you get a trash bag for me, please? I want to clean out this truck. And can you bring the broom, Windex, and paper towels? Dad got potato chip bags, McDonald's and Burger King bags, and Baby Ruth and Butterfinger wrappers in

167

here. I think I saw a couple of chicken bones on the floor, too!" We both laughed hard.

I helped him clean out the truck. Myles stepped back when we were done and said, "You know what? It doesn't look bad, now that it's clean. Get in. Let's go for a ride. Come on, Spot. Jump in." We drove to Wendy's on the other side of town.

"Are we going in?" I asked.

"Not this time. I am going to the drive-thru, get our food, park, and sit in my dad's truck while I eat my food and watch my beautiful wife do the same."

"You're such a smooth talker."

"Only to you, Babe. Only to you." He squeezed my hand, and Spot licked it from the back seat.

While we ate our food, a woman exited Wendy's. She was carrying a bag of food and holding a little boy's hand. Myles said, "Wow! That's Maya. I haven't seen her since we were in high school. I used to have a crush on her. I see she's put on a little weight." We watched as she walked to the car parked next to us. She opened the rear door, and the little boy climbed into his car seat. When she turned to open her door, Myles spoke.

She turned around and said, "Myles Ferguson! Is that you? Long time, no see! How have you been doing?"

"I'm good. I haven't seen you since high school. How's Andre?"

"He's good," she replied.

"Maya, this is my wife, Lexie."

She looked past Myles at me and said, "Hi! Nice to meet you! I've seen you somewhere before. Where have I seen you? Oh! I know! Do you work downtown?"

"Yes, in the Human Resources building."

"My aunt works there. Do you know a lady named Paula Jones?"

"Yes, I do! She works in the office next to mine."

"I knew I'd seen you before!"

"It's nice meeting you, Maya. I'll be sure to tell Mrs. Jones I met her niece when I see her again." She smiled before turning away. The little boy was opening the door, trying to get out.

"Close the door. We are getting ready to leave," she commanded.

Myles waved bye to the little boy. "Maya, tell Andre hello for me."

"I will," she said as she got into her car and then drove away.

Chapter 59

"Myles, how do you feel about seeing someone you dated?"

"We didn't date, Lexie. We happened to be at the movies at the same time and sat together. Her entire conversation was about Andre. She said he was coming with her, but his job called him into work at the last minute. I never bothered to tell her how I felt about her because she was all in with Andre."

"Did you...you know?"

"No, I never slept with her or even kissed her. Remember: I said I had a crush on her. She wasn't thinking about me." He laughed and said, "The Lord blessed me with the woman I love. She's sitting here beside me and having my baby." He squeezed my hand as we drove away. He looked over at me and said, "You are so beautiful. You make me very happy. And now, you are having my baby. Could things get any better than that? I love you, girl!"

No sooner than we turned into our subdivision, a policeman pulled in behind us and turned on his flashing lights. "Oh, my God. Why is he stopping me?" Myles wondered. When the officer walked up to the truck, he asked to see Myles' driving license, which he removed from his wallet and handed to him.

The officer looked past Myles, saw me, and said, "Ms. Lexie, how are you doing?"

"I'm doing well, officer Brown."

He handed Myles his license back and said, "Mr. Ferguson, your right taillight is out."

"Thank you, officer. I had no idea."

"See you on Monday, Ms. Lexie. Man, get that taillight fixed."

"Yes, sir. I will," Myles responded. When the policeman pulled away, Myles asked, "He talked to you and didn't even glance at the registration. Where does he know you from?"

"He's my supervisor's husband—and he's the same one who came out when I called the police on Keith."

Myles looked at me seductively when we finally got home and pulled into the garage. "Put Spot in his cage and get the sauna ready. I am going for a run. When I get back, I want us to spend some time in the sauna to relax. This has been a long day for me."

"No sauna for me, Myles. I can't get in because I'm pregnant." The disappointment was evident by the look on his face.

Later that night, while lying in bed, Myles said, "While doing inventory today, I moved some boxes. Behind them, dad had two pickle jars full of quarters, dimes, and nickels, and one jar filled with pennies."

"For real? What are you going to do with all that change?"

"I'll give Mae one jar filled with silver and keep the other one. I'll bring the pennies jar home to give to KJ. He can roll them and start a savings account. I'll take my jar to the bank and have them deposit the money to start a savings account for the baby. What do you think?"

"That sounds good to me…but KJ already has a savings account."

"Well, he can add the pennies to it. I'll tell him Pawpaw left the money for him," he said, laughing.

"What about Sharon?" I asked.

"She wouldn't want any. She got the house in Myrtle Beach, Mae got the house here, and I got the shop. Plus, each of us received $20,000.00 from his life insurance policy. Sharon will be just fine without the change," he said, kissing me good night.

I laid in bed thinking about what I would wear to KJ's graduation. I remembered Myles had given me a cream-colored pants suit and a pair of cream-colored shoes with polka dots for my birthday. I could match the outfit with the hat I bought while at the retreat. It was brown with cream polka dots. To top it off, I could carry my brown purse. I fell asleep thinking about KJ telling me his daddy told him I was mad at him.

Later that night, I was awakened by Myles talking in his sleep. I heard him say, "Daddy! Daddy!" and murmuring something. He then began to cry and sob in his sleep. I called his name and gently shook him to wake him up. He turned on his side away from me, but I could still hear him sobbing. A few minutes later, he got up, sat on the side of the bed, and put on his house shoes.

"Myles, where are you going? Are you alright?"

"Yes, I'm okay. I'll be in the garage."

I got up to peek at what he was doing and saw him sitting in his daddy' truck, crying. I knew that truck brought back a flood of memories. Finding those jars of coins didn't help. I got back in bed and waited for him to return. Roughly 25 minutes later, he climbed back into the bed. He held me close, and I finally fell back asleep.

Chapter 60

On Sunday morning, I got up while Myles was still asleep. I got dressed in the bathroom, and when I came out, he was sitting on the side of the bed with his face buried in his hands. He looked up at me and asked, "Why are you wearing your birthday outfit?"

"Although my birthday isn't until May, I won't be able to fit into it by then with me being pregnant."

"Oh, that's true," he said, rubbing my belly. "Babe, you are looking good with your hair hanging down. That hat is beautiful! Where did you get it?"

"From a little boutique when I was on the retreat."

"I like it," he said before going to get dressed. When he came back out, I told him how good he looked. "Thanks, my lady!"

We never ate on Sundays until after church. He fed Spot, took him outside to do his business, and put him back in his cage. We walked out of the house, leaving for church. On the way to Pearl, I looked back and saw Myles standing near his dad's truck with a curious expression. "Myles? Are you alright?"

"Yes." He opened the vehicle's door so that I could get in. As we rode to church, he reached over, held my hand, and said, "I had a dream about my dad last night."

"I know. Maybe you dreamed about him because of the truck and those coins."

"Maybe so," he said thoughtfully. I looked at him closely and commented on how we were wearing the same colors. He laughed and replied, "I promise I didn't plan this." He was wearing brown slacks, a brown turtleneck, brown shoes, and a cream-colored jacket with a brown and cream polka dot handkerchief in the pocket.

Church service that Sunday was wonderful. The pastor's message was "Let Jesus Be the Center of Your Life." He called Myles to the front to sing a solo. Myles whispered something to the pianist, and the man nodded yes. His song choice was "He Wouldn't Let It Be" by Beau Williams. After singing, virtually everyone was on their feet. Before Myles could head back to his seat, the pastor asked him to sing "Tomorrow Might Be Too Late." The pastor called the congregants to the altar for prayer as he sang.

"Thank you for singing those songs, brother. We really needed to hear them," the pastor said.

When he sat back down next to me, he whispered, "I wasn't expecting that. Those were my dad's favorite songs. I remember singing both of them the Sunday before I left for Iraq."

I had to compliment him. "You sounded so good! I didn't know you could sing like that!" He smiled and returned his attention to the remainder of the service.

After church, Myles met with the pastor and secretary to program the computer. Afterward, we went to the Fire Mountain Restaurant for dinner. "Myles, were you afraid when the pastor called you to sing?"

"No, I wasn't. Before leaving for Iraq, I was a member of the choir."

"Say what? For real?!"

"As a matter of fact, the pastor asked me if I wanted to rejoin the choir. I told him I had to pray about it before answering."

"That would be great, Myles! Do it!"

"Maybe I should tell him you can sing, too," he joked.

"Don't you dare do that!" He laughed hard at the serious expression I beamed his way. On our way to Mae's house to pick up Chyna for KJ's program, it started to rain. I couldn't help but laugh. "We have two umbrellas, and they are home. Now, we need them."

"Look. Chyna is waiting for us with hers," Myles said, laughing.

When Chyna got in, she said, "Uncle Myles, I've never been to a graduation at a church before."

"Me, neither." It was still raining when we arrived at Pastor Montgomery's church, so Myles dropped us off as close to the door as he could get and then went to park.

We stood in the interior doorway, waiting on him. Some of the ladies remembered me from when I used to attend service there and spoke, saying it was nice to see me again. When Mother Hamilton saw me, she came over. "Sister Lexie! It is you! How are you doing? Girl, you are looking good!"

"I am doing well, Mother Hamilton! How have you been?"

"I've had my good days and bad days, but I feel good today! Thank You, Lord!"

"Mother, this is my husband's niece Chyna."

"Hi, Chyna! What a pretty name for a pretty young lady. Look at all that hair on your head!" she said with a smile.

"Thank you," Chyna replied, blushing.

Just then, Myles walked in and handed Chyna her umbrella. "Thanks, Chyna."

I then introduced Mother to Myles. "Mother Hamilton, this is my husband, Myles."

"Myles, is that you?" You are looking good, son." She turned to me and said, "I've known him since he was in high school."

"Ms. Hamilton, it's so good to see you," Myles said, hugging her.

She stepped back to look at him. "Boy, you got muscles now! So, you married Sister Lexie?"

"Yes, ma'am."

"Well, it's so nice seeing you again," she said while hugging him again. "Lexie, you look so happy. I'm glad you married Myles. He's a nice young man. We'll talk later, okay? Let me go in and get off my legs."

"It's nice to see you again, Ms. Hamilton," Myles said as she walked away. We entered the sanctuary and were led to our seats by an usher. Myles leaned over and whispered, "Ms. Hamilton was sweet on my dad." I smiled at the thought.

I could see First Lady Brenda looking toward us from where we sat. I know she remembered me from how she treated me and that day she came to my house with Keith.

The program started with prayer, a scripture reading, and a song from the choir. The graduating children marched in and stood in place in their pews until Pastor Montgomery came in and took his place behind the podium. As he looked over the congregation, he paused before speaking.

"Thank you to all of our guests who found it not robbery to share this time with us. This will not be a long service. We are here to show our love to these young people for their accomplishments. They have done a tremendous job learning the Books of the Bible and scriptures, and a couple of the students had perfect attendance." He then called two students to the front to recite one passage of scripture each had to remember. Another two sang solos. KJ was called on to recite both the Old and New Testament Books of the Bible. When he finished, he waved to us, and Myles responded with two thumbs up. He smiled, showing his gratitude for us being there.

All the students stood and went to the front to receive their certificates from First Lady Brenda. Once each had their certificate in hand, they remained standing and then sang "I Need You to Survive." Three of the girls did a praise dance while the others sang. For the six students with perfect attendance, the pastor called their names and gave them a plaque.

When the program was over, First Lady Brenda announced there were refreshments in the Fellowship Hall for everyone. I walked over to her and told her how much I enjoyed the program. "Are you staying for refreshments?" she asked.

"No, thank you. My husband is ready to go. I just wanted to say hi to you before we left."

"Okay. I understand. Thanks for coming."

As I turned to leave, Sister Owens approached me with her arms outstretched for a hug. "Sister Lexie! It's so good to see you! I miss you! You are looking so good."

"Thanks, you are looking good yourself! Call me sometime. I gotta run. My husband is waiting for me. It's nice seeing you."

"What? Your husband?!" she exclaimed as I walked away.

"Yes, girl. Call me so we can talk." I walked over to where Myles and Pastor Montgomery were talking.

Once at his side, Myles took my hand and asked, "Are you ready to go now?"

"Yes, I am." Pastor Montgomery looked at me from head to toe.

KJ came over to us and asked his dad, "Can I go home with Mama?"

He looked at me before replying. "Yes, if it's okay with her."

176

"Can I come with you, Mama? Please?"

"Yes, you can come home."

A man walked up behind the pastor. "May I speak to you for a minute?" he asked. He was the same man I saw Pastor Montgomery with at the store.

"Okay, I'll be right there." He turned to us and said, "Thanks for coming. See you next week, KJ."

"Come on, Peanut," Myles said, reaching for KJ's hand. Chyna already held his other one. The rain had stopped, so we walked to the SUV together. Myles helped me get in. Once settled inside, KJ and Chyna asked if we could stop at Taco Bell. Myles didn't reply, acting as if he had something on his mind.

I interrupted his thoughts. "Myles? Are you going to stop?"

"Oh. Yes, I am. What do y'all want to eat?"

"Nothing for me," I answered. "But the kids want Taco Bell. Get yourself something, too." When we turned onto Riverside, Chyna asked me if KJ could come to her house. "Ask your uncle."

"Let me call your mom and ask if he can come over," Myles replied. He called Mae, who said yes. In his deepest voice, he looked at KJ and said, "Peanut, you behave yourself. You hear me?" Both children thought that voice was hilarious.

"Uncle Myles, you're so funny!"

In the same deep voice, he replied, "I am not funny, my little Cupcake. I am your uncle!" More laughter between the two younger ones roared throughout Pearl before they got out. "See you in two hours, Peanut! Bye, Cupcake!" They went inside the house, still laughing.

Chapter 61

Driving home, Myles finally shared what was on his mind. "Pastor Montgomery is very crafty and conceited. Something about him is strange. I saw how he looked at you when you talked to his wife. And when you came over to me, he couldn't take his eyes off you."

I had to laugh. "Are you jealous? Be fore real, Honey. All I can say is that he is a sick man for telling KJ what he did. I don't care a thing about that man. I wasn't in love with him when we were married, and I don't like him now. We just have a son together. I think he needs to find himself."

It was Myles' turn to laugh. "To answer your question: No, I am not jealous. I just didn't like the way he looked at you. Period." He drove into the garage, got out, and opened my door. "Mrs. Ferguson, you know you look good, right?" He knew how to make me blush.

Once inside, Myles sat at the kitchen island to eat his food. "You want a bite?" he offered.

"No, thank you." I could tell he had something on his mind. When he finished eating, he went into the exercise room, and I went to our bedroom to get ready for bed.

After about 15 minutes, he walked in. "Babe, are you asleep?"

"No, just relaxing," I replied.

"Can I relax with you?" he asked while lying on the bed.

"Yes, after you pick up KJ." I could tell he had been crying. "Are you alright?"

"Seeing Ms. Hamilton today made me think of my dad again. She really liked him. She used to cook for us, help Sharon clean the house, and wash our clothes, but daddy never married her. I wonder why."

"Maybe she was there for companionship. Some older people are lonely and just need to be around other people their age," I replied thoughtfully.

"Well, she must have been really lonely because she was at our house all the time!" We laughed. "It's time for me to get KJ. Can you call Mae to let her know I'm on the way? Do you want to ride with me?"

"Yes, I will call. No, I don't want to ride. I am not getting out of this bed until the morning."

He kissed me on the forehead and said, "I'll take Spot with me."

I called Mae and then went right to sleep. It seemed like Monday morning came quickly. When I woke up, Myles had already left to drop off KJ at Mae's house to catch the bus. I had to make it to work by 9:30, so I hurried to get ready.

That day in the office started out rough. I was informed two ladies were fired for fighting on the job. Plus, I had over 20 files on my desk that needed to be transferred to my computer. Then, I had two interviewees coming in that afternoon for a secretary position we posted.

I called Myles on my lunch break to see how his day was going. His secretary said he was with a customer and that she would have him call me back. Twenty minutes later, that call came. "Are you alright?" he asked.

"Yes, I'm doing great! How's Spot?"

"Spot is fine. I'm not."

"What's wrong?" I asked with concern.

"I miss you," he said, laughing.

"You just left me four hours ago!"

"Nooooo... It's been five hours, 32 minutes, and six seconds!"

"You're so funny, Myles! I miss you, too. Listen, I gotta run. The office phone is ringing. See you at home. Love you!"

On my way home from work, I stopped by Subway to pick up dinner and then Walgreen's to pick up the photos I had printed from Myles' sister's house. I also had our wedding picture enlarged. I purchased frames off eBay two weeks prior and was excited about finally putting the pictures in them. Even after making those stops, I made it home before Myles. When he got in, he called out to see where I was in the house. "I'm in the hallway."

He came in and kissed me. "How was your day?"

"Busy. So busy!" I said tiredly.

"Oh, my. The pictures look nice, Lexie! Who is this?"

"She is the lady who helped me in Germany. Her name is Gina."

"Oh, okay." He looked at me as if he wanted me to say more.

"Remember: You don't want me to talk about Germany." He laughed and nodded, affirming I was correct. "Where's KJ?"

"Outside with the dog."

I went into the living room to put our enlarged wedding pictures on the table in front of the couch. I then put Myles' parents' and my parents' wedding pictures on the end tables at each end of the sofa. Myles stood back and watched me work. "The pictures look nice in those expensive frames. I really like that ivory and gold," he mentioned.

KJ came in and said, "Mama, I'm ready to eat. I'm sleepy, too."

"We have Subway sandwiches and soup in the kitchen for dinner," I replied. Myles chose that moment to come over and play around with me, trying to kiss me.

"There you two go again! Yuck! I'm ready to eat," KJ teased. Myles laughed and rubbed him on his head.

I sat at the piano. "Let me play this song my Mama taught me, and then we'll eat." I got up off the piano bench to look inside for the book. "I haven't looked in this bench since Mama died. She has so many song sheets and books in here." I finally found the one I was looking for: "I Come to the Garden." "KJ, your grandmother would always play the piano, and we would sing this song together." Myles sat beside me, and KJ stood on the other side of me. When I opened the music sheet, an envelope fell out with my name on it. I pulled the card out and saw it was a birthday card my mom bought for me before she died. I opened the card, and a bouquet of flowers popped up, along with 50 one-dollar bills that fell to the floor.

"Look at all that money!" KJ exclaimed.

I opened the card all the way, and a recording of my mother's voice singing the birthday song flowed through the room. "Oh, my God. That's Mama's voice singing to me for my 27th birthday. This must have been the surprise she said she had for me, but she died two weeks before she could give it to me. KJ, that's your

180

grandmother's voice singing happy birthday to me." I began to get emotional, so Myles hugged me close.

"Mama, you don't have to play the song now. I'm hungry and sleepy." The way he whined made Myles and me laugh.

"I know you're tired. Mrs. Riddle said you were playing your game all night when Myles and I went to Las Vegas for the weekend."

"I like staying at her house. I had a lot of fun with Dexter and Carl," KJ said. (Dexter and Carl are Mrs. Riddle's 20- and 22-year-old sons.)

"Okay, let's go eat so you can go to bed."

Myles helped me up and asked, "Are you okay?"

"I'm alright. I felt a bit emotional after hearing my mom's voice sing to me."

We ate our dinner in the breakfast room. When we finished, KJ went upstairs and then came back with his homework. After I checked it, I complimented him. "Excellent job! Every answer is correct!"

"I can now take my shower and go to bed," he said.

"Yes, you can. And don't forget to say your prayers!" I instructed.

Myles had disappeared into my office for his Bible study time. KJ hugged me good night and yelled, "Good night, Myles!" before going upstairs.

Chapter 62

I cleared the table and then went into the living room. I sat on the couch and listened to my card sing to me. Myles called to me and asked, "Are you alright?" He knew I hardly ever spent time in the living room.

"Yes, I'm okay." But I wasn't okay. I started to cry as I sat there listening to my card sing happy birthday in my Mama's voice. I went into my bedroom, laid the card on the dresser, and went to take my shower. When the water hit my stomach, I felt the baby moving inside me. I stood there with the water running down my body and cried, thinking about how much I missed my mom. I wished she were there with me so that I could tell her all about her grandson and the wonderful husband God had blessed me with…and let her know I was pregnant. Through my tears, I whispered, "Thank you, Mama, for my birthday song. I loved hearing your voice." Once out of the shower and ready for bed, I picked up the card and listened to it sing to me again. I turned the card over and saw "R and L Publishing Company." I thought, "That's Rose and Lexie Publishing Company. Did she copyright this?"

Myles came in and said he had checked on KJ, who was asleep with his coloring book in the bed with him and his crayons on the floor.

"Myles, I felt the baby move when I took my shower."

"For real? How did it feel?"

"Like something fluttering in my stomach."

"Wow!" He placed his hand on my growing belly to see if he could feel anything. He was disappointed when he didn't. "I'm going to take my shower now. Maybe I will feel a baby move in my belly while I'm in there." We laughed.

When he exited the shower, I told him I believed Mama had published her voice. "Look on the back of this card."

"Are you saying she recorded her voice and published it, too?"

"I believe so. She said she was going to do birthday and Mother's Day cards. If not, why would it be imprinted with "R and L Publishing Company"?"

"Where is the envelope the card was in?" Myles asked.

"On the piano or in the song sheet."

He retrieved the envelope, returned to my side, and said, "There's a contract from a publishing company in here." He handed it to me.

"There's an account number and a bank's name on the contract. It says 20% of sales are to be donated to the Heart Foundation, 50% is to be deposited into the above account for Lexie Rose Harris, and the remaining 30% is to be used to pay off the investors. Once they're paid in full, all monies will go into the account listed above."

"Oh, my God! Let me see, Lexie! She did this nine years ago. You need to go to this bank and check on it."

I started to cry and laid back on the bed. I felt the baby moving. "Myles, lay your hand on my belly. I feel the baby."

"Oh! Yes! I feel my baby, too!" He kissed me. He was so happy about finally feeling the baby move.

As for me, I cried because I missed my mom. Finding out about the card with her voice and the money mentioned in the contract was the icing on the cake.

Chapter 63

On Wednesday morning, I reminded Myles about our doctor's appointment at 2:00 p.m. I worked a half-day since the doctor's office was far from my job. Myles worked a half-day, too, so he left the dog home. I left work early to stop by the bank and check on the account mentioned in the card contract. I learned Mama had made a Mother's Day card, too. There was over $40,000.00 in that account! It made me feel good, knowing Mama's voice was all over the world.

By the time I made it to my appointment, Myles was already there. I told him how much was in the account and informed him that the investors were paid off already. "Wow! You were making money and didn't even know it!" he said, laughing. He then told me he had hired Ron full-time. "Ron and Mrs. Clark work well together. Both are dependable and honest," he stated. I was glad Ron accepted the offer to work full-time because Myles had been busy trying to keep up with the workload ever since his dad died.

When it was our turn to go back, we followed the nurse into room three. She instructed me to put on the gown that was on the bed. "The doctor will be here in a few minutes."

The doctor came in and introduced herself. "I'm Dr. Smith. Dr. Jessica was called away to the hospital. I'm taking care of her patients today." She looked at my chart. "Everything looks good. Your temperature and blood pressure are perfect. Can you sit on the bed, please?" Myles helped me stand so I could sit on the bed, never letting go of my hand. "Okay. Now, lie back, please." She placed gel on my stomach to do an ultrasound and smiled as she warned, "The gel is a little cold." She then rubbed the monitor over my belly and then paused. "Hmm... Do either of you have twins in your family?"

"Not in mine," I answered.

Myles said, "I think one of my cousins on my mother's side has twins."

"Well, you guys are having twins!" the doctor reported.

Myles used his free hand to rub his hair back. "Lexie, she said we are having twins!"

Dr. Smith smiled as she continued to move the monitor over my belly. "See? There's the boy." She moved the machine again to the other side. "And there's the girl."

"A boy and a girl? Oh, my God!" Myles said, smiling from ear to ear.

"From the size of the babies and what has been annotated in your chart, I would say you're at 25 weeks. Keep doing your monthly check-ups. Your doctor has a note in your file for you to continue taking your vitamins."

Leaving the doctor's office, Myles held my arm as we walked to Pearl. In a muffled voice, I heard him say something. "What did you say?" I asked.

"I just thought of my dad right then. Do you want to drive the truck home? It's easier to get into."

"No, I'm alright." Before driving off, I saw Myles on his phone. I knew he was calling his sisters to tell them what the doctor said. He was close to both of them and often said Sharon practically raised him and Mae when they stayed with his Uncle Eddie. He then called me and said he would pick up KJ from Mae's house. He told me to go home, get off my feet, and said he would pick up dinner so that I didn't have to cook.

In the middle of the day on Thursday, Myles called me at work to tell me he had picked up KJ from school and was at work with him. "Why did you pick him up? Is he sick?" I asked with concern.

"He's fine. He'll tell you about it when he gets home."

"Myles, what did he do?! Is he alright?"

"He's fine, Lexie. We'll see you at home. I'll bring home fried chicken for dinner, and you can make some sides to go with it," he said, hanging up the phone.

Myles and KJ were already home by the time I arrived. KJ was sitting at the island in the kitchen. "Hi, KJ. Where is Myles?"

"In the exercise room."

I set my purse and attaché case on the island, sat beside him, and said, "This has been a busy day. I am so tired. How was your day at school?" I didn't let him know Myles had called me earlier.

"Mama, don't be mad at me."

"Mad at you for what? What did you do?" He handed me a small envelope. "What's this?" I looked inside and saw the tennis bracelet my mom had given me. "Where did you get this, KJ?"

"Out of your jewelry box," he replied with his head hung low.

"Why is it in this envelope?" He looked at the floor and rubbed his hand nervously over the countertop. "KJ, why is my bracelet in this envelope?" I couldn't hide my rising anger.

"I gave it to my girlfriend."

"You did what?! You went into my jewelry box and gave some little girl my bracelet?! Do you know that is called stealing?! My Mama gave me this bracelet. Oh, my God!" I sat there speechless. "You know what? Go upstairs right now. Pack your clothes. You are going to your daddy's house. I can't believe you're up in here stealing!"

He started to cry. "I'm sorry, Mama. I'm sorry. I don't want to go to daddy's house!"

"You are going. Get out of here. Go pack your clothes," I said with finality. He cried all the way up the stairs. When I turned to go to my bedroom, Myles was standing behind me.

"Babe, don't be so hard on him," he said lovingly.

"No, Myles. He's stealing my stuff and giving it to some little girl. My mom gave me that bracelet. Do you know how expensive this thing is?! I lost it and found it, only to have my child steal it and give it away?" I couldn't believe I was even having this conversation.

Myles hugged me close. "Pray about your decision and calm down. He took it, and now, you have it back. The teacher said the little girl was showing it to a group of girls in the back of the classroom. She went to see what they were looking at and asked the girl where she got the bracelet from. The girl said Keith gave it to her. The teacher said that she could tell it was expensive when she looked at it. She tried to call you first, but you were in a meeting, so she called me. I have already talked to him and told him he can't take things that don't belong to him." He rubbed my back gently as he spoke. "They don't have school tomorrow. I told him he would come to work with me and clean up my workroom. Babe, he's sorry. Please don't send him away. I know he's your son, but I think he has learned his lesson."

186

As we were talking, KJ came downstairs, still crying. "Mama, I'm so sorry. Please don't make me go to daddy's house. I will never steal again."

Myles looked at me, nodded his head toward KJ, then said, "I'm going to take the motorcycle out for a ride. I'll be back in a bit."

Once alone with KJ, I looked at him with rage. "Go back upstairs. I don't want to see you right now. I'll call you when dinner is ready." I was so upset with him. After taking my purse, attaché case, and bracelet into my bedroom, I returned to the kitchen to start dinner.

I saw the chicken and biscuits Myles bought sitting on the stove. I put on the rice, peeled sweet potatoes to make yams, and cooked some fresh green peas. While waiting for the food to cook, I called Mrs. Riddle to tell her what KJ had done and that I was sending him to his daddy.

"Calm down, Lexie. Did you pray about that decision first? Do you really think that's the right thing to do?"

"I don't know, but he's here stealing! I won't deal with that."

"Lexie, let Myles deal with him. Thank God you got the bracelet back."

"But Mrs. Riddle, it was the bracelet my Mama gave me."

"But you got it back, Lexie. Let Myles deal with him, okay?"

"Thank you for talking to me, Mrs. Riddle. You are right. I'll let Myles deal with him." We said our goodbyes and hung up the phone.

When Myles returned from his ride, he stuck his head in the door and asked, "Is it okay for me to come in?"

"Yes, you can come in. It's safe," I said with a sigh. "I spoke to Mrs. Riddle, and she suggested I let you handle it, so it's now out of my hands."

"Are you still sending him to his daddy?"

"It's in your hands now. I'm still going to punish him. He can't watch TV or play his games for two weeks."

Myles came over and hugged me. "I'm going up to let him know he doesn't have to go to his dad's."

I could tell he was happy I changed my mind about sending him away. I yelled, "When you come back down, dinner should be ready."

Chapter 64

After dinner, I didn't see KJ until the next morning. He was up early, ready to go to work with Myles. I worked a half-day on the job and was back home before Myles and KJ returned.

Walking in, KJ said, "Mama, I'm never going to mess with your stuff again. I'm tired. Myles had me working all day. I had to sweep and mop the whole floor, take out the trash, and take down everything on the shelf to dust it off. I didn't even get to play with Spot. I was only allowed to stop working when I had to use the bathroom and eat lunch. Guess what, Mama? Myles told me I had ten minutes to use the bathroom and 30 to eat lunch!" I laughed at his expression as he spoke the latter. His facial expression changed once again when he said, "And now, I can't play with my games or watch TV for two weeks." He walked away with his shoulders slumped. After dinner, he took his shower and was in bed by 5:00 p.m. I didn't see him again until the following day when he came down to eat breakfast.

On Saturday morning, Myles was up early and cooked breakfast. After eating, he left to meet a man who was dropping off 55 tablets that were in a warehouse fire. The man wanted them checked for damages. He told Myles, "If they aren't damaged, I will send them to the children in Africa." Although he was at work, it was like he was home. He called every two hours to give me an update. "The tablets are all in good condition. They were packed in a Styrofoam tray and wrapped in plastic. None of them got wet or were damaged." He said he would ask the man to sell him two; one for KJ and one for Chyna. "So, my lady, what are you doing today?"

"I'm having a picnic," I replied.

He laughed. "Where are you going for this picnic of yours?"

"Me, KJ, and Spot's picnic will be in the theater room. We are going to watch a movie and eat hot dogs, chips, and cookies. Then, we're going to put the train set together that you bought KJ three weeks ago."

"Okay. I was looking at all those small pieces on that box and thought about taking it back! I'll call you later to see if you got it put together. Enjoy your picnic! Love you!"

Around 2:00 p.m., we gathered our food and went into the theater room for our picnic. We were still in our PJs while watching Lion King and eating our snacks. When the movie ended, we went into the sitting room, sat on the floor, and put the train set together. Spot got in on the fun by moving and hiding the small pieces from us. I noticed how easy it was for KJ to connect the pieces and thought, "He doesn't need my help. He is doing it all by himself!" I would read the instructions, and KJ would say, "Mama, I did that already!"

One small piece was missing, which KJ found under the table. When he went to retrieve it, he asked, "Mama, why is there pink paper stuck under here?"

"Paper? What paper?" I asked.

"There's a piece of paper taped under here."

I looked where KJ pointed and saw a pink envelope taped to the bottom of the table. I gently pulled it down and saw my name on it in my mom's handwriting. I opened the envelope, and a note with some other papers fell out. It was a life insurance policy for $50,000.00. The message read, "This is for my grandchildren. I know I will never live to see them because of my heart problems. Use it as you see fit. I love you, Lexie." I began to cry.

"Mama, why are you crying? What did the note say?" KJ cried with me and hugged me. "Tell me, Mama! What did the note say?"

"Your grandmother left you some money."

"That paper is my money?" he asked, obviously confused.

"Baby, go watch another movie. I'll explain it later. Right now, I need to be alone." He walked out, and shortly after, I heard voices in the theater room. I laid on the floor and cried my eyes out. I heard Myles ask KJ, "Is the picnic over already? Where's your Mama?"

"She's in the room, crying." He didn't specify which room.

Myles went to KJ's room first and then called out for me. He found me in the sitting room. "What's wrong, Lexie? Are the babies okay?" I couldn't say anything. I just handed him the note. He sat on the floor beside me as he read it and held me while I cried. "Lexie, your mom loved you and the grandchildren she knew she wouldn't live to see, so she wanted to leave them something just from her." KJ came in and sat on the floor with us. Spot jumped on his lap.

"I thought you were going to call me," I said.

"I thought your picnic was still going on or that you were putting the train set together. I didn't want to disturb you." He then laughed as he said, "I ate a hot dog and some chips before coming up here. I know what we can do now. Let's go for a ride!"

"Myles, we aren't even dressed to step outside!"

"Well, get dressed! We are going out for ice cream!"

"Ice cream? Yay! Can Spot come with us?" KJ asked.

"Yes, he can, but you can't give him any ice cream," Myles replied. KJ ran into his room to get dressed, full of excitement. Myles helped me off the floor, and we went downstairs to our bedroom.

I laid the note and policy on the dresser and began to cry again. "Myles, she left me her state retirement insurance from her job, the policy she had for her and daddy, the money she received from the sale of her house, and her car, which I sold. Here it is ten years later, and I find an envelope with a $50,000.00 insurance policy in it for grandchildren she knew she wouldn't live to see. And I can't forget about that birthday card."

"Lexie, she knew you would have children one day. And the situation with the birthday card? She just didn't live long enough to give it to you and tell you about the publishing aspect." I laid across my bed and cried as Myles rubbed my back.

A few minutes later, KJ ran downstairs and shouted, "I'm ready!"

I got up and went into the bathroom to put on jeans and a t-shirt. I heard Myles say, "Peanut, we'll be there in a minute. Go into the family room and watch TV." I was so emotional, I couldn't stop the tears from falling. Once I pulled myself together, we left to get ice cream. Along the way, I thought about the conversation I had with my mom about that table and shared it with Myles.

"Myles, I had to promise Mama I would never sell or give that table away."

"Why would she make you promise that?" he asked.

"She told me when Leon was about 15 months old, my dad took her on a stroll in downtown Nashville. They walked and window shopped as they passed stores while pushing Leon in his stroller. When they passed the furniture store—the one only wealthy people shopped in—Mama saw that table sitting in the window and told my dad she really liked it. 'The price of that table is two of my paychecks. I can't afford that!' he said to her. Mama told me she thought of that table every day and could see it sitting in her house, so she started saving her own money to get it.

"On her birthday, a box was delivered to the house. Daddy called her from work and asked if a box had been delivered. She told him yes, and he asked if she had opened it. She said, 'No, my name wasn't on it.' He told her to go ahead and open it. 'It's your birthday gift.' When she opened the box, inside was that table. She said she cried and reminded him that he said it cost too much. He replied, 'I saw how much you liked it. I put it on layaway and made payments on it.' Mama went on to tell me, 'That was the night you were conceived.'"

"Wow! She told you that?" Myles said, laughing.

"Yes." I laughed along with him. "That's why she told me not to sell or give it away. It held irreplaceable sentimental value—and apparently, it also held an insurance policy taped to it."

Myles laughed again and said, "I remember the night you conceived the twins."

"No, you don't!"

"I do! It was the night of my surprise party. Just count back."

KJ chimed in. "What does conceive mean?"

We needed to change the conversation, so Myles asked, "KJ, what kind of ice cream do you want?"

"Superman ice cream!"

"I want a banana split," Myles said.

"Mama, what kind do you want?"

"I want a scoop of butter pecan, a scoop of strawberry, and a scoop of cookies and cream." They laughed at me.

Myles and KJ went inside to get the sweet treats. When they got back, we sat in the SUV, ate our ice cream, and talked. KJ thought he was slick, slipping Spot some of his Superman ice cream. "You are going to clean up behind him," Myles said to KJ.

After finishing our ice cream, we drove around town, ending up on the southside. As KJ looked out the window, he pointed and said, "That's Mama Brenda's old house, and that's the school where we used to play."

"Mrs. Brenda doesn't live there anymore?" I asked.

"She lives in a big house by daddy's church now."

"Oh, okay. She's living in your dad's old house now," I stated.

"Yes, and I have my own room with two beds! Brandon has his own room, too. And Mama Brenda and daddy have their room. There is another room Mama Brenda said she might use for our playroom when it's raining outside, but we mostly play in the backyard."

"I thought someone else lived in your daddy's house."

"They moved out. Daddy had to paint every room and put down new carpet in all the bedrooms. He said he would never let anybody else move into his house again because those were some messy people." Myles and I laughed at what KJ said.

When we got home, Myles and KJ played kickball in the backyard with the dog running around after them. I started dinner and thought about Mama and that insurance policy. All the while, my phone kept ringing off the hook. Every time I answered, the caller would say, "Congratulations on the twins!" Myles told his sisters, and the news spread like wildfire. I wondered how KJ would take it when he found out he would have siblings soon, especially since he had been the only child for so long. When the boys came inside, they got cleaned up, and we sat down for dinner.

"You didn't have to cook," Myles said.

"I am not sick, Honey. I'm just…" I stopped talking because KJ was there. Myles started laughing.

KJ went upstairs when he finished eating, and Myles said, "I already told him about the babies, but he is not going to say anything to you because I told him it was our little secret."

"How did he take it?"

"He sounded excited, Babe! Like I said, you didn't have to cook tonight. We could have eaten hot dogs and chips again. I enjoyed the one I ate!"

"Well, I was hungry. After all, I am eating for three now."

He came over and hugged me. "Yes, you're right. You and my babies gotta eat!"

Chapter 65

Going into my seventh month, I was getting bigger by the day.

One Sunday after church, Myles got a call from Sharon, saying they were planning a baby shower for us the weekend after the 4th of July holiday and wondered if we could make it. Myles told her we would have to talk to the doctor first to see if I could travel.

Two weeks later, it was time for my next check-up. Myles asked the doctor if I could travel to Myrtle Beach, and she said, "I don't see why not. You just need to make sure you stop so she can stretch her legs. Lexie and the babies are doing great." When we arrived home, Myles called Sharon right away and told her we would be there.

The Monday afternoon that followed, Myles called me from his cell phone to tell me that when he picked up KJ from Mae's house, he was crying and said he never wanted to go back to his dad's house. "He'll tell you about it when he gets home. Do you need anything from the store?"

"Yes, please. Butter pecan ice cream."

He laughed and replied, "That sounds good to me! I'll get myself some, too. See you in a few."

KJ was still crying when he walked into the house. "What happened? Why are you crying?" I asked.

"I don't want to go to daddy's house anymore."

"Why?"

"Mama Brenda yelled at me for no reason. I didn't even do anything!" He started crying harder.

"We need to see what went on over there," Myles said with concern.

"Let's eat our ice cream before it melts. Then, I'll give Mrs. Brenda a call," I replied.

We finished, I cleaned up, and KJ went upstairs to do his homework. Myles headed into the garage to detail his truck. When he came back in, he checked KJ's homework. "I'm ready to call Mrs. Brenda to see what happened at your dad's house," I told KJ as I headed into my office.

I called Pastor Montgomery's house from my office line. Myles was in the bedroom with me on one phone, and KJ was in the kitchen on the other phone. Mrs. Brenda answered. I told her who I was and added, "I hope I'm not calling you at the wrong time."

"No, it's okay," she replied.

"I'm calling because KJ came home crying this afternoon, saying he doesn't want to come back to your house anymore. He said you yelled at him for no reason."

She started to laugh and said, "I didn't only yell at him, I yelled at Brandon, too. Did he tell you why I yelled at them?"

"No, he didn't, but he's listening on the other phone. KJ, what did you do?" I asked.

"Nothing!" he yelled.

Mrs. Brenda said, "KJ, be truthful. Tell your mom what you did."

He started to cry. "I didn't do anything."

"KJ, what did you do?" I asked, demanding an honest answer in my tone. He didn't say anything. He just kept crying. "KJ, tell…me…what…you…did!"

He cried as he said, "I was walking in the living room, and Brandon jumped on my back. I fell on the table, and the lamp fell off and broke."

Myles hung up his phone and shook his head, taking a seat beside me. "KJ, don't you owe Mrs. Brenda an apology for breaking her lamp?" I asked.

"No, because it wasn't my fault!"

Myles walked into the kitchen. "KJ, tell Mrs. Brenda you are sorry for breaking her lamp," he insisted. KJ remained silent. "KJ, I said to tell her you're sorry."

In a muffled voice, he said, "I'm sorry." He then hung up the phone and ran upstairs to his room. I waved to Myles to go and check on him.

196

I told Brenda I would pay her for the lamp, to which she replied, "You don't have to do that. I'm always telling those boys about running and playing in the house."

"I'll still put something in the mail for your lamp. It was nice talking to you."

"Same here," she replied.

"Oh! Before I go… KJ will not be there next week because we're going out of town."

"Okay! Are you going to Disney World?" she asked.

"No, we're going to Myrtle Beach. My sister-in-law is hosting a baby shower for me."

Brenda laughed and said, "KJ told me a couple of months ago that Myles was taking him to Disney World. That's why I said that. Then last weekend, he told me, 'My Mama's tummy is bigger than yours.'"

"He said that?"

"Yes, he did. I'm pregnant, too. I'm having a girl in about six weeks."

"I am due in about two months. I'm having twins."

"Congratulations!" she replied.

"Congratulations to you on your little girl! Okay, I gotta run. Be on the lookout for something in the mail for that broken lamp."

"You don't have to do that," she said again.

"I insist, Brenda. It will be taken out of KJ's allowance, so he will be paying for it himself," I said with a laugh as we hung up.

I sat there thinking about Brenda. She seemed to be a nice woman who cared about my son. I enjoyed talking to her. I thought, "She's not the woman who took my husband away; she's the woman who rescued me from a man who didn't love me and thought he would take my house." I paused and wondered what he told her for her to be out here with him looking at my house. I suppose he told her it was his. I smiled as I thought about the man God blessed me with to marry, who loved my son and me. Outside of God, Myles and KJ were the best things to ever happen to me.

Walking into the bedroom, Myles said, "KJ cried himself to sleep, saying it wasn't his fault. He's upset because you made him apologize, but he wasn't sorry." Myles was laughing when he said, "I wasn't any help, Lexie. I told him it wasn't his fault either and that Brandon shouldn't have jumped on his back."

"Myles Lee Ferguson!"

"Well, I don't think it was his fault. It was an accident," he replied. "Come on. Let's go to bed. Don't worry your pretty little head about it."

Chapter 66

After I made KJ apologize to Mrs. Brenda, I noticed he had little to say to me for the rest of that week. He depended solely on Myles to check his homework and wanted only Myles to play games with him. That Friday night, we all watched a movie together in the theater room and ate popcorn. KJ and the dog were playing around until Myles told KJ they were being too loud and needed to go into his room to play. When the movie ended, I peeked into KJ's room. He was sound asleep, and so was Spot.

Myles climbed into bed with me and said, "I'm going to surprise KJ tomorrow and take him fishing. Lexie, it really wasn't his fault that the lamp got broken." He laughed, kissed me, and played in my hair. "Lexie Rose Harris Ferguson…"

I cut him off. "Why are you calling me all of my names?"

He laughed harder. "Wait a minute! I'm going somewhere with this." He pulled me close. "Lexie Rose Harris Ferguson, if we weren't already married and you were single, I would ask you to marry me."

I looked into his hazel eyes and replied, "And I would yell yes! Yes! Yes! I want to marry you!"

He ran his fingers through my hair. "And I would still be the happiest man alive to have you lying beside me." He then kissed me and whispered in my ear, "Oh, my God. You smell good."

On Saturday morning, Myles was up early and made breakfast so that he and KJ could get an early start on fishing. I called for KJ to come down for breakfast, but he didn't respond. "What is that boy doing up there?" I asked.

"Maybe he's still asleep. I'll go up and see what he's doing," Myles said as he made his way upstairs doing a silly dance. He was up there for a while before he came back down with a sad look.

"Well, is he still asleep?" I asked.

"Lexie, he's not up there."

"He's not?! Where is he?!"

"I don't know. I looked in all the rooms up there but couldn't find him."

"Where could he be?!" I was freaking out, running from room to room, holding my belly. We both called out for him, shouting his name. "Why is he not answering me?!" Myles rubbed his hair back, looking nervous. We looked everywhere for him, even going back upstairs to look in every closet, under the beds, and in the theater room. We then went downstairs and looked in every corner of the garage, underneath the vehicles, and all over the backyard.

"He might be in the shed house," Myles suggested.

"He can't be in there. That door is always locked."

"Maybe he got the keys and unlocked it." I looked in the drawer where the keys were kept. They were still there.

My thoughts then went to Pastor Montgomery. I thought, "Did I leave my door open, and Keith came into my house and took my baby? What if someone else came in and took him?"

Myles tried his best to relax me. "Lexie, calm down. Call the police. I'll go to the Johnson's house to see if they have seen him. Wherever he is, Spot is with him."

I called the 911 operator. "May I help you?"

"Yes, my son is missing!" I screamed into the phone.

"Calm down, ma'am. What is your son's name?"

"Keith Allen Montgomery, Jr. He's eight years old. My address is 2622 Riverside, off Highway 23. My name is Lexie Harris Ferguson."

"Lexie Harris, you said?"

"Yes."

"This is Irma. I will get someone out there right away."

"Thank you." I hung up the phone, trying to recall who Irma was. I remembered her being in my class when I was in high school, and she dated my brother Leon before he was killed. I went into my bedroom to get dressed. All the while, I prayed my baby was alright. I then stepped outside to wait on the officer to arrive. I looked out toward the lake and prayed aloud, "Lord, please don't let my son be in that lake. Lord, please let him be alright."

As Myles walked back home from the Johnson's house, he shook his head and rubbed his hair back. He walked up to me and said, "They haven't seen him. Did you call 911?"

"Yes, an officer is on the way."

He held me, saying, "He's alright, Lexie. I have faith that he's alright. Lord, we pray in Your name, let our son be safe and help us find him."

Through the trees, we saw the police officer's car turn off the highway. When the car drove up, there were two officers inside. Myles and I met them at the end of the driveway. I was so nervous, I had to hold up my belly as I walked. I could hardly talk, so Myles was the one to explain that when we got up this morning, our son and the family dog were gone.

One officer asked, "What was he wearing?"

Myles answered. "When he went to bed last night, he had on his Mickey Mouse PJs, but they are lying on his bed. I don't know what he's wearing now."

The other officer looked at me and said, "Ma'am, we need to have a look in your son's bedroom."

We went inside the house. The officers asked us questions as if we were guilty of doing something to KJ. I finally replied, "Mister, you need to be out there looking for our son. We can't find him!" I busted out into tears.

"Calm down, Babe," Myles said.

"I can't calm down! I don't know where my baby is!"

"Babe, they are just doing their job." Myles' voice cracked, sounding as if he were about to cry, too. "Maybe he's at the other house over there," he said, pointing toward the house on our left. "They have a little boy. Maybe he's over there."

One of the policemen asked for a picture of KJ and the color of the dog. I gave them a photo I had taken of the two of them together a couple of weeks ago. They then left, going from house to house, looking for the pair. Myles went with them.

Myles told me to stay home, just in case KJ came back and I could call him to let him know. I stood outside, walking up and down the driveway, praying KJ was alright. I thought that maybe his dad picked him up early that morning, and KJ took the dog with him. Maybe he thought he didn't have time to tell me. I didn't know what to think. All kinds of crazy thoughts flowed through my mind.

I called Pastor Montgomery's house, and KJ's' little brother answered the phone. "Hello?"

I didn't want to ask if KJ was there, so I just said, "Hi, I'm KJ's mom."

"My mom's not here," he replied.

"What's your name?" I asked.

"Brandon. You want to talk to my dad?"

"No, thank you. Bye." I hung up the phone but heard Keith ask, 'Who is it?' before ending the call. If Brandon knew KJ was there, he would have asked if I wanted to speak to my son. My hands shook so badly, I could barely get the phone onto its cradle. I then called Mrs. Riddle, crying. "KJ is missing! We can't find him!"

"Lexie, Baby, calm down and take a deep breath. Now, tell me: What's going on?"

"We got up this morning, and KJ is missing."

Mrs. Riddle immediately began praying: "Lord, please let KJ be alright. Keep him safe. Lord, do not let any harm or danger come to him." Before I could say anything else, she said, "I'm on my way out there. Let me get dressed."

"Thank you, Mrs. Riddle." As I walked back outside, my cell phone rang. It was Myles.

"We found him, Lexie. He was at Mae's house."

I started crying. "Thank You, Jesus! Thank You, Jesus!"

"Babe, he's okay. The dog is, too. I sent the police away, so you'll have to drive down to pick us up. Mae said she tried to call us, but we didn't answer. She was just getting dressed to bring him home when we knocked on her door."

"Okay, Myles. I'm on my way." Before leaving, I had to sit down for a moment. My legs were shaking so badly, I could hardly walk, let alone drive. I couldn't believe that boy walked all the way to Mae's house! Why didn't we think to call her first? I called Mrs. Riddle to let her know KJ was at Myles' sister's house.

"Thank You, Jesus! I was just getting ready to walk out the door. Do you still need me to come?"

"No, ma'am. Thank you. I'm alright now." I heard her repeatedly say, 'Thank You, Jesus,' as we hung up the phone. After calming myself down, I stopped by the

Johnson's house to let them know we found KJ, explaining that he was at Myles' sister's house. I then went to Mae's to pick up Myles and KJ. I was so happy to see my son. Without a word, I went inside and sat next to him in a chair by the door. Spot jumped all over me. I was overjoyed to see my baby was truly alright.

Myles was sitting beside KJ on the sofa, hugging him. "Peanut, you had us upset when we couldn't find you." He never raised his voice, even while KJ sat there like he had done nothing wrong. "Why did you leave the house and not let us know?"

"I was mad at Mama," he admitted.

Myles looked at me before asking, "Why were you made at your mom?"

"Because she made me say sorry to Mama Brenda, and I didn't want to. I didn't do anything wrong. It wasn't my fault that the lamp got broken," he insisted.

Myles gently rubbed KJ on the head and agreed. "It wasn't your fault; it was an accident. But you were the one who fell on the lamp, which was why Mrs. Brenda said you broke it."

"I was just walking, minding my own business when Brandon pushed me. That's why the lamp got broken. If he hadn't pushed me, the lamp would have been just fine." Myles had to turn his face toward the wall to keep KJ from seeing him giggle.

I got up and went to sit next to KJ on the couch. "Honey, don't be angry at me. I thought apologizing to Mrs. Brenda was the right thing to do. Sometimes, you must apologize for things that aren't your fault." I hugged him and said, "I love you. I'm sorry I upset you."

"Now, tell your Mama you are sorry for running away and getting her upset," Myles coaxed.

"Mama, I am sorry for running away and getting you upset." I hugged him and planted a kiss on his cheek. "Still, the broken lamp wasn't my fault."

Myles couldn't hold his laughter any longer. "Come on, Peanut and Spot. Let's go home."

"Hold on. I gotta grab my bookbag," KJ stated.

"You were going to run away with a bookbag and the dog?" I asked.

"That way, if I got tired, I could sit down, lean against Spot, and read my book!"

"Boy, come on. Here I was, worried about you, and you had a bag of books to read!" Myles kept laughing. "Thank you, Sis."

"At least he knew where to come," Mae replied.

"Indeed. We'll talk later," Myles said.

Chapter 67

During our short ride back home, KJ broke the uncomfortable silence. "I wrote you a note and told you I was running away."

"Where did you leave the note?" I asked.

"Under my pillow."

Myles laughed so hard that he had to pull the vehicle over and stop.

I looked back at KJ in utter surprise. "Boy, who is going to look under a pillow for a note when you call yourself running away?!"

He shrugged his shoulders and replied, "I don't know."

"I know one thing: You better not ever put us through this again," I said sternly.

As we pulled into the garage, Myles said, "KJ, we still must talk about what you did today."

"Okay." Once inside the house, KJ sat at the table in the breakfast room and said, "Mama, I'm hungry."

"Go take your bookbag of books upstairs and wash your hands." I grabbed the Frosted Flakes and milk.

"I don't want cereal today, Mama. I want a big breakfast because I walked a long way this morning."

I turned on him in a flash with fire in my eyes. "Boy, like I said, take your stuff upstairs and get cleaned up!" I poured his cereal and milk and then went into the bedroom, where Myles was laughing. "What are you laughing about now?"

"I was thinking back to when I was KJ's age. I ran away, too."

"What did your daddy say?"

"Nothing. I ran away to the third house from Uncle Eddie's. There was an older couple who lived there named Mr. and Mrs. Riley. As I walked by their house, Mr. Riley asked where I was going. 'I'm running away from home,' I replied. 'You are?' he asked. 'Yes, sir.' I then asked him for some water. He said that Mrs. Riley was in the house and that I needed to ask her for a cup of water. I went inside and asked her for some water. She was sitting at the table eating ice cream at the time. She gave me a cup of water and asked if I wanted some ice cream. 'Yes, ma'am!' She set the sweet treat and four cookies on the table and told me to wash my hands first. When I came back to the table, she asked, 'Where are you going?' I remember saying, 'I don't know.' She didn't ask me anything else. She just finished her ice cream, then got up and washed her dish. I finished my ice cream and then sat on the floor to play with her cat and my Rubik's Cube. I thought it was strange that I had been gone a long time, but no one came looking for me. I thanked Mrs. Riley and told her I was going home. 'Okay, thanks for stopping by,' she replied.

"When I got back home, Uncle Eddie was working on his car in the garage. 'Uncle Eddie, I'm back!' He simply responded, 'Okay.' I then went into the house. Sharon was in the family room lying on the couch, reading a book. 'Sharon, I'm back,' I announced again. 'Umm-hmm,' she replied. She never even looked up at me. My last chance to see if I was missed came when I walked out to the patio where my Aunt Ruby was. She was teaching Mae how to make a flower arrangement. 'Aunt Ruby, I'm back!' Well, I was disappointed yet again. 'Alright,' she said. I went to my room, sat on my bed, and cried. I couldn't understand how nobody missed me when I ran away from home. When I heard my dad laughing while talking to Uncle Eddie, I ran to him and said, 'Daddy, I ran away!' He said, 'Okay.' Lexie, I thought no one cared if I ran away or not. I was sad, but I never ran away again!"

I was laughing so hard, I thought I would go into early labor. My midsection was so sore. Myles had a good laugh, too. KJ was standing in the doorway, looking at us act a fool. "Myles, lay your hands on my belly. I feel the babies moving. KJ, come over here and feel the babies."

KJ laid his hand on my belly and smiled. "Mama, that feels funny. I'm sorry for running away."

"Okay, son."

Myles rubbed him on his head. KJ asked, "Why do you always rub my head?"

"Because I love you." That was followed by another head rub.

KJ hugged him tightly. "Pawpaw always rubbed my head at church."

"Yes, he sure did. That's because he loved you, too!" Myles replied. When KJ left the room, Myles thought aloud, "I wonder what made him think of my dad."

"Well, you always rub KJ on his head like your daddy did before meeting you. Maybe he is missing your dad. KJ really liked him."

Myles smiled. "One day, I'm going to tell him some stories about my dad, including how often he rubbed my head, letting me know he loved me. Lexie, remind me to thank our neighbors Mr. James and Mr. Hill for helping us look for KJ today."

Later that evening, after dinner, the three of us put on our PJs and went into the theater room to watch a movie and eat popcorn. Before the movie ended, KJ was already asleep. Myles carried him to his room, put him to bed, and then retired to our bedroom.

I had a little light cleaning I wanted to do before going to bed. I didn't want Mrs. Riddle to have a heavy workload when she came for the weekend while we were out of town. I cleaned the theater room and the sitting room. KJ had stuff everywhere. Toys, books, candy wrappers, empty chips bags…you name it, it was on the floor in the sitting room. Downstairs, I cleaned my office.

Satisfied that Mrs. Riddle wouldn't have much more to do, I went into the bedroom with Myles. He was already asleep. I laid beside him, watching him while he slept and playing in his hair. I was grateful for the good man the Lord had blessed me with. He was compassionate, caring, and wise. I laid back and reflected on the day's events. I liked the way he handled KJ. He treated him as if he were his own son. I heard the sadness and fear in his voice when we didn't know where KJ was, yet he remained strong for me. I got up, grabbed my camera, and took a photo of Myles as he slept. I thought, "He is such a handsome man, lying there sleeping peacefully." I had to laugh to myself as I thought about his own running away from home story. Whether true or not, he made me laugh.

I went upstairs to check on KJ and took a picture of him sleeping, too. I stood in the hallway and looked at my son with love—the same one who had worried me almost out of my mind today, yet there he lay, sleeping peacefully. I whispered, "Lord, I thank you for protecting him. When he wasn't in my care, he was in Yours." I thought about the note he said he wrote to me. I walked back into his bedroom and eased my hand under his pillow, feeling for the note. He shifted his head slightly, and then I felt the paper. I pulled it out slowly and went back into the hallway to read it. Just like he said, it was a simple message saying he was running away. I folded it and slid it back under his pillow.

Chapter 68

On Wednesday morning, I got up feeling good. I only had two more days to go before we left for Myrtle Beach. Myles and Spot dropped KJ off at the bus stop, and then the duo went to work. As I got dressed for work, I thought about what had taken place that weekend and thanked God again for allowing us to find KJ safe and sound. He had walked far to get to Mae's house, including passing by the lake. So much could have happened to him along the way, but I pushed those bad thoughts to the back of my mind and just thanked God for His protection.

Getting to work, I passed by Mrs. Jones' door and spoke morning greetings. "You are looking pretty today. New outfit?" she asked.

"No, I have worn this before, Mrs. Jones." I continued to my office, laughing. I thought to myself, "If I didn't have this meeting today, I could have worked from home." Myles called, as usual, to see how I was feeling and ask how my day was going. I was pleased to report that all was well.

I was in the middle of transferring files on my computer when the building's power went out. I sat in my dark office, waiting for it to come back on. After about 15 minutes, Mrs. Jones came to my office and said, "We can call it a day. There's a power outage on this side of the street, and they said it won't be back on until 4:00 this afternoon at the earliest."

"What happened?" I asked.

"I don't know, but I'm going home to bake my husband a sour cream pound cake that he's been asking for." She smiled as she left my office.

"Bring me a slice tomorrow!" I yelled to her.

"Okay!" she yelled back.

At the time, it was approaching 10:30 a.m. My meeting was scheduled for 11:15. I called the woman from my cell phone, letting her know the building had no power and that I needed to reschedule for the next day at the same time.

As I drove home, I decided to stop by Myles' shop. He typically closed at 1:00 p.m. to complete his paperwork, so he would be surprised to see me. Pulling up to the shop, I looked out the rearview mirror and saw Pastor Montgomery's car stop behind me at the hardware store near the bank. The first thing I thought was that he was following me again. I stared in the mirror until he got out of his car with the same man I had seen him with before. They entered the bank together. Pastor Montgomery carried a money bag in his hand. "Why is he doing his banking at this bank when the same bank is a block from his church?" I wondered aloud. I parked and got out of Pearl. Mr. Ron was coming out of the shop at the same time I was going in, so he held the door open for me.

"It's nice to see you, Mrs. Ferguson. You're looking nice."

"Thank you, Mr. Ron. Have a good day!" Once inside, I noticed Mrs. Clark wasn't at the front desk. I went into the back room where Myles was and saw him with a lady I had never seen before. They were talking and had their backs to me. Both were smiling as they chatted. I stood there looking at them engage in an animated conversation. "Why is she back here alone with my husband? And where is Mrs. Clark?" I wondered.

At that moment, I thought about the time a waitress left her name and number on a napkin when she gave Myles the receipt. I took the napkin, wiped my hands on it, and left it on the table. Another time, we were at Red Lobster. A woman sitting at a table across from us tried to get Myles' attention, and when she got up to leave, she brushed against him and said, "Excuse me. You have pretty eyes." She walked away, swaying her hips.

I found myself having flashbacks of those times as I stood in the shop's back room observing how that woman looked at my man—and he was grinning from ear to ear! What were they saying to each other? There I stood, pregnant and ready to drop, and there she stood by my man!

I yelled, "What's going on here? Why is she back here?!" Both of them jumped.

Myles turned around and said, "Babe, I'm working. Are you alright?"

"Answer me! Why is she back here?!" I yelled louder. The lady stood there in total shock.

Mrs. Clark came out of the bathroom and asked if I was alright. "Come and sit down," she coaxed. She caught me by my arm and led me into the breakroom.

I started to cry. "Why is she back there?!" I yelled even louder than before.

"Calm down, Lexie. I told her to go back there so that Myles could show her what's in the back of her computer." I was crying so hard that Mrs. Clark had to rub my back and remind me to breathe. Myles called for Mrs. Clark to ring up the lady customer a few minutes later.

He came into the breakroom and hugged me. "What's wrong with you? Why are you here? Are the babies okay?"

I was so embarrassed. "I'm sorry. Mr. Ron was leaving when I came in, and I didn't see Mrs. Clark at the desk. When I saw that lady standing beside you, I lost it. I'm so sorry."

He wiped my tears away. "When I looked up and saw the look on your face, I thought you were going to use some Karate chops on that lady and me!" he said, laughing.

Mrs. Clark yelled into the room. "Mrs. Ferguson, are you alright in there?"

"Yes, ma'am. I'm good. Sorry for the way I reacted." I heard her laughing at me.

"Myles, I'll see you tomorrow. It was good seeing you, Mrs. Ferguson."

"Okay, see you tomorrow, Mrs. Clark," Myles replied.

"Bye, Mrs. Clark! It was nice to see you, too," I called out. Her laughter continued as she walked out the door.

"For real, Lexie. Why are you here?" In his hand, he held the money for the day's deposit.

"The lights are out at work and won't be back on until 4:00 at the earliest, so they closed the building. I decided to pop in to see you."

He sat down to fill out the deposit slip. "That lady came in with her computer and waited until I could look at it. She thought she might have had a virus. I turned the laptop around and saw some sticky, syrupy stuff running out of it. I told Mrs. Clark to tell the lady to come and see what the problem was. When she saw it, she explained that a couple of days ago, her son was eating a popsicle at the same time he was using her laptop. When he went outside to play, he put the popsicle on her laptop, which leaked into her system. I told her I had a son, but he knew not to touch his mother's computer. If he did, my wife would get him good! She laughed and told me she took care of him. He's on punishment for a whole month and can't play any of his games or watch TV. Then, you came in and ran the lady off!" He started laughing again.

"Myles, I'm sorry. Stop laughing at me!"

Just then, the phone rang. He went to answer it. "FCC... Sorry, we're closed for the day... No, she's not here... I'll look to see if I can find it... Yes, it's here on the floor in front of the desk... Okay, I'll wait for you to pick it up... Five minutes? That'll be fine. I'll be here."

He came back into the room and said, "That was the lady you ran off. She said she went to pay for her groceries but didn't have her debit card. She called to see if it was here. She's coming to get it. Behave!" He laughed again—hard. When the lady arrived, he handed her the card, and she was gone.

Myles helped me into Pearl and put the dog in there with me. I headed home, and he went to the bank down the street to make the deposit. He called me from his cell phone, saying, "I'm calling in for carry-out from Cracker Barrel. I want a catfish dinner. What do you want?"

"Get me the chicken dinner. I can share mine with KJ."

"Are you sure?"

"Yes, one chicken dinner will be enough for both of us. And can you see if they have banana pudding for KJ, please?"

"I think I want some of that, too!" he said, laughing. "Okay. You go on home. I'll pick up KJ on my way in. Remember he had a half-day today."

"Oh! I forgot!"

"I know why you forgot. You're too busy running people off!"

I laughed at what he said. "Myles, don't play with me. I will put you on punishment until after the babies are born!"

"You can't do that!"

"Watch me! I love you. See you when you get home."

Chapter 69

I felt sorry for how I reacted when I saw that woman standing by Myles. "Am I a jealous woman, or did I act that way because I'm pregnant?" I pondered.

When Myles walked in with lunch, he told KJ to wash his hands so that we could eat. We sat in the breakfast room to eat. There was so much food on our plates, we had leftovers. After eating, KJ went outside to play with his ball and Spot.

Myles reached across the table to hold my hand. "Lexie, have I ever given you a reason not to trust me?"

"No, you haven't. I don't know why I reacted the way I did. Again, I'm so sorry."

He scooted his chair closer to mine. "Before leaving for Iraq, I was in a relationship with another woman. I asked her to wait for me until I got back, but she said three years was too long to wait for anybody. She said she had to get on with her life. That hurt me. I cared for her. We had been together for over two years. Then, I saw you riding your bike before I left. Something about you stayed in my mind, even when I was in a warzone. I thought of you, not her. When I got home from the war, I was in the shop with my dad. Mrs. Clark came in the back and said someone was there to see me. When I walked out, it was the same woman who said she couldn't wait for me. She said, 'I heard you were back home. I was at the bank and thought I'd stop in to see how you are doing.' She then asked if I was in a relationship. I told her, 'Yes, I am. Why do you want to know? Remember: You said you couldn't wait for me.' She said she made a mistake and wanted me back. She even offered that I could stop by her house if I ever got lonely. I didn't say anything more because my feelings for her were gone. I thanked her for stopping by, and she left.

"Three weeks later, I was in the bank down the street from the shop making a deposit for my dad. There was a lady who worked there and would make it a point to talk to me every time. One day, she asked if I worked down the street because I always came to that bank, and I told her I helped my dad in the computer shop. So, when daddy got sick one day and wanted to go home, I told Mrs. Clark I would trail him home to make sure he arrived safely and that I'd be back to lock up the shop. When I got back, Mrs. Clark told me the white lady who works in the bank was looking for me. Later that day, when I walked out to my car to go home, she was outside waiting for me! She said, 'I thought you weren't coming back. I need some company tonight. Do you want to come over?' I kindly told her my girlfriend wouldn't approve."

"So, wait. You had a girlfriend?" I asked.

"Yes, I did. You."

"But I wasn't your girlfriend then."

"Yes, you were. In my heart, I knew I was going to marry you. I went out and got your ring, waiting for you to fall in love with me so that I could ask you to marry me. You see, I had to keep the vows I made to the Lord to not mess around with any other women when I got home. Yes, temptations were great, but I had to keep the vows I had made to the Lord for bringing me home alive when men all around me were dying.

"The week before we were to be married, this lady asked me to go on a cruise with her to the Bahamas. She told me I didn't have to pay anything; she just wanted a nice-looking man to be in her pictures when she showed them to her friends. She added that she would 'show me a good time.' I told her to look elsewhere because I was getting married that weekend. Lexie, I must be honest and tell you that it was hard for me to turn down an all-expense-paid trip, but I wanted you." He kissed me on my nose.

"What if I would have said no to your proposal? Would you have dated one of those ladies?"

"No matter what, I wanted you, not them. I knew you would say yes because God designed you just for me and honored my commitment. The point here is that you do not have to get upset whenever you see me talking to another woman. I loved you and sacrificed for you. I don't want you to ever doubt that." He pulled me into a warm embrace and kissed me. "Let's go for a walk. I'm glad we're going away to Myrtle Beach this weekend. I think it will be good for us to get away. Wait. Are you really putting me on punishment?"

"No, I'm not."

"I should punish you for running that lady off!" he said, laughing at me again.

"Watch yourself, Mr. Ferguson. I could change my mind!" We shared a good laugh.

Chapter 70

Early Friday morning, we dropped Spot off at the doggie daycare on our way to Myrtle Beach. I enjoyed riding and listening to Myles and KJ sing and engage in conversation. Every few miles, Myles would ask if I needed to stop and stretch my legs like the doctor ordered. A couple of hours into the trip, I took him up on the offer. He called Derrick to let him know we were stopping at the next rest stop. We pulled into Roadside Park, where both carloads of people exited the vehicles. Mae, Trina, and I walked around while Derrick, Rodrick, and Myles sat on a bench talking. Chyna and KJ were running around playing. We were there for about 30 minutes before getting back on the road.

Roughly 30 minutes into the drive, KJ said, "I have to use the bathroom."

"Why didn't you use it when we stopped?" I asked.

"I didn't have to use it then," he whined.

Myles called Derrick again to let him know we would be stopping when we found somewhere to pull off because KJ had to use the bathroom. Eventually, we found a small gas station. It looked like one the farmers used to fill their tractors. Myles and KJ went in and came out with a key to unlock the bathroom door that was on the side of the station. Once done, he returned the key, and the two of them climbed back into the vehicle. Myles was laughing and shaking his head. I had to admire the patience and compassion he had for my son. It was apparent the love was reciprocated.

"What are you two laughing about now?" I asked.

"That boy didn't use it!"

"What? Why not?"

"KJ looked at the toilet and said, 'The toilet is dirty. I don't want to put my clean pee in that dirty toilet.'"

I laughed so hard, it made my belly hurt. We then drove until we saw a sign for McDonald's. At that stop, everyone went in to relieve themselves.

Sharon had already booked our hotel rooms at the Holiday Inn, so when we arrived in Myrtle Beach around 4:00 p.m., we quickly settled in our rooms and then went out to eat. Sharon told me the baby shower would be held in the hotel's Banquet Room. I smiled because I could imagine just how grand an affair it would be.

After eating, the men and children went to the movies. The women gathered in my room, and we played Monopoly until the others returned. I enjoyed my time with them, getting to know them better. By the time I went to bed, I was exhausted from the day's activities.

On Saturday morning, I woke up craving grits and raisin toast. We chose Waffle House for breakfast. After eating, Mae and her family went to Sharon's house, and Myles and I took KJ sightseeing, ending up downtown. "I had told that man whenever I came back to town, I would look him up. Since we're down here, let me swing by Subway to see if he got the job," Myles said.

"Are we going to the movies?" KJ asked.

"Not right now. I'm going to check on someone."

"You want me to go with you?" he asked.

"No, Peanut. Stay in the SUV with your Mama. I won't be long." He went into Subway and was in there for a while.

"Mama, maybe you should see what's taking him so long."

"It's okay, he'll be out soon," I stated, although I did wonder the same.

Myles emerged about 20 minutes later, carrying a bag and drinks. He was smiling. When he got inside with us, he said, "Lexie, Ivory got the job and an apartment! He said he gave his life to the Lord and is getting married in two months!"

"Really? The homeless man you met?"

"Yes! I didn't even recognize him at first, but he remembered me. Believe me: If you saw him, you wouldn't recognize him, either. The beard is gone, and he has a nice haircut. If I must say, he's a nice-looking man. He's the Assistant Manager now. After asking how many people were riding with me, he gave me three combos and cookies and paid me back the $50.00!"

"Myles! For real?" I exclaimed.

"Yes! He said if it weren't for me, he wouldn't have that job. He also invited us to his wedding. I told him we'd have to miss it because we'll have newborn babies by then. He congratulated me and asked me to tell you hello. And check this out: When I tried to give him the money back, he said to keep it as a gift for the babies! What a guy!"

Getting back to the hotel, I quickly dressed for the baby shower. Myles rode down the elevator with me to the Banquet Room. The women had decorated the space beautifully, including a balloon arch we had to walk through at the room's entrance. Blue and pink balloons were everywhere. The spread of food was immense. Nearly anything a person's heart could desire was on the tables lined against the far wall. There was also a table with various candies so that the guests could help themselves to a bagful when they left.

"I'm going back upstairs where the men are. I'll keep KJ with me. If any other men show up in here, send them upstairs. Call me when it's almost over so that we can come down and grab some food," Myles said.

"Okay, Honey. See you later."

Over 35 ladies attended the party. Sharon shared with me that some of the teachers and students from the college where she worked decorated and set up the food and games. I met more of Myles' family and friends and had an amazing time. I called Myles to let him know the party was almost over, and I was getting ready to open the gifts.

When Myles and the men walked in, Sharon announced, "Everybody, this is my brother and the twins' father, Myles Lee Ferguson." He blushed at the suddenness of the attention.

"Thank you all for making this day special for my beautiful wife and me," he stated. He walked over to me and whispered, "I'm ready to eat. Look at all of that food!" KJ was right behind him, looking in awe at the food spread.

Above the roar of conversations in the room, Sharon yelled out, "All the men can help themselves to something to eat. There's a lot of food over there." Including KJ, about 16 men rushed the food tables.

The way Myles and KJ interacted remained mind-blowing to me. At one point, I motioned for Myles to send KJ to me, but he mouthed the words, "He's alright."

When it was time to open the gifts, Myles and KJ sat beside me. We received two of virtually everything a baby needs, down to two car seats. Trina was tasked with writing down the name of every gift and giver so that I could send thank you cards. I thought to myself, "I'm glad Derrick is driving his Tahoe and that we're in the Escalade. There's no other way to get all these gifts home in one trip."

Once the gifts were opened and organized off to the side of the room, Sharon said, "We have one last game to play: Make a Donation to Winner Takes All." One of Sharon's students named Tae had a clear bowl with some money in it. "Okay, who wants to donate to this game?" Sharon asked. Another one of Sharon's students named Shannon walked behind Tae with a bag and a roll of tickets. As people made donations, Shannon handed them the top half of the ticket and put the other half in the bag for the drawing.

Everyone waited anxiously to see if their number would be drawn. It was pin-drop quiet in the room for the first time that day. Sharon yelled, "What did I say the name of this game is?"

"Winner Takes All!" everyone yelled back.

Sharon asked Chyna to come and pull a ticket out of the bag. She also asked Myles and me to come to stand by her. Myles had to help me up, with KJ trying to assist. Sharon called out, "The number is 346!" The woman who had the lucky number came running to the front, reaching for the money bowl. Sharon stopped her short—and handed her a large bottle of "ALL" laundry detergent. The moment was absolutely hilarious! After everyone quieted down, Sharon said, "Thank you for your donations, everyone. The money will be given to the real winners here tonight, Myles and Lexie, to help with diapers and wipes. We know they will need a lot of them!" She placed the money into the bag with the remaining tickets and handed it to me. Everyone clapped and commented about how good of a game that was.

The lady who won the game said, "You know, I needed some detergent to wash clothes when I get home. Now, I don't have to stop at the store!" She was so funny, hugging the bottle and kissing it.

Out of all the games we played that day, the Winner Takes All was my favorite— not because we "won" the money, but rather because of the look on the lady's face and her reaction when Sharon handed her that bottle of detergent. I thanked everyone for coming and Sharon for hosting the baby shower for us.

I pulled Sharon to the side and asked if she was the one who had prepared all the food. "I told my colleagues I was hosting a baby shower for my brother and his wife, who are expecting twins, and they all offered to bring a dish. The only things

I supplied were the plates, cups, and plasticware. Mae picked up the cake this morning. A bonus was that one of the teachers who works with me has a brother who manages this hotel. He said we could have the room for free if the out-of-town guests booked rooms here. The only other thing he asked was that we clean up after the event, which the men agreed in advance to do." I couldn't thank her enough for all she did to make the party a success.

Once the Banquet Room was clean, some of the party-goers helped load up our SUVs with the many gifts received. Sharon was the last to leave. We counted the money from the game, which came to $98.00. Sharon added $2.00 to make it an even $100.00, hugging both of us before leaving. "I don't want you to leave," Sharon playfully whined.

"Sharon, we'll be back when the babies are old enough to travel," Myles replied.

Tears began to stream down her cheeks. "I want to be there when the babies are born, but I don't know how I would feel coming home, and daddy isn't there." Those words brought tears to Mae's eyes.

"Let me walk you to your car, Sharon. We gotta get up early in the morning to leave," Myles said.

"Are you putting me out, Myles?" Both of them laughed.

"No, Sis! We have a 10-hour drive tomorrow, and we need to get some sleep!"

Sharon gave a final round of hugs to us all, and then Myles and KJ walked her to her car. I was in bed by the time they came to the room. Myles laid behind me and asked, "Babe, how are you feeling?"

"I'm feeling good, just big!" Myles laughed as he rubbed my belly.

Chapter 71

On Sunday, we were on the road at 5:00 a.m. We drove until we saw the same Cracker Barrel where Myles and I ate on our way home from our honeymoon. We stopped, ate breakfast, and walked the strip mall next to the restaurant. I bought a gift for Mrs. Brenda's baby, and Mae picked up a couple of things for Chyna before getting back on the road.

Myles told me he didn't want me to drive; all I needed to do was sit in the passenger's seat and look pretty. I added, "And big!" He laughed and reached over to rub my belly again. We rode along in comfortable silence, enjoying the scenery. I thought KJ was asleep, but when we passed by the gas station with the dirty toilet, he said, "Mama, that's the place with the dirty toilet." I guess he needed to see that place one more time because afterward, he went to sleep.

"I enjoyed spending time with my family. It was so nice seeing everybody," Myles said. "You know, we haven't picked any baby names yet. What do you think?"

I looked in the backseat, got a sheet of paper out of KJ's writing tablet, and tore it into ten strips. "Give me five boy names, and I will do five girl names. I'll put them in the bag and see what comes out!"

The first boy's name I pulled out was Karson. "I like that one," Myles commented.

"Me, too."

The first girl's name I pulled out was Kaylin. We both said together, "I like that one, too!"

"So, what do you think about Karson Lee? He will have my middle name and my dad's first name."

"That's a beautiful name," I replied. "What do you think about Kaylin Rose, after my mom's first name and my middle name?"

"I love the sound of that. Karson Lee and Kaylin Rose Ferguson. Sounds good to me! I wonder what Peanut will think about those names," Myles said thoughtfully. "Karson and Kaylin! Come here!" he said playfully. "Yes, that has a nice sound to it. But let me sleep on it." I shot him a quick look and saw he was driving with one eye open, playing like he was asleep.

"Myles, stop playing!" He laughed so hard at the expression on my face. "Wow, Myles! Think about it: All of our children have names that start with a K!"

He smiled and started singing, "When I Found Love, I Found You."

"That's the same song you sang when you married Mama," KJ stated.

"That's right! I thought you were asleep, Peanut."

"Nope! I was listening to you sing."

"Do you know a song to sing?" Myles asked.

"I know 'I Believe I Can Fly'!" KJ replied happily.

"Okay! Let's hear you sing!" I encouraged.

KJ sang his little heart out, knowing every word. "Peanut, you sound good!" Myles said. KJ beamed his brightest smile my way and said, "Mama, I sang a song, and Myles sang a song. Now, it's your turn!"

"Yes, it's your turn to sing, Lexie," Myles said with a laugh.

"Okay. Hmm... Let me see..." I started singing "Addicted Love" by CeCe Winans.

"I remember that song, Mama! You used to sing that to me!"

"Yes, I sure did!"

"I didn't know you knew that song. I love it!" Myles said.

"Mama, how about you sing the lady's part and let Myles sing the man's part?" That's just what we did. I must admit: Myles and I made that song sound good!

Chapter 72

After an eventful ride home, we finally made it in around 5:00 that evening. Derrick followed us home, and the men and KJ took all the gifts out of both vehicles and put them in my office. While they did that, Mae, the girls, and I separated the food we brought home from the baby shower.

When they left, I took my shower and got ready for bed. Myles yelled from the kitchen, "I'll bring your food to you if you are ready to eat."

"Yes, I am," I yelled back. He came in with a plate full of spaghetti, a seven-layer salad, lemon pepper chicken, stuffed eggs, and two slices of turkey roll.

"KJ convinced me to let him sleep in the office. He already took his shower and got his clothes ready for school tomorrow," Myles said, passing me the plate.

"How is he going to sleep on the couch with all those gifts?" I asked.

"He already made enough room for him to sleep in there." We laughed.

After eating, I was full and exhausted. I can't recall much of anything Myles said because I went right to sleep. When I woke up at 8:00 a.m., Myles and KJ were already gone. I walked into the kitchen and saw Myles had made breakfast. I hurried to get dressed, put my food in a carry-out container, and left for work, making it there at 9:30. I was late, so I went straight to my office, barely speaking to anyone along the way.

I walked into my office and was shocked at the sight before me. My computer, papers, pictures of Myles and KJ, and plants were strewn across the floor. All the drawers in my desk were open. I placed my food on the desk and went to find out what had happened. I went to Mrs. Jones' office and immediately noticed her office was in total disarray as well.

Before I could open my mouth to ask, she answered my question. "Someone broke into five of the offices in this building on the weekend, and all of the offices were on this floor only. My small TV and computer are missing, my filing cabinet was overturned, and some checks are missing. Fortunately, I recorded the check numbers on a paper file in my desk, so if anyone tries to cash them, they will get caught immediately. I don't know why they took the computer. They can't access it without the password."

I went back to my office, warmed my food, and sat down to eat. I looked around the room at all that had to be done to get it back in order. My cell phone rang, interrupting my thoughts. It was Myles. "How are you feeling today? I thought you were going to sleep in today, which is why I didn't wake you."

"Well, I was feeling great until I got into my office this morning. Someone broke in over the weekend and trashed the place. My office was one of them."

"Oh, no. I'm sorry to hear that. Maybe you should take a leave of absence until after the babies are born," he suggested.

"Myles, I'm alright. I'm not going to clean up this mess. They have maintenance men here to do that."

"Did you grab some of the breakfast I made?"

"Yes, I'm eating now. I gotta go, Honey. The men are here to clean my office. Love you."

"Okay. Love you, too. Bye."

As the men cleaned, one mentioned they had the two guys on camera who broke into the building. It turns out the same men broke into another office building down the street that same night.

I worked in my office all that day. Myles called to let me know that he, KJ, and Spot were home. When I got home that afternoon, Myles had made homemade chicken noodle soup and a salad. I was grateful that he did. As my pregnancy progressed into my 8th month, I grew bigger by the day. My back hurt, and my feet began to swell, causing me to move a bit slower than normal.

That Thursday, I was away from my office most of the day. I met with my supervisor to discuss my maternity leave, as I decided Friday would be my last day. I also had an appointment to sit in on a meeting at 2:00 p.m. for a former employee who claimed he was wrongly terminated. I didn't see him getting his job back because he did things such as not turning in his timesheets and, when he did, he had times handwritten that were inaccurate (many people witnessed him leave the job early a lot of the days he wrote on his card that he worked all day). The last meeting I had was with my replacement while on leave. That was scheduled for 4:00 p.m.

When I had a moment, I checked my cell phone messages. Myles had called me three times to tell me he was taking KJ to a parent meeting at his school at 5:30

222

p.m. I had actually forgotten all about that meeting. I sat in my office and thought about how blessed I was to have Myles help me with KJ. I arrived home a little after 6:00. Myles and KJ weren't there, so I let the dog out and waited for him to come back in. I then sat on the couch in my bedroom and went to sleep, waiting on Myles and KJ to come home.

I was awakened by Myles kissing me on my forehead and KJ saying, "Mama, I'm doing good in all my classes! Here. Look at my progress report card!" Myles stepped away and went into the kitchen. KJ was so excited for me to see his report card.

"Baby, you are doing great! Give me a hug. I'm so proud of you!"

Myles yelled from the kitchen, "KJ's teacher said they are getting ready to start an accelerated program, and KJ will be one of its students. She'll let us know when the program begins."

"She said that, KJ? Wow, son! I'm so proud of you!"

"Mama, can I look at a movie in the theater room?" he asked.

"Yes, you can."

"Do you want to watch a movie with me?" he asked excitedly.

"No, baby. Mama is tired. I had a busy day and don't have the strength to walk upstairs."

"Myles already bought me a kid's meal at McDonald's. Can I pop some popcorn?"

"Yes, you can, but I don't want you dropping popcorn on the floor."

"I won't," he answered.

Myles came in with my food and set it on the serving tray in front of me. "Young lady, here is your food. How was your day at work?" he asked as he kissed me on the cheek.

"Busy. I had three meetings today. One of them was with my supervisor. I told her I would be taking maternity leave starting tomorrow."

"So, you decided to go on maternity leave? That's good." He paused and then said, "Oh. Before I left to take KJ to the parent conference, Keith called and said Mrs. Brenda went into the hospital to have her baby, so he won't be able to get KJ on Friday."

"Good for her. I put a check in her card for the lamp. I know she got it because the check was cashed. She also sent me a thank you card for the baby gift."

"Don't let KJ hear you say that! Remember: It wasn't his fault that the lamp got broken." Myles was laughing so hard at his own joke.

"Did you talk to him again about that?" I asked.

"Yes, but he still insists it wasn't his fault." He suddenly stopped laughing and looked at my face.

"What's wrong? Are you looking at my nose? I know it's gotten big since I've been pregnant."

"I love your nose, and I love you, too."

"What brought on that look?" I pried deeper.

"Nothing. Nothing. I just feel like the luckiest man alive. I am married to a beautiful woman who's having my babies."

I shook my head at him. "Myles, let me eat my food. I love you, too."

"Okay, I'm going to check on KJ."

I finished eating and then went to take my shower. When I got out, Myles was lying across the bed. "KJ was asleep, wrapped in his blanket. The movie was still playing, and he was holding his bag of popcorn. I removed the bag from his hand and left him sleeping right where he was." I had to laugh. "Did KJ tell you a little boy at school keeps messing with him?"

"No, he hasn't said anything to me about that."

"I told him I would look around for Karate classes and enroll him to go on Saturdays."

"You told him that? Why?"

"Lexie, I don't want anybody messing with him. He needs to know how to protect himself. If he doesn't, he will soon be afraid to go to school." He got up to take his shower, just as the news reported they had caught the men who broke into our building and the Civil Rights Center downtown. They were caught trying to break into the Citizen Bank. One man was shot.

"Myles, did you hear that?"

"When will these people realize when you do wrong, they will eventually get caught?" he replied.

Chapter 73

I fell asleep that night thinking about my last day of work and what I had to do before the babies came. I woke up to Myles singing to the babies in my belly. "Today is your Mama's last day at work. Thank You, Jesus!"

KJ was sitting at the table eating his breakfast. He came into my room and said, "Mama, I didn't get to watch my movie last night because I went to sleep."

"I know. Listen, today after school, get on the bus and come back home. Mrs. Brenda went into the hospital to have her baby, so your dad's not home."

"Good. I didn't want to go over there anyway." Myles gave me a curious look.

"KJ, why don't you want to go to your dad's?" I asked.

He shrugged his shoulders and replied, "I just don't want to."

"We'll talk about it in the car. Hug your Mama so we can go. Babe, I'll call you when you get to work," Myles said.

After they left, I thought, " I do not like KJ's attitude right now. Hopefully, Myles can get to the bottom of what's going on with him."

Arriving on the job, I was so happy it was my last day for a while. I went straight to my office to get the paperwork set up for the lady who would be replacing me while I was on maternity leave. I also worked on the thank you cards to mail off to those who attended the baby shower. At 11:00 on the dot, Myles called to see how I was feeling. "I'm feeling heavy and moving slow. Since you put the running boards on the truck, can you come here and switch out vehicles? It's so hard for me to step up into Pearl."

He laughed and said, "I'll bring it at noon. You want me to bring you lunch?"

"Yes, please. That sounds good."

"What do you want to eat?"

"A pepper steak meal and an egg roll from the Chinese restaurant."

"Chinese food it is! I have never even seen you eat Oriental food before."

"Well, that's what the babies say they want to eat!"

He was cracking up. "Okay, my lady. See you at noon."

I finished writing the thank you cards around 11:45, right when someone knocked on my door. "Come in," I said, not even sure who was on the other side. It was Mrs. Jones.

"Did you hear they caught the men who broke into the building?" She had mail in her hand.

"Yes, I heard it on the news last night."

"What are you doing here? I heard this is your last day for a while."

"Yes, this is my last day. These twins are getting the best of me. My legs swell, my back hurts, and I really don't feel comfortable driving with the seatbelt. It barely fits across me."

"I know the feeling, Lexie. I carried one and felt that way. And you are having twins? Lord, help you!" We laughed. "Do you feel like walking with me? I have to mail these newsletters before the new month comes in."

"Sure. I can mail my thank you cards at the same time. I just finished with them and need to stretch my legs anyway." I used the desk to help me stand. Mrs. Jones laughed as we walked out of my office. "I'm sure I look like a big elephant walking down this hallway."

"You look fine," she said, still laughing at me. We dropped our mail in the box, and I turned to go back to my office. "Are you tired?" she asked.

"No, I'm not tired. Myles is bringing me lunch. I need to meet him in my office."

"Walk with me to the conference room. I need to pick up some papers, and then we'll walk back together." We entered the room, and I realized the company was throwing me a surprise baby shower.

"Mrs. Jones! You tricked me!" I was so overwhelmed with joy, I began to cry.

She laughed and told me, "Have a seat before you fall."

The room was set up nicely. It was decorated from the front to the back. They also provided food and had a gift table stacked from the floor to the ceiling. It looked like everyone who worked in that building had bought me a gift. About 20 minutes later, my secretary brought Myles to the conference room. "Mrs. Ferguson, this gentleman was looking for you."

As Myles walked toward me with a smile plastered on his face, my supervisor asked, "So, this is your twins' dad?"

"Everybody, this is my husband, Myles." They all spoke, and he responded in kind. I noticed some of the women were practically drooling over him.

My supervisor, Ms. Ellis, told Myles to get something to eat. "Here is the hand sanitizer," she said. I know Myles felt uncomfortable with all eyes on him.

He smiled at her and said, "Thank you." He grabbed a plate of food and then came to sit beside me. He whispered, "I wasn't expecting this."

"Me, neither. Mrs. Jones tricked me into coming down here. I didn't call you because my phone is in my office."

"Well, I left the Chinese food on your desk."

I asked him, "What happened to your ponytail?" I could see his hair hanging loosely from under his cap.

"My rubber band popped when I got out of the truck." He looked at me closely. "You are looking extraordinarily nice today."

"Thanks, Honey. You are looking rather dapper if I must say so." We smiled at each other.

Out of nowhere, a lady I'd never seen before came over and sat beside Myles. She looked over and spoke to me. I heard her ask him something about school. Mrs. Jones approached us and asked Myles, "So, are you ready for two babies?"

He laughed and said, "Yes, I think so. I survived Iraq. I imagine the babies will be a piece of cake!" We all laughed and nodded in agreement.

The lady sitting beside Myles asked only him if he wanted something to drink. He shook his head no. I spoke up, though. "You can get me a cup of punch."

When she got up to get it, Myles murmured, "Don't you drink it."

"But she already went to get it," I said, confused.

"I said don't drink it, Lexie."

228

"Okay, I won't drink it," wondering why he would order such a thing. When the lady returned with the punch, I was talking to Mrs. Jones. She handed me the punch and sat back down beside Myles. He removed the drink from my hand and set the cup on the floor as she was saying something to him. He stood suddenly and retrieved a small bottled water for me.

"Open this and drink it. You don't need the sugar." He picked up the cup of punch and said, "Babe, it's time for me to get back to work. Call me when you get back to your office. Remember: No sugar." He kissed me goodbye, walking out with the punch. Before exiting, he turned and thanked everyone for the baby shower and food.

That lady watched Myles closely as he walked out. She then moved into the chair he was sitting in, looked at me, and asked, "Do you want me to get you some more punch?"

"No, thank you. I'll drink this water."

"Your husband looks familiar. Does he lift weights?"

"Yes, he works out."

"He looks like it by the way he is built. He's bowlegged, too. Umm. So, how long have you been married?"

Before I could answer, two ladies came over and said they were leaving to go back to work. I thanked them for coming and for their gifts. When I turned around, the lady was gone. Mrs. Jones instructed everyone to take a plate with them because there was a lot of food left. Some people grabbed a plate to go. "Before you all leave, I want to thank you for the gifts and food. This was truly a surprise. Thank you all so much," I said.

The room emptied, leaving me with Mrs. Jones and Mrs. Ford. They put the leftover food in the refrigerator, and I placed the gifts in trash bags to make them easier to carry out to the truck. I thanked Mrs. Ford and hugged her. "You take care of yourself and those twins."

Going down the hall back to my office, Mrs. Jones said, "When it's time to leave, I'll help you take the gifts to your vehicle."

"Okay, thank you. But know this: I will get you back for tricking me!"

She laughed and replied, "It won't be today, with that load you're carrying! See you later."

"Thank you for all you've done for me, Mrs. Jones."

Chapter 74

I went into my office, and, just as Myles said, there was Chinese food sitting on my desk. It was almost 1:30, so I sat down and called him. His secretary said, "Mrs. Ferguson, he wants you to call him on his cell phone."

"Okay, thank you." I called his cell.

"Are you just getting back to your office?" he asked.

"Yes."

"Who was that lady sitting by me?"

"I don't know. I guess she works down the other hall. I know everyone who works in my area. I thought you knew her."

"I have no idea who she was. Did you drink any punch?"

"No! You told me not to."

"That lady sitting beside me kept looking at me with those false eyelashes, winking her eye at me, and trying to touch my hair."

"No, she didn't!"

"That's not all. When she gave you the punch, she whispered in my ear and said she liked the way I looked. She then asked me if I wanted her to show me a good time and rubbed my thigh."

"She did what? She put her hand on you?!"

"Yes, which is why I stood. I felt violated." The way he said that made me laugh. "That's not funny!"

"No, it's not. It's the way you said it." I calmed my laughter. "I don't want another lady putting her hands on my man. After you left, she asked how long we've been married and if you lifted weights. She also commented about your bowlegs."

"Wow, she said all that?"

"Yep! She probably would have said more, but some other ladies came over to talk to me. I didn't even see where she went. I'm going to look for her and tell her I don't appreciate her flirting with my husband."

It was his turn to laugh. "No, Babe. Don't do that. Leave it alone."

"Myles, she was hitting on you right in front of my face!"

He chuckled and said, "I know. She was up to no good. Leave it alone, though. She's not worth it. I'll see you at 4:30 to pick up the gifts."

"It's okay. You don't have to come back. Mrs. Jones said she would help me load them up in the truck."

"You don't understand. I have to come back. I'm in the truck, not Pearl. That lady had me so nervous, I forgot to switch. I'll see you soon. Don't worry about KJ. I already talked to Trina, and she agreed to keep him until we get there. Love you, Babe. Bye."

I sat there thinking about what Myles said about that lady. I wondered if she followed him out when he left. I was curious about who she was and where she came from. I walked to Mrs. Jones' office. Her door was open, but she was on the phone. She waved for me to come in and have a seat. I sat in the chair in front of her desk. When she got off her call, she asked, "Are you alright?"

"Yes, I'm okay. I was wondering: Do you know who that lady was in the blue top who sat at the table beside Myles?"

"I thought she was from one of the offices on the other hall. When we were setting up the food, she came in and helped us."

"Well, she was hitting on my husband."

"She did what?!" Mrs. Jones looked shocked.

"Myles said she was trying to put her hands in his hair, rubbed his thigh, and asked if he wanted her to show him a good time. That's why he left when he did."

Mrs. Jones stood, obviously upset. "Where did she come from?"

"I'm not sure, either. She sat down beside him and started talking. I thought they might've known each other. At one point, she got me a cup of punch, but Myles told me not to drink it."

"Did you?" Mrs. Jones asked.

"No, I didn't. He actually took it with him when he left, but not before giving me a bottle of water."

"I wonder if she saw us bringing in the food and walked in off the street. Did you see her leave?"

"No, I didn't see where she went. Mrs. Jones, I have to go. I have a meeting with Ms. Hall at 4:00 to go over a couple of things before I leave on my break."

"Okay, we will talk later," she said as she helped me up.

On my way back to my office, I ran into Ms. Hall. She was on her way to my office. When our meeting was over, I put my Chinese food and the things I was carrying home into my rolling cart. Mrs. Jones was locking up her office at the same time. We walked to the conference room together, still talking about that mystery lady. When we entered the room, Mrs. Jones gave me some of the food that was left over. Mr. Lee, Mr. Mattix, and the maintenance man were waiting to help me carry the bags to my vehicle.

As we walked out the front door, Myles drove up in the truck. He got out and thanked everyone for their help. When he got to the maintenance man, he said, "David, how are you? I haven't seen you in a while." They shook hands.

"I'm good, man. I have been working here for about six months now. Things are looking up for me. Are you still at the computer shop?" he asked.

"Yes, I'm still there. Man, it's nice to see you. Call or stop by sometime."

"Okay, I will. And congratulations on the babies!"

"Thank you," Myles said while helping me into the truck.

While trailing Myles home, he called me from his cell phone. "Babe, you look tired. I'll get KJ. You head on home."

"I feel tired, heavy, and ready to have these babies."

"Maybe we should cancel Bible study tonight," he suggested.

"No, it's too short of a notice. After tonight, we'll stop hosting until after the babies are born. I didn't know you knew Mr. Lee."

"Yes, I know him from school. We played football together."

"He's a nice man. He hasn't been working there long."

"I know. He said it's only been about six months. It was nice to see him." I heard a beep on his line. "Babe, I got a call coming in. We'll see you at home."

When I got home, I was drained. I sat on the stool as I put the leftover food from the baby shower into plastic bowls and then into the refrigerator. Myles and KJ came in shortly after I arrived. "You should be resting, Babe."

"I wanted to put the food away before I got settled."

KJ said, "Mama, I've missed you."

"I've missed you, too. Give me a hug. My baby boy is growing up!"

He hugged me and said, "Mama! I'm not a baby!"

"You're right. My KJ is growing up and doesn't want to be my baby anymore," I said sadly. Myles laughed at us and went into our bedroom while snacking on a carrot from the vegetable tray. I followed him and sat on the side of the bed.

KJ came in and sat on the couch. "Mama, can I get a ponytail like Myles?"

"The last time you said you wanted a mohawk!"

"Yeah, but this time, I want a ponytail."

I looked at him, imagining him with a ponytail. "You will have to let your hair grow out long enough to make a ponytail. We'll see if you still want one when your hair gets longer."

"Okay!" he said, prancing his way outside. I was sure Myles told him they were going to get their hair cut.

As Myles exited the bathroom, he asked, "Lexie, what are you doing tomorrow?"

"Nothing. I'm too big to go anywhere. I'll be here waiting for Mrs. Riddle to come and clean. The yard man's coming tomorrow, too. Why do you ask?"

"KJ and Chyna have convinced me to take them to the circus." By then, KJ was back inside. I asked him if he wanted Myles to ask his dad if Brandon could go to the circus with them.

"No, we will be okay without him."

"You don't want your little brother to go? All kids like the circus," I replied.

"I just want it to be me, Myles, and Chyna."

234

"KJ, you're being selfish."

Myles chimed in. "Maybe we'll ask your dad if your brother can come next time."

KJ took that exact moment to redirect the conversation. "Myles, do you want to come outside and play basketball with me?"

"Not now, Peanut. I need to talk to your mom and rest a little before Bible study."

"Okay." He called for Spot and went upstairs.

"Myles, he doesn't want to share you. At the baby shower in Myrtle Beach, I noticed how he followed you everywhere you went."

He smiled as he said, "He'll be alright. Hey, did you find out who that lady was?"

"I talked to Mrs. Jones about her. We both think she was someone who walked in off the street."

"Umm…and found it appropriate to put her hand on me?"

"She might be a lady of the night and wanted to try and steal my husband," I replied. He looked at me, frowned, then closed his eyes. Bible study was 45 minutes away. "I wonder if the group wants to stay for snacks tonight." Myles didn't respond because he was asleep. I laid beside him, too tired to stay awake and too tired to nap. Forty minutes later, the doorbell rang. "Myles, get up. They're here."

He got up quickly to let them in. We prayed, and Myles read the scriptures. Before I knew it, our study on "How Important It Is to Live by Faith" was over. I told everyone we wouldn't meet at our home again until after the babies were born.

One of the ladies said, "We talked about that on our drive here. We understand."

"Would you like to stay for snacks?" I asked. Brother Sam said everyone rode in with him, and he had somewhere else to be by 8:00. I told them to take some of the food with them. Myles handed each of them a carry-out plate.

After everyone left, I called KJ down so that we could eat our Chinese food. "Myles, what if KJ doesn't like it?"

"If he doesn't, he can eat chicken and spaghetti salad. We know he likes them!"

KJ came into the kitchen, saw the food, and exclaimed, "Yes! I love Chinese food!" Myles and I both sighed with relief.

We finished our dinner, the three of us did the dishes, and then we went into our bedroom to watch a Charlie Brown movie. I sat on the couch, Myles sat beside me, and KJ sat in the big chair. We chatted while waiting for the movie to start. By then, KJ was asleep. Myles and I kept talking. I reminded him about our upcoming doctor's appointment on Thursday. He didn't reply. When I looked over at him, he was asleep, too! I took my shower and, when I exited the bathroom, covered them with a blanket. I climbed into bed and watched Charlie Brown until I fell asleep.

Chapter 75

I woke up on Saturday morning, only to find Myles and KJ were still asleep. Around 10:00 a.m., the doorbell rang. It was Mrs. Riddle coming to clean. The landscaper was already working in the yard. I walked back to my room and woke up Myles.

"What time is it?" he asked groggily.

"10:00."

"Oh, my God. Why didn't you wake me?"

"The two of you were sleeping so well, I decided to let my guys rest."

"Is KJ still asleep?"

"Yes, he's over there in the chair. Mrs. Riddle is here now. She's cleaning upstairs first."

Myles took his shower, got dressed, and said, "I told Mae I'd pick up Chyna at 11:45. The circus starts at 1:00. We need to leave early so that we can find parking." He headed upstairs and called out, "Mrs. Riddle, I am coming up!"

"Come on. I'm in the theater room," she replied. I heard him greet her when he got to the top of the stairs.

He came back down with KJ's change of clothes. "Get up, KJ. Go into your mom's bathroom and get dressed." He asked if I wanted something to eat on his way to the kitchen.

"No, thank you. I already had orange juice and toast. I still feel full from last night."

"Are you alright?"

"Babe, the babies moved around all last night. It felt like they were pressing on my spine."

"Do you want to go to the doctor?" he asked with concern.

"No, I'll call Jessica today and let her know how I'm feeling."

Myles rested his chin on his hand, thinking. "Next week, I'm installing an intercom system. You won't have to walk upstairs, and you can talk to KJ from down here." He came over, rubbed my belly, and the babies started moving, "That's right, Karson and Kaylin. Daddy's here."

"Keep talking to them, Babe! They are finally moving off my spine!" Myles rubbed my back as he talked to my belly, which confused KJ.

"Mama? Are you sick?" he asked.

"No, I'm fine. The babies are pressing on my spine, and Myles is rubbing my back and talking to them, trying to get them to move."

"I'll be glad when they come out," KJ said.

Myles started laughing. "Me, too, Peanut! Me, too. Are you ready to go?" He nodded yes. "We'll stop by McDonald's to grab breakfast. Lexie, if you need me, call. And don't go upstairs."

"Okay, Dr. Myles. I won't."

He kissed me before leaving. He stuck his head back in the door and said, "The checks for the lawn man and Mrs. Riddle are in the red vase."

Around 12:30, Mrs. Riddle came downstairs, saying she was done upstairs. "Come. Sit and have lunch with me." I tried to stand but felt pressure on my back again. "Oooo!"

Mrs. Riddle told me to stay seated. "I'll get the food. Maybe you are putting pressure on your back when you stand." We sat together and ate some of the leftover food. "Thanks for lunch. Let me get back to work."

I slowly made my way to the patio, wondering why I was in so much pain. It wasn't time for the babies to come yet. While I sat there, Sharon called. "I received the thank you card today. How are you feeling?" she asked.

"I'm feeling okay now, but these babies moved around a lot last night. My back is hurting, but I feel a little better today."

"Maybe you are doing too much standing."

I started to laugh. "My housekeeper said the same thing."

"Lexie, I really would like to be there when the babies are born. How many more weeks do you have to go?"

"Three weeks or less, but I'm ready now!" We both laughed. "You are always welcome to stay with us. We live down the street from Mae, so you can see her, too. I have a doctor's appointment on Thursday. I'll call and let you know what she says."

"Okay. Let me know as soon as you can so that I can put in for time off from work. Is Myles there?"

"Not right now. He took Chyna and KJ to the circus."

"Please tell him I called. I'll be looking to hear from you guys soon."

"Okay, love you. Bye."

Myles called shortly after to let me know they were leaving the circus. "We're going to stop by the barbershop to get our haircuts."

"Okay, but remember KJ's ponytail?"

He laughed. "How are you feeling?"

"Still hurting a little."

"I'm on my way home!" he said in a panic.

"No, Myles. I'm okay! You don't have to come home. Mrs. Riddle will still be here for a while."

"Have you eaten anything?" he asked.

"Mrs. Riddle and I ate lunch together."

"Do you want me to bring you anything special to eat?"

"No, but I would like you to make some of your famous chicken noodle soup when you get home!"

I could hear the smile in his voice when he asked, "Is there anything else you want or need?"

"No, nothing else."

"Oh! I saw KJ's dad."

"Was he at the circus with Brandon?"

"He was riding in the car with some guy. I saw him at a red light."

"Oh, okay. Honey, we'll talk later. Mrs. Riddle is saying something to me."

When I abruptly ended the call, Mrs. Riddle said, "You didn't have to get off the phone. I was just saying I'll be done for the day when I do the patio."

"I'll go into the family room to get out of your way." As soon as I stood, the pain moved to my back again.

Mrs. Riddle noticed I was in pain. "Are you alright?"

"Yes, ma'am. The babies are pressing on my spine." She helped me stand.

"You don't have long to go. Those babies are ready to come out of there!" We both laughed. She finished around 5:00 and prepared to leave. I handed her the check. "Thank you. See you in two weeks—if you're still here!" When she went outside, I heard her talking to someone. It was Myles and KJ coming in.

KJ came inside, excited to tell me all about the circus. Myles came over, kissed me, and said, "I've missed you," as he handed me a fish sandwich.

"Is this all?" I asked, confused.

"That will hold you over until my famous chicken noodle soup is ready. You know what I meant when I said I've missed you, don't you?"

I laughed. "I always miss you when you're away, Honey."

KJ showed me the coloring book Myles bought him at the circus. "Did Chyna get one, too?" I asked.

"Yes, she got one, but she's a scaredy-cat. She cried when the elephants and tigers came out."

"I'm afraid of them too!" I exclaimed.

"You're a scaredy-cat, Mama?!"

"I guess I am!"

He shook his head and walked away. "I'm going upstairs to color." He stopped, turned around, and said, "Mama, I saw daddy at the red light today."

"That's good. Did he see you?"

"I don't know. I don't think so."

"I like your haircut, KJ."

"Thank you, Mama." He then ran upstairs as fast as his legs could carry him.

"Myles, can you help me to the island so that I can sit on the stool? Oh. And I like the way your beard and hair are cut, too," I said with a smile.

"Thanks," he replied, rubbing his beard.

I sat down and ate my sandwich while chatting with Myles. "I enjoyed myself at the circus. I noticed KJ wouldn't let Chyna sit next to me. He sat so that she was on the other side of him, not me. I ended up sitting in the middle."

"I see he is getting attached to you. That's likely why he doesn't want to stay at his daddy's house too long."

"He's attached to me like I'm attached to his Mama." He came around the island, rubbed my belly, and sang to the babies: "He's attached to me like I'm attached to his Mamaaaaa."

"Oh! Before I forget. Sharon called and said she wants to be here when the babies are born. I told her she could stay with us."

"She just wants to come so she can boss me around," he replied, laughing.

"You did say she was your sister-mom!" He cracked up over that comment.

Chapter 76

"Ta-da! Here's a bowl of my famous soup!" Myles announced as he placed the bowl on the kitchen island in front of me.

"I'm ready! Wait. Where are the crackers?" He handed me the crackers, and I called for KJ to come down.

"He has already eaten, but he might want a small cup of soup," Myles said.

We all sat around the island, eating soup. "Myles, this is good!" KJ said with a mouthful of soup.

Myles smiled. "I'm glad you like it, Peanut."

As I sat there, I didn't feel the pain in my side and back like I did earlier that day. It was 6:30 p.m. when we finished eating and cleaning the kitchen. "Do you want to go for a walk with me? I haven't been out of the house all day."

"Sounds good to me!" Myles said.

"Me, too!" KJ stated.

As we walked, KJ bounced his basketball, and the dog ran behind him every step of the way. Myles and I walked and talked, discussing the lady at the baby shower. "I believe that lady just walked in off the street."

He laughed and said, "She was bold, putting her hand on my thigh like she did!"

"What did you do with that cup of punch?"

"I poured it out. She probably put some date rape drug in it." He said that with a stank face. I laughed at him.

We walked for about one-third of a mile before I grew tired and wanted to return home. It was around 8:00 when we walked back through the door. I was tired, so I immediately took a shower and prepared for bed. KJ asked if he could sleep in my office again. "Yes, you can, but go take your shower and get your clothes ready for church tomorrow."

"I took a shower this morning, remember? I haven't done anything to get dirty."

"Myles, please talk to KJ. He doesn't want to take his shower."

"Peanut, go. Put on your PJs when you get out. You can forget about sleeping in the office tonight."

"But Mama already told me I could sleep in there!"

I could tell Myles was losing his patience when he rubbed his hair back. "KJ, bring me your game, take your shower, put on your PJs, and go to bed in your room," he commanded.

"But Mama…"

"I'm going to count to five. Bring me your game, take your shower, and go to bed!"

He stomped away, going upstairs to get the game. He came back down and handed it to Myles. "I'm going to keep it until you apologize to your mom for not doing what she asked you to do. I am disappointed in you for not listening to your Mama and me. When you are told to do something and don't, you lose privileges. What you did is called being disobedient. Now, go upstairs and do what you've been told to do. I will be upstairs to check on you when I get out of the shower," Myles said sternly.

KJ walked away slowly and then turned around to ask, "Can Spot come with me?"

Myles and I both said no at the same time. Myles started counting, prompting KJ to walk faster until he was out of sight. "I don't like being mean to him," Myles said.

"You're not being mean; you are addressing his behavior." He nodded his head in agreement and then went to take his shower. When he got out and got dressed for bed, he went upstairs.

He came back into the room. "KJ took his shower and was in his bed. He told me he was sorry and will tell you he's sorry when he gets up in the morning." We talked until I fell asleep.

Around 1:45 a.m., I woke up with my back, side, and chest in severe pain. I woke up Myles, telling him I was hurting. "Is it the babies?" he asked.

"I don't know. It feels like everything is hurting right now."

"Do you think it's your heart?"

"I'm not sure. I remember Mrs. Riddle telling me that I might be standing too much, causing my back to hurt. But my chest and side are hurting now. This is new."

"You are going to the ER," he replied. I heard him on the phone with the 911 operator. "My wife is 37 weeks pregnant and having chest pains... My house address is... Yes, that's correct. Off Highway 23... You can only turn left onto Riverside. We're in the second house from the end of the street. My garage door will be up." He hung up and asked, "Babe, can you walk?"

"I think so. But what about KJ?"

"Put your robe on over your PJs. I'll go and get him." I could tell he was nervous because he pushed his hair back repeatedly. He came downstairs with KJ, who had his shoes on and a jacket over his PJs. Myles slipped on a pair of jeans and a sweatshirt and then helped me walk into the family room. I sat on the couch while he went to let the garage door up.

"Mama, are you going to have the babies now?" KJ asked.

"I'm not sure."

Within a matter of minutes, the ambulance pulled up. The two EMTs came in with the cart, helped me onto it, and loaded me up inside. Myles and KJ followed behind us in the truck. I heard one of the EMTs talking to someone at the hospital, saying, "We're coming in with a lady, 37 weeks pregnant, age 32, with chest, back, and side pains." As soon as we pulled up to the hospital, the medical team was there, waiting to take me in. They checked my heart and hooked me up to a bunch of monitors. I remember seeing Mae working with a patient as they rolled me down the hall.

The nurse working on me gave me a short for the pain. "Are my babies alright?" I asked.

"Yes, the babies are okay," she replied, patting me on my hand.

"Is that shot going to hurt my babies?"

"Not at all. Just calm down. You and your babies are going to be fine." After the shot, she hooked me up to an IV and gave me some liquid antacid medicine.

I went to sleep before Myles and KJ came in. Myles was sitting beside the bed when I woke up, looking at me. "You're finally awake. How are you feeling?" he asked as he rubbed my hair back.

"I'm okay. Where's KJ?"

"Mae took him home with her. He didn't want to go, but I told him you were alright and that we'd see him later. I stopped by Mae's to check on him when I went home to change my clothes. I grabbed you some clothes to wear home and KJ's clothes for school tomorrow." He let out a slight laugh. "When I got to Mae's house, KJ asked, 'Why are you coming to pick me up so soon?' I told him I was just dropping off his clothes."

I smiled. "What time is it?"

He looked at his watch. "It's 3:35, Sunday afternoon."

"What? I slept all last night and most of today, too?!" I was taken by surprise when he said it was Sunday afternoon.

"Yes, you did. The pastor and his wife came by to see you, but you were still sleeping."

"You called him?"

"No, he actually called me when I was home picking up the clothes. Since I wasn't at church, they thought you were in the hospital having the babies."

"What did the doctor say is wrong with me?"

"You were full gas." He laughed so hard. "You were diagnosed with acute indigestion. You had bombs going off all day while you slept."

"For real, Myles? Oh, my God! Did the pastor and his wife hear them, too?"

He was laughing so hard, he had to take a moment to compose himself. "They weren't here long. They were on their way to another service that the pastor had to speak at this afternoon."

"Did they say when I can go home?"

"Tomorrow. They want you to stay overnight to make sure all the bombs are out."

"Myles, you are silly! Stop it!" I laughed and let out a couple more bombs. Myles was laughing hysterically by then.

"Dr. Jessica was in to see you, too. She wants you to come in on Wednesday." Just as he placed his hand on my belly, I felt one of the babies' elbows or feet poking me in my side. "I can feel one of them moving. They know daddy is here."

"Myles, Honey, it's getting late. You can go home. I'll be fine."

"No, I am going to stay right here with you. KJ is at Mae's, so there's no reason for me to leave you."

"Are you sure? Where are you going to sleep?" I asked.

"This chair lets out to a bed, and here's my blanket." He spread the blanket on the chair bed, watched TV for a while, and then fell asleep.

Chapter 77

When I woke up the next morning, the nurse was taking my blood pressure. Myles was gone. His chair bed was back in place, and the blanket was folded neatly on the chair. I was sure he went to work. The nurse asked, "What would you like for breakfast?"

"Orange juice, oatmeal, one boiled egg, and a slice of toast. Can I get all of that?"

"Yes, you can."

"I am really hungry since releasing all that gas. Can you bring me a slice of bacon, too?" The nurse was laughing. When I got up to go to the bathroom, I paused to look at my belly in the mirror. It had gotten bigger and dropped since I first arrived. I thought to myself, "I had no idea my belly could stretch this far! I had a nice shape. I wonder if I can get back to the size I was." I used the bathroom and slowly made my way back to the bed. Around 8:30, the nurse returned with my breakfast.

At 11:00, Myles called my cell phone. "I didn't want to wake you before I left for work. How are you feeling?"

"Pretty good. I just ate a good breakfast."

"Oh, no. Not more bombs on the way!" he said, laughing. "Call me when they're ready to release you. Love you. See you in a bit."

The nurse came in and told me I could go home once the doctor issued the release papers. I was still there at noon, so I ate lunch. I chose Salisbury steak, mashed potatoes, green peas, a roll, and applesauce. After lunch, I put on the clothes Myles brought for me to wear home. I was ready to go by the time the doctor came in at around 2:30. I called Myles to let him know he could come to pick me up. No sooner than I hung up the phone, he walked into the room. He didn't tell me he was in the hospital when I called.

As we turned onto our street, the bus had just dropped off KJ and the other children. When he saw the truck, he stopped and waited for us to pick him up. He ran to the truck and asked, "Mama, are you alright?"

"Yes, I'm alright.'

"Come on. Get in," Myles said.

KJ turned and waved bye to Chyna and Trina before getting in. "Mama, did you get sick because of me?"

"No, but you did disappoint me by how you acted."

Myles pulled into the garage, got out of the truck, and went inside the house. KJ and I remained in the truck, talking. "Mama, I am sorry I didn't do what you asked me to do."

"Okay. I forgive you."

He hugged me and asked, "Do you want me to help you get inside?"

"Yes, please. Come around and help your Mama."

He got out, walked around the truck, and held my hand. "Don't walk too fast, Mama. You can't see your feet."

I looked down. "You're right! I sure can't!" Walking into the house, I immediately noticed the bouquet of flowers Myles had placed on the kitchen island. "They're beautiful."

"You are beautiful," he said, hugging me and planting a kiss on my lips.

"Yuck!" KJ said before running upstairs to put his bookbag away.

"I missed you when you were in the hospital, my lady."

"You were right there with me!"

He laughed and said, "I still missed you."

KJ came back downstairs and said, "Myles, you said I could have my game back when I apologized to Mama. I apologized, didn't I, Mama?"

"Yes, you did."

"Okay. Look on the table in your Mama's office. Your game is there." KJ found his game and went back upstairs. Myles laughed and said, "That's your son!"

"I know. He's growing up so fast."

"Come and sit down. Remember: You just got out of the hospital. Do you want anything to eat?"

"Not right now. I need to lie down for a while. When I get up, I'm going to want some chicken noodle soup and a salad."

"I know I keep asking, but I need to know: Are you sure you're alright?"

"Yes, Honey. I just want to relax in my own bed." He helped me into bed and then went into the sitting room to read his Bible. I laid there, thanking God for such a caring husband as I drifted off to sleep.

When I woke up, Myles was lying in bed beside me, moving my hair away from my face. "You are so beautiful. Your skin. Your lips. Those beautiful brown eyes. I love lying here looking at you. You don't know how bad I felt while you were in the hospital, thinking it was my fault."

I started to laugh. "I don't want anything to eat that will give me indigestion ever again."

He laughed so hard and agreed. "By the way you were sounding in that hospital room, I had to duck left and right, making sure those bombs didn't hit me!" I laughed as he tried to kiss me.

KJ came in just then and said, "Y'all are at it again? Yuck!" He quickly turned to leave, but Myles stopped him.

"What's up, Peanut?"

"My tablet doesn't work."

"The one I gave you just the other day?"

"Yes, it won't come on."

"Let me see it. Did you plug it in?"

"No, I need batteries."

Myles corrected him. "No, this doesn't take batteries. You must plug it in for a while and let it charge. Have you done your homework?"

"Oh, my goodness!" KJ said, stomping his feet as he walked away.

"Come back here right now!" Myles yelled. KJ returned with his lips poked out. "Where did that attitude come from? Didn't we just talk about that on Saturday?"

KJ started to cry. "I'm sorry, Myles. I'll do my homework." He went upstairs, grabbed his homework, and then sat at the island in the kitchen to work on it.

"Are you ready to eat yet? The soup is ready. No onions this time. I went to McDonald's and bought you a Southwest salad, too," Myles said.

"When did you have time to do that?" I asked.

"When you were in here sleeping, looking pretty. I bought apple pies, too. Do you want me to bring it in here?"

"No, but can you help me up, please? I want to make sure KJ is doing his homework." He helped me over to the chairs that sat lower in the breakfast room. "Thanks, Honey." I ate my food and watched KJ do his homework.

"I'm not ready to eat right now," he said.

"You're not hungry?" I asked.

"No." After finishing his homework, I checked it, and then he went back upstairs.

"Myles, something is going on with KJ. He doesn't want to eat."

"He probably ate something at Mae's house. After I get back from my run, I'll check on him and help him get his clothes ready for school tomorrow."

I put the dishes in the dishwasher and then went into my bedroom to read my Bible. Once again, I started feeling pressure in my back. I took a quick shower and then sat on the bed so I could hear Myles when he came in from his run. When he got back, and after he checked on KJ, he came into the room and asked, "How are you feeling?"

"I can feel the babies pressing against my spine again."

"You want me to rub your back?"

"Please? I hope that will make the pressure go away." As he rubbed, I felt the babies moving. "Thank you so much. They are moving off my spine. How's KJ?"

"He's okay. He's feeling like I am taking you away from him. He said I'm always kissing you and saying I love you. I told him that I loved you and then asked if he wanted me to kiss on him. He frowned and said, 'No way. You can keep rubbing my head, though.' He's alright Babe."

"Did he say why he didn't want to eat?"

"It's just as I suspected. He already ate at Mae's house."

Chapter 78

The following morning, I woke up earlier than usual, so I headed to the kitchen to make breakfast. The babies moved around all night, so I didn't rest well. When Myles walked into the kitchen, he said, "I knew I smelled food. I see you're up and made breakfast."

"Yes, I was hungry. I guess the babies were hungry, too. They moved around all last night."

"Well, I'm ready to eat, too! Are you going to join me?"

"I already ate. I told you I was hungry!"

He laughed and asked, "What is that boy doing up there?" He called for KJ to come down to eat.

As KJ ate his food, he said, "Mama, this food is good!"

"I'm glad you like it. Be good in school today, okay?" He nodded yes.

"Hurry up, Peanut! You're going to miss your bus!" Myles called out from the patio.

"I'm coming!" KJ hugged me and said, "Bye, Mama! See you later!" Myles came back in, kissed me, and said he would call when he got to work.

Once alone, I did my morning devotion and then walked through the house, looked out of the windows, and walked around the backyard. "This is going to be a long day," I thought to myself. I went back inside to my office and began separating the boy's clothes from the girl's clothes. I didn't realize just how much we received. By the time the sorting was done, I had two containers full—one for each baby. In another container, I put the 9-12-month-old clothes. In addition to what I put in the containers, each baby had about a dozen outfits hanging in the closet. We were gifted 25 boxes of diapers and wipes. I found a small container to house the baby oil, lotion, shampoo, hairbrushes, baby bottles, bottle cleaning brushes, pacifiers, socks, and washcloths. There were safety pins, Q-tips, cotton balls...you name it, I had it. There was so much stuff, the babies would be two years old before they used it all!

After putting the babies' things away, I sat at the computer. Going through the drawers, I found a CD I forgot I had. I recalled attending a 6th-grade graduation at the school where my mom taught. The class sang a song to their parents that I really liked. After the program was over, I asked the music teacher for the name of that song and the artist. A couple of weeks later, I went to the music store and purchased the single. I used to listen to it while driving in my car. The song was "Because You Love Me" by Celine Dion.

After moving into my house, Mama retired from her job. About a year later, I knew she missed going to work and being around the children. I came home from work one day, and before going upstairs to see my mom, I put my hair in pigtails— the same way she used to do when I was a little girl. I then put on white bobby socks, white gym shoes, and a skirt. I walked upstairs to her sitting room. "Hi, Mama!"

She looked at me strangely and asked, "Did you wear that to work today?!"

"No, I'm taking you back to where you want to be." She continued looking at me with a funny grin. I put on the CD and sang "Because You Love Me," along with the song. She sat there laughing at me, shaking her head.

When the song finished, she said, "I needed that, but I don't want to return to school. I'm happy here, sitting and reading my Bible and working in my flower garden."

Myles' call interrupted my moment going down memory lane. "I'll be home around 1:00. I have someone coming to install the intercom system at 3:00. I'm going to have them check the batteries in the camera because we seem to have a Lover's Lane in the cul-de-sac."

"In the what?"

"At the end of the street, Babe!"

"For real?"

"Yes, I've seen a couple of unusual cars sitting down there. There's one particular dark-colored car that's been passing by lately. It goes to the end of the street, drives slowly, stops for a few minutes, and then leaves."

"Wow, really?" My first thought was that KJ's dad was probably driving by, looking at my house.

"How are you feeling today?" Myles asked.

"Better today than yesterday."

"Okay. I miss you, my lady. I'll see you at 1:00." I heard him laughing as he hung up the phone.

I sat there trying to figure out how I could surprise Myles when he got home. I put the CD in the player in our bedroom, took the ponytail out of my hair to let my hair hang down, put on lipstick, and sat on the stool, waiting for him to come in. "Because You Love Me" was on repeat. When he came in, he hugged me and said, "I love that song! Where did you get it?" I told him the short story of how that song came to be. "Wow! Now, every time I come home, I want that song playing—and I want you looking just like you are now!" he said with a kiss. "I've missed you, my lady."

"You just left me five hours ago!"

"I know, I know. Still, I've missed you."

At 2:45 p.m., we received a call from the intercom company letting us know the technicians would arrive in 15 minutes. Getting dressed, Myles said, "You won't believe this. I got a call this morning from a man who said he dropped off his child's iPad nine or ten months ago, and he's ready to pick it up!" We laughed. "He said my dad accepted the device and that he still had the receipt. I told him I'd have my secretary look into it and call him back if we locate it. You should have seen Mrs. Clark's face when I told her. She couldn't believe it! We looked everywhere for that darn thing, finally locating it at the very bottom of a box my dad kept for overdue pick-ups. Lexie, that thing had been there for a year and two months!"

"For real? That man owes y'all for storage!"

"Right?! Well, I'm glad we found it. That prompted me to ask Mrs. Clark to go through that box and try to contact the owners, informing them that if they did not claim their items, they would be sold. We'll get our storage money one way or another!" We were cracking up by then. "When they finish installing the system here, I'm going back to the shop to meet the man, give him his iPad, and lock everything up. Oh! I'm going to have the technicians check all the smoke and carbon monoxide detectors while they're here."

DING, DONG! DING DONG!

"That must be them," Myles said, going to open the door. I heard him say, "This way."

One of the men said, "Nice house!" From their conversations, I could tell it was two techs. The man must have seen the picture of me sitting on the table and asked, "Is this a picture of your wife?"

"Yes, it is," Myles replied. Even from the confines of the room, I could hear the smile in his voice when he spoke. The trio went upstairs. I sat there wondering who the man was asking about me. His voice sounded familiar. The men were upstairs for about 30 minutes before coming back down. They headed into the family room.

I then heard that same man ask, "Is that your wife's dad?"

"Yes," Myles answered.

"Is your wife's name Lexie?"

"Yes."

"Man, your wife is my cousin!" I heard the excitement in his voice. "Is she at work?"

"No, she's in the back. I'll get her." He came into the room and said, "A man out there said he's your cousin and wants to see you." Myles helped me up and held my arm as I wobbled into the family room.

When I saw my cousin Matthew, I cried. "Oh, my God! Matthew!"

"Lexie! I haven't seen you since before you went into the Air Force. Girl, you are looking good. Carrying a little weight in the front of you, I see!"

"Hmph! Not a little weight; a lot of weight! I can't believe you're here! Is so nice to see you. Matthew, this is my husband, Myles."

"We've met," Myles said. "I wondered why this man was asking questions about my wife when he saw your picture." We all shared a laugh.

"So, how are Kathy and Liz?" I asked.

"Kathy is doing well. She has five-year-old twin girls, and I have twin boys. They are eight years old. Liz is doing well, too," Matthew said with a smile.

"Well, I'm having twins, too. A boy and a girl. I also have an eight-year-old son. He's at school right now."

The other man was hard at work and said to Matthew, "I need your help with this wire."

That was my cue to end our chat. "It was nice to see you again, Matthew. Please leave your number with Myles."

The men were finished within the hour. Matthew yelled back to me, "Take care of yourself! I'll be in touch with you again soon!"

"Okay, Matthew! Good to see you!"

After they left, Myles came into the room. "Here's his number. I know you were happy to see your cousin."

"Yes, I was. Before my dad died, we were together all the time. When my dad died, they stopped coming around. I would only see my cousins at school. Their mother didn't like my mom because she said my mom thought she was better than they were."

Myles laughed and replied, "You know, I thought that about you when I saw you running with that ponytail sticking out of your cap, bouncing as you ran. I thought to myself, 'She's fine, but she looks stuck-up.'"

"What?! You thought I was stuck-up from a simple run down the street?!"

"I sure did!" I threw a pillow at him. He came over, hugged me, and said, "I thought that about you then, but I now know you are for sure!"

"No, I'm not!" He laughed and landed pecks all over my face, knowing I was helpless and couldn't fight him off.

"I'm getting ready to go pick up KJ. I'll take him with me to meet the man at the shop and then turn on the alarm. There are too many computers in that place for someone to break in and clean me out. Before I leave, let's try the intercom system. When I get upstairs, push this button and talk." He ran to the top of the stairs and spoke softly into the intercom. "Can you hear me?"

I pushed the button. "Yes, I can."

Talking on the intercom, he replied, "Now, you don't have to come upstairs while you are carrying Karson and Kaylin!" He came back down and said, "I like that system. The men confirmed all the detectors are working properly, too. I gotta run now. I'll see you around six. Oh! And don't cook. I'll make a taco salad for dinner when we get back."

When he left, I remained sitting in the room, thinking about how nice it was to see Matthew. I reminisced about how Kathy and I used to play together when their dad would bring them over to our house. I thought to myself, "Once I have these babies, I want all of us to get together again so that I can meet their twins." I laid back, closed my eyes, and went to sleep.

Chapter 79

I was awakened by KJ saying, "Hi, Mama! I had a good day at school!"

"Give me a hug. I'm glad you had a good day."

"Mama, I'm going upstairs to do my homework so that I can play on my tablet when I'm done." He took off, running up the stairs.

Myles came into the room, taking a quick break from making dinner. "Watch this," he said. He went to the intercom and pushed the button. "KJ, what are you doing? I see you!" He then ran back to the kitchen, working on the salad.

KJ came running downstairs, freaking out. "Mama! Somebody is up there! They said they see me!"

I couldn't keep a straight face. "They did?"

"Yes! Somebody is up there!"

"Son, there's no one upstairs but you. There are only three of us in the house. You are here, I am here, and Myles is in the kitchen."

He was insistent. "But Mama, I heard a voice up there!"

"Boy, there's nobody else here. Go upstairs and finish your homework." He left the room, walking very slowly. Myles came back. "Stop scaring my baby!"

He was laughing so hard. "Just one more time." He pushed the button again and said, "KJ, are you doing your homework?"

That time, KJ came down crying. In his hand, he held his homework. "Mama, there is somebody up there!" He was hysterical.

"Go and tell Myles someone is upstairs." I could hear Myles in the kitchen, laughing his heart out.

"Myles, somebody is upstairs and keeps calling my name!" KJ said through his sobs.

Myles hugged him and said, "Calm down Peanut. It was me." He had KJ follow him into the sitting room. "Stand here and push this button. Wait for me to get upstairs. When I get up there, tell me to come back downstairs." He went up and instructed KJ to talk into the intercom.

"Come downstairs, Myles."

Myles' voice floated through the intercom, "Okay, KJ. Here I come."

When he got back downstairs, KJ said, "That's cool!"

"So, you see? No one else is in here. And now, we don't have to yell for you. We can speak directly into the intercom, and you can push the button upstairs to talk to us down here!" Myles said, adding a rub to KJ's head.

Around 8:30 p.m., we settled down for the night. KJ took his shower and went to bed. I took my shower and then tried to find something to wear to the doctor's appointment the next day. "Myles, what am I going to wear tomorrow? I can't fit any of these clothes anymore. Everything is too small!"

He got up, looked through my closet, and pulled out a loose-fitting dress. "What about this?"

"That's too small now, too."

"I have a new V-neck t-shirt. It's a size 2X. Maybe you can fit it and wear these black pants," he said while holding up the pants.

I looked down at my immense belly and asked, "Do you think I can fit a 2X?"

"I'll get it so that you can try it on." He laughed at the expression on my face.

I tried on the shirt, and it fit perfectly. "Thanks, Honey. This will work. You're a life saver. I refuse to buy any more big clothes at this point."

Myles nodded and laughed at me. Going to the intercom, he said, "KJ, what are you doing?"

We waited for a few seconds and then heard, "I'm getting ready for bed."

"Okay, son. Goodnight," Myles replied.

Before he released the talk button, I said, "Goodnight, baby. I love you."

"Mama, I'm not a baby anymore!"

"You're right. Goodnight, KJ."

"Goodnight. I love you, Mama. Tell Myles I love him, too!"

"He hears you!"

On Thursday morning, I woke up extremely hungry. I made pancakes, eggs, and bacon for breakfast. I called KJ through the intercom and told him to come down to eat. He was fully dressed when he came into the kitchen. "KJ, you are looking nice this morning!"

"I know," he replied. He sat down to eat, looked at Myles, and said, "I need to tell you something when you pick me up later."

"About what?" Myles asked with a grin on his face.

"What do you need to tell Myles?" I asked.

KJ looked at me in all seriousness and said, "Mama, you wouldn't understand."

"Okay, Peanut. We'll talk in private later. Let's go so you won't miss your bus." Myles cleaned up our dishes, putting them in the dishwasher. "Are you ready to go, Lexie?"

"Yes, I am." We dropped off KJ at Mae's house and then headed to the doctor's appointment. "I wonder what KJ wants to tell you."

"I have no idea. We will see this afternoon—if he still wants to talk about whatever it is."

We made it to the doctor's office and signed in. Before we could sit down, the nurse said, "You can follow me back, Mr. and Mrs. Ferguson. We're going into Room 2. How are you feeling today?" she asked, smiling at me.

"Pretty good, but I'll feel better when these babies are born."

She smiled at me while taking my vitals. "The doctor will be here in a few minutes," she said before leaving.

Dr. Jessica came in with a big smile on her face. "How are you feeling, Lexie? The last time I saw you, you were in the hospital full of gas." We all laughed. "Come. Have a seat on the bed." Myles helped me stand and then sit on the bed. "Well, your blood pressure is good. I see the swelling in your feet has gone down. Your weight is 180, which isn't bad. What's your normal weight?"

"140 to 145 pounds."

"35 pounds or so isn't bad for someone carrying twins. Lay back. Let's see what these babies are up to in there." Dr. Jessica rubbed the gel on my belly, and the babies started moving around. "Wow! They sure are active! Did you choose names for them yet?"

"Yes, we have. Kaylin Rose and Karson Lee. My eight-year-old's name is Keith."

"Beautiful names, all beginning with Ks!" she replied. The monitor sprung to life, and we could see the babies, looking like they were in there playfighting. "The babies are big. If I don't see you before then, I'm looking at doing a C-Section on you on the 19th to get them out of you."

"The 19th? Of this month?" I asked.

"Yes, Mrs. Lexie! In less than two weeks, these babies should be here." Myles looked like he was about to faint as he rubbed his hair back. "Do you have any questions for me?" she asked.

"Not right now. On or before the 19th," I murmured.

"Yes, ma'am. You can get dressed now," Dr. Jessica said, patting me on the back.

Myles helped me off the bed and said, "Babe, I'll bring the truck closer so you won't have to walk as far."

As I waited for him to pull the truck to the front door, I had a chance to talk to Jessica. "Guess who came to my house yesterday?"

"Who?"

"Matthew."

"For real?! Matthew? That man was almost my husband."

"He asked you to marry him?" I asked with surprise.

"Well, we talked about it," she said sadly.

"I know you two were dating when I went into the Air Force. What happened?"

"I went out with James. That's what happened."

"Jessica, you didn't even like James!"

"I know. Do you remember Sonya from school?" she asked.

"Yes, I remember her."

"Well, she had a get-together for our graduating class. She told me that if I saw any of our classmates, let them know about the party because she didn't have everyone's number. The week before the party, I saw James at the store, told him about it, and he said he wanted to come. On the day of the party, I didn't have a ride, so I called and asked James if I could ride with him. He said yes. That night, I think somebody spiked the punch because I somehow ended up drunk and in the backseat of James' car. That would have never happened in the right state of mind because I was dating Matthew."

"Jessica, no you didn't. In the backseat of his car?"

"Yes, I did. Two months later, I found out I was pregnant."

"How did you know it wasn't Matthew's baby?"

"Matthew had been out of town for four months at that time. I was pregnant and married by the time he returned. Lexie, I didn't know what else to do, so I married James. Although I didn't love him, I knew he loved me—and had gotten me pregnant. Girl, when I ran into Matthew a year or so later at Walmart, my oldest son was almost two years old. He asked me why I didn't wait for him."

"What did you say?"

"The only thing I could manage to say was sorry. Lexie, how is he doing? How does he look now?"

"I guess he's doing okay. In high school, he was skinny, but now, he's muscular. I must say, he looks good. He said he has twin boys, but he didn't say anything about a wife."

"Girl! For real? Did he say anything about me?"

"No, we didn't talk long because he was at my house to install an intercom system. It was my first time seeing him in over ten years."

"Wow…" she replied.

"Jessica, before Myles, I married someone I loved, but I wasn't in love with him. We were best friends, and I enjoyed his company. After my mom died, I was so lonely, and he was the one there for me. We were married for a little over a year before he asked me for a divorce. Divorcing him was the best decision I could have made. It allowed Myles to come into my life. He loves me, and he loves my son. At least your husband loves you."

"Yes, he's a good husband, but if I'm honest with you and me, I'm not in love with him. I never was. I'm trying to make it work for our son's sake. I think I still have feelings for Matthew," she replied.

"Jessica, forget about Matthew. You have a husband who loves you. That should count for something."

"I know what you mean."

I changed the conversation because I saw that she was getting emotional. "How's your mom?" I asked.

"She's great! As a matter of fact, when I told her you were one of my patients, she told me to tell you hello and that she would love to see you."

"Please tell her hello for me. After I have the babies, I'd love to visit her, if that's okay with you."

"Girl, you are welcome to come out any time you want!"

Myles came in and asked, "Are you ready to go?"

"Yes, I am." I turned to Dr. Jessica, hugged her, and said, "I enjoyed our conversation."

She smiled and replied, "You will get a call or letter from my office to let you know what time to come to the hospital on the 19th."

"Okay. Thank you, doctor."

"I'll see you on the 19th or before!"

Chapter 80

Myles asked if I wanted anything to eat on our way home before he dropped me off. "No, we can have Sloppy Joes, fries, and salad for dinner. I have all the ingredients at home. I need to call Sharon to let her know when I'm scheduled to have the C-Section. Myles, do you realize we will have Kaylin and Karson in less than two weeks?!"

"I don't even know how to think clearly right now," he said, rubbing my hand softly.

"I think Jessica is still in love with Matthew," I said out of nowhere.

"Who? Your cousin Matthew?"

"Yes."

"Why do you think that?"

"She was in love with Matthew but slept with another man and got pregnant."

"Wow, that's messed up. Didn't you say she's married now?"

"Yes, she married the man who impregnated her."

Myles rubbed his forehead, turned to me, and said, "Lexie, stay out of it." We rode the rest of the way home in silence. It was obvious both of us had things on our minds. When we pulled up to the house, he helped me inside to get comfortable. "I need to run to the shop. I'll be back around 4:00 with KJ and Spot." He kissed me and left.

I sat there thinking, "In eight days, I'll have my babies. Thank You, Jesus!" I decided to call Sharon after baking a chocolate cake, giving her time to get home from work. I knew Myles and KJ would be surprised to see a cake in a flavor they both loved. My thoughts diverted to what Jessica said about Matthew and how she wished they were still together. Just then, my phone rang. I looked at the caller ID and saw it was Kathy, Matthew's sister. I answered the call.

"Lexie? This is Kathy. Matthew said he was at your house yesterday."

"Yes, he was. How have you been?" I asked.

"I'm good. Girl, it's been a long time since I saw you. It's been what? Over ten years? Matthew told me you are pregnant with twins! Congratulations!"

"Thank you. And yes, it has been too long since I've seen you guys. It was nice to see Matthew after all those years. I'm scheduled to give birth to my twins in eight days or less," I replied.

"I have twins, and so does Matthew. It must be a family thing. Twins run in the Harris family," she said, laughing.

"We must get together after I have my babies. I'll invite you guys over so I can meet your twins. Kathy, how is Liz?"

"She's doing good."

"How's your mom?"

She paused before answering. "Mom passed away a year ago."

"Kathy, I'm so sorry to hear that. I didn't know."

She quickly changed the conversation. "Matthew told me you live in a mansion!"

"I won't call it that. It's just a big house," I said, laughing at the tone in her voice.

"Well, I must make the trip to see your big house," she said, joining me in the laugh. "Since I now know how to get in touch with you, I'll call again soon. I'm at work right now, so I gotta run. I enjoyed our chat!"

"We'll talk again soon, Kathy. Bye for now."

I then called Sharon to let her know when the babies were scheduled to be born. "Okay! Great! I'll fly in on the 18th. Tell Myles I'll call him with my itinerary once I get the flight information."

"Okay. We'll be happy to have you here. You're planning on staying with us, right?"

"Of course!"

"Great! I look forward to you coming!" We said our goodbyes and hung up.

After the call, I decided to go upstairs to make sure the suite was ready for Sharon. Plus, I wanted to see where they installed the intercom system. I thought to myself, "I'll make sure I'm back downstairs before Myles gets back." Slowly, I made my way upstairs. I saw where they placed the intercom and then walked into the suite. Everything was in order. On my way back, I peeked into KJ's room and saw he had made his bed, although he had left his toys all over the floor. Suddenly, I started feeling dizzy. I went into the upstairs sitting room and sat down. "I can't let Myles catch me up here," I said aloud. As I walked out of the room, fear came over me, and a flood of thoughts entered my mind.

What if I get dizzy and fall down the stairs?

I shouldn't have come up here!

What was I thinking?

Lord, help me!

I was truly fearful that I would fall when I walked down the stairs. The thoughts kept coming.

What will Myles say if he catches me up here?

He told me not to go upstairs.

I supported my belly with one hand and held the railing with the other, trying to take that first step down. I couldn't do it. I couldn't even see my feet! I then sat at the edge of the steps and considered scooting my way down but couldn't do that, either. I was too heavy to lift myself.

The house phone rang. There was no way I could get to it in time. A few seconds later, my cell phone rang. I knew it was Myles calling. I sat there with a dilemma: If I stood, I might fall and kill my babies and myself. I froze in place. Both phones rang again, back-to-back. I was in a panic.

I remained sitting on the edge of the steps for about 20 minutes until I heard KJ run into the house, calling for me. I saw him run past and go into my bedroom. When Myles called out for me, I yelled, "I'm up here!"

"Up where?!" he yelled back. He finally found me, sitting motionless at the top of the stairs. "What are you doing up there?! Didn't I tell you not to go upstairs?!" He had never yelled at me before. By the expression on his face, I could tell he was angry. I started to cry. He stood at the bottom of the stairs, rubbing his hair back and looking at me while shaking his head. He walked up to help me back down, instructing me to hold onto the railing. KJ was right there to help.

"I am sorry, Myles. I wanted to see the room where Sharon will be sleeping and see where they put the intercom." He helped me get settled on a stool at the island in the kitchen. He didn't say anything in response to me, though. I knew he was disappointed in me for not listening to him. He just rubbed back his hair, which let me know he was not happy. He walked into the bedroom without a word, with KJ walking behind him. After a few minutes passed, he came back to the kitchen and just stared at me.

"Myles, are you going to punish Mama for not listening to you?" KJ asked. "Mama was hardheaded, wasn't she, Myles?" Myles had a discouraging look but didn't say anything.

I looked at my husband, knowing he wanted to laugh at what KJ just said, but he didn't. When he finally spoke, he directed his question to KJ. "What punishment should I give her for not listening to me?"

"Maybe she can't kiss you for two weeks," KJ said with all seriousness.

"That's not punishing her, Peanut; that's punishing me."

"Well, how about you can kiss her, but she can't kiss you back?" Obviously thinking he solved the issue, he quickly turned and went back upstairs.

Myles finally looked at me and said, "Do you now see why I told you not to go upstairs? What if you would have fallen? When I called the house and cell phone, and you didn't answer, I immediately thought the worst."

"I'm sorry. It won't happen again." I slowly stood, wobbled over to him, and attempted to kiss him.

He threw his hand up, saying, "Remember: You are on punishment. You can't kiss me."

"Myles, I just wanted to see how it looked up there before Sharon got here. I talked to her, and she said she would be here on the 18th. You'll have to pick her up, but she will call you with the time and flight information."

"You going upstairs was reckless. It could have waited until I returned." After those words were spoken, he turned and went into the bedroom. I had never been the target of Myles' anger before. I disliked how I made the love of my life feel toward me.

Chapter 81

KJ came to sit beside me at the island with his progress report and homework. "Mama, I'm doing good in all my classes. Here's my homework."

"Let me see. Wow, you are doing good!" I kissed and hugged him as we wiped my kiss away. I sat listening to him tell me all about his day at school.

"Mama, this boy said he was going to beat me up."

"Why does he want to fight you?"

"I don't know. What should I do?"

"Tell your teacher."

"But he still might want to beat me up, and I don't want to fight him."

"KJ, I don't know what to say. How about talking to Myles when he wakes up? For now, go wash your hands so we can eat. And can you stop by the room to let Myles know the food is ready, please?"

As Myles walked out of the room, he said, "You made a chocolate cake."

"Yes, I hope you like it."

When KJ came back, he asked Myles, "What do I do when somebody wants to fight me?"

"Who is this somebody, KJ?" Myles asked as he reached for his plate.

"This boy in school keeps following me, saying he's going to beat me up."

KJ and Myles continued their conversation while eating. I thought to myself, "Maybe he has forgotten about me going upstairs." I broke into their chat. "Myles, you need to call KJ's dad to see if he wants his son to go over there tomorrow."

"I don't want to go over there," KJ said sadly.

"Why not? You haven't been over there since Mama Brenda had the baby. That was six weeks ago. You don't want to see your brother and baby sister?" I asked.

"No."

"You will only be there for three nights."

"I still don't want to go."

Myles stopped us both. "Lexie, I'll talk to him when I get back from my run and call his dad." He then turned to KJ. "When you finish eating, empty all the trash cans upstairs and downstairs. Put the trash in the big trash can in the garage, and we will take it to the curb when I get back from my run. Making sure the trash is out of the house is your job from now on. Now, go upstairs and do your homework."

"I already did my homework while you were asleep."

"Good. Then bring it down so Mama can look over it. Then, you can go outside. We'll talk when I get back."

"Mama already looked over my homework."

Myles looked at me and said, "When I get back, I might want another slice of that cake." I could tell he hadn't completely forgiven me for going upstairs, but at least he smiled.

"Me, too!" KJ said.

While Myles was out on his run, I prayed, "Lord, help him forgive me for going upstairs." I waited to see if KJ would do what Myles told him to do. When he finished his piece of cake, he grabbed a plastic bag and went upstairs. He returned with the trash from the upstairs and downstairs rooms and then put the bag in the big trash can in the garage. I thought to myself, "My baby is growing up."

He came back inside and said, "Mama, I finished what Myles told me to do. Are you done looking over my homework?"

"Yes, I am. Put it in your bookbag, and then you can go outside." I was surprised he did everything Myles told him to do. I thought, "That Karate class he's in is helping. His whole attitude has changed. I can see he's following instructions better."

I thought back to the day we went to his Karate playoff program. He didn't win, but I saw he had increased confidence in himself. When he lost, he didn't even get upset. He told Myles, "I will win 1st Place the next time."

Myles laughed and rubbed his head. "Peanut, 3rd Place is not bad. Keep practicing, and you'll do better the next time. Plus, those were some big boys you were up against." KJ was so happy. That day, Myles dropped me and my big belly off at home, and the two of them went to Applebee's to celebrate KJ's 3rd Place win.

By the time I finished cleaning the kitchen, I looked out of the window and saw Myles returning from his run. He and KJ were outside horseplaying, putting the trash on the curb. I was in the bedroom when they came in. I heard Myles talking to KJ's dad on the phone.

"How are you and the family?... I am calling to see if you want KJ this weekend... Okay, he will see you tomorrow... Thank you... Bye."

As he walked into the room, Myles said, "There's something about that man. I can't put my mind on it right now, but for one, he is conceited." He went to take his shower.

I laid there, thinking about KJ not wanting to go to his dad's house. I already knew Keith would ask him all kinds of questions about us.

When Myles exited the shower, he said, "You know, that run tired me out! I'm coming to bed, so I need the three of you to move over." He kissed me goodnight and was sound asleep within a matter of minutes. I thought to myself, "Thank You, Jesus! He didn't say anything more about me going upstairs."

The next morning, I was up early so that I could talk to KJ before he left for school. I knew I wouldn't see him again until Monday afternoon. When Myles got ready to leave, he kissed me on my forehead and said, "Please don't go upstairs." I hugged KJ, and they left.

I went back to bed. As I laid there, I felt the babies moving around. "We only have seven days to go," I said to them. My rest was interrupted when the phone rang. I looked at the caller ID and saw it was Pastor Montgomery calling me from his church. "Maybe he is calling to say he doesn't want KJ to come over this weekend," I thought. I picked up the phone. "Hello?"

"Hi," he replied.

"Why are you calling? Did you change your mind about KJ coming?"

"No, I want to know why you have that man calling my house about my son. I know when I want to see my son."

"My husband's name is Myles, not that man. And I asked him to call because I don't want to talk to you. Do you want KJ to come over or not?"

"Yes, but I want you to ask me, not that man. Plus, I love hearing your voice."

"Bye, Pastor Montgomery." I hung up the phone, and he called right back. I didn't answer.

Around 11:00, my doorbell rang. I peeked out of the window and saw Mrs. Riddle standing at the door. When I opened the door, she looked at me wide-eyed and said, "Girl, you look too big to be walking!"

"Mrs. Riddle, you're not supposed to come until tomorrow."

"Can't I stop by to see how you are doing?" she asked.

I started to laugh, making the connection. "Myles called you, didn't he?"

"Well, yes, he did. He thinks you will do something you are not supposed to do—like going back upstairs and being afraid to come back down. You know, you really shouldn't have gone up there, Lexie."

"Yes, ma'am. I know. I was just being nosy."

"Tell me what you need to have done. I will be here until 4:00."

"Mrs. Riddle, you don't have to babysit me."

"Look, I was hired by the boss to come here today instead of tomorrow," she said, laughing.

"In that case, can you make sure the upstairs suite is ready for our guest? Myles' sister will be here on Wednesday. Did he tell you we are scheduled to have the babies on Thursday?"

"Yes, he did. How do you feel about that?"

"Honestly, I'm just ready for this to be over with," I said, pointing to my belly. Myles called at 12:30. "I don't need a babysitter, Myles."

He was laughing and said, "So, she's there?"

"Yes, she's upstairs, making sure the suite is ready for Sharon. Myles, Keith called me this morning."

"What's wrong? Did he change his mind about KJ coming?"

"No, he wanted to know why you're the one calling him about his son and then said he just loves hearing my voice."

"What did you just say?!"

"It's okay, Babe. I told him I didn't want to talk to him and hung up the phone. He called right back, but I didn't answer."

Myles paused and then said, "I'll talk to him."

"What are you going to say?"

He didn't answer that question. Instead, he asked me one. "Do you want to go out on a date tonight?"

"As big as I am?"

"You'll be with your husband, my lady!"

"Okay. Sure. Let's go out. I'll be happy to go as long as you don't mind me wobbling around behind you." We both laughed, imagining the wobble. Getting off the phone, I said aloud, "Thank You, Jesus! My husband has forgiven me and is taking me out to dinner!" I used the intercom to ask Mrs. Riddle if she could come down and wash and blow dry my hair.

She came to the edge of the stairs and asked, "How do I answer you using this thing?" We both busted out laughing.

"Push the red button and talk."

She pushed the button and replied, "I'll be right down." When she got downstairs, she said, "I like that!"

"Myles had it installed to keep me from walking upstairs."

"Lexie, you got a good husband—much better than that other one you were married to."

"Talking about Keith… He's been harassing me."

"What?!"

"It started before he found out I was going to marry Myles. He stopped for a while after that, but he started again. At first, I didn't even tell Myles about it because I figured he would stop once we were married, but he didn't. Once I told him about the harassment, he started dropping off KJ at his dad's house and picking him up so that I wouldn't have to see or meet him anymore. Well, last night, Myles called Keith to see if he wanted KJ to come over this weekend. Mind you, we haven't heard so much as a peep from Keith in almost two months, and this will be his first weekend with KJ in six weeks. Anyway, Keith called today and asked me why I had Myles calling him about KJ and not me, adding that he loves hearing my voice. I told him I didn't want to talk to him and hung up the phone. He called back, but I didn't answer."

"Did you tell Myles he called you?"

"Yes, Myles said he will talk to him."

"Your husband is a smart, saved man. He knows what to do."

I enjoyed talking to Mrs. Riddle while she did my hair. When she finished, I did my nails and makeup. As I looked at myself in the mirror, I said, "I do look cute—big belly and all!"

Chapter 82

At 4:00 p.m., Mrs. Riddle left. Myles came in at 4:15 with a dozen red roses and said, "Babe, you look good, and I love your hair."

"Thank you. Mrs. Riddle always does an excellent job with my hair. Look at my fingernails! I did them myself."

"They look good, too. Let me snap a couple of pictures of us before we leave." After taking our pictures, he asked, "Are you ready?"

"Yes, I am—and we're ready to eat," I replied, pointing to the babies.

"Me, too!" Myles said.

We went to Outback Steakhouse. "You always eat at Cracker Barrel. Why Outback Steakhouse tonight?" I asked.

"I wanted a steak and large baked potato, so here we are!"

"Whatever I eat, I hope it doesn't give me indigestion."

He laughed and said, "I hope so, too! That day when you were in the hospital, I thought I was back in Iraq!"

"Stop it, Myles!" We were laughing so hard, tears were coming out of our eyes.

After giving the waitress our order, we sat there talking. Myles said, "I talked to Keith today."

"What did he say?"

"It's not what he said; it's what I told him. Let me say this: I don't think he will be calling you again." Just then, the waitress returned with our food.

My seat was facing the door. "Myles, don't turn around. Keith's here with a man."

"Does he see you?"

"No, the waitress is showing them to their seats."

"When I am done eating, I am going over to speak to him."

"Myles…"

"I got this, Lexie. I'm sure what we talked about today is still fresh in his mind."

I watched as the waitress took their order. Just like Myles said, when he finished eating, he stood and said, "I'll be back in a few minutes." I sat there thinking, "I've seen that man Keith's with somewhere before." Myles approached their table, said something, and then pointed toward me. After a few minutes, Myles turned and walked back to our table, smiling. When he sat down, I asked, "What did you say?"

"I went over and said, 'Hi, Pastor Montgomery. How are Mrs. Montgomery and the new baby?' 'They are good,' he answered. The other guy was just sitting there, playing with a spoon on the table. Keith looked at me like he didn't know who I was and even asked me, 'Who are you?' I said, 'Remember we spoke today?' He said, 'Ooooh.' I then asked him to tell his wife hello from Lexie and me. I introduced myself to the other guy since Keith seemed to have left his manners outside somewhere. He said his name was Sam. After a few more nice words, I turned and walked away."

"You know, I think I've seen that man somewhere," I said.

"I can't believe Keith acted as if he didn't' know me. How could he forget what I looked like after six weeks? As many times as he saw me drop off KJ… Lexie, I'm telling you: There is something about him," he said as he rubbed his hair back.

When Sam suddenly left, he had a carryout box in his hand. "Now I know where I've seen that man. Before I married Keith, we were in the mall. I went into the shoe store, and Keith went into Blackstone's. When I came out, they talked until I started to approach them. Keith said the guy was one of his friends from school who was moving to Arkansas. I also saw him with Keith on your birthday at the store."

"Well, Sam is back in town visiting, I guess. Come to think of it, he's the same guy I saw with Keith a couple of weeks ago when I picked up supplies for the shop," Myles said. "I saw him going into the bank with that man the day you ran that lady out of the shop." Myles was laughing so hard.

"Stop saying I did that!" I joined in the laughter.

"Well, you did run her away!"

When we left, Keith was still sitting at the table.

"It's early. Do you want to go to the movies? There are no stairs to walk up." Myles asked.

"I don't feel like walking anywhere else but into our house."

"Okay. No more walking. Let's go for a ride around town. That way, you don't have to walk anywhere. You can just ride and look pretty."

"That sounds good to me. Anything's better than walking."

We drove past the old Opry House, and he showed me where they lived when they first came to Nashville to live with his Uncle Eddie. They lived in the suburbs, northeast of the big water slides. Once I got tired of riding around, I told Myles I was ready to go home. When we arrived, Myles had to help me inside. That night, as I tried to sleep, the twins moved around like they were playing ball in my belly.

Chapter 83

Waking up early Saturday morning, I made breakfast: oatmeal, wheat toast, eggs, turkey bacon, and orange juice. After eating, I sat out on the patio, reading my devotions. I heard Myles calling out for me. "I'm on the patio."

He came out and asked, "How long have you been up?"

"Since 8:30. Breakfast is ready."

He looked at his watch. "It's almost 10:00. I told Rodrick to come over at 11:00 to help me move the couch to make room for the nursery and mount the TV on the wall over the fireplace. If he has time, we'll put the babies' crib together. Once we start, I want you to stay out here until we are done."

"But I want to see what you're doing!"

"No, I want you to be surprised when you see it!" he said, eating his breakfast.

"Do you think we need to put up both cribs right now?" I asked.

"No, I think they can sleep together until they start standing on their own."

At 11:00 sharp, the doorbell rang. Myles said, "The little lawyer is on time." He went to let him in. "Hi, Rodrick! Are you ready to work?"

He laughed and replied, "Yes, I am here to work. Where's Aunt Lexie?"

"She's on the patio."

"Hi, Aunt Lexie!" he yelled.

"Hi, Rodrick!" I yelled back.

I could hear them talking and laughing as they worked. "Uncle, this is a large bedroom back here!"

"Yes, it is. Let's put the couch here, and we will move the table over there by the window. Do you think you have time to help me put one of the cribs together?" Myles asked.

"Sure! That's easy to do," Rodrick replied.

They were chatting and laughing while putting the crib together. I then heard Myles say, "I'll call you back in six to eight months to put the other crib together."

"Okay. You know, it really looks good back here. It looks like you have more space with the way you rearranged everything."

"Yes, it does," Myles responded.

I couldn't wait to see what they had done. I called out and asked Myles to look in my office, get the babies' dressers, and put them in the nursery. I added, "Their names are already on them."

When they finished, Myles came to help me up so that I could see the room. I walked into my bedroom and saw how they had transformed my sitting room into a nursery. It was beautiful! "How do you like it?" Myles asked.

"It's amazing!"

"I thought you would like it," he said, kissing me on my forehead.

"Rodrick, since you helped Myles, I'd like to invite you to dinner after church on Sunday."

"I'd like to come, but may I bring my girlfriend? She comes to church with me on Sundays."

"Does your mom and dad know you have a girlfriend?" Myles asked jokingly.

"Yes, uncle. This is my second year in college. I am almost 20. They know I have a girlfriend. As a matter of fact, she comes to our house nearly every Sunday. She's from Saginaw, Michigan, and doesn't go home until the Thanksgiving and Christmas holidays."

"What's her name?" I asked.

"Ashley Marie James."

"Ashley is a pretty name," I replied.

"She's a year older than me. She transferred from Michigan State and is studying to be a pediatrician. I really like her. I met her parents. Her mother is a nurse. Her name is Marie. Her father is a General Foreman at the Cadillac plant in Lansing, Michigan. His name is Jack. She has two brothers and a younger sister." He looked at Myles as if he wanted Myles to ask him something else. "So, do you approve, uncle?"

"Hey, I just asked you one question, and you gave us your girlfriend's life story." We all started laughing. "But yes, I approve. We'll be glad to meet her."

Rodrick was laughing so hard, he had to sit down. "I suppose that's the lawyer in me, pleading my case." He left around 2:30, saying he had football practice starting at 4:00.

After he left, I sat in my bedroom and looked around at the babies' nursery. KJ suddenly crossed my mind. I missed him.

The phone rang. On the other end was Sharon, calling to tell Myles what time to pick her up from the airport on Wednesday. When he got off the phone, he was laughing and said, "Sharon will be here on Wednesday to boss me around." He came and sat next to me, looking around at how the sitting room was transformed into a nursery. "Only five more days, Lexie, and we'll have two babies in that crib."

"I am getting excited and nervous. Two babies? Oh, my Lord!"

"You will be alright. I'm here. We'll do this parenting thing together. Are you sure you will feel okay having people over for dinner on Sunday? I already paid Rodrick for the work he did."

"Right now, I'm feeling great. Tomorrow, I don't know how I'll feel, but I'll make it happen," I replied.

"Do you need me to pick up anything from the store?"

"No, not for tomorrow, but I know we'll need some things before Sharon arrives. I'll get a grocery list together for you."

On Sunday morning, Myles was up early for Sunday school and church. He brought me breakfast in bed. "Myles, you are so sweet."

"Yes, I know. Are you sure you don't want me to pick up something from the store for our dinner guests?"

"No, I have everything I need for dinner tonight."

"What are you going to cook?" he asked.

"It's going to be a surprise. I hope you like it."

He kissed me and said, "I love everything you cook, just like I love everything about you."

"Okay, lover boy. You better get going, or you'll be late for Sunday school." After he left, I ate my breakfast and stayed in bed, thinking about me having the babies on Thursday. At some point, I dozed off. When I woke up, it was 12:30. I got dressed, seemingly moving even slower and feeling even bigger since going to bed the previous night.

For dinner, I made meatloaf, baked mac-n-cheese, green peas and steamed carrots, rolls, lemon iced tea, and banana pudding for dessert. I thought of KJ. Banana pudding was his favorite, and he wasn't there to enjoy it with us. I missed my baby, although he didn't want me to call him my baby anymore and had some little girl following him around. I had to laugh at the thought.

I was sitting at the island in the kitchen when Myles got in from church. He said the service was good and that the pastor's message was "When Jesus Returns, Will You Be Ready?" "Babe, how are you feeling?"

"I'm not hurting, just feeling heavy and big."

"You know you didn't have to cook, right?" he asked with concern.

"I know, but I wanted to do it."

"What do you need me to do?" he asked.

"Nothing. Everything is ready." I told him all that I had made.

"That sounds good! I'm ready to eat now!" he replied. "Guess what? The pastor called me up to sing again."

"He did? What did you sing?"

"I sang "God Is Real." When I was singing, I felt the Spirit of the Lord all over me. I really felt good. By the way, I have about 45 or more packages of diapers and wipes in Pearl. It looks like everybody in the church discussed it and gave them to us as gifts."

"For real, Myles?"

"When I got ready to leave, the pastor, his wife, and all the deacons gathered around me and prayed for us. Meanwhile, the members loaded up the bags for me."

"I'll be sure to send a thank you card to the church next Sunday, thanking everyone for the gifts."

Myles looked around. "When Rodrick gets here, I'll ask him to help me bring them in and put them in your office for now."

"Okay. Can you set the food on the table in the dining room for me? They should be here soon." No sooner than those words left my mouth, the doorbell rang. Rodrick, Ashley, and Chyna had arrived.

"I hope it's okay to bring Chyna. She wanted to come," Rodrick said.

"Yes, my little Cupcake is always welcome," Myles assured him. Chyna giggled at him calling her Cupcake.

"Aunt Lexie, you got so big!" Chyna said as she hugged me.

"Yes, I am big, but I won't be for much longer."

"Excuse me, everyone. This is Ashley. Ashley, this is my Uncle Myles and Aunt Lexie." She was a pretty girl and well dressed.

"It's nice to meet you, Ashley. Welcome to our home," I said.

"Thanks for inviting me. You have a beautiful place," she replied, looking around.

"Rodrick, show Ashley around while we get the food set up on the table. When you get back, I need your help bringing in some bags from the SUV. And yes, Ashley. You and Chyna can help, too," Myles said.

"Okay, Uncle Myles," Rodrick replied, walking toward the living room.

Chyna walked into the family room, came back, and asked, "Uncle Myles, where is KJ?"

"He's visiting his little brother. You'll see him tomorrow."

"Okay," she said, leaving to join Rodrick and Ashley.

When they returned to the dining room, Ashley said, "I love your house. I really like your living room."

"The tour isn't over. You haven't seen anything yet!" Rodrick said with a knowing smile. "Aunt Lexie, can I show Ashley your bedroom, the babies' nursery, and the exercise room?"

"Yes, you can." Chyna followed them.

"When you guys finish the tour, head to the garage," Myles called out. After they finished unloading the packages, he told them to wash their hands for dinner. "Sit down, Lexie. I got this." Once seated, Myles blessed the food, and we dug in. I smiled, watching everyone enjoy the meal. "We have banana pudding and ice cream for dessert." Ashley wanted just pudding, and Rodrick and Chyna wanted both.

After eating, Rodrick and Ashley cleared the table and put the dishes in the dishwasher. We then played a couple of games of Connect 4. Myles cheated—like he always did. "I let you win," he said when he lost. We ended up playing Monopoly until it was time for them to leave. Chyna wasn't ready to go, though. "Aunt Lexie, can I stay here a little while longer?" she asked.

Myles spoke up. "Rodrick, call your mom and ask if Chyna can stay. I'll drop her off at home."

Ashley hugged me and said, "Thanks, again for inviting me to dinner. I enjoyed everything. May I come back to see the babies?"

"Yes, you are always welcome. I might want you to babysit sometimes."

She smiled and said, "Okay! I'd love that!"

Rodrick ended his call, turned to Chyna, and said, "Mama said you didn't do your homework. You have to go home. So, little one, let's go." Chyna laughed, hugged us, and walked out with Rodrick and Ashley.

Chapter 84

Monday morning, Myles went to work. Around 11:00, Mrs. Riddle arrived to sit with me again. Walking in, she said, "Good morning! Here is your mail." She leaned in to hug me.

"This is the letter I was waiting for, letting me know what time to be at the hospital on Thursday morning. It also outlines what I need to bring."

"Are you ready?"

"Yes, ma'am. I was ready two weeks ago!"

She laughed and said, "I'll be here until 4:00 again today. Myles called and asked me to come and clean the stove, throw out the leftover food in the refrigerator, and mop the bathroom floors. He doesn't want you doing it."

I was laughing as she walked into the kitchen. "Don't tell Myles, but I have already done the stove and refrigerator, and I'm feeling just fine."

"Lexie, you are hardheaded," Mrs. Riddle replied with a disappointed look. "Sit down, looking like you're ready to pop any second." I laughed, and she just shook her head at me.

"I know I must look like the Goodyear Blimp. My nose has gotten bigger, and I can't see my feet!" She laughed so hard at what I said.

Around noon, Myles called to check on me. "Stay off your feet, Lexie. Don't cook anything. I'm bringing dinner home from Cracker Barrel. I have a taste for fried chicken. What do you think?"

"Fried chicken sounds good to me, and KJ loves their chicken, too."

"Get a grocery list together. I'll go to the store on Wednesday before picking up Sharon from the airport. Starting Wednesday, I'll be home with you and the babies for three or four weeks. Ron and Mrs. Clark can run the shop. If they need me, they know how to reach me. I want you to rest now. You have three more days to go."

"Myles, I am doing fine."

"Yes, I know. That's why Mrs. Riddle will be there tomorrow, too. Babe, I gotta go. I hear an angry customer. Love you."

Mrs. Riddle finished mopping the floors. I asked her, "Would you like a sandwich, some chips, and a glass of iced tea to wash it down?"

"Yes, that sounds good—but you sit, and I'll fix it," she replied.

"Before you leave, Mrs. Riddle, I'd like to show you the babies' nursery. Myles and his nephew fixed it up on Saturday."

She finished eating and followed me into my bedroom. She stopped in the sitting room (turned nursery) and said, "This is beautiful! I have always liked the size of this room. I love the nursery. When did you get the new comforter set?"

"Myles got it the other day. He said, 'New babies, new comforter set.'"

"Well, I love it! It makes everything pop in here. The colors are beautiful," she said.

"Thank you. We are going to put up the other crib when the babies get bigger."

About that time, Myles and KJ came home. KJ ran in, calling out for me. "Mama, where are you?"

"I'm in here!" I yelled.

"Mama, I've missed you!" he said, hugging me.

"I've missed you, too."

"Hi, Mrs. Riddle!" he said, hugging her, too.

"Boy, you are getting tall!" she said, hugging him back.

He looked around the nursery and asked, "Mama, who did this?"

"Myles and Rodrick. Do you like it?"

"Wow! It's off the chain!" he said, walking over to the babies' crib. We all started laughing.

Myles was standing in the doorway and asked him, "Where did you hear that?"

He looked at Myles and replied, "It just means I like it."

Mrs. Riddle threw up her hands. "I have heard it all. Let me go home." She left, laughing hard.

Myles walked her out to her car. "Will you be here tomorrow?"

"Yes, at 11:00."

When he came back inside, he kissed me. "Yucky yuck," KJ said and then ran upstairs. "Babe, KJ really doesn't want to go back to his dad's house anymore. He asked me if I would adopt him."

"What? He asked you that, Myles?"

"Yes, he did."

"I wonder what's happening over there to make him ask that."

"Well, you know he didn't want to go over there in the first place," Myles reminded me.

"Did he ever tell you what he wanted to talk to you about?"

"Yes, we had our little talk," he replied, laughing.

"Well? What was it about?"

"I'm not sure you're ready for this, but…" He started laughing again. "He told me that sometimes, down there sticks up, and he doesn't have to pee." Myles was laughing so hard, he was bent over at the waist, holding his side.

"What did you tell him? I hope you didn't tell him one of your 'when I was your age' stories!" I shuddered at the thought.

"No, I told him little boys go through that. It just means he's growing up." As he talked, his laughter grew in intensity.

"Myles, stop laughing at my baby!" Unfortunately, I was no help because I was laughing, too.

"Lexie, you should have seen how he was looking when he told me! He told me not to tell you because you wouldn't understand." We couldn't stop laughing.

KJ came on the intercom and asked, "Who's been in my room, coloring in my circus coloring book?"

"Myles, that's on you," I whispered through my laugh.

"Chyna came over yesterday, looking for you."

"Can she come back tomorrow?" he asked.

"Come down so that you can eat dinner."

"Okay."

Still laughing, Myles went into the kitchen to reheat the food from Cracker Barrel. I called for him to come and help me up. KJ was downstairs by then and said, "Mama, I can help you."

"No, Babe. I'll bring your food in there to you," Myles replied.

"But I want to come and sit in the breakfast room. I want to eat with you guys," I whined. I glanced at my son and thought, "Oh, my God. He's growing up." Myles came and helped me go into the breakfast room.

Chapter 85

"So, KJ, what did you do at your dad's house?" Myles asked.

"Nothing. And I don't want to go back there anymore."

"You don't? How did you like your baby sister?"

"She's alright." KJ wasn't smiling at all.

I asked, "What's her name?"

"Breonna."

"That's a pretty name. Why don't you want to go back over there?" I asked, needing to know what was wrong.

"Mama Brenda treats me different from Brandon. She always yells at me, but when Brandon does something, she doesn't say anything to him."

Myles looked over at me and then got up to get the pudding and ice cream.

"What does your daddy say?" I pried.

"He doesn't say anything. Sometimes, he's not even there." When he saw the banana pudding, he said, "Wow! Banana pudding? Mama, you made this for me?"

"Yes, I had you in mind when I made it."

"Thank you, Mama!"

Myles reminded KJ, "Before it gets too late, you need to do your homework. Bring it down so your Mama can check it, and then take your bath. You can watch TV for an hour and then go to bed. Oh, yeah. And bring down those dirty clothes you brought home from your dad's house and put them in the washroom."

"I did my homework when I first got home," KJ said proudly.

"Great! Your Mama needs to see it, though."

KJ finished his food, put his plate in the sink, hugged me, and then went upstairs to get his homework.

"I don't like him being mistreated at that house. That explains where his rebellious attitude is coming from," Myles said.

"What do I do?"

"Nothing. We'll pray about it and know that God will work it out."

KJ returned with his homework, handed it to me, and then put his dirty clothes in the washroom. He came back and stood by me. I put one of my arms around him while going over his homework. "You did an excellent job on your math sheet, but you need to read this one again on your science sheet. All of them are correct except for this one," I said, pointing to the one he had wrong.

"Oh," he said, correcting it right then and there.

"Your English paper is correct, too! Have I told you lately how smart you are?"

Out of nowhere, KJ said, "Mama, can Myles be my daddy?"

"You already have a daddy." KJ hung his head low, got his homework, and went upstairs.

Myles looked over at me. "Lexie, he can have two daddies."

"True, but I wonder what really happened that bad over there to make him even ask that."

"I don't know, but he'll be alright," Myles said with surety. He put all the dirty dishes in the dishwasher, came over to me, and said, "Let me help you into the bedroom."

Once in the room, I put on my nightgown and got into bed, thinking about what KJ had asked. Myles turned on the TV to watch the news. "Babe, how are you feeling?"

"Big and heavy. I didn't know my belly could stretch this big!"

He smiled as he rubbed my big belly, saying, "Well, there are two little babies in there."

A few minutes later, KJ came in with his blanket. "Mama, can I sleep down here?"

"Why don't you want to sleep in your own bed?"

"I just want to sleep down here tonight," he answered. I figured with him just getting home from his dad's house, he wanted to be close to Myles and me.

"Okay, you can sleep down here." He walked over to my side of the bed. "Where are you going? There's already a lot of people in this bed!"

Myles was laughing so hard. "Peanut, get a sheet from the closet and get on the couch."

"I already have my blanket, though."

"Still, get a sheet to lay on." Myles changed the station from the news to the movie "NCSI."

I thought KJ was already asleep, but he said, "Mama, why didn't you answer your phone when I called? I wanted you to come and pick me up."

"Pick you up when?"

"From daddy's house. I wanted to come home early."

"Why?"

"Because Mama Brenda was mad."

"What are you saying, KJ? She didn't want you to be over there?" I asked, afraid of the answer.

"No, the baby wouldn't stop crying, and she couldn't get daddy to answer his phone."

"When was this?"

"On Friday. When daddy dropped me off, I wanted to come home, but you didn't answer your phone."

"On Friday, Myles took me out to dinner, KJ."

"Well, when daddy got home, it was late. Mama Brenda was mad. She asked daddy where he was, and he told her he was at the church. She said, 'You weren't at the church. I called the church. I called your cell phone, too. Are you back at that mess again?' Daddy asked her what she was talking about, and Mama Brenda said, 'You know what I'm talking about! That down-low mess.'"

I nudged Myles—hard.

KJ continued. "Daddy told her to lower her voice because she was going to wake up Brandon and me. I was already awake because she was talking loudly, and I couldn't go to sleep. Mama, what does down-low mess mean?"

I didn't say anything. I just laid there in disbelief at all KJ just said because we saw Keith out with a man Friday night. "KJ, I think your Mama is asleep." I wasn't, though. I laid there reminiscing about how every time I would run into Keith or see him, he was with that same man we saw him with at the restaurant. I thought about what those ladies were saying at Mother Stone's dinner, and the day he called me and said that I was the reason he started doing what he used to do. Was that what he was trying to tell me?

Before we got married, when we were shopping, he said that same man was his friend who was moving to Arkansas. He never told me his name, and I never asked. Myles said that man introduced himself as Sam. Oh, my God! That's what the 'S' stood for on those Valentine's Day flowers and candy and the 'S' on the mail that came to my house after Keith moved out! That must've been who he visited when he said he was out of town. Was Sam his lover? Oh, my God! Does Keith like women and men?! I wondered if that's what those ladies were saying when they said he made his mother cry…

KJ was quiet for a while before asking, "Myles, what does down-low mess mean?"

"Peanut, go to sleep now. We'll talk about that in the morning." Myles turned over and whispered in my ear, "Did you hear what he said? That explains why he doesn't want to go back over there anymore. They were arguing and fussing over Keith's behavior. Oh, my God! That had to be his down-low lover we saw him with Friday night. I'm here thinking he's after you, but that's a front. That arrogant, sneaky, backsliding preacher! I knew there was something strange about him. Now, how am I supposed to explain to KJ what that mess means if he asks me again tomorrow?"

I had no answer to give. I laid there, listening to Myles pray while I thought of my son's father—a preacher—being on the down-low. I wondered if KJ was telling us the truth, although there was no way he would have thought of anything like that on his own. Eventually, I drifted off to sleep.

Chapter 86

The following morning, by the time I woke up, Myles and KJ were already eating breakfast. I called out to KJ, reminding him not to forget his homework. Myles came in and laid on the bed beside me. "I pray he doesn't ask me again about what he talked about last night."

"He probably forgot what he said. I must admit that I was shocked by all he said." I had to push the memory to the recesses of my mind. "I received a letter from the hospital, letting us know what time to be there on Thursday morning and what to bring with me."

"Okay. I'll look at it when I get home. Where is it?" I pointed to the dresser. "I gotta go. I'll call you later. Mrs. Riddle will be here soon to take my place." He kissed me and told KJ it was time to leave.

I stayed in bed until 10:00, thinking about what KJ had said. I then thought about Mrs. Brenda, wondering if she married him, thinking she could change him. I imagined what she was going through was hard on her.

It took me longer to get out of bed. When I stood, I felt so heavy and bigger than when I laid down the night before. I managed to shower and then ate the breakfast Myles left for me in the microwave. I then called Mrs. Riddle and asked her to stop by the store on her way to pick up something she could prepare for us for dinner. "I'll pay you back when you get here," I added.

When Mrs. Riddle arrived, I immediately paid her for the food. "I hope you like what I picked up for dinner."

"Whatever you cook will be okay with me," I replied.

"Is there anything else you want me to do?"

"No, just cook for me, please."

"Myles told me he didn't need me to come tomorrow or next week because he'll be here."

"He told you that?"

"Yes, he said he would call and let me know when to return to work and asked if I might be available a couple of days a week to come and help you with the babies."

I started to laugh. "He doesn't want me to do a thing!"

"Lexie, you have a man who loves you." She went upstairs to see if there was any cleaning to do but came right back down. "Everything up there looks okay, but KJ's room has toys everywhere, and his bed wasn't made."

"Don't you clean his room, Mrs. Riddle. He can put his own toys away and make his own bed."

"Sorry. I already did it."

"Myles told that boy his bed should be made and that his toys are to be put away before he leaves for school."

"We'll just say he forgot to do it today," Mrs. Riddle replied, laughing. She went into the kitchen to start cooking. I followed her and sat on the stool at the island, watching her prepare the meal.

I told her what KJ said about his daddy and that he wanted to know what down-low mess meant.

"Did you tell him?" she asked.

"No, I'll let Myles talk to him about that."

"Lexie, I knew there was something different about that man the first time I saw him. Remember me telling you that? I just couldn't put my finger on it. You married him anyway, even though you didn't love him," she said, laughing.

"Mrs. Riddle, you should have insisted on me not marrying him. We were good friends, though. When he asked me to marry him, I was lonely. I wanted to be well-known, so I married the pastor's son, which was a mistake. Still, I had my KJ, the joy of my life, even when he's a spoiled brat. I love that little boy so much."

"Yes, I know you do," she replied. "What did Myles say when KJ told y'all about Keith?"

"I can't repeat what he said."

Mrs. Riddle laughed so hard, she could hardly catch her breath. "Well, I agree with whatever Myles said. I'm glad you can't read my mind!" Once she calmed down, she asked, "How did Keith act when y'all were married?"

"When I married him, he was my friend and a lot like a brother. We didn't love each other for sex, either. During the year and three months we were married, we slept together twice, and I got pregnant the second time. It just didn't seem right, sleeping with my friend and someone I thought of like a brother. When he lived here, he had his bedroom, and I had mine. I knew he went out of town a lot, but that didn't bother me. After hearing what KJ said, I think he was going to meet up with his down-low friend."

Mrs. Riddle let out a laugh before saying, "All things worked out for the best. His down-low mess has nothing to do with you. He was that way when you met him."

"But why does he keep calling me and he got a wife?" I asked, confused.

"It has nothing to do with you, Lexie. He is hiding, and you are his shield. Just let Myles deal with him, and Keith will stop." She looked at her watch. "Well, so much for this conversation. I have an appointment at 4:30 today. Is it okay for me to leave at 3:45?"

"Yes, you can leave when you put the food on. I can finish."

She started laughing at me. "Oh, you must want Myles to be angry at me for having you in here cooking. No, ma'am!" We shared a laugh as she cooked. She made grilled pork chops, a cheesy rice casserole, and steamed broccoli, cauliflowers, and carrots. For dessert, she made a strawberry cheesecake from scratch. As she cooked, she looked at me and said, "Lexie, you are a beautiful woman. I have known you for a long time. When I first met you, you looked like you had just stepped out of a fashion magazine. Who was that other man that kept calling you after your divorce?"

"Are you talking about Albert?"

"Yes, that's him. I am glad you let him go. That man was a mess!"

"I didn't like Albert. He was weird in high school and acted even weirder when he came to my house. I hadn't seen him since we graduated. One day, he came by my office to put in an application for a job we had posted for a Custodian. After completing the application, he insisted on giving it to me personally. I told him to give it to my secretary because I was busy and couldn't see him right then. He gave it to her and left. That following Saturday, I had just finished eating my dinner and put KJ down for his nap. Just as I was getting ready to do my exercises, Albert rang my doorbell. I asked through the door, 'What do you want?' He said he wanted to talk to me and asked if he could come in. I told him I was busy and that he'd have to call my office to make an appointment with my secretary. I thought he was there to discuss his job application. He asked for my number, saying he wanted to call and talk to me. I thought he wanted me to put in a good word for him at the job, so I called out my number through the closed door. I watched him pull a pen from his coat pocket and write the number on his hand. He said he would call me soon, got in his car, and left. I was hoping my number would have sweated out of his hand because I didn't want to be bothered with him." Mrs. Riddle was obviously tickled by my story, so I continued.

"I was happy when I hadn't heard from him. A couple of weeks later, he called me from his cell phone on a Saturday morning. He said he was sitting in my driveway and told me to open my garage door so that he could pull his car in. I told him, 'You're not putting your car in my garage! You don't live here! Why are you here anyway? If you're checking on the job, someone else was hired.' He replied that he was in the area and thought he would just stop by. Being polite, I told him to come in.

"I looked at the window as he got out of his car. He was dapping his way up to my house, tilting his head to one side, wearing some silly superfly hat, and smoking a cigarette. I opened the door and told him he couldn't come into my house smoking, so he dropped the lit cigarette on the ground. When he walked in, he was looking at me, licking his lips, and said, 'Girl, you know you look good.' I thanked him and invited him to sit down. He didn't sit, though. He just stood there looking around, saying, 'Umm-hmm. Nice house. I can put a music studio in there (he pointed to my office), and I can put some different colored lights in the ceiling.' Then, he looked at me and said, 'I think you need to take that mirror from over there and put it on that wall. And those plants are in the wrong place. They need to be over there.' His finger was pointing all over the place, Mrs. Riddle!" She had actually stopped stirring the vegetables to look at me, shocked.

"I stood there looking at him while he talked and then politely walked to the front door, opened it, and told him to leave my house. 'You are not welcome back here anymore. Lose my phone number and forget where I live. And on your way out, pick that cigarette butt off my sidewalk.' He didn't move right away. He just stood there looking back at me and then said, 'You are just mean. Just plain mean. You think you are too good for a brother.' He then dapped his behind out of my house, picked up that cigarette butt, got in his car, and sped off."

Mrs. Riddle was laughing so hard, she couldn't stand straight. The tears were running down her face. "Did you ever hear from him again?"

294

"He called a couple of times. I wouldn't answer the phone, so he stopped calling."

"Good. I didn't like him anyway," she said, still laughing at the story.

"You know, Mrs. Riddle, after my divorce, I didn't want a man in my life. I was going to enjoy being single and raising my son alone. Then, the Lord sent Myles to me."

"Lexie, I have been married for 40 years this year and have enjoyed every minute. Now, every day wasn't a great day, but we iron out our differences and make our marriage work. I want your marriage to last as long as mine has or longer. You have a good man who loves you and your son. Feed him, love him, keep your marriage exciting, talk out your differences, communicate with each other, and keep him happy. Most of all, keep God in your lives and pray together. Once you have those babies, get back to the woman who looked like she stepped out of a magazine. Keep him interested in you and you alone. There are a lot of women out there who would love to have a man like Myles." She paused to let out a laugh. "Myles is a very good-looking man. Keep him wondering what's going to happen next." She looked at her watch again. "Look at the time. It's 3:40. All the food is ready. Let me get out of here before I'm late for my appointment. Myles should be pulling up in a few minutes. Don't you do a thing!" she ordered.

"I won't do anything but sit here and wait for my boys to get here. Promise. I'm ready to eat as soon as they walk through the door," I said, rubbing my belly. "Thank you for your advice. I needed to hear that. Don't forget the envelope Myles left for you."

She opened the envelope and said, "It's a thank you card with a check for $300.00! Oh, my God! He didn't have to give me this much money!"

"Mrs. Riddle, you deserve whatever he gave you. We are so thankful for you and all you do for us." She hugged me tight and then left. She gave me a lot to think about.

I heard Myles and KJ pull into the garage a few minutes later.

Chapter 87

When Myles and KJ walked into the house, both hugged me before KJ went upstairs. "I've been missing you all day. Have you been missing me?" Myles asked.

"Yes, I always miss you."

"What's that cooking that's smelling so good up in here?" He went to the stove to peek at the food.

"Wash your hands first! Mrs. Riddle cooked a delicious meal for us."

Myles went to the intercom. "Come down and wash your hands so that we can eat." He then went into the hallway bathroom to wash his. As he came out, he said, "KJ told me he was hungry when I picked him up. I'm hungry, too."

When KJ made it downstairs, we sat together and ate the tasty meal Mrs. Riddle prepared for us. The strawberry cheesecake was right on time.

While we talked, Myles said, "I am here with you for the next three or four weeks, as long as you need me."

"Is that why you told Mrs. Riddle she didn't have to return until you called her?"

"Yep! I'll be here to take care of you."

KJ wasn't saying anything. He concentrated on eating his food.

"KJ, are you alright?" I asked.

"I'm sleepy."

"I know you are. You talked all last night."

"Tonight, you sleep in your own room," Myles said.

"Can I go to bed when I finish my food? I don't have any homework to do."

"KJ, when you get home tomorrow, I want you to take all the diapers and wipes out of my office and place all the newborn sizes and ten packages of wipes in the babies' nursery. Everything else goes upstairs in the green bedroom," I instructed.

He stood there looking as if he were asleep. "Do you understand what I am saying?"

"Yes, I understand. Can I go to bed now?" he murmured.

"Yes, you can go to bed."

He hugged me, turned to Myles, and said, "Bye, Myles."

"Goodnight, Peanut. Don't forget to say your prayers."

I got up to do the dishes. "Babe, I got that. You don't have to do the dishes."

"Honey, all I have to do is put them in the dishwasher and clean the island."

"Sit down. I can do it." He cleaned the kitchen and then said he was going for a run. He helped me to my room, where I sat on the couch, watching TV.

While waiting for him to get back, I had a sudden urge to use the bathroom, but I couldn't get up from the couch or make it to the intercom to call KJ down. He was probably asleep by then, anyway. As soon as Myles opened the front door, I called out, "I need you to help me up! I gotta go to the bathroom! Hurry!"

He ran into the room, helped me up, and asked, "Why didn't you call me? I was standing outside talking to Mr. Hill." I didn't respond because I had no good reason.

When I came out, I sat on the side of the bed, and Myles went in to take his shower. It was getting increasingly hard for me to walk. The babies were pressing on my lower back and stomach. Myles finished showering and then went up to check on KJ. When he came back, he said, "KJ is out for the night." He came over to me, hugged me, and rubbed my hair back. "Babe, lie down. You look tired."

"If I do, I'll have to get right back up again."

"Whenever you have to get up, I'm right here to help you."

I laid there listening to Myles talk about his day. "I told you I was outside talking to Mr. Hill earlier. Well, he was telling me about our Lover's Lane at the turnaround at the end of the street. He said he saw as many as six cars sitting there once, with young people smoking, playing music, and leaving trash behind. A few months ago, he put a motion-sensor light in front of his house, and now, he doesn't see those cars out there anymore. He said all he sees now are deer on his surveillance camera. He even mentioned that every now and then, he sees a dark-colored car drive past slowly, enter the turnaround, and then leave out the same way—slowly. I told him I hoped it wasn't anybody casing our homes. He said, 'If it is, he will be leaving my house in a body bag!' I had to laugh at that and replied, 'Me, too! And what I have, I'm not afraid to use!' Think about it, Lexie: I'm an Iraqi war vet!"

I thought to myself, "That's probably Keith passing by, looking at our house." I turned my head toward Myles and asked, "Did KJ say anything to you about what he said last night?"

"Yes, he did."

"What did you say?"

"I was honest and told him that low-down is when a man has affection for women and men. He then asked, 'Is that when you have a best friend and a wife?' I told him yes, it was something like that. He sat there for a while, thinking, and then asked, 'What does affection mean?' Just then, his bus drove up. When he got out, I said aloud, "Thank You, Jesus!"

Chapter 88

On Wednesday morning, we were all up early. KJ had gone downstairs to handle the task I asked him to do with the babies' diapers and wipes and then ate his Frosted Flakes.

"I was hungry when I got up," Myles said. "Do you realize we were all in bed before 8:30 last night?"

"We must've needed those extra hours of rest," I replied.

KJ said, "Mama, I've been up a long time. I took some of the diapers upstairs already."

"Thank you. I heard you in the kitchen."

"Are you ready to go, Peanut?" Myles asked.

"Yes." He hugged me and said, "Bye, Mama!"

"Bye, son."

Myles leaned over, kissed me, and said, "I'll be back in a few minutes," smiling as he walked out the door. When he returned, I was sitting at the island in the kitchen. "How are you feeling today?"

"You know, I feel good. I got a good night's rest and didn't have to get but once last night."

"Did you miss me?"

"Myles, you weren't gone for more than 20 minutes!"

He came over, hugged me, and said, "Well, I still missed you." I thought about Mrs. Riddle telling me to keep my marriage exciting.

At 11:00, Myles was ready to go grocery shopping. I was back in bed. I told him I wanted him to get two 12-inch Subway sandwiches for when Sharon arrived. "I wonder if Mae's family would like to be here when Sharon gets in?" he asked. "I'll just stop by on my way out and ask her. I know she's off work today." He looked up at the clock on the kitchen wall and said, "Okay. It's noon now. I should be back in about two hours."

"Okay, Honey. I'll be right here in this bed until you get back." I watched The Chew until I fell back to sleep. When I woke up, Myles was lying on the couch, watching TV. "Myles, why didn't you wake me when you got back?"

"You were sleeping so peacefully, Babe. I didn't want to wake you. I talked to Mae and told her we wanted her and the family to be here when Sharon arrives."

"What did she say?"

"They'll be here around 5:30. She seemed excited, knowing her big sister was coming to town. I asked her to bring KJ home when she comes."

"Umm… Do you see what time it is now?" I asked.

He looked at the clock and said, "Oh, my God! It's 4:15! Let me get out of here. Sharon's flight arrives at 5:00!"

When he left, I got up and packed what was on the list for me to take to the hospital. I then wobbled into the kitchen, cut the sandwiches, and put toothpicks in them. Myles had already prepared his chicken noodle soup, which was warming in the slow cooker. I sliced the cake, made lemon iced tea, and set out the vegetable tray and chips in the breakfast room.

At 5:20, Myles called and said they were on their way back. At 5:30, Mae and her family arrived, with KJ in tow. All of them hugged me as they came inside. Mae said, "Lexie, look at you! I haven't seen you since you were in the hospital. Those babies are ready to come out of there." We all started laughing.

Derrick chimed in, asking, "How in the world are you even standing right now?"

"Barely. I can't even see my feet. Are they still down there?" Everyone busted out laughing even harder. "Y'all have a seat."

"Mama, where is Myles? Why didn't he pick me up?" KJ asked.

"He went to pick up his sister from the airport. He should be pulling up in a few minutes. Y'all can wash your hands. The food is ready." Derrick didn't hesitate. He got up, washed his hands, and grabbed a plate of food.

Mae replied, "I can wait. Kids, wash your hands. When Aunt Sharon gets here, y'all can eat." About that time, Myles and Sharon walked through the door. Everyone was excited to see Sharon and gave her hugs.

"How was your flight?" I asked.

"It was good. I went to sleep. Thankfully, the lady sitting beside me woke me up when we landed," she said, laughing. "Girl, how are you walking? Sit down somewhere!" I started to laugh, holding the underside of my belly. "I love your mansion," she commented.

"Thank you, but it's a house."

"If there are more than five bedrooms in here, it's a mansion!" she said, laughing.

"Well, y'all can eat now," I said.

"I'm ready!" Sharon replied.

Myles had already washed his hands and had joined Derrick at the table. After everyone had their food, we sat down to eat and talk.

"Myles, thank you for making the soup," I said with a smile.

He smiled back and whispered, "You're welcome," kissing me on my cheek.

Sharon seemed happy to be with her brother and sister. Mae asked, "Lexie, what time do you have to be at the hospital tomorrow morning?"

"At 6:00. We have to be there one hour early, so we'll be leaving around 4:30," I answered.

"We can keep KJ overnight. That way, you won't have to get him up that early," Mae offered.

"Thank you, Mae. That would be great," Myles said.

"Derrick can bring the kids to the hospital to see you and the babies when he gets off work. I'll already be there, working," Mae said.

"Okay! Sounds good to me!" I replied.

When everyone finished eating, Sharon said, "I want to see the rest of your mansion!"

I looked over at Myles and laughed. "I can't go upstairs. Myles will have to show you."

Myles started to laugh, telling them what had happened and why I couldn't go upstairs. "So, KJ had me put her on punishment. She can't kiss me, but I can kiss her." Everybody started laughing at what he said. "Okay, Sharon. Let's go." When

Myles got upstairs, he used the intercom to say, "KJ, bring Aunt Sharon's bag up here and get your clothes ready to take to Aunt Mae's house for school tomorrow."

As Derrick and Trina did the dishes, I told Trina to be sure to take some of the leftover food. I didn't want it to go to waste and spoil while I was in the hospital.

Sharon and Myles came back downstairs. "Lexie, it is beautiful up there! Did you do the decorating?" she asked.

"No, I had an Interior Designer do it. I just added a couple of pieces here and there."

She walked around the downstairs area, heading toward the living room and my office. She stopped, looking at my picture wall. "You were in the Air Force?" she asked.

"Yes, for eight years."

"Hmm… I see you made copies of the pictures you took at my house. Those frames look expensive."

"Well, I wanted them to match the frames I already had."

"And I see you were in a beauty contest," she said while looking at the photo.

"Yes, when I was stationed in Germany. I came in 2nd Place out of 50 women."

"Wow! You are a pretty lady!"

"Thank you," I replied, smiling.

"It's going on 9:00. We better go," Mae said.

KJ had already taken his shower and had on his PJs and shoes. While upstairs, Myles helped him pack his clothes for school. He came over to hug me. "Bye, Mama." He hugged Myles as well. I could tell he didn't want to go.

When they left, Sharon got up and walked toward my office. I thought she was heading back to the picture wall. From where Myles and I sat, I saw the light come on in the living room. In there, everything was in cream with a gold-trimmed French provincial furnisher, a China cabinet with my mom's antique doll collection, and a cream-colored Baby Grand Piano that belonged to my mom. In addition to the wedding pictures I had added recently, over the sofa was a large gold mirror with cream trim and angels painted on the mirror.

I sat there and thought about how Mama loved the living room. We used to sit in there after church on Sundays, and she would play the piano while we sang together. Mama had a beautiful singing voice, and she loved relaxing in that room when she read her Bible. After she died, I would sit and play the piano, crying and remembering our time together. When Mrs. Riddle cleaned the house, she would clean the living room, too, and say it was a peaceful room. Myles often went in there when he wanted time alone to think and pray.

After some time, Sharon turned off the light and joined us in the family room. She sat in the big chair by the door. She didn't say anything right away; she just looked around at the furniture, the pictures on the wall, the winding staircase, and the mirror. She then looked up at the chandeliers hanging from the ceiling and then down at the floor and my exotic plants by the window.

Myles whispered, "What's wrong with Sharon?"

I shrugged my shoulders and replied, "I don't know."

She heard us talking about her and laughed. "Lexie, I like your living room."

"Thank you."

"I'm not getting in your business, but…are you rich?" she asked. Myles and I laughed at the curious look she had while awaiting my answer.

"All I can say is the house is paid for, we don't owe anything on our vehicles, and the Lord has richly blessed us. Why do you ask?"

She started laughing. "Girl, I'm taking all of this in. Where is the babies' nursery? I know you have one in this mansion." We were laughing as Myles helped me up, and we walked/wobbled to our bedroom suite.

Sharon barely stepped foot into the bedroom when she exclaimed, "Oh, my God! It's beautiful and big back here. Everything is in cream, just like in your living room. Girl, I like your bedroom set! It looks so expensive, and the nursery is amazing! I love the way you guys have it set up."

"Thank you. Myles and Rodrick did it. Myles, show Sharon our sauna room."

She started to laugh again. "Yes, y'all are rich. I played that game at the baby shower to help you with diapers, and you guys are loaded!" We laughed together so hard that tears were coming out of our eyes.

A few minutes passed. I settled my eyes on the sliding doors in my bedroom, which were mirrors painted with my dad, mom, and brother, with an angel taking them up into Heaven. I used those doors to access the patio and exercise room. Sharon followed my eyes and asked, "What's behind that mirror?"

"The patio, exercise room, a half-bath, and laundry room," I replied.

Sharon and Myles went to explore the rooms on the other side of the sliding doors, returning through the garage. I heard Myles laughing as they walked back into the bedroom. "Sharon asked me if the garage door led to a swimming room!"

"I thought it was going to open to an Olympic-size pool! I've seen everything a mansion could have, except for a pool!" Sharon explained. "Lexie, this is a mansion. I counted six toilets in this place: three upstairs and three down here." Myles was laughing so hard, he had to sit down. Sharon was laughing, too, and sat on the couch beside him.

"Sharon, by the time you come back, I will be sure to have a pool installed in the backyard," Myles said, getting up to walk over to me. "That was supposed to be your surprise, my lady."

"For real? You're going to put a pool in?"

"They break ground on it the last week of April next year!" he said excitedly.

Sharon smiled at us and said, "I like the color scheme you used in your exercise room. It's so relaxing."

"You are welcome to use it while you're here," Myles offered.

"Are you calling me fat?"

"Not fat, just a little fluffy."

She laughed and threw a pillow from the couch at him. "For that, I'm going to my apartment upstairs!"

Myles laughed at her. "We are leaving at 4:30 a.m. Be ready."

"Okay. Good night, you two." We watched as she walked out, paused to marvel at the nursey again, and then turned the corner to head upstairs.

Lying in bed, Myles asked, "How are you feeling?"

"I feel okay."

"Just think, when we come back home, we will have our babies with us," he said, kissing me on the cheek.

"Are you really putting in a swimming pool?" I asked.

"Yes, you said you wanted one, didn't you?"

"I don't recall telling you I wanted a pool. I think you're the one who wants it, and you're putting it on me. When did I ever say I wanted a pool?"

"When we were on our honeymoon. Your wish is my command," he joked.

"Maybe you mentioned wanting a pool because I looked good in that two-piece swimsuit you bought me."

He tried to wrap his arms around me, which was funny because his arms weren't long enough to wrap around my belly. "Okay. I'll buy you a larger size two-piece swimsuit after you have the babies. It'll be just like the one you have."

"No, I'm going to get this weight off me and get back into the one I already have! I'm lying here looking like a pregnant elephant." He laughed so hard, still trying to wrap his arms around me.

Once he gave up on his efforts, he laid back and said, "I'm glad Sharon is happy now. When I turned off the highway and passed dad's house, she started to cry, saying how much she missed daddy. We had to sit in the garage for a while before she stopped crying. I knew it would be hard on her to come here and not see him. Truth be told, I think about him every time I pass by his house. I miss him so much, too." He fell quiet for a minute. "She said her plane leaves at 1:30 p.m. on Sunday because she has to be back in her class Monday morning." Within minutes, he was asleep.

At 12:30 a.m., I had to use the bathroom, so I woke up Myles. "I'm sorry to wake you. I need help getting up."

"There's no reason to be sorry. That's why I'm here."

I went to the bathroom, returned to bed, and fell right back to sleep. It seemed as if I was asleep for a few seconds when Myles woke me up, saying, "It's time to get ready to leave." He walked over to the intercom. "Sharon, wake up. We will be leaving in 45 minutes."

"Okay!" she replied.

With Myles' help, I got dressed and grew extremely nervous. He was already rubbing his hair back. I knew he was nervous but wasn't letting on just how nerve-racking the upcoming day would be.

Sharon came downstairs, ready to go. "Lexie, I love that room. I slept like a log."

"I had the entire upstairs designed specifically for my mom. After she retired, she came to live with me. She was surprised at how spacious it was up there and couldn't believe it was all hers. She loved it, especially the bedroom suite that you're sleeping in."

"Well, I'm with her on that! I love the room. As a matter of fact, I love your whole mansion!" she said, laughing at her use of the word mansion again.

"It's time for us to go," Myles said nervously. We climbed into Pearl and headed to the hospital. We arrived at 4:50 a.m.

Chapter 89

Dr. Jessica and her staff were waiting on me. She asked, "How are the two of you doing?"

We both replied, "Okay." Myles then introduced Sharon to Jessica.

"I can tell you are brother and sister. You look alike. Nice to meet you, Sharon," she said as they shook hands. She then looked at me and smiled. "Are you ready? We have everything set up for you. This is Dr. Collins, Nurse Green, Nurse Griggs, and Nurse Practitioner Sanders is on her way. They will be in the delivery room with us." She looked at Myles and Sharon. "The two of you can wait in the Labor and Delivery waiting room. Someone will come to get you when the babies are here."

About that time, Mae came in, hugged Myles and Sharon, and spoke to everyone else. "I made it!" She looked at me and asked, "Lexie, are you ready?"

"Yes, I am." She smiled and patted my hand before leaving to scrub in and prep for my surgery.

Myles kissed me, told me he loved me, and whispered a prayer in my ear as he held my hand. He didn't let go until they rolled me into the delivery room. I remember passing two incubators in there.

Once on the delivery table, I was given a shot in my back. I felt numbness and pressure pressing on my stomach. The next thing I knew, I heard my first baby cry.

"It's Karson!" Mae exclaimed.

A few minutes later, I heard another cry.

"It's Kaylin!" Mae exclaimed again. "Lexie, they're both beautiful!"

"I want to see them."

"They are getting them cleaned up right now and taking their weight and length. You'll see them in just a moment. I'll go and let Myles and Sharon know they are here," Mae said.

Tears of joy were running from my eyes. Karson Lee weighed 6 lbs., 14 oz., and was 21 inches long. Kaylin Rose weighed 6 lbs., 6 oz., and was 20 inches long. The date was September 25, 2018, at 6:36 and 6:37 a.m.

Dr. Jessica came over, held my hand, and smiled. "They are perfect, but the boy has six fingers on each hand."

"My baby has six fingers?!"

"Yes, there's no bone in them. We'll tie them off, and they will fall off soon. He will never know they were there unless you tell him."

I was hurt by her report but happy the extra fingers would fall off. "I want to see him."

She looked at me, sensing my hurt. "Lexie, don't worry. They will fall off. Promise."

When Myles and Sharon came in, the babies were already in their incubators. Myles stood in between them with tears streaming down his cheeks. He came over and kissed me. Sharon planted a soft kiss on my forehead, smiling. I told them what the doctor said about Karson having six fingers.

"Myles, you were born with six fingers on each hand, too," Sharon said.

He looked closely at his hands. "Seriously? I had six fingers?"

"Yes, and daddy was born with six fingers on each of his hands, too!"

Myles looked at his hands in amazement. "Wow. I never knew that."

"Dr. Jessica said they will fall off, and Karson will never know they were there," I stated.

The doctors and nurses left the room, leaving Myles and his two sisters to spend time looking at the babies. Myles started crying again and prayed, "Lord, I thank You for our babies. They are beautiful." He came over and kissed me again. He then thanked his sisters for being there for us. "Let us pray and thank God for these babies." We all held hands, and Myles prayed aloud, giving God praise and thanks for two healthy, perfect babies.

Chapter 90

A few hours later, Dr. Jessica came in. "I needed to get some rest. The Nurse Practitioner will be in at 2:00 to show you how to breastfeed the babies." On her way out, she said, "Nurse Griggs will remain with you for the next four hours to make sure you and the babies are alright."

Myles said to me, "I gotta go anyway to meet with KJ's teacher at 9:00 about the accelerated classes he will be taking this Fall."

"Oh, my. Myles, I forgot about that meeting."

"Don't you worry about it. I have it covered. You get some rest, and I will be back after getting KJ off the bus."

Nurse Griggs checked my and the babies' temperatures and confirmed what Dr. Jessica said: She would be with us for a while. Mae stopped in to check on us, too. I was glad when she came. My midsection was hurting so bad, it felt as if all the organs in my body had moved to my back. I asked Mae to look in my hospital bag and get my belly wrap. She and Nurse Griggs wrapped it around my waist, fastening it with the attached Velcro.

"Don't wrap it too tight. Remember: You have stitches. Where did you get this from?" Mae asked.

"I ordered it from Amazon. I read a book that recommended using a belly wrap to help strengthen stomach muscles after having a baby. I'm glad I remembered to bring it with me." Mae had to leave and said she would be back on her next break. I went to sleep. Mae returned just as Nurse Griggs was preparing to leave. I thanked them both and added, "My belly feels much better with the wrap."

Breastfeeding the babies wasn't hard. They latched on well. The problem was that I had two babies to feed.

Mae came in later and said she had called home and told Derrick not to come to visit me until Friday so that Myles and KJ could bond with the babies first. "Plus, you need your rest, Lexie." When Myles and KJ arrived, I had already finished feeding Karson and Kaylin.

KJ was so happy to see his new brother and sister and wanted to hold them. I explained they were too small right now and that he would have to wait. I asked Myles, "What was Sharon doing when you left?"

"She was in the sitting room upstairs, watching TV." He then gave me the update from the meeting with KJ's teacher. "KJ is doing good in math and science. The accelerated classes will be in the same school. He'll be in a class with nine other students who scored high on their testing. You will be proud to know KJ was the one who scored the highest out of the ten!" He reached over and rubbed KJ's head.

"I'm so proud of you, KJ!" He paid my comment no attention. He was focused on his siblings, not on what I said.

The first time Myles held the babies, he was so nervous. KJ hugged me and said, "Mama, they are pretty." He pointed to them. "That's Karson, and this one is Kaylin."

"Wow! You can tell them apart?" I asked, surprised.

"Yes, Karson looks like me!" he said, laughing. KJ didn't see Karson's six fingers because the baby had on mittens.

The nurse came in to check on the babies and take my temperature. Myles asked if she could take a couple of pictures of the four of us. I held the babies, and Myles and KJ were on each side of me.

It was getting late. Myles had to leave to take KJ home and get him ready for school. KJ didn't want to leave. "Mama, I can miss school tomorrow. I don't have any homework to turn in."

"No, you go to school. I'll see you tomorrow when you come back here."

Myles didn't want to leave, either. He just sat there, looking at the babies as they slept in their incubators. "Goodnight, you two." He kissed his hand and then placed it atop each incubator. He came back to me, kissed me, and said, "I will be back in the morning after I put KJ on the bus."

"Don't forget: Tomorrow is Friday, and KJ's supposed to go to his dad's house after school."

"He's not going, Lexie. I will not put him through whatever they have going on over there anymore. If he doesn't want to go, we are not going to make him go.

KJ will let us know when he is ready to see them, or his dad will call for him." I could tell he was putting his foot down once and for all.

"Okay, I will see you tomorrow." He kissed me again, KJ hugged me, and they left. I was left in the room alone with my two babies. Shortly after, one of the nurses came in to observe as I nursed the babies. Afterward, she had me get up and walk around the room. I was glad I had on the belly wrap.

Karson and Kaylin woke up every hour, needing to be fed and changed. It was tiresome. When I did manage to get some rest, the nurse would come in to take my temperature.

Myles returned around 9:00 a.m. on Friday. He came in with a sad face.

"What's wrong? Is KJ alright?"

"Yes, he's fine. Last night was the second night we've slept apart since getting married. I didn't like it."

"I will be coming home tomorrow. The babies and I are doing well. Didn't you say your duties with the Army Reserves are starting back up this month?"

"Yes, I did, but I got an extension," he answered.

"Can you do that?" I asked, confused.

"I contacted the Reserves when I found out the date the babies would be born, and they extended my time for eight months."

As we sat there and talked, Myles removed the mittens off Karson's hands so that we could see what Dr. Jessica was talking about. She was correct: There was no bone in the sixth finger. It was just long skin with a small nail at the end. Myles said, "I can't believe I was born with six fingers, too," as he looked at his own hands again. Karson started to cry.

"Okay, daddy. Give him to me. I'll feed him, and you can change him."

Picking him up, Myles said, "Lexie, his eyes are open. He's looking at me!" Just as he passed Karson to me, Kaylin started to cry. "Her eyes are open, too! Babe, we made some beautiful babies."

The nurse came in with my breakfast. Myles told me he had already eaten. "Oh, when I made it home last night, Keith had left a message saying he would be out of town. His wife had a death in the family, so he wouldn't be getting KJ this weekend."

"Okay. That worked out well."

Myles reminded me, "He wasn't going over there anyway."

Around 11:30, the pastor and his wife came in for a visit. They "oohed" and "ahhed" over the babies, saying how beautiful they were and commenting about all the hair they had on their heads. When they left, I decided to sleep while the babies were sleeping. When I woke up, Myles was asleep, too.

When it was dinnertime, the nurse brought in my food. I offered to share with Myles, but he said Sharon was bringing him and KJ something to eat when she came in. He fell back asleep until Mae, her family, and KJ came in. Mae said Sharon had stopped by Subway to get Myles and KJ's food. "We're not going to stay long," Mae stated. "Trina has a basketball game tonight."

"If you want to hold the babies, go wash your hands first," Myles said to the children. Trina and Chyna got cleaned up and held the babies. After KJ washed his hands, he held Kaylin. He was so happy and felt like such a big boy.

"Chyna, this is my sister. Her name is Kaylin," he announced. We all laughed.

Derrick stood and said, "We better get going so that we can get to the game on time." We said our goodbyes, and I told them I would be home tomorrow.

They left, leaving me, Myles, KJ, and the babies in the room. KJ stood by me and asked, "Mama, do you love me?"

"Yes, I love you. Why did you ask me that?"

"I don't know. It was just in my head."

"Don't you ever think I don't love you. You are my baby. I will always love you." I found myself getting emotional. I didn't know where that question of his came from.

"You love Myles, and now you have Karson and Kaylin to love."

"KJ, I love you, too. You are my oldest son."

"Daddy said the same thing, but Mama Brenda still treated me differently than she did Brandon."

"Give me a hug. I will never treat you differently. Do you hear me? The babies will require more of my time than you because they are babies, but I'm going to need your help. You're their big brother!"

"Mama, I put the diapers upstairs and put the right ones in the nursery like you asked. Aunt Sharon helped me."

"Thank you, Mama's big boy."

Myles didn't say anything during my conversation with KJ. He just sat and held Karson. When Kaylin started to cry, I told him it was time for them to be changed and fed. I asked him to take KJ to get a treat from the snack room for doing good in his class and doing what I had asked him to do at home for me. Honestly, I wasn't ready for KJ to see me breastfeeding the babies.

They were going out the door, and Sharon came in with their food. The three of them went into the waiting room to eat. The nurse came in with a few tiny baby bottles that held two ounces of milk. She handed them to me and said, "The babies can't get the proper amount of milk with just breastfeeding. I need you to alternate their feedings with the bottles. They will sleep a little longer when they are full." Before leaving, she let me know that Dr. Jessica would be in soon when she made her rounds.

When Myles, Sharon, and KJ returned, I had finished feeding and changing the babies and had put them back in their beds. Sharon said, "All I can say is I have the most beautiful niece and nephew in the world. Now, I have another handsome nephew." She wrapped her arm around KJ. "Are you ready to go home?"

"Is Myles coming?" he asked.

"No, Peanut. I'm going to stay here with your Mama tonight."

"KJ, if the doctor says everything is fine with the babies and me, I'll be home tomorrow. I don't know what time that will be, though."

He looked over at the babies and said, "Aunt Sharon, I'm ready to go now. I'm getting sleepy."

"Come and give me a hug, Peanut. You know I love you, don't you?" Myles asked.

"Yes." Myles gave him one last rub on the head before he left.

"Bye, Myles. Bye, Mama. Bye-bye, babies," KJ said in a sleepy voice before walking out the room.

Once alone, I told Myles what the nurse said about alternating the babies' feeding times with the bottles. As we discussed that, there was a knock at the door. In walked Matthew, Kathy, and Liz. I was surprised and happy to see them. Myles stood and shook Matthew's hand. Kathy came in smiling and said, "Lexie, you are still pretty. It is so good to see you."

"I don't remember you," Liz said.

"You don't remember me?" I know you are a little younger than I am, but I remember you telling on Kathy and me." She started to laugh. "Kathy and Liz, this is my husband Myles."

They shook hands and sat in the two chairs, and Matthew sat beside Myles on the couch. Before Myles or I could ask them to wash their hands first, Kathy said, "Let me wash my hands so I can hold those babies."

Matthew asked Myles, "Do you own the computer shop on Shelby Drive?"

"Yes, I do."

"I thought I'd seen you there one day. I remember playing football against you at school, too."

"Aww, man! I remember who you are now! You were a bad behind running back!" Myles said, smiling.

Matthew smiled back, replying, "You were good, too." He got up and came to my bed. "It was so good seeing you that day I was at your house. I thought of you often, hoping I would run into you someday. After I left your house, I thought about all the fun we had growing up and how you got Leon and me in trouble." He started laughing. "Like the time you got Leon and me in trouble when we beat up that boy for you. Did you tell Myles how you got in trouble for bringing that boy into your house?"

"Matthew, please. Don't go there. Why do you have to bring that up? You and Jessica were the reason I got in trouble anyway!" We were all laughing.

"What happened, Matthew?" Myles asked.

"I'll tell you," I responded. "This new boy from Detroit, Michigan, enrolled in the Skill Center. He drove a black convertible Mustang. The car was pretty. One day, we were waiting for the bus to take us back to school from the Skill Center. The boy pulled up and asked if we wanted him to drop us off at school. Matthew wanted a ride in the boy's car and said, 'Yes, come on, Lexie. Get in, Jessica.' I told him I would wait for the bus, but Jessica begged me to join them. The boy dropped the top back on his car and drove us to school. Matthew asked him to drop us off at the store on the corner near our house. Once there, Matthew and Jessica got out of the car. I didn't get out. I wanted him to drop me off at home. When we made it to my house, he asked if he could come in to use the bathroom. I told him yes. He came inside, took off his jacket, laid it on the chair, and went into the bathroom. I kid you not: As soon as he closed the bathroom door, Mama walked in, asking me, 'Whose car is that in front of the house?' I started explaining how my ride home came to be. 'I know you don't have some boy in my house!' she hollered."

Matthew cut me off. "Jessica and I were walking toward the house and saw Aunt Rose drive up. A few minutes later, that boy came running out the house, putting on his jacket." We were cracking up!

The door opened slowly. Dr. Jessica stood in the doorway, listening to us talk. When she saw my visitors, she looked surprised. She came all the way in and hugged each of them. "It's so nice to see you guys! Yes, Lexie got into big trouble for having that boy in the house. She didn't even know his name!"

"It was your fault that I even got into that boy's car, Jessica. You couldn't go anywhere without Matthew. And that boy's name was Frank," I replied sarcastically.

Jessica came over to hug me. "You guys, Ms. Harris was so mad at Lexie. She tore that behind up and put her on punishment for a month!" Myles found that part of the story the funniest out of it all.

"Y'all, stop laughing at me!" I looked at Jessica and then at Matthew. "You two were the reason I got into trouble. I was going to wait for the bus, but y'all insisted on riding in that boy's car." They were laughing so hard.

Jessica said, "You know you liked riding in that boy's car with your hair blowing in the wind. You talked about it for days after you got that butt whooped!" More laughter followed.

Matthew had another story. "Lexie, do you remember when we were in 8th grade, and your daddy chased you home for hanging with that girl? I think her name was Diana. Jessica, you remember that day, I'm sure."

"Yes," I replied. "Her name was Diana. We were walking around the corner. I saw daddy coming with Leon in the car. Daddy stopped in the middle of the street, jumped out of the car, picked up a stick, and ran toward us. I took off running, with daddy hot on my heels. He chased me all the way home!" I had to pause my storytelling because I was laughing, and it hurt my belly. "When I ran inside, Jessica was standing there, laughing at me. 'I told you not to go with her. I saw y'all running across that vacant lot,' she said." At that point, everyone had fallen to their knees, laughing.

Myles asked, "What did your dad say when he got home?"

"He said, 'I told you about being with that girl. You're out there walking down the street like a streetwalker. If I catch you with her again, I'm going to beat you good!' I remember Leon having to drive the car home that day after daddy left him and the car in the middle of the street."

Jessica stopped laughing for a moment, looked over at Matthew, and said, "Boy, you can't laugh! Do you remember when you and Leon came home with a cigar? Each of you had one, sitting in the family room, puffing away. Lexie kept saying, 'I'm going to tell daddy! You know you're not supposed to smoke!' Leon told her she talked too much. We heard the side door open, knowing it was Mr. Harris coming home early from work. 'Do I smell smoke? Who's that smoking in my house?' he yelled. You should have seen Matthew and Leon trying to fan the smoke out of the room with books. Mr. Harris walked into the room and hollered, 'Y'all are smoking in my house?' He made the two of them sit right there and smoke the entire thing! They were so buzzed by the time they finished. Mr. Harris took off his belt and started whipping both of them. Matthew was crying and saying, 'Uncle Dee, I gotta pee! Please, let me go pee! I won't smoke anymore!' Every time he tried to stand and run, he would fall back onto the couch, begging, 'Please don't tell Mama!' Leon was lying on the floor, laughing at Matthew. He couldn't stand, either. Every time he tried, he would fall." There wasn't a dry eye in the room. Everybody was laughing ridiculously hard.

Matthew went over to Jessica, trying to put his hand over her mouth, but she was still laughing. "You know, I don't remember how I got home that day. I just remember waking up in my bed. My bed was wet, and I was sick as a dog."

"And Mama whipped your behind for peeing in the bed," Kathy added.

"Look, all I know is that I never put another cigar—or anything else that would have given me a buzz—in my mouth to this day," Matthew replied.

Once the laughter quieted down, we marveled at the fact that the babies didn't wake up. Jessica said, "Let me get out of here so I can finish my rounds and go home."

"Yes, you go home thinking about all that stuff. Remember: You got in trouble, too," Matthew replied.

She winked at him. "All the trouble I got into, I was always with you. That's our secret." She glared at him, daring him to say another word.

"Yes, it's our little secret," he agreed.

"Anyway, Lexie. I came in to give you this." It was a breast pumping kit with 12 bottles. "You will really need this when you get home. Did the nurse explain about alternating their feedings?"

"Yes, she did."

"I have enjoyed myself going down memory lane with you guys. Matthew, Kathy, Liz… It was nice seeing you, although Liz doesn't remember me," Jessica said with a laugh as she headed for the door.

"Myles is putting in a pool next Spring. I'll be on my feet, and the babies will be older. I'm going to invite all of you to our house for a cookout and pool party. You are welcome to bring your families," I announced.

"Sounds like a plan!" Matthew replied.

Jessica stopped in her tracks, turned around, and said, "I'll be looking for my invitation! Lexie, I will see you tomorrow after 3:00 so that you can sign your discharge papers, but you can't leave the hospital until Sunday after 12:00. Myles, you will need to have the car seats installed properly to take the babies to their new home."

"Yes, I know. They are already secured in the car."

"Jessica, I thought I was going home tomorrow," I responded.

"No, you can't go home tomorrow. Because you had a C-Section and twins, those are the hospital's rules."

"Why are you coming to release me tomorrow, but I can't go home until Sunday?"

"I'm off on Sundays," she answered.

"Okay. I'll see you tomorrow," I replied, very disappointed.

The way Jessica and Matthew eyed each other as she walked toward the door did not go unnoticed by me. "Okay. Tomorrow it is," Jessica said, finally walking out the door.

"Okay, guys. It's time for us to get out of here, too," Matthew announced.

"Wait. How did y'all know I was here?" I asked.

"I called your house, and a lady told me you were in the hospital. I called Kathy and Liz, and here we are!" Matthew started to walk out of the door, stopped, and said, "Lexie, I saw LT a couple of weeks ago."

"Who is LT?" I asked.

Matthew looked curiously at Kathy and Liz. "I'm sorry. You don't know LT. He's Leon's son."

"Leon's son?!" I asked in disbelief.

"Yes, you didn't know he had a son?" Kathy asked.

"No, I didn't! Where is he?"

"He lives on Darrel Drive. Leon was about to marry a girl who was three months pregnant when he was killed," Kathy replied.

"Was the girl's name Irma?" I asked.

"Yes," Matthew answered.

"I knew he was dating a girl named Irma before I left for the Air Force."

Matthew spoke slowly. "Leon really loved her. He was so excited when he found out she was pregnant. After he died, she moved out of town. Two years later, she returned with LT. I've kept in touch with her. Lexie, that boy is the spitting image of Leon. You need to see him."

"Oh, my God. Leon has a son. Do you have his number?"

"No, but he lives in the same house Irma grew up in. Her parents moved out, and Irma and LT live there now," Kathy replied.

I sat there in a state of shock. "Oh, my God! Leon has a son! I have a nephew!" I said, smiling.

Chapter 91

Time seemed to creep by slowly as the reality set in that I still had my brother Leon here with me. I couldn't believe it! Reality returned when Matthew lightly touched my arm.

"We're getting ready to leave now, Lexie. This is my weekend to get my twins," he said.

"I thank you all for coming by to see us. Thanks for the information about Leon's son. What does LT stand for?" I asked.

"Leon Tremaine, but they call him LT for short," Matthew replied. He and Myles shook hands and gave each other a brotherly hug.

"I'll be sure to keep in touch with you guys about our get-together," I stated.

"I can't wait. I have really enjoyed myself here tonight," Kathy commented.

"Next time, we are going to talk about you. You got into trouble, too!" I said, laughing. After getting hugs from everyone, they departed. The smile remained on my face as I thought about meeting my nephew. My protective brother left a piece of him behind just for me.

"Myles, can you help me up to go to the bathroom?"

As he helped me out of bed, he noticed the belly strap. "What's this thing you're wearing?"

"It's the belly strap I ordered off Amazon. I was hurting so bad, I had to put on this wrap. I'm glad I remembered to pack it because it's really helping my belly. Before I put it on, it felt like every organ in my body moved to my back." He looked at me with so much love and concern. "Myles, I will be okay. Remember: Two six-pound babies were cut out of me yesterday."

When I came out of the bathroom, I sat on the couch beside Myles. "How are you feeling now?" he asked.

"My midsection hurts a little. I'm surprised and disappointed that we can't go home until Sunday afternoon. I'm also excited to learn I have a nephew!" Myles rubbed my back lovingly. "Myles, my mom and dad thought Jessica was an angel because she never got in trouble. She was the sister I didn't have. Matthew was like a brother to Leon. I remember how close they were before my brother died. Mama and daddy didn't know that Matthew and Jessica were like peanut butter and jelly together. Jessica was always at our house, just so she could be with Matthew. I was really surprised when Jessica told me they weren't together."

Both babies started to cry. Myles passed me Karson, and he held Kaylin. We changed and bottle-fed them. As I fed Kaylin, he stared at me. "Why are you looking at me like that?" I asked.

He smiled, moved my hair back from my face, and replied, "I enjoyed seeing you laugh and enjoy time with your family and friend tonight."

"You're such a hopeless romantic."

He kissed me and said, 'Yes, I am, but only for you."

"Okay, Mr. Romantic. It's time to burp our babies." It was funny to me as I watched him lay the burping cloth and his should and burp Kaylin. I was grateful to have Myles remain in the hospital with me and see how he was bonding with the babies. That night, I slept well. When I woke up, Myles was changing one of the babies. Around 8:00 am. Saturday morning, the staff brought us both a breakfast platter. Dr. Jessica made sure we both had enough to eat. They served us oatmeal, eggs, turkey bacon, toast, and coffee.

"This hospital food is good!" Myles said.

"You're just hungry," I replied, but I had to agree with him. We watched TV and talked. "Myles, Sharon is leaving tomorrow around the same time I'm scheduled to be released."

"You're right! She sure does. I guess I can ask Mae to drop her off at the airport."

"Are you sure? You can always drop her off a little early and pick me up after. I remember Mae saying she has to work this weekend."

He sat back and started rubbing his hair back. I knew he was trying to figure out what to do. "Okay, I'll go home and talk to Sharon. I'll let her know I'll take her to the airport at noon. Her plane leaves at 1:30. I'll drop off KJ at Mae's, and he can stay there until I pick up you and the babies."

"I think that's the best way."

"I think so, too. God will work it out for us," he replied with surety.

Myles left around 1:30 p.m. I got up on my own, walked around the spacious room, and changed and fed the babies. I was so grateful for the belly wrap, as it really helped me navigate the early days of motherhood. "Thank You, Jesus!" I whispered.

Around 5:00 p.m., Dr. Jessica came in with my discharge papers to sign, telling me the dos and don'ts of motherhood as I healed from childbirth. I enjoyed sitting and talking with her as we reminisced about our time seeing Matthew, Kathy, and Liz. As she walked out, she said, "I'll be waiting on my invite this Summer."

"For sure, Jessica! You are at the top of the list! I want you to be there."

Myles was coming in as Jessica was leaving. "Sharon, KJ, and I went out for dinner and ended up in the mall." He handed me a shopping bag. As he took a seat on the couch, he said, "KJ told me Bella dumped him today for the boy who wanted to beat him up."

"Who is Bella?"

"The little girl who was following him around at school. The same little girl he gave your bracelet to." He was laughing so hard. "Babe, you should have seen the expression on his face when he told me!"

"Stop laughing, Myles! What did you say to him?"

"I told him I got dumped by a girl when I was his age. He said he's not going to tell you about it, though."

"Why not?"

"He said you won't understand because you're a girl." I laughed so hard! "But he did say he'll be glad when you come home."

"Aww, his first little heartbreaking moment came from the same little girl he gave the stolen bracelet to. Did Sharon hear him tell you about it?"

"No, he whispered it to me when we were eating dinner. Sharon was talking to Isaac at the time."

I laughed as I dug into the bag and pulled out the outfit he had bought for me to wear home. "Thank you, Myles. It's beautiful. I like the colors." He had picked out a pair of dark gray pants and a loose-fitting gray and white top.

He barely heard me because his attention was on the babies. "My beautiful babies. Thank You, Lord, for healthy babies."

I was glad he came back. After eating my dinner, I breastfed the babies and went to sleep, resting well most of the night. When I woke up refreshed on Sunday morning, the nurse was bringing in breakfast.

As planned, Myles left in time to get Sharon to the airport by 11:30. While he was gone, I got everything together so that when he returned, I would be ready to leave. I took my time dressing the babies and myself. When I turned around and looked in the mirror, I said to myself, "Lexie, you look good!" My nose still looked large, but I thank God the pain in my midsection had diminished a lot. The babies fell back to sleep, so I laid down and took a nap. When Myles got back at 1:30, I woke right up, ready to go.

"Lexie, that outfit looks nice on you," he said, coming over to kiss me.

"Yes, I love me in it. And this belly wrap is really helping me. I can stick the Velcro on the second strip now. That's a size 40." I showed him what I was talking about. He laughed.

"We stopped by to see you before Sharon left, but you and the babies were asleep."

"Why didn't you wake me?"

"I wanted to, but Sharon told me not to wake you. She just wanted to peek in on you guys before she left. As I drove her to the airport, she said you are a beautiful lady and that while you slept, she saw just how much KJ looks like you, but that he has his daddy's eyes and mouth."

"Where did she see Keith to know KJ has his eyes and mouth?"

"She said Keith stopped by the house to see KJ because he was going out of town for a week and wanted to see him before he left."

"What?! He stopped by our house?!" I was livid.

"Yes, he did. Sharon said they were upstairs and after he left, KJ told her his dad saw all the diapers and wipes in the bedroom. He walked in and said, 'This was my old room when I lived here.' KJ said his daddy looked in the closet and made a funny face and then said, 'You were a little bitty baby when I lived here.' She said KJ laughed for a long time after that visit. About 30 minutes after he left, Keith called back, saying he had left his boarding pass on KJ's dresser. Sharon said she looked for it but didn't see it. When she got back on the phone, he said, 'Never mind. It's in my pocket,' and then hung up."

I sat there thinking, "KJ must have told him I was in the hospital. Keith knows he's not welcome inside my house. And why was he looking in my closet?"

Myles laughed and said, "Before Sharon got out of the truck, she told me I better treat you right."

I asked, "Why would she say that?"

He said, "She knew me when I was wild and foolish," kissing me on my forehead.

The nurse knocked on the door, entered the room, and asked, "Are you ready to go, Mrs. Ferguson?"

"Yes, I am."

Myles helped me into the wheelchair. Once settled, the nurse placed the babies in my arms and pushed us to the hospital's exit doors. Myles walked beside us, carrying the bags. The nurse helped us secure the babies in their car seats, ensuring we buckled them in correctly. The four of us pulled away, and I thanked God I was finally free from that place.

Chapter 92

As Myles drove, I told him I wanted to go by and see the house where my nephew lived. "Are you sure you feel like going by there? That's on the other side of town."

"I know where it is. It's about four blocks from my old house."

We drove down the street where the house was. Passing by, there was a boy and two girls outside playing basketball. "That's it," I said, pointing.

Myles drove slowly as we passed by. "Do you want to stop?"

"No, let's go around the block. We'll come back and ask where is Warrington Avenue. That's the street I used to live on. I just want to get a closer look at him. Hopefully, they're still there when we return."

We went around the block, saw the children were still playing, and stopped. Myles yelled, "Young man, can you tell me where Warrington Avenue is?"

The boy approached us but didn't get too close. He pointed, "Go down to the end of the street..." While he was talking, one of the girls ran inside the house and then came out with a woman. It was Irma. I sat there in shock, knowing for sure the boy was my nephew. She came over and gave us directions.

"Thank you, ma'am," Myles said. To the boy, he said, "How good are you with that basketball?"

He smiled and replied, "I think I'm pretty good."

"Alright, now! Keep up the good work," Myles said before driving away.

I sat there and cried. It was like I was looking at Leon. The boy's smile, the way he stood, the deepness of his young voice... Oh, my God! He looked just like my brother! "Myles, when we get home, look on the picture wall and see how much Leon's son looks like him."

By the time we picked up KJ from Mae's house, I had calmed down. I was so never so glad to see our house. When we pulled into the garage, KJ grabbed the food Myles picked up from Cracker Barrel, I carried in the things I got from the hospital, and Myles had the babies.

Once inside, Myles laid Karson and Kaylin in their crib and stood looking at them. I washed my hands and prepared the table for dinner. Myles bought so much food, we were sure to have leftovers. On the table stood the cake plate. I took a peek. Sharon had baked a cake with the words "Welcome Home" on it. I thought that was so sweet of her.

Myles went to look at the pictures on the wall. When he joined me in the kitchen, he said, "Oh, my God! Lexie, that boy looks just like that picture of Leon!"

"I told you."

I then noticed the flowers on the table in the breakfast room. "Myles, you got me fresh flowers?"

"Yes, I picked them up on my way to get Sharon."

"I love them. Thank you."

"You're welcome, and thank you for my beautiful babies."

"Are you ready to eat?" I asked.

"Yes, but I need to change Karson first. I'll be right back."

"KJ, what are you doing?" I yelled.

"I'm helping Myles change Karson," he yelled from the nursery.

I sat at the island, waiting for them to come so that we could eat. When they came in, we sat and talked. Myles said, "Lexie, you need to go and rest when you finish eating."

"I will."

We sat there and listened to KJ tell us what he and Sharon did. "She took me shopping and let me pick out my own outfit!" After dinner, he excitedly ran upstairs to get his clothes to show us.

"I like them, KJ!" I said. It was black jeans and a red and black top.

"Aunt Sharon let me pick it out all by myself. Myles, do you like it?"

"Yes, man! That's a cool outfit!"

"Did you tell her thank you?"

"Yes, ma'am," he said, smiling.

I asked Myles to help me off the stool so that I could go into the bedroom. KJ wanted to help by holding my other hand. "KJ, I can make it."

"Call me Keith," he replied.

"Okay, Keith. I can make it."

He smiled and asked, "Mama, can I sleep down here tonight?"

"You'll have to ask Myles, Keith."

He turned to Myles. "Can I sleep down here tonight?"

"Yes, you can sleep down here, but you'll have to sleep in the office. Your Mama and I will be getting up through the night with the babies."

"Okay," he answered.

"Your room needs to be cleaned. Pick up the toys off your floor, make your bed, and drop all the dirty clothes and towels down the chute," Myles said.

"Okay," he answered again.

When KJ went upstairs, Myles said, "I wonder why he wants you to call him Keith all of a sudden."

"Probably because of the babies." I took my time climbing into bed. "Oh, my God! It feels so good to be in my own bed!" The phone rang. It was Sharon letting us know she had made it home and asking how the babies and I were doing. "We are all doing great. Thank you for the cake and KJ's outfit."

"The cake was KJ's idea. I hope you like it."

"Yes, I do. It's delicious."

"Lexie, we'll talk later. Someone is at my door. Love you guys! Bye."

When Sharon called, Myles was in the kitchen, putting the food away and cleaning up. I yelled to him, letting him know Sharon had arrived home safely.

"Okay, thanks for letting me know!"

I heard Myles talking to someone. I thought it was KJ, but it was Mae and the girls. Chyna ran into the bedroom. "I want to see the babies!"

Mae hollered at her. "Girl, take off your shoes! How are you feeling, Lexie?"

"I'm doing good. Thanks for asking."

Myles yelled from the kitchen, "If you want to hold the babies, go wash your hands!"

Mae yelled back, "Myles, who are you talking to? I'm a nurse, remember?"

"Yes, I know you're a nurse. You wash your hands, too!" We all laughed. Mae and Trina went to wash their hands. Chyna remained standing at the side of the crib, looking down at the babies.

"Where's KJ?" she asked.

"He's upstairs somewhere."

"Can I go and play with him?"

"Yes, if it's okay with your mom."

"You can go, but don't be running around up there," Mae said as she picked up Karson. Trina was holding Kaylin.

Myles yelled from the kitchen, "Babe, I'll be in the exercise room."

"Okay!"

Mae asked, "Does he always tell you where he's going?"

"Yes, if he doesn't, he will always call to let me know where he is." We shared a laugh.

Myles came into the room when he finished exercising. "I hate to break up your little get-together, but Lexie needs to rest. She has two four-day-old babies who will need her attention soon," he said, smiling.

"Are you telling us to leave?" Mae asked.

"No, not leave the house, just the room."

"Myles, you're running my company away!" I said.

"Lexie, you haven't rested at all since we got home." Mae started to yell for Chyna to come downstairs. Myles stopped her. "You are going to wake the babies.

There's an intercom right there," he said, pointing to the device on the wall. I was laughing.

Mae got on the intercom and said, "Chyna, come down. Uncle Myles is putting us out of his house. Lexie, we'll be back when Myles isn't here," she said, laughing hard. "I know you need your rest. I'm just joking."

"Thanks for coming," I replied, hugging her and Trina.

Myles and KJ walked them to their car. I got up, went to the bathroom, and climbed right back in the bed, hoping to rest before the babies woke up. When the guys came back in, Myles went to wash his hands. Suddenly, both babies started crying simultaneously. KJ thought that was so funny.

"Can I help?" he asked.

"Yes, pass me the diapers, please." He was so happy to help Myles and me. He was right there being the big brother. He even helped Myles change Karson while I worked with Kaylin. It was around 9:00 p.m. when we put the babies in their crib. I laid down, and KJ and Myles watched TV.

I woke up around 2:30 a.m. to Myles changing one of the babies. "I've done what I had to do. I am going to sleep now," he said. He kissed me on my forehead as he handed me the baby. As I breastfed them, I thought about how good of a man the Lord blessed me with.

Chapter 93

On Monday morning, Myles was in the kitchen early. I got up, took a shower, did my breast pumping, and joined him after getting dressed. "Good morning, sleepyhead! You smell good!" he said, coming over to kiss me.

"Good morning, Honey. You cooked all this food?"

"Yes, I made biscuits, grits, hashbrowns, eggs, and bacon. There's a fruit dish in the refrigerator. Let me grab it."

"You are spoiling me—but pass me a plate! I am ready to eat. Everything looks so good," I said, complimenting his cooking skills.

The doorbell rang, and Myles went to see who it was. Looking at the clock, I saw it was only 10:30. KJ came in from the office and said, "Good morning, Mama!"

"Good morning, K... I mean Keith!" I hugged him before he went into my bedroom to check on the babies.

Myles came back with Rodrick following him. "Rodrick wanted to see you and the babies before going back to college this morning." Rodrick hugged me. "Have you eaten breakfast?"

"No, not yet."

"Well, get a plate and eat with us," Myles offered.

"Thanks, I will." He went to wash his hands. As he walked back in, he asked, "How are you feeling, Aunt Lexie?"

"I'm feeling good. Thanks for asking."

"Rodrick, when you finish eating, wash your hands again and go see the babies," Myles said.

"Okay, I will."

After breakfast, Myles and Rodrick went into the nursery. I heard Myles say, "What are you doing, KJ?" I ran as fast as I could to see what he was doing. KJ was sitting, holding Karson, giving him his bottle.

"I'm feeding the baby," he replied nonchalantly.

I reached for my baby and shouted, "You are not to pick him up! You are too small! Do you hear me?!"

"Calm down, Lexie. He's not going to hurt the baby," Myles said. KJ started to cry and ran out of the room.

"Oh, my God. I am so sorry." I handed Karson to Myles and went after KJ. I found him in my office, hiding under his blanket, crying. "Keith, I'm sorry for yelling at you. Mama doesn't want you picking up the babies by yourself. They're too small for you to pick up and take out of their crib without Myles or me telling you to do it. Do you understand?" He didn't answer and refused to take his head out from under his blanket. "Baby, please come out from under there. I have something to tell you."

He slowly moved the blanket away. "Mama, I'm sorry for picking up the baby. I was just giving him his bottle," he said sadly. He started to cry.

"Give me a hug. I'm so sorry for yelling at you," I said, kissing him on his forehead. "What I wanted to tell you is that you have a cousin."

"I have a cousin?!" he asked with a surprised look.

"Yes, and I saw him yesterday. Myles took me by to see him, but he doesn't know I am his auntie yet."

"Where is he? Can I go and see him?"

"He's at his mother's house. His daddy was my brother but was killed before your cousin was born."

"How did you find him?" he asked.

"Your cousin Matthew told me about him while I was in the hospital," I replied, rubbing him gently on his head. I started to feel the hurt all over again from the loss of my brother, but I held it together. "When the babies get bigger, we all are going over to meet him."

"Mama, what's his name?"

"Leon Tremaine Harris, but they call him LT. His dad's name was Leon, too." I needed to change the conversation. I bopped KJ on the nose and said, "Myles cooked a big breakfast for us. Are you ready to eat?"

He sat there for a while in silence. "Yes, ma'am. I'm ready. And I won't pick up the babies unless you tell me."

I kissed him on his forehead and said, "Let's go eat."

When KJ and I walked into the kitchen, Myles and Rodrick were there, sitting at the island. I said, "I want to apologize for what just happened. Keith and I have talked about it, and he knows not to pick up the babies unless he's told, right Keith?"

"Yes, ma'am. Look at all this food! Myles, you cooked all this food for us? Wow!" He grabbed a plate, loaded it with food, and went into the breakfast room to eat.

I sat there, listening to the men talk, but my mind was on KJ. I wondered if he would try to run away again like he did when I made him apologize to Mrs. Brenda. "What's he thinking right now?" I thought. I heard one of the babies crying, so I got up to check on the crying baby. Myles was right behind me. Making it to the room, I picked up Kaylin and then started to cry myself.

"What's wrong, Babe?" Myles asked.

"It seems I'm always doing something to make KJ upset with me. I'm scared he might try to run away again."

Myles came over and hugged me. "He's not going to run away."

"I'm sorry for reacting the way I did when I saw him holding the baby. You saw him first. Why didn't you say something?"

"What I saw was a big brother sitting down feeding the baby. There was nothing to say. He did what he sees us doing."

"I bet Rodrick thinks I'm a mean lady."

He laughed and replied, "You are not mean."

KJ ran into my room laughing. "I just beat Rodrick in Connect 4! Myles, he was cheating like you do."

Myles laughed along with him and said, "When Rodrick leaves, I will beat your socks off!" The three guys went into the exercise room for about an hour. When Myles and KJ returned, Rodrick wasn't with them. "Rodrick couldn't come back in. He had to hit the road but said when he comes back again, he'll bring Ashley over to see the babies."

"I like that idea. Both of them are pleasant to be around," I replied.

Chapter 94

Life was different, having two babies in the house. Changing diapers, breastfeeding, and waking up every three to four hours was something to get used to, but Myles was a major help. After four straight weeks at home with me, he returned to work part-time but called every two hours to check on the babies and me.

It was my first time out of the house since the babies were born when it was time for our six-week checkup. I was so happy to get out and ride with the sun shining on my face. Arriving at the doctor's office, we ran into Keith and Brenda coming out as we were going in. Myles and I spoke to them. Brenda spoke, but Keith didn't.

"Let me see these twins," she said, peeking under the blankets at the babies. I held one, and Myles held the other. "They are beautiful!" She looked at me and said, "It doesn't look like you just had these babies. How did you lose your weight so fast?"

"Working out in the morning and evening. Cutting back on what I eat. Breastfeeding is helping, too."

"Well, girl, you look good."

"Thank you, Brenda. How's your baby?"

"Growing like a weed. She's at daycare right now." Keith stood there looking at us before walking away. He still hadn't spoken one word.

"It's nice seeing you, Mrs. Montgomery. Babe, I'll see you inside," Myles said, walking away.

"Brenda, I didn't know this was your doctor's office."

"My insurance transferred me over here right before Breonna was born."

"You're going to like coming here," I assured her.

"I already do! They have some good doctors here, and everybody is so nice," she replied, smiling.

Just then, Myles called me on my cell phone, saying they were ready for us. "Well, it was nice seeing you, Brenda. I gotta go now. They're ready for us."

"I'll be looking forward to seeing KJ this weekend. Bye!"

The checkup with the babies and me went well. The doctor looked at Karson's hands and said, "His hands look good. You can't even see where the other finger was."

Myles laughed and said, "I never knew I was born with six fingers until my sister told me."

"Every now and then, we get babies born with six fingers. I must say this: Karson looks like his daddy, and Kaylin looks like her mother with all that hair on her head. Lexie, I see you are getting your girly shape back. You were full of babies anyway. Now that they're here, you are getting back down to the size you were," she said, laughing.

"I exercise twice a day and eat healthily. Breastfeeding is helping with my weight, and next week, I will resume jogging."

"Keep up the good work. I'll see you at your next appointment," she replied.

When we got home, there was a message on the phone from Mae saying Rodrick got hurt while playing football and was at the hospital. Myles asked if I wanted to go. "No, you go. Call and let me know how he's doing."

"I'll pick up KJ and take him with me," Myles replied. About an hour later, Myles called and asked how I was doing.

"I'm doing good, but how's Rodrick?"

"I left KJ at Mae's. Trina and Chyna were home, so Trina said she would keep him for me. She didn't want to come to the hospital."

"Myles, calm down. How is Rodrick, Honey?" I could tell he was a nervous wreck.

"I gotta go, Lexie. The doctor is coming out now to talk to us. I'll call you back." About 15 minutes later, he called back and had calmed down a lot. "Rodrick is okay. He has a slight concussion and a fractured arm. When he first got here, Mae said he didn't recognize anybody, but he's doing better. His memory is back, and he remembers what happened to him. I think Derrick and Mae are doing worse than Rodrick," he said with a nervous laugh. "Ashley is here, too."

"I'm glad he's doing well. I gotta run. Both babies are crying."

"Okay, see you in a few. Love you," he replied.

"Love you, too." When I hung up, I thought back to the time Leon got a concussion while playing football. After that, Mama wouldn't sign the paper for him to play the game again. Leon was angry at her for a long time, but she let him run track and play basketball.

By the time Myles and KJ got home, the babies and I were sound asleep.

Chapter 95

Time progressed, and we adjusted to having the babies in the house. Myles returned to work full-time, and Mrs. Riddle agreed to come over every Wednesday to help with the babies and every other week for housekeeping. Her coming in on Wednesdays gave me time to get out of the house for some me-time.

Rodrick was doing well, but Mae had yet to sign the papers for him to play football in the Fall. Needless to say, he wasn't happy about that.

One Wednesday, when Mrs. Riddle arrived, the babies were asleep. I used that time to try on clothes to see what I could fit since I was almost back to my normal size. Myles didn't seem to notice the weight loss because I was so self-conscious about my after-baby weight, I wore oversized clothes. Even when I went to bed, I wore the same pregnancy gowns. I tried on the two-piece bathing suit Myles bought for me on our honeymoon, and it fit! I was glad Mrs. Riddle told me about putting pure cocoa butter and olive oil on my stomach and back. I didn't have as many stretch marks as I thought I would have after giving birth to twins. I worked out morning and afternoon to tighten my stomach muscles, and the belly wrap helped a lot as I jogged up and down the long driveway. I still had a little fat to get rid of, but I could say I looked good. Plus, my nose went back down to its former size, and my hair was growing, hanging down my back.

Myles called earlier to check on us. He said Mr. Ron was out of town for a funeral and wouldn't return until Friday. My husband needed some cheering up. I thought, "I'll make today 'The New Me Day'! I'm going to surprise Myles at work."

I put on the two-piece bathing suit under my sweats and gym shoes. I grabbed my red high-heel shoes and put on my trench coat. Leaving out, I told Mrs. Riddle I would be back in an hour or two. She smiled a knowing smile at me. I stopped by Subway to get lunch and then went to Dollar Tree to have the sales clerk blow up 25 small red, white, and blue balloons to put in trash bags and three big ones that had "I Love You" printed on them. I made it to the shop at around 11:30, placing the lunch and balloons on the table in the breakroom. Mrs. Clark followed me, telling me how good I looked, and asked about the twins. I thanked her, told her they were doing well, and said, "Take the rest of the day off. I want to surprise Myles."

"For real?" she asked.

"Yes, and I'll pay you for the time." She smiled, hugged me, and left. After retrieving the bags of balloons, I went back inside and locked the door behind me, turning around the sign on the door to 'Closed.' I went into the bathroom, removed my sweats and gym shoes, put on my high heels, and sprayed some perfume I knew Myles liked.

I walked down the hallway, peeking into the workroom where Myles was dutifully working on a laptop. He was listening to music with his back to the door. I stood there, looking at him hard at work. I forgot Spot was at the shop with him. I could see him asleep in his cage with the door open. I quietly took the bags with the balloons and released them low to the floor. As if magnetized, they started rolling toward the dog's cage.

The phone rang three times. Since Mrs. Clark didn't answer, Myles picked it up. I heard him say, "No, it won't be ready until tomorrow… I'm working on it now… Yes, tomorrow around 10:00… Thank you, Mr. Horton."

The phone ringing woke up the dog. He started barking at the balloons. Myles asked, "What are you barking at, Spot?" without looking up. When Spot started running around, chasing the balloons, Myles turned to see what the commotion was all about. That's when he saw me standing there in my two-piece bathing suit and red high heels. In my hand, I held the three "I Love You" balloons. His mouth fell open, and he shouted, "Lexie, where is Mrs. Clark?!"

"I gave her off for the rest of the day with pay," I replied seductively.

He stood, looked at me, and smiled. "Spot, get in your cage," he ordered. He then covered the cage with a cloth lying on a nearby chair. "So, you can fit it. Babe, you look good! Oh, my gosh!" he said, kissing me.

"Yes, I can wear it. Now, you can put your arms around my waist."

"What brought this on?" he asked, running his fingers through my hair.

"You brought this on. I want to keep our marriage exciting. Today is 'The New Me Day'!"

He couldn't stop laughing and kissing me. "I can't believe you! Did you come out of the house looking like this?"

"No, my sweats are in the bathroom. I did this just for you."

He pulled me close and inhaled deeply. "Mmm… You smell so good."

I knew he had work to do, so after a bit of play, I went into the bathroom to put on my clothes. I stayed with him, watching him work on computers. I answered the phone for him, repeatedly having to say, "We are closed for today. Call back tomorrow after 9:00." I felt obligated to do that, only because I had sent his secretary home for the day. He finally took a break, and we ate lunch together. I ended up staying with him until it was time for me to pick up KJ from Mae's house.

When we got home, Mrs. Riddle said, "I enjoyed the babies. They ate, slept, and played. They weren't any problem at all."

"Mrs. Riddle, can you make me banana pudding?" KJ asked.

She bent at the waist, looked him in the eyes, and said, "The next time I make it, I will be sure to save you some."

"Okay, thank you." He hugged her and ran upstairs.

"I gotta bring that boy some pudding soon. He's growing so tall so fast," she said, laughing. I paid her for the day, and she left.

Myles arrived shortly after Mrs. Riddle left. He came in with a dozen red roses and a box of chocolate candy. As he handed the gifts to me, he asked, "When are you going to surprise me again with 'The New Me Day'?" He pulled me close, kissed me, and played in my hair.

"It wouldn't be much of a surprise if I told you, Honey!"

"Well, I enjoyed being surprised!" He tapped me on my butt, smiling.

Chapter 96

One Saturday, Myles and KJ went out for bonding time. I sat in my bedroom, thinking about Leon's son—my nephew. I still couldn't believe it. I dialed 911, hoping Irma would answer the phone, and she did. I told her who I was and asked for her number or for her to call me back. "I'll call you on my break. Your number showed up on the ID. Bye." She ended the call so abruptly, I wasn't sure she'd even remember I called.

I waited for her return call and was glad to see when her name showed up on my caller ID. "I'm sorry for hanging up so fast, but we are swamped today," she said. I told her Matthew was the one who told me about Leon's son and asked her why she didn't let us know. "Lexie, when Leon was killed, I immediately left town and stayed gone for two years. I was hurt and pregnant. The man I loved was gone. I just had to get away. When I moved back, I saw Matthew and Kathy, but they didn't know where you were. They did tell me your mom had passed away and that they didn't know if you were still in the Air Force or not."

"After retiring from the Air Force, I didn't know where any of my family members were when I got back in town. A month ago, Matthew came to my house to install an intercom system. That was my first time seeing him in about 11 years. Matthew, Kathy, and Liz came to see me in the hospital after giving birth to my twins. That's when Matthew told me about LT. The day we left the hospital, I had my husband drive me by your house. Your son was in the yard, playing basketball with two girls. Do you remember the day you gave a stranger in a truck directions to Warrington Avenue?" I asked.

"Yes, someone in a blue truck," she replied.

"That was my husband and me. Kathy told me where you lived, which I recognized as your parents' house. Irma, when I saw your son, I knew he was my family. He looks just like Leon. He smiles and walks like him, too."

"Yes, he does look like his daddy," Irma said.

"I would love to meet him and let him know I'm his aunt."

"Right now, he's out of town visiting my sister for a couple of weeks. I'll have him call you when he gets home. Here's my home number. You can call him any time you'd like. Lexie, thanks for calling me. I must get back to work now. Bye."

I was so happy to talk to her and know she was receptive to me meeting my nephew, I cried when I hung up the phone.

When Myles and KJ got home, Myles kissed me, and KJ hugged me. "Mama, can I take a nap in your office? I'm too tired to walk upstairs to get in my bed."

Myles laughed. "Boy, you slept through the whole movie!"

"Yes, you can take a nap in my office. Take the papers that are stacked on the couch and put them on the computer table," I answered. He walked over to the crib, looked down at the sleeping babies, and went into the office for a nap.

Myles told me about their day. "We went to the movies, and, on our way home, we stopped by the flea market. We stopped by this one table with a man sitting behind it, looking down, counting something in a box. He had Black art merchandise, Obama calendars, wristbands that said 'What Would Jesus Do?', Bible covers with scripture on them, and a lot of other things. The man heard me talking to KJ and looked up. Lexie, it was the same man we saw Keith with at the restaurant!"

He asked, "Do you see anything you like?"

"No, we are just looking," I replied.

"I like your t-shirt," he said.

"Then, he read the words on my cap aloud."

"'Daddy Touch.' I like that cap, too."

"I thanked him for the compliments. Lexie, he was talking and moving his hands all around. I couldn't look at him, so I kept looking down at the table. When we started to walk away, he said, 'I have seen you somewhere.' He stood and looked at me as if he were trying to think of where he's seen me. 'I know where! You were at Outback Steakhouse. You're Myles,' he said. 'Yes, and your name is Sam,' I answered. He looked down at KJ and said, 'And you must be KJ.' 'Yes, sir,' he replied. The story doesn't end there.

"As we were walking away, guess who we ran into?"

"Who?" I asked.

"Keith."

"For real? What did he say when he saw the two of you together?"

"He spoke, looking like the canary that swallowed the fish. He asked KJ if he was having a nice day, and KJ told him he was. That was it. That was the extent of the father-son interaction. I watched as he walked toward Sam's table. He kept looking back at me with an evil look because the last time we spoke, it didn't go too well."

"Myles, when did you talk to him?"

"Not long after KJ asked us what low-down meant."

"What?! What did he say?" I pressed.

"Wait, Lexie. Let me finish telling you about what happened today, and then I'll tell you about that day."

I sighed. "Okay."

"So, when we passed by KJ's dad today, KJ said, 'That man at the table is at my daddy's church all the time. He was at my daddy's house when Mama Brenda moved into her apartment by the Walmart store.' I asked, 'Mrs. Brenda doesn't live in your daddy's house?' 'Nope.' I asked him what he does when he's at his daddy's house, and he said, 'Sometimes, daddy takes me to Mama Brenda's apartment, and sometimes, he drops me off at the daycare at church.'"

I was looking at Myles. As he talked, he was rubbing his hair back. I could tell he wasn't pleased with hearing what KJ told him.

"Lexie, I don't like what's happening. You need full custody of KJ. We have no idea what he sees or hears when he's at that man's house. One day, he told me he was in the daycare and went looking for his daddy. When he got to his dad's office, the door was locked. He said he heard his daddy talking to somebody, but he wouldn't open the door to let him in. He even said he was knocking hard on the door."

"I wonder who Keith was talking to that kept him from opening the door for his son," I said.

"That's what I want to know! Who was he talking to...or what was he doing?" I just sat there, shaking my head in disbelief. "Okay, I didn't tell you this, but a week after KJ asked us what down-low meant, I saw Keith at Subway with Sam, and we had a talk."

"For real? What happened?"

"After I placed my order and turned to walk out, Sam got up and walked toward the bathroom. I don't think either of them saw me because when I first went in, they were huddled up next to each other with their heads down, looking at some papers. You should have seen the way Keith smiled as Sam walked away. Anyway, when he saw me walking toward him, his smile faded. I could tell he was surprised to see me. We engaged in some small talk—you know, how's the family and whatnot—but I noticed he kept looking down at the paper in his hand. He wouldn't look at me to save his life.

"I asked him, 'Keith, what does down-low mean?' He finally looked up at me and asked, 'What do you mean?' with a curious look. I told him, 'That's what your son came home asking us. I don't believe in your lifestyle, but you'll have to answer to God about that. In the meantime, you have a confused son who's asking me questions about what he hears when he's with you.' He resumed looking down and asked, 'What do you mean about my lifestyle?' 'You tell me, man. I see you all the time. I'm downtown nearly three times a week, going to the parts shop. I have seen you two coming and going from the hotel across the street from my shop. I have seen you coming out of the grocery store around the corner together, getting into a red car just like the one parked out front. Now, it's not my business what you do, but when KJ comes home confused and asking his Mama and me questions, that's when it becomes my business. What am I supposed to tell him? Do you think you should think about giving Lexie full custody of him?' He never looked up when he said, 'He's my son.' I told him, 'Yes, he is your son, so you be the one to tell him what down-low means and why Sam is following you around at your house and the church.' He looked up at me and said, 'I'll think about it.' 'Yes, you think about it before the news get back to your church, since you seem to be hiding out on this side of town.'"

"Wow, Myles. What did he say about that?" I asked, concerned about the direction their conversation took.

"He didn't say anything else because Sam had come out of the bathroom. I just waved at both of them, turned to Keith, and said, 'Nice talking to you, Mr. Montgomery,' before walking out the door." Finished with the play-by-play, Myles got up and went into the kitchen. "That man is so conceited, proud, and on his

342

way to Hell." I knew he was upset, having to relive the moment to tell me about it.

I sat there thinking, "I felt better with KJ going over to his dad's house when Brenda was there. Now, she has moved out, and I don't know what to think."

Myles came back into the room, eating an apple. He had one in his other hand for me. "Would you like an apple?"

"No, thank you."

"Babe, when I finish this apple, let us pray that the Lord will give us direction on how to deal with the situation."

Chapter 97

The Monday before Thanksgiving, Myles had to pick up KJ from school because he was sick with a headache, stomachache, and was vomiting. On Wednesday, Myles came home from work with the same symptoms, adding that his joints were aching, and he had a sore throat and fever. He slept in one of the bedrooms upstairs, not wanting to give whatever he had to the babies and me. Mae brought him over some of the medicine she had given to Derrick when he was sick two weeks prior. When KJ felt better, he took food and water up to Myles. I used a lot of Lysol spray during that time.

On Thanksgiving Day, I ordered out for a Thanksgiving dinner from Cracker Barrel. I made a lemon pound cake and two sweet potato pies. Myles slept all day and didn't eat anything, so KJ and I ate.

On Friday, Myles was up early, making a pot of vegetable soup, saying he felt better. On Saturday, he felt much better and spent the day disinfecting the bedrooms and theater room and washing all the bedding. When he was done, he indulged in eating a lot of the leftover food from Thanksgiving.

Two weeks before Christmas, Myles called from work. "How are you and the babies?"

"We're doing good."

"I received a call from KJ's dad today. He wants to meet with us at his church Sunday after service around 2:00. He wants to talk about KJ."

"He does?"

"Yes, I told him we would be there. I was thinking we could drop off KJ at Mae's house. I don't think he should go with us, especially when we have no idea what that man is going to say. I asked him if Mrs. Montgomery would be at the meeting, and he replied sarcastically, 'She told me that she would be there.' For some reason, I just don't like his arrogant attitude. I definitely don't like his lifestyle."

"Okay, Honey. I'll see you when you get home. Let me check on the babies," I replied, not knowing what else to say.

"Do you need anything from the store?" he asked.

"No, nothing I can think of." After hanging up the phone, I thought, "What does Keith want to talk to me about?"

That Sunday after service, we dropped off KJ at Mae's house and drove to Keith's church for the meeting. When we arrived, people were still exiting the church. We sat in the parking lot until Keith opened the door and waved us in. Walking into his office, we saw Brenda was already there. She smiled, hugged me, and shook Myles' hand. "Have a seat," she said with a smile. She peeked at the babies and said, "They are some beautiful babies."

"Thank you," I said, returning the smile.

Keith came in, shut the door behind him, and took his seat across the table from us. "I'll get right to the reason I wanted you all here," he began.

Myles stopped him. "Do we need to pray first?"

"I have already prayed, which is why we are here," Keith replied. Myles squeezed my hand.

I heard Brenda say in a muffled voice, "I have prayed, too. That's why I am here." She was mean-mugging Keith the whole time.

Keith continued. "Lexie, I was thinking I want to give you full custody of KJ. I'm busy going out of town to different church meetings ever since they made me a superintendent over a district, and I won't be able to spend much time with him. I'd feel better if he didn't have to depend on me. I'd still like to see him from time to time and I don't want you to change his name."

"I won't change his name," I replied.

Brenda was looking angry as she kept looking down. I noticed Keith kept looking at her as he talked, not at us. Suddenly, the door to the office opened. It was Sam. "Excuse me, I'm sorry. I didn't know you were in a meeting."

Brenda turned, saw Sam, and murmured, "What is he doing here?" The mean-mugging was nonstop.

Keith smiled and said, "Brother Sam, I'll be done here in a few minutes. Come back later."

When Sam closed the door, I said, "Keith, if that's what you want to do, that will be fine with me."

Keith looked over at Myles and asked, "Is that okay with you?"

"It's your decision, but it sounds good to me," he replied. I knew that arrangement sounded very good to Myles, especially after the talk he had with Keith in Subway.

"Keith, once the paperwork is completed, you don't have to pay me child support anymore. I'll contact my lawyer and have him draw up the paperwork tomorrow."

"Okay, you can call and let me know the cost. Whatever it is, I will pay it," he responded.

Myles spoke up. "No, we'll take care of the cost."

I could see Brenda glaring at Keith, looking like she had something on her mind. I reflected on how they disrespected me at Mother Stone's dinner party and how she slipped in and out of his office at the church. I definitely couldn't forget her coming to my house with him, but I felt sorry for her at that moment.

Keith looked at Brenda and said, "I should have let you know I was thinking about giving Lexie full custody of KJ. What do you think?"

She pulled papers out of her purse and said angrily, "He's your son. I think you should give her custody—with that lifestyle you're living!" She stood, walked to his desk, and slammed the papers, scattering everything within reach of their wind. "I am asking for a divorce. When I moved out of your house, I prayed about my decision to stay with you or leave. Today, I got my answer!"

Keith stood, looking shocked. "You want what? You said you were moving out to give you time to think!"

"I did think, and this is my answer," she replied while tapping the divorce papers with the tip of her finger.

That was our cue to leave. Myles started wrapping up the baby he was holding and whispered to me, "We better go."

By then, Brenda was screaming at the top of her lungs. "I am asking you for a divorce. I can't stand seeing you that that man. You seem to be happy with him, and he always follows you around like a little puppy. I want you to know I am not going to be like Lexie. When you sign this paper, you will be paying me a hefty amount of child support!" Keith stood there, taking the verbal onslaught and trying to get her to lower her voice, to no avail.

Myles and I gathered the babies and our things and walked out. When we opened the door, Sam was standing on the other side, listening. We hurried out of there, not wanting to bear witness to anything else that was surely about to happen in that office.

As we put the babies in their car seats, Myles asked, "Lexie, what just happened back there?"

"I don't know, but I'm glad he's giving up custody of KJ. Thank you, Jesus."

"That was the Lord's doing, and it is marvelous in our sight," he said, laughing.

"Myles, are you sure we should pay all the fees for the custody hearing?"

"Yes, Babe. I don't want Keith to change his mind."

"Do you think I should tell KJ?" I asked.

"No, not yet."

When we made it back to Mae's house to pick up KJ, Chyna came out with him. "Where are you going?" Myles asked her.

"KJ said I can come with y'all," she answered.

"Does your mom know you are gone?" I asked.

"No, KJ told me to come on." We laughed.

"Where is your mom?" Myles asked.

"She's asleep."

"And where is your dad?"

"He went over to grandma's house."

I had to stop the madness. "Girl, let me call your mom to see if it's okay for you to come with us." After a quick call to Mae, I hung up and said, "Yes, you can go."

Driving away, Myles asked, "Where do y'all want to go for dinner?"

KJ and Chyna yelled, "McDonald's!"

Myles laughed and said, "No McDonald's today. I need a meal."

"Let go to your favorite place, Cracker Barrel," I suggested.

"Yay!" Myles said, clapping his hands.

"You are so silly!"

He squeezed my hand and said, "Is that why you love me?"

"Nope, I love you because God sent you to me. Remember what the scripture says: 'He that finds a wife finds a good thing and obtains favor from the Lord.' I have favor!" He and KJ thought that was so funny.

Chapter 98

As the Christmas season rolled in, I could see how much Myles loved the holiday. He and KJ put up Christmas lights all around the inside of the house and large Christmas trees—one in the living room and one in the family room. The twins enjoyed sitting in their walkers, looking at all the blinking lights on the trees. Spot did, too.

On Christmas Eve, Mae's family, Uncle Eddie, Aunt Ruby, and a couple of their cousins came to our house for a gift exchange. I called Irma to ask if LT could come over, but he was spending the holiday in Memphis with her sister. We took family pictures, ate until we were full, played games, and went upstairs to watch The Christmas Story move in the theater room. I was surprised to learn Myles and Mae had never seen it before.

While watching the movie, I thought about my dad. Every Christmas before he died, we would sit and watch that same movie together. My dad loved that movie and laughed all the way through.

After the movie, our guests gathered their gifts, said their goodbyes, and left. It was a fun, memorable night.

It was just Myles, the kids, and me on Christmas Day. We slept in that morning but had a big Christmas lunch to make up for not eating breakfast. Before we ate, Myles told the story about the birth of Jesus. After we ate, we opened our gifts. Myles gave me a gold necklace with all the children's birthstones and a short black leather jacket. I gave him a gold watch and black jogging suit with two white stripes on each leg, and a pair of Jordan gym shoes. KJ gave Myles and me matching red sweaters. KJ and the twins got so much stuff, I cannot even begin to remember it all. Once we tidied up after unwrapping gifts, Myles came over and gave me the best Christmas gift ever.

"This, my lady, is the house gift." He handed me the receipt for the pool's installation. It was paid in full and scheduled to begin in April, just as he promised.

The three of us played games until the early evening. Once it grew dark outside, we drove around the city, looking at the Christmas light displays. It was beautiful. Driving back home, not one house was without holiday lights and decorations in their yard. When we pulled up to our house, it was the first time I saw how Myles and KJ had decorated our home and yard. It was amazing! Before pulling into the garage, we stayed outside for a while, admiring their hard work. Together, my guys decorated the mailbox and the tree in the center of the circle driveway and used a boatload of lights on the house's exterior. I was so proud of them.

Chapter 99

On Saturday, around 1:00 a.m., I was awakened by Myles doing something in the kitchen. "Myles, what are you doing?" I called out.

"Just putting some meat in the slow cooker. Go back to sleep. I'll tell you about it in the morning."

While I was up, I changed and fed the babies and then went right back to sleep. Around 8:30 that morning, Myles was up again, cooking breakfast for us. "Is that the meat I smell?" I asked.

"Yes, it is. I had a taste for my Grandma Rosa's tamales. The other day on my way home, I stopped by the store to pick up everything I needed to make them today. After eating breakfast and tidying up the kitchen, he made four dozen tamales, putting them in the steamer to cook for about an hour. The three of us waited patiently to taste them.

When they finished steaming, Myles unwrapped one, tasted it, and exclaimed, "Oh, my God! It tastes just like Grandma Rosa's! I did it!" He then shared his with KJ and me.

After tasting it, KJ said, "I want one of my own!"

We spent the next 30 minutes or so sitting around the island, eating tamales.

"Myles, these are really good!"

"So, y'all really like them?" We both nodded, unable to speak because we had meat in our mouths. "You know what? I'm going to take Mae a dozen and see what she thinks about them. I'll surprise Uncle Eddie with a dozen, too." Myles was so happy they turned out the how they were supposed to. "I can make this a New Year's Eve tradition! We can all get together and make tamales!"

When the twins woke up, we loaded all the kids into Pearl and went to Mae's house. KJ and I remained in the vehicle with the twins while Myles took the tamales inside to her. At Uncle Eddie's, we all went in. Myles handed him the tamales, and he responded, "Boy, where did you get these from?

"I made them, Uncle Eddie!" he said proudly.

"Here, Ruby. Heat these up!" As he ate one, he paused, looked at Myles closely, and asked, "Myles, did you really make these?"

Myles laughed and said, "KJ, tell Uncle Eddie I made the tamales."

"Yes, sir, he made them—and I helped."

"Myles, these are good. They are really good," Uncle Eddie said, smiling.

Aunt Ruby agreed. "Yes, they are."

"I remember standing around at the table, watching my Grandma Rosa make them. I would wash the corn husks, and Lee, your daddy was the one who tied and put them in the pot," Uncle Eddie explained. "You know, Myles, we should make this a family thing. We should get together and make your Grandma Rosa's tamales every New Year's Eve!"

"That would be great! I was thinking the same thing," Myles replied.

Aunt Ruby wanted to hold the babies before we left. "Lexie, which one of these babies do you want to leave here with us?" I laughed but didn't say anything.

Myles said, "Aunt Ruby, you can keep them when they get bigger."

"They sure are some beautiful babies," she said.

"Ruby, what does being a beautiful baby have to do with it? You know you can't keep no baby! You can hardly stand up yourself," Uncle Eddie stated. We were all laughing at their playful exchange. By the time we left, they were arguing about her keeping one of the babies as he was saying she could hardly keep herself.

Once back home and as we were getting the twins out of the SUV, we heard the house phone ringing. I ran inside and checked the caller ID. Mae had called twice and left one message. The message was short and sounded urgent: "Myles, call me when you get home." He called her back immediately.

"Myles, do you have any more tamales? Rodrick stopped by, and he and his daddy ate all of them except one!" Myles laughed so hard.

"Uncle Eddie liked them, too. He said he wants to make it a family thing and suggested we get together every New Year's Eve to make them like they did when he was younger."

Mae replied, "I can't wait until New Year's Eve! I want some now!"

Laughing, he replied, "I'm on the way." He hung up and grabbed all the tamales we had left to take over to Mae's house. He paused and counted them. "There's only eight left." KJ was cracking up, laughing at the expression Myles had on his face. He immediately called Mae back, telling her he only had eight left and would make more soon. Hanging up the phone, he said, "Mae sounded sad but said she understands." We ate the last eight tamales: Myles had four, and KJ and I had two each.

"Honey, you'll have to make some more soon. They are good," I replied. He smiled.

"Good night, Mama," KJ said suddenly.

"Good night, Keith. Give me a hug." KJ hugged me tightly.

"Good night, Myles. I liked your tamales. They were good."

"Thanks, Peanut. Good night."

Chapter 100

KJ couldn't wait for February 13th to come. He was going to spend the night with his brother on his birthday and, on the 14th, go to Jolly Junction Playhouse for the birthday party. On the 13th, he stayed on the bus and rode it to Mama Brenda's house after school.

On Valentine's Day, I was surprised by Myles serving me breakfast in bed. He said he wasn't going to work and that it was my day to relax. "I'll be right here to sit with the twins today," he said. For my gift, he had made an appointment for me to get my hair done at 11:00, and at 1:00, I was scheduled to get a full body massage. "By the time you make it home, dinner will be waiting." I finished my breakfast, got dressed, and headed out to start my day. I was so excited to get my day started!

When my day out was over, I walked into the house to balloons everywhere. On the island, there was a note that read, "Go get dressed in the office." I entered the room and saw a big box on the couch. Inside, there was a beautiful long cream-colored dress with gold rhinestones down the front. Under the dress was a pair of cream-colored heels with gold trim. I quickly cleaned up and changed into the dress.

Walking out, Myles stood there, looking at me from head to toe. "Lexie, you look beautiful. Tonight is your night. Hurry before the babies wake up." No sooner than those words escaped his mouth, one of the babies started to cry.

"That was not supposed to happen," he said. We had to laugh.

As I entered the nursery to get the baby, I saw a heart made of red rose petals in the middle of our bed and a box of candy in the center of the heart.

While changing and feeding the babies, I asked, "When did you have time to do all this?"

He kissed me and said, "I have magic, remember?" He went into the bathroom and emerged wearing a white leisure suit. He looked really good.

"Myles, you look so handsome. Is that new?"

He just smiled and replied, "It's Valentines' Day, Baby!"

He grabbed his camera and took pictures of the twins and me. "I really like you in that dress."

"I like me in it, too. Thank you," I said, laughing.

After the babies were full and back to sleep, he escorted me to the breakfast room, where he had a big bouquet of red roses sitting in the center of the table. "Sit here. I will be right back." Suddenly, the song "When I Found You, I Found Love" began floating through the air. He returned with a marvelous steak dinner, complete with a strawberry shortcake for dessert. I was so surprised, I cried. He sat there smiling lovingly at me. "You are such a good wife to me and a good mother to our children. I wanted this day to be special for you and show you how much I love and appreciate you. You are the best, my lady." I was so emotional as he spoke each word.

After dinner, we took more pictures and then went outside to sit on the patio and look into the star-filled sky. The night was so romantic. I enjoyed my husband and the many laughs we shared.

That Monday, I was up early, made breakfast, and waited for Myles and KJ to finish eating. I sat at the island, looking at Myles's pictures of us on our romantic Valentine's night. "Myles, the pictures are beautiful. Look at this one." It was a photo of him holding the babies.

"Wow," he said, looking at the picture. "That's a handsome man right there!" he said, laughing. "KJ, come on. Let's go before you miss your bus."

"Okay, coming!" he said, kissing me on the cheek.

Myles kissed me on the lips and said, "I love you. Come on, Spot."

"Love you, too. See you at three this afternoon." I put the dishes into the dishwasher and then tended to the twins. I changed, fed, and played with them for a while and put them back in their crib. I had some work to do that needed to be completed for the job before 5:00 p.m. I finished around noon and submitted it online before the babies woke up. "Thank You, Jesus," I said aloud.

The sound of sirens sounded, breaking the peaceful bliss I was experiencing. I looked out the window and saw the sky was getting dark. I turned on the TV in the family room to see if I could catch an update on why the sirens were sounding. A bulletin flashed on the TV, advising residents to take shelter because a tornado had touched down Southeast of Nashville. My heart started racing. I grabbed the twins and their tie blankets and laid them in the tub in the hallway bathroom attached to the family room because there were no windows in there. I then ran to get their mattress to cover us in the tub and pulled the comforter off my bed to wrap us all up. As soon as I closed the bathroom door, everything went dark. I climbed into the tub with the twins and covered ourselves. I heard the wind howling and the rain hitting against the house.

My cell phone started ringing. I remembered I had left it on the table in the family room. I quickly retrieved it and answered. It was Myles, screaming into the phone. "Grab the babies and go into the hallway bathroom away from the windows! A tornado has touched down. I'm turning onto Riverside now." His phone went dead. I called back and got a busy signal. I crawled back to the bathroom, climbed back into the tub with my babies, and prayed, "Lord, please protect us." I knelt over the babies, shielding them with my body and the mattress. I prayed that Myles wasn't caught up in the tornado and that the Lord would protect us and KJ's school. I didn't know where the tornado was headed. It was so dark in the bathroom, I couldn't see my babies but I knew they were there. "Myles should be here by now. Lord, where is he?" I wondered. I was outright scared and felt helpless. One of the babies started crying, so I had to breastfeed the crying baby in the dark. For 30 minutes or more, we stayed in that tub. "Where is Myles, Lord?" I kept asking.

My cell phone rang again. I hoped it was Myles calling, but it was Mae. "Are you guys alright?" she asked.

"Yes, the babies and I are okay, but I don't know where Myles is!" I yelled, panicking. "He called over 30 minutes or so ago and said he was turning onto our street, but he hasn't arrived yet. And I don't know how KJ is doing."

"Lexie, calm down. KJ is okay. I talked to Trina. She got him. And Myles is okay, too. Stop worrying."

"She's said that to calm me down," I thought to myself.

"I gotta go now. They are bringing people in that are hurt from the tornado. Don't worry. Myles is okay. Bye for now."

I remained under the mattress and comforter, breastfeeding the crying baby while crying myself. I laid there, listening to the howling wind and crackling sounds that accompanied it. There was a hard knock at the front door. I opened the bathroom door slowly and saw that the sun was shining, and everything was calm again. Leaving the babies in the safety of the bathroom, I went to the front door, looked out, and saw it was Myles. I was so happy to see him. His hair was wet, curly, and

356

in total disarray. He had mud on his clothes, and his arm was bleeding. He hugged me, saying, "You all are alright. Thank God. Where are the babies?"

I hugged him back and told him, "They're in the tub."

"I had to walk home. A tree fell in front of the truck, and I had to take shelter under it and the tree. Once the storm passed, I had to climb over branches and limbs to get over the tree. I had Spot with me, but he jumped out of my arms and ran. I looked and couldn't find him," he said sadly. He went into the laundry room to change his clothes. I got the first-aid kit to tend to his wounds. When he exited the room, he walked into the bathroom to see the twins. "I got this scratch on my arm when climbing over the tree. The cut isn't as bad as it looks." He paused and said, "We can't stay here tonight in the dark. Pack a bag for the babies, and we will find a hotel. Bring the Lysol and grab my phone charger. My cell phone is dead."

"We can't get Pearl out of the garage. The power's off."

"I'll let it up manually," he replied.

We drove to where the tree had fallen across the road, blocking Myles' return trip home. Leaving the SUV, Myles carried the diaper bags and I carried the babies. I walked behind him as he broke away branches so that we could get across to his truck. Getting to the truck, we buckled the babies in, making it to Mae's house just in time to see the children get off the bus. I was so happy to see them. Looking at Mae's house, it didn't look damaged at all.

"Get in, KJ. We're going to look for a hotel," Myles said.

We stopped at three hotels, but they were already full of people needing shelter after the tornado. At the Holiday Inn across the street from Walmart, we managed to get the last double-bed room available. We stayed in the truck until Myles sprayed down every inch of the room. Once settled, Myles left to check on Trina and Chyna at Mae's house. I knelt beside the bed and prayed, thanking God for blessing us to be together and sparing our lives.

KJ was crying when he said, "Mama, I was scared at school. They made us all go into the gym and get under the bleachers. Everybody was crying. I thought I was going to die."

I hugged him close and replied, "Thank God, we are all together and safe."

When I called to check on Mrs. Riddle, she said, "I called your house to see if y'all were alright and didn't get an answer."

"We're staying in a hotel. Our house is damaged, and the lights and phone are off."

"It got dark over here so fast. The wind was blowing hard, but we don't have any damage, just a lot of rain," she replied.

"I don't know how long we'll be here, but I'll call you to let you know when we are back in our house."

"Y'all can come over here," she offered.

"Thanks, Mrs. Riddle, but I know Myles won't come." We laughed. "Thanks, anyway, for offering." I then called Myles' Uncle Eddie. They were okay. I thought to call Irma, but I had left her number at home.

Myles made it back to the hotel around 6:00 and said, "When I got to Mae's house, Derrick was there with the girls. He said their house wasn't damaged, but their lights were off. Mae was still at work. She told him she'd meet them at his mom's house and stay there until their lights were back on. Rodrick called Derrick to let him know he was okay. Derrick rode with me to check on the shop. It didn't look like anything even happened over there, but it did rain. The southeast side of Nashville looks like a warzone. It's being reported that 25 people lost their lives, and they were still looking for others.

"We checked on our house, and Babe, it needs a lot of work. All the windows at the back of the house need to be replaced, and the lamps are broken in your Mama's suite. In the theater room, the screen is split in half. The patio and exercise room need a new roof and part of the garage. The toolshed is gone. Everything in the shed is now scattered across the backyard. The big tree that was in the backyard is now in the front.

"Once the lights are back on, the garage door will be okay. I called the insurance company when I was at the shop. They are sending an adjuster and contractor on Wednesday. I'll walk through the house with the adjuster to see what other damage there is, just in case I didn't write everything down. Hopefully, the power will be restored by Wednesday. I was thinking since I've already paid for the swimming pool to be installed, maybe when the work is done on the house, we could get in touch with the pool company to see if they can install it earlier than April. There's a pretty big hole in the backyard with that tree gone." Myles laid back on the bed with his head in his hands. "We need to pray."

The three of us held hands and prayed. Myles started by quoting Psalm 40:1-3. After he finished praying, he hugged both of us and said, "I thank God for blessing us to be here together. When I was under the truck, I thought I would never see either of you again. It was like I was back in Iraq." He started crying, saying, "Lord, I'm so thankful to be alive and with my family."

KJ started crying again. "I thought I was going to die, Myles."

Myles hugged him and said, "I thank God we are all alive, Peanut. I thought I was going to die, too." They hugged and cried together, bringing tears to my eyes at their love for one another.

Chapter 101

"Let's go across the street to Walmart to get some clothes. None of us has a change of clothes except for the twins!" Myles said, laughing.

At the store, we picked up PJs, a change of clothes for the next three days, snacks, and a case of bottled water. Although I had packed enough clothes for the twins, I bought them an outfit, too. KJ was happy to get new clothes and wanted everything he had to match what Myles chose.

After clothes shopping, we went to Applebee's for dinner. Once back in the hotel, KJ did his homework and took his shower. When he exited the shower, he asked, "Where is Spot?"

"KJ, he got away from me during the tornado. I looked for him but couldn't find him," Myles answered.

"You don't know where he is?" KJ asked, near tears.

"No, Peanut, I'm sorry. I don't know where he is right now."

KJ started crying. "We gotta pray for him. Can we go look for him when I get out of school tomorrow?"

"Yes, tomorrow we will go and look for him," Myles replied.

That night, KJ cried himself to sleep.

While in the hotel, Myles and KJ shared a bed, and the babies and I were in the other. Since I had to breastfeed them, that was the most convenient arrangement. Myles turned toward me from their bed and asked, "Babe, do you miss me?"

"No, you're right over there. Go to sleep."

He laughed hard, saying, "I love you and miss you lying beside me."

"I love you, too. Now, go to sleep." I thought to myself, "My husband is so hilarious. I love him so much. He's my knight in shining armor."

The following morning, we ate breakfast and then dropped KJ off at school. The twins and I went to the shop with Myles and, at 2:00, went to see if the tree had been removed so that we could get the SUV and get back to our house. When we got to the tree, Mr. James and his brother were there with their chainsaws, cutting limbs off the tree. Mr. James said his patio was torn off his house, and his gazebo was damaged. His brother said he didn't have any damage to his home, but they got a lot of wind and rain. He was surprised at the level of damage in our area. The man who lived next door to us, Mr. Hill, drove up with his chainsaw, prepared to start cutting off limbs because he needed to get past the tree, too. He reported his house had damage, and a couple of trees had fallen, but it wasn't as bad as our house.

Myles said, "My chainsaw was in our toolshed, but the toolshed is gone. All of the contents are spread out over the backyard. I'll be back to help you guys in the morning."

One of the babies started to cry. "Do I hear a baby?" Mr. James asked, looking around.

Myles said, "Yes, we have twins in the truck—a boy and a girl."

All three men came over, looking at the babies in their car seats. Mr. James was the first to speak. "They are beautiful babies! I didn't know you had twins. I remember your little boy, though. He's the one who ran away with his dog." They all started to laugh.

"Yes, that dog got away from me when the tree fell in front of my truck. I couldn't find him. I got to go pick up my son from school and let him know I still can't find him. I'll see you guys in the morning around 9:00. Remember: That vehicle sitting there is mine."

"Yes, I know," Mr. James said. "It will be safe until you get back here tomorrow," he said assuredly.

On our way to get KJ from school, Myles said, "Lexie, when we moved out here, I was 12 years old. There were only four houses on the street: ours, the two houses beside us, and the Johnson's house. Only three black families are living out here. To tell the truth, I didn't know your house and Mr. Hill's house were back there until the day my dad came to work on your computer."

"Is that right?" I asked. "Look, KJ is getting off the bus now."

When KJ got in, he looked directly at Myles and said, "I'm hungry."

"We'll stop at Pizza Hut and get a bite to eat."

"Yay! Then, can we go and look for Spot?" KJ asked.

"We have already looked for him today and didn't see him. I will be back in the area in the morning to help our neighbors remove a tree. I'll look for him again then, okay?" Myles asked.

"Okay," KJ replied sadly.

Wednesday morning, Myles took KJ to school and brought breakfast back to the room for us. Finishing our food, he said, "Babe, I gotta go so that I can help the men with the tree and meet with the adjuster and contractor at the house at 11:00. I also need to keep looking for Spot." He kissed the babies and me and then left.

About 30 minutes later, Myles called. "We were picking up the last branch of the tree when I saw something white. It was Spot, covered in blood. One of the men picked him up and said I needed to carry him to the vet's office quickly because he had lost a lot of blood and would need stitches. He's at the animal hospital across from the hotel we're staying in. I didn't stop by to let you know because I had to hurry back to the house to meet with the men at 11:00. I gotta go now, Babe. I love you. Kiss the babies for me." I heard the happiness in his voice.

Hanging up the phone, I prayed. "Thank You, Lord, for letting him find the dog. And Lord, please let him be alright." I couldn't wait to tell KJ the good news. I knew he would be happy to hear Spot had been found.

That afternoon, around 3:30, Myles called. "What are you up to?"

"Just finishing up some work I had to complete by today for the job."

"How are the babies?"

"They're fine. They are sleeping right now."

"How do you feel about us going to Bowling Green tomorrow? KJ doesn't have school, and the dog will still be in the hospital." I heard KJ in the background, screaming excitedly.

"That sounds good to me," I answered.

"I'm driving Pearl so that we have more room. Chyna wants to come with us."

"Hey, that's okay with me, if it's okay with Mae. I just need to get out of this room!"

"I know what you mean. We're going to stop by the hospital to check on the dog on our way in. I'll bring KFC for dinner."

"Hurry, Honey. I'm hungry!" We both laughed as we hung up the phone.

When Myles and KJ finally arrived with the food, I was ready to dig in. "The nurse said the dog needed blood and had a cut on his side that required eight stitches. He's recovering well, but they are keeping him until Monday. And yes, KJ cried when he saw him."

"You cried, Keith?" I asked.

"Yes, I was happy to see him." We laughed at his expression as he talked and ate his food. "Mama, they were happy tears, not sad ones."

Myles rubbed him on his head. "Peanut, I was happy to see him, too. Thank God I thought to get pet insurance. I know the cost of him being in the hospital for a week is going to be expensive."

"You got insurance on a dog?" I asked, confused.

"Yes, the guy I got him from said I should get some insurance. I'm glad I listened. It's only $17.00 a month."

"Honey, you're so smart. I would have never thought to get insurance on a pet." Myles smiled and laughed—and then playfully patted me on the head like one would a dog. I smacked his hand away and threatened to Karate flip him again, causing us to bust out laughing.

Chapter 102

"I have more good news," Myles said. "The lights are back on in the house! The insurance adjuster and contractor said they will start working on the house tomorrow."

"Tomorrow, as in Friday?" I yelled excitedly.

"Yes, tomorrow. The cost of all the repairs is $12,500.00."

"Wow, that's a lot of damage!"

"Yes, it is. Fortunately, our insurance will cover it at 100%, along with the cost of our hotel stay. You'll have to choose the color paints you want for the bedroom, patio, and exercise room. They are going to replace the screen in the theater room and the broken lamps," he replied. "Talking about insurance…" He pulled a check from his pocket. "I got the payoff check for $12,200.00 for my car."

"For real, Myles?"

He was grinning and replied, "Yes, ma'am! I'm thinking about buying a new car. You can come along to pick out the color."

"What are you going to do with the truck?"

"I'm going to keep it. The other thing I wanted to ask you is…" He was looking at me with begging eyes as he spoke. "After the insurance adjuster left, I talked to the contractor to see if he could connect another car and a half garage to the old one. He said they could do it. I told him I needed to talk to you first. He said they could add it on while working on the roof of the old garage. They would simply knock down the wall, dig up the ground, pour the new driveway, and put up the frame. By the time they're done, it will look like it was built at the same time the house was built. The only difference is there will be a different remote to control the new garage. The cost is $4,000.00 out of pocket. What do you think?" He looked directly in my face to gauge my reaction the whole time he was talking.

"Myles, it's our house. You didn't have to ask me that. I think it's a great price for the addition. You'll need somewhere to park your new car," I said, laughing. He laughed and kissed me on the cheek.

"KJ, you have a good Mama!" He was smiling from ear to ear. "Okay, I'll call and tell him he got the job!" It felt good to see him so excited after all we'd been through that week. "Babe, they're going to replace the toolshed and everything that was in it, too."

"Do you remember what was in there?" I asked.

He laughed. "No, I don't, but I will make a list of what goes in a toolshed and add the three bikes that went flying into the lake. They'll give you a check to replace everything. As I passed by the Johnson's house, they were just returning from their cruise. Mr. Johnson said they only had damage to the patio and roof and that the patio furniture was destroyed. He said they didn't even know about the tornado until they landed at the airport."

On Friday, the repair work began on the house. We picked up Chyna and drove to Bowling Green, which was a couple of hours away, checked into the Holiday Inn, and then went out to dinner and a movie.

On Saturday, we were away from the hotel all day. We spent our time at Beech Bend Park and Splash Lagoon. The kids truly enjoyed themselves. We were all exhausted when we returned to the hotel. We had pizza for dinner and went straight to bed.

On Sunday, we slept late, waking up around 10:30. We got dressed and checked out of the hotel, stopping at Cracker Barrel for breakfast. After eating, we went sightseeing around the city. We made it back to Nashville around 4:00 that afternoon. I told Myles he could drop the twins and me off at the hotel, and he and KJ could take Chyna home.

"Okay, KJ and I will stop by the hospital to check on Spot on our way back."

When they got in, KJ was so excited. "Mama, I saw Spot! He's up and running around. The lady said he can come home tomorrow!"

"Wow, baby! That's good!" I replied, sharing in his excitement.

"I have some good news, too!" Myles said. "We went to see what the men had done at the house on Friday. They were getting ready to leave. The foreman said they worked through the weekend and would be finished before the end of the week! In the morning, I'll drop off KJ at school and come back to pick up you and the babies so that you can pick the paint colors you want for the rooms."

"Oh, my God! That's great news!" I was so excited to hear that update.

"When I pick up KJ from school, we'll go and get the dog. Would you believe eight men are working on the house? I don't want you to go over there because you'll probably slow them down, telling them what to do."

"I don't want to see it until it's time for me to move back into our house."

On Monday morning, after taking KJ to school, Myles picked us up so that we could go get the paint. Afterward, we stopped by the shop so that Mrs. Clark could see the twins. Ron came from the back room, saying how big they were getting and that they looked like both of us. While there, I helped Mrs. Clark declutter some paperwork and organized the computers, iPads, and other stuff on the shelves that people hadn't picked up. When the babies got restless, Myles took us back to the hotel.

Three nights before moving back into our house, Karson woke up crying and pulling at his ear. I told Myles he was acting as if he had an earache. "Call the doctor so that she can take a look at his ear," Myles said, leaving to take KJ to school. When he returned with my breakfast, Karson was asleep. Before heading to work, he reminded me to call the doctor. Spot went to work with him for the first time in a week.

Just as I was getting ready to call Mae, she called to check on us. I told her about Karson. "It sounds like an ear infection. Do you have a microwave there?" she asked.

"Yes."

"I'll bring some ear drops and Acetaminophen for fever. In the meantime, put a warm towel on his ear. I'll see you in a few minutes. I'm leaving the hospital now." When she got there, I had put Karson back to sleep with a warm towel on his ear. "Oh, my God! Lexie, they have gotten so big! They are some beautiful babies. Look at all that hair on Kaylin's head! They are looking just like you and Myles," she said, giving Kaylin's braids a gentle tug.

"I knew something was wrong with my baby. He would cry and pull at his ear. He's not a crying baby. He smiles a lot like Myles."

She checked his ears. "He does have an ear infection. There's a little bit of irritation in both of his ears, but his fever isn't high. Warm this oil and put two drops in each ear." She then gave him a drop of medicine in his mouth to keep him from getting a fever. "Once the medicine gets in his system, he should get over this quickly." She looked at me cradling my son. "Lexie, y'all could have stayed at our house. We have an extra bedroom."

"Girl, you know your brother won't stay," I replied, laughing.

"You're right. When Myles came back from overseas, daddy tried to get him to stay with us, but he went and got an apartment."

"I wonder if he had a girlfriend staying with him."

"I don't know. I don't think so because he never told us about a girlfriend."

"I'm going to ask him if he had anyone living with him." She laughed. Just then, Myles called, checking to see if I had called the doctor, and said he was bringing KFC for us to eat. "Do you miss me?"

I laughed and replied, "Mae is here now, checking on Karson. She said he has an ear infection in both ears, but it's not bad."

"Okay, let me speak to her."

When she got off the phone, she said, "Myles was concerned about Uncle Eddie. He said he called but didn't get an answer. I told him I talked to him yesterday, and they were fine. Well, Mrs. Ferguson, I'm going home. My bed is calling my name. I pulled an all-nighter and need to sleep."

"Thank you for coming by and bringing the medicine for Karson."

"He'll feel better when he wakes up. Use all the drops for his ears two times a day until it's gone. The other medicine is for fever. Only give it to him if he needs it. Oh, Chyna said she had a good time with you guys. She said Myles gave her and KJ $10.00 to buy anything they wanted."

"I'm glad she went. KJ had someone to go on the rides with. They had a ball eating cotton candy, hot dogs, and everything else their little tummies could hold. I have some pictures of her to give you when I go through my camera." I hugged her and thanked her again for coming.

After Mae left, I changed and fed Kaylin and then put her back in bed. I decided to take a quick shower before Myles got in with the food. When I ran out of the shower to grab my clothes, a man jumped from behind the wall and bear-hugged me. I screamed, turned around, and started punching him. My heart was beating so fast, for a brief moment, my mind flashed back to the attack in Germany. I was fighting my assailant so hard in that hotel room, I didn't hear Myles saying, "Lexie!

Lexie! It's me! Open your eyes! It's me!" He was holding my hands, trying to keep me from hitting him.

"Myles! Oh, my God! You scared me! Don't you ever do that again!" I held my hand over my heart and was shaking and crying. As he hugged me, I repeated, "Don't you ever do that again!"

"I'm sorry. I'm so sorry."

He was standing there naked. "Where are your clothes?!" I asked.

He laughed and said, "I was coming in to take a shower with you."

"Why didn't you call my name or something? How long have you been here?"

"Long enough to take my work clothes off. I came in when Mae was leaving."

"Where's my lunch?" I looked around the room, not seeing any sign of fresh food.

"I wanted to surprise you and take you to Red Lobster."

"Oh, my God. I'm hot," I said, fanning my face with my hand.

He laughed, hugged me, and asked, "Babe, you know how to fight with your eyes closed?"

"That's not funny. I was trying to protect myself and the babies."

"Did you miss me?" he asked, kissing me on my neck.

I didn't answer. I was still shaken up. He could tell I was still upset.

"I told KJ to go to Mae's house after school, and we'll pick him up when we close up the house and get the dog." He looked into my eyes and said, "I'm really sorry for scaring you. It wasn't supposed to turn out like that."

Around 2:30, we got dressed, got the babies ready, and left for Red Lobster. I was thinking about what Mae and I had discussed. "Myles, why did you move into an apartment when you got home from overseas? Why didn't you just stay with your dad and Mae?"

"I didn't want to stay with them."

"You didn't answer my question. I asked why you didn't stay with them."

"Where is this coming from? What did you and Mae talk about now?"

"She said they wanted you to stay with them, but you chose to move into an apartment. Did you have a woman living with you?"

"No, I didn't have a woman living with me. I wanted to be by myself and spend time with God, thanking Him for blessing me to come home safe." He squeezed my hand and apologized again for scaring me. "Do you forgive me?"

"Once we leave Red Lobster, I'll give you my answer," I teased. "It will be based on how much I enjoy my food." I looked at him and smiled. While putting the babies in their car seats after our meal, I told Myles I enjoyed the food and thanked him for taking me out to eat.

"So, do you forgive me?" he asked.

"Yes, I forgive you."

He smiled, escorted me to the passenger side door, and helped me get in. "I have something for you."

"You do? What is it?"

"Get in, and I will give it to you." He reached under the seat and handed me a box. "Open it."

Inside was a diamond bracelet with three charms hanging from it. "Oh, Myles, it's beautiful! I love it!" I said, kissing him on the lips.

"I wanted to celebrate the day!"

"What day is it?"

"We found out you were pregnant a year and eight months ago. Now, our babies are in the back seat!"

"You remember that day?" I asked.

"Well, to be honest, I found an old calendar in the shop. When I looked at the date, it was circled with the words "We Are Pregnant!" written there. So, I went by Kay's and got you this bracelet."

"Thank you for my bracelet. I'm sorry, but I don't remember that day at all." He laughed.

"I forgot to tell you: One of the men working on the house wants to buy my motorcycle."

"I didn't know you were interested in selling your toy!"

"I was thinking about it. It's just sitting there, taking up room. Plus, I'm a family man now. I was single and wild when I bought it!" he said, laughing.

We went to pick up KJ from Mae's house. When he came out, he asked, "Are they finished with our house?"

"No, not yet, Peanut. Get in. We're going to pick up Spot and lock everything up at the house. How was your day at school?"

"Good," he replied. He immediately noticed my new bracelet. "Mama, that's pretty. Is it your birthday?"

Myles answered for me. "No, I gave that to your Mama because she makes me happy."

"Do I make you happy, too?" KJ asked. "I don't get into trouble, and I do what you ask me to do."

"Yes, you make me happy, but not like your Mama." I hit him on the arm and gave him a side-eyed look. He was cracking up.

As we approached the house, I thought, "It does look good. All they need to do is put the bricks on the new garage."

"Wow!" KJ said. "They are putting another garage on our house?"

"Yes, they are so that I have somewhere for my new car," Myles answered excitedly.

"You're getting a new care, Myles?" KJ asked.

"Yes, as soon as they finish, I'm buying a Chrysler 300."

"Wow!" KJ said again. He held Myles' hand as they walked toward the house. I stayed inside Pearl with the twins.

When they got back inside, Myles said, "They are doing the finishing work on the patio. The painters have to paint the rooms, and then they'll be done on the inside. The last thing they have to do is put the bricks on the garage."

"I don't want to go in yet. I'll wait to see it all when we move back home."

That weekend, we moved back into our house. I was one glad sister. My paint choices were beautiful, making the entire atmosphere look different. We had help from Mae's family, Mr. and Mrs. Riddle, their two sons, and Ron to assist with the general cleaning. Mrs. Riddle filled the role of supervisor, instructing everyone on what to do. Her husband made everyone laugh when he said, "She's bossing everybody around like she does at home."

At some point, the general clean up turned into a picnic party cleanup. Myles grilled the meats, and I made the sides. When I learned Rodrick and Ashley were on the way, I called and asked him to pick up some additional items, including a vegetable tray and watermelon. I enjoyed my helpers and appreciated being back home. By the time we finished, everything was back to normal—except for the big hole in the backyard where the tree once stood.

Before everyone left, Myles invited everyone to dinner on Sunday after church at Cracker Barrel. He told Rodrick and Ashley they were welcome to join us, if they hadn't left for college by then. I called Irma to invite my nephew, but she said he was away at basketball camp. I thought, "That boy is into his sport, just like his dad." She said he would return home in three weeks and asked that I call him then.

That Sunday, we enjoyed each other's company once again, giving God thanks for bringing us together one more time.

Chapter 103

Two months had passed. The babies were growing fast, walking, pulling things down, and sleeping all night. As planned, we put up the other crib so that they had room to sleep.

I gained full custody of KJ. When he wanted to see his brother and sister, he would go for visits at Mama Brenda's, and when she took her kids to see Keith, KJ went, too. KJ told us the last time they went to see his dad, they were arguing because his dad told her Sam was renting a room and some lady named Kellie was renting a room, too.

"Mama Brenda was angry and called daddy a sneaky snake. That's living a double life and being a backsliding preacher who doesn't want to pay child support," he repeated, likely verbatim. "Myles, what does a backsliding preacher living a double life mean?" KJ asked.

The expression on Myles' face said he didn't know how to answer that question. He quickly replied, "We'll talk about that later, Peanut. Go look in my truck and get the bag of Hot Cheetos I bought for you," he said, smiling. After KJ left the room, Myles said, "I don't like him going over there, Lexie. He doesn't need to be hearing all that. How in the world do I explain that mess to him?" He sat there frustrated, rubbing his hair back. "I know what we can do. You call Brenda and ask her if it's okay to meet us at a play place—like at McDonald's or Burger King— when KJ wants to see her kids. We'll pay for everything. She can stay or leave. And when his daddy calls to see him, we'll drop off KJ at his church and pick him up from there. He'll get to see his brother and sister at church, too."

"No, KJ said Brenda goes to another church now," I answered.

"Oh, my God. I wonder how the members of the church feel about that."

"From what I've heard, some people have already left the church. People talk, you know."

"Well, we will leave that alone and let God deal with him and his situations," Myles replied.

Thankfully, when KJ came back inside, he didn't say anything more about what he asked. He ran upstairs, eating his Cheetos.

Two weeks later, on a Saturday afternoon, we met Brenda and her kids at McDonald's. She chose to drop off Brandon and take his sister with her. She returned in a couple of hours to pick up her son. As we were leaving, KJ said, "I had fun playing with my brother. He's so funny!"

"I'm glad you had fun with him," I replied.

When we got home, Keith had left a message saying he wanted to see KJ. Myles called him back and told him we would drop him off at his church at 10:00 a.m. on Sunday and pick him up at 2:30 on our way to dinner.

Everything went as planned. We picked up KJ at 2:30 sharp. "So, Keith, how was your visit with your daddy?" I asked.

"Good, but daddy asked me a lot of questions. While we were talking, two men came into daddy's office, so he told me to go to daycare and wait for you to come pick me up."

"Where do you want to go for dinner?" Myles asked.

"How about Red Lobster!" KJ yelled. "I'm ready to eat!"

"I was talking to your Mama, Peanut," he said, laughing.

"Mama, say you want to eat at Red Lobster."

"Boy, you need a job! Do you have any money?" Myles asked. KJ laughed at him.

We had Red Lobster for dinner.

A week later, Myles and I were sitting in the living room, watching KJ play ball in the driveway with the dog. The twins were in their walkers in the living room with us. We saw a red car turn into Mr. Johnson's driveway, but no one got out. "The Johnsons have company," I said.

"Mr. Johnson is out of town. He said they were driving to Oklahoma to visit his daughter for a week and asked me to watch his house for him." Myles got up, walked out to the driveway where KJ was playing ball, and looked directly at the driver of the red car. They quickly backed out and drove away. When he came back inside, he said, "That was KJ's daddy."

"How do you know it was him?"

"I remember that car from when I dropped KJ off to him. It has a big American flag on it above the license plate. I saw him get into that same car with Sam after talking to him at Subway."

"I wonder why he's down here. I'll bet you my bottom dollar that KJ told him you bought a new car."

"He knows I have a new car already. He saw it when we dropped KJ off at his church. Maybe he's showing his friend your house," Myles said, laughing.

"No, maybe he's showing his friend our house—the one he thought he would take from me in the divorce. He loves this house." When KJ came inside, I asked him, "What do you and your daddy talk about when you visit him?"

"We talk about a lot of stuff, and he asks me a lot of questions."

"Questions about what?" I asked curiously.

"Daddy saw you and Myles in the new black car when Myles dropped me off at his church. He asked me, 'Was that Myles' new car?' I told him yes and that we got a new garage, too. He asked me about every car in our garage and if I liked the new car. I told him I do and that Myles sold his motorcycle."

"Does your daddy have a new car?" I asked.

"No, he still has his black Impala. Sometimes, he drives a red car, but it's not his. He said he doesn't have enough money to buy a new car because the church doesn't collect a lot of money to pay him. Now that he has two people renting rooms in his house, he said he would get a new car."

"Okay, KJ. You can go back outside and play with Spot," Myles said, trying to keep from laughing.

When KJ left the room, I said, "Keith asked KJ a couple of questions, and that boy told all our business. That explains why he was down here, sitting in that man's red car watching our house again."

Three weeks later, Myles went for his run after work. When he got back, he said, "Mr. Johnson stopped me and told me to be careful because a red car parked with two men inside sits down the street and watches our house. When he and his wife got home a few weeks ago, he said that car was sitting near their house. They walked out to the car, thinking it was someone looking for them. When they approached, they saw two men sitting in there. The man who was driving told them they were looking for land to buy and said they liked the quietness of the area. He said when they went back inside the house, his wife asked him if he knew the man in the passenger seat, and he told her no. She said, 'That's that Montgomery man. He has grown a beard, but he looks the same. You know what they are saying about him, and I know the Lord is not pleased.' Mrs. Johnson put up a Private Property sign and said she would call the police if she saw them sitting there again. 'I don't want a man like that to build a house near us,' she said."

"What did you say?" I asked.

"I told him I saw that sign but thought they had purchased the land," Myles said, laughing at the whole situation. "Mr. Johnson said that they haven't seen that car sitting there ever since his wife put that sign up."

Chapter 104

On Sunday, I didn't get to go to church. Both babies were teething and had kept us up most of the night. While Myles and KJ were getting ready, Keith called and asked Myles if he could drop off KJ at his church for the Children's Church service. He told Myles all the churches in his district would be there, and he wanted his son to participate, apologizing for the short notice. "Yes, I'll drop him off at 10:00 and pick him up at 2:30," he replied.

When they left for church, I put the babies back to sleep and started Sunday dinner in the slow cooker. While they slept, I climbed back into bed to take a nap. When I woke up, Myles and KJ were already home. KJ was asleep in the big chair in the nursery, and Myles was sleeping next to me. The aroma of the pot roast in the slow cooker filled the house.

One of the twins started to cry, so I got out of bed to check on them. Myles stirred out of his sleep and said, "I enjoyed service today. We had a guest preacher, and the pastor called on me to sing again."

KJ woke up, saying, "Mama, I had a good time at daddy's church today."

"Good, what did you do?"

"Mama Brenda dropped off Brandon. We sang songs, ate hot dogs, chips, and cookies, and drank punch."

"That was nice. You were able to spend some time with your brother today."

"Before I left, daddy kept asking Brandon, 'Where's your Mama? What's taking her so long?' Then, Myles came and picked me up."

Myles went into the kitchen to check on dinner.

KJ whispered to me, "Mama, is Myles rich?"

"Why do you ask? Did your daddy say that?"

"Yes, he asked me if Myles was rich because he got a new car and a new garage." By then, Myles was standing behind KJ, listening to our conversation.

"What did you say when he asked you that?" I asked.

"Well, I told him I think he is because he put a basketball hoop in the backyard, a swimming pool with a fence around it, and a little pool for Karson and Kaylin. I told him I was taking swimming classes so that I could learn to swim in the big pool. I told daddy that Myles signed me up for Karate classes and buys me whatever I want, so he must be rich. Mama, I told daddy I helped Myles and the yardman plant a flower garden in the front yard with a water fountain, too," he finished with a proud smile. Myles stood behind him, shaking his head and chuckling. "Mama, I told daddy me and Myles were going on a camping trip and sleeping in the tent he bought, but we'll probably go to the lake where we fish all the time."

I smiled at my son. "Keith, please go and take Spot outside. He hasn't been out to play today."

He got up, called for Spot, and then turned to add, "I also told daddy Myles got me a dog."

"Keith, I think you tell your daddy too much. Did he ask you all that?" I asked.

"No, but he was listening, so I kept talking."

"Boy, go take the dog out, please!" I said, laughing.

When KJ left the room, Myles was laughing so hard. "Oh, my God! That boy tells his daddy everything we have going on over here!" He took a seat next to me. "When I went to pick up KJ from the church, Sam was sitting in the parking lot in that red car under a tree. He had a newspaper open, looking like he was reading, but I'm sure he didn't want anyone to see him. I guess he was waiting for his Boo-thang to come out." Myles was laughing so hard, tears fell down his face.

"Did Sam see you?"

"I'm sure he did, especially when KJ got in the car. I was leaving just as Brenda was driving up."

Chapter 105

Two weeks later, Myles left for his Army Reserves weekend. Trina and Chyna stayed with me at night to help with the twins. Myles called often, saying he missed the children and me. I told him he had to get used to being away from us with him back in the Reserves. He replied, "I didn't know it was going to be this hard being away from you guys. I might have to get out of the Reserves when I get home," he said with a laugh. "Lexie, are you sure you want to return to work?" he asked during one of his calls.

"Yes, I spoke to my supervisor last week. She said I can work two days a week in the office and two from home, just like I'm doing now. The only difference is that I will work nine hours per day at the job and five hours on Fridays. I should be home by 1:30 on Fridays. I was thinking you could pick up the twins from daycare and get KJ when you get off work on Mondays and Tuesdays. The other three days, I'll be home to get them. I'll be sure to schedule all my meetings and training on Monday, Tuesday, and Friday mornings. My supervisor agreed to the arrangement, as long as the work gets done." Myles didn't say anything at first. I knew he was taking in all I had just said.

After a brief silence, he replied, "Lexie, you don't have to work. I'm making more than enough money at the shop, getting rent from the house on Mary Street, both of us have investments, I'm in the Reserves, and you have that monthly check from those Birthday and Mother's Day cards coming in. Why do you want to work?"

"Myles, I like my job. I have 14 years' worth of experience in Human Resources, including the time I had in the Air Force. I don't want to quit now when I can retire in six and a half years."

"Why do you have to work until you retire? You don't need the retirement money."

"Myles, I'll only be out of the house two and a half days a week."

"Okay, if that's what you want to do."

"We can put the twins in daycare during those days. It will cost $50.00 a day for both and $35.00 on Fridays. That's only $135.00 a week. Mrs. Watkins said the days KJ is out of school, he could attend the after-school program at the same price. He could get off the bus there instead of going to Mae's house all the time."

"I don't think Chyna would like that," he replied, laughing.

"I know, but KJ will be turning ten soon. He needs to be around boys his age."

"Okay, it sounds like you have it all planned out."

"It will work out, Honey. Just think: You will come home to a hot meal three days a week! On Saturdays, we'll have leftovers, and on Sundays, we'll go out to eat after church."

Laughing, he replied, "Babe, I gotta go now. I love you. Kiss the babies and rub KJ's head for me."

When we ended our call, I thought, "Myles is jealous! He doesn't want me working outside of the house." I recalled the day we were out, and some man kept looking at me. I could see Myles looking back and forth at the man and me out of the corner of my eye.

"Do you know that man?" he asked.

"No, I don't know him."

"Why is he looking at you like that?"

"Honey, I don't know," I replied, kissing him on the lips.

The man eventually walked away, but not without looking back in our direction.

Then, when the men were repairing our home after the storm, Myles said there were too many men working for me to be there and that he knew I would be telling them what to do. I believe that was his excuse to have me stay in the hotel and not be at our house around all those men.

Myles came home after his Reserves duty on Sunday afternoon. I was happy to see my husband, and he was glad to be home. He didn't say anything more about my plans to start working outside of the house in September.

On the 4th of July holiday, I was surprised to receive a call from Irma. "Lt says he wants to come over, if that's okay."

"Yes, y'all can come! Bring the girls with you. I have a pool, so they can go swimming. You and your husband are welcome to swim, too. When it gets dark, my husband's going to set off a huge fireworks display in the backyard."

She started laughing. "My husband went to visit his mon. It will be just the kids and me. Oh. And I can't swim." We both laughed.

"Can y'all be here around 4:00? We will be grilling in the backyard, and my husband's sister and family will be here."

"Yes, is there anything you want me to bring?" she asked.

"Yes, you and the kids!" I replied, laughing.

"No, Lexie, I want to bring something."

"Okay, bring a watermelon."

I heard the smile in her voice when she replied, "I know you live on Riverside. What is the address?"

"3622 Riverside. Once you turn into the Riverside subdivision, come around the curve, and you will see my house. I'm the only one with a three-car garage."

"Okay, we'll see you at 4:00!"

After ending the call, I told Myles. "That was Irma on the phone. She wanted to know if it was okay to bring LT by. He wants to see me. I told her they were all welcome to come. Oh, my God! I'm so excited! LT wants to come and see me!"

"And I get to see how good your nephew is with that basketball," he replied, hugging me.

When they arrived at 4:00, I introduced everyone. Irma mentioned she had seen Mae before at the hospital. While everyone else was outside, I invited Irma and her children inside for a tour of the house. "Lexie, I love your house," she said.

"Aunt Lexie, you and your husband must be rich!" LT exclaimed.

"All I can say is the Lord has blessed us, LT."

As we passed by the picture wall, LT stopped. He stood there, looking at the framed images. I pointed to each one, telling him who they were—with a particular emphasis on the pictures of his grandparents and father. He looked at me and said, "I wish I could have met them, Aunt Lexie."

Every time he called me Aunt Lexie, my heart grew ten sizes. I hugged him and said, "I wish you could have met them, too."

Myles came in and said, "Come on, LT! Let me see how good you are with this basketball." Myles and LT teamed up against Derrick and Rodrick.

Matthew surprised us when he joined the festivities in the backyard. "Wow! I didn't know all this was back here! This is richness!" he said, hugging and laughing. He shook Myles' hand, and Myles introduced him to everyone. "So, you found him?" Matthew asked.

"Yes, I did. Thank you for telling me about LT." He went over, hugged Irma and LT, and then saw the twins in their playpen. "My goodness! The babies are big, looking like you and Myles. They sure are pretty babies!"

I called for KJ to come and meet Matthew. "Keith, this is your cousin Matthew."

KJ was so excited to play with the other kids in the pool, he quickly shook Matthew's hand, said, "Hi!" and then ran back to get in the pool.

"He's a nice-looking boy. I've seen him somewhere," Matthew said, looking at KJ as he ran back to the pool. "I know where I've seen him. He comes to the third house from my twins' mama's house—the house where a preacher lives."

"Yes, that preacher is his daddy," I replied.

Matthew's hands flew up to his mouth. He had a puzzled look when he asked, "You married Keith, the preacher man?!"

"He wasn't a preacher when I married him. It's a long story," I answered.

"Oh, my God. I dated Keith's sister, Barbara, about 11 years ago. She moved away to Chicago. Man, she was a fine little thang then. I heard the preacher man is a fine little thang now," Matthew said, laughing. I slapped him with the paper plate I had in my hand. He and Myles were laughing so hard, I thought they were going to wet themselves.

"Matthew, I'm glad you stopped by, but don't be up here starting something!" I said, laughing.

Once he regained his composure, he replied, "I hope you don't mind me dropping in on you guys like this. I dropped off my twins at their mom's house and didn't want to go home, so I decided to ride out here to see what y'all were up to." He struggled to keep from laughing again as he watched Myles continue to laugh.

"Man, I'm glad you stopped by," Myles managed to say. "You can drop in any time. Do you want to eat first or play a game of basketball?"

"I don't want anything to eat yet. I remember you were a bad running back in school. Let me see how good you are with that basketball." The two new teams were Matthew and Rodrick against Myles and Derrick.

"Phew! Now, I can swim and cool off," LT said, happily climbing into the pool.

Mae, Irma, and I sat around the pool, watching the kids play and watching the men play basketball. Trina spent her time in the kiddie pool with the babies. After eating, it was near dark. Myles had already set up the fireworks, so we just waited for it to get dark for him to set them off. From start to finish, the fireworks were amazing. Everybody said they enjoyed them.

Later, as Matthew prepared to leave, I reminded him to keep an eye out for a letter regarding the get-together. He hugged me, shook Myles' hand, and replied, "Okay, I will."

Mae and her family left shortly after Matthew's departure.

When it was time for Irma to leave, she said, "I enjoyed myself. Thank you for having us over."

"Y'all are welcome to come back any time." I turned to my nephew and said, "LT, if you want to spend the night sometimes, I have plenty of room. The girls can come, too," I offered. They all hugged me on their way out the door.

Myles walked with them to their car, he had a one-on-one chat with LT. "You are pretty good with that basketball. Next time, we're going to beat Derrick and Rodrick! I gotta get a little more practice in. Your uncle was a little slow."

LT laughed and replied, "You're good! They were cheating anyway. We'll get them next time. I see how they play." He gave Myles a thumbs-up as he got into the car, looking just like Leon.

After everyone left, we put the twins down for the night. KJ was already asleep upstairs in his room. Myles and I went for a swim in the pool. It was a peaceful night. We sat in the pool, looking up at the beautiful stars and talking about how we had enjoyed our guests.

"When we were walking out to play basketball, Matthew said he didn't know you had a child by the preacher man. He said when he was dating Keith's sister, the talk was that Keith was gay, but when he got a girl pregnant, the rumors stopped—until word spread that the story about the child was just a front to stop the rumors."

"For real? Matthew said that?" Myles nodded his head yes. "Maybe Brenda knew Keith liked men and thought she could change him. She must have known Keith was up to no good again when she had that argument in front of KJ. Now that I think about it, when we were married, Keith's whole attitude changed when Brenda came back into town, like she was holding something over him. I remember him telling me she helped him through some challenging times."

Myles sat there, thinking. "Matthew did say that's why Barbara left town to go live with her sister. She didn't like what was happening to her mom because of him."

"Is that what Matthew said? Wow, Keith! Skeletons are leaping out of the closet! You know, when I married him, it was a friendship marriage. There were never any romantic feelings between us. I loved him as my friend, but I wasn't in love with him. I'm in shock. I didn't see that other side of him at all."

"That's why they call it down-low," Myles said, laughing. When I suddenly got out of the pool, he asked, "Where are you going?"

"I'm going to check on the kids."

"Okay, hurry back." Returning to the pool, he asked, "What took you so long?"

"When I went inside, I saw Spot's cage open. I looked upstairs and saw KJ's light was still on, so I went up there to see why. The dog was asleep in the basket in KJ's room and had ketchup around his mouth. KJ was asleep with ketchup on his face and hands."

"I bet you KJ was eating a hot dog and gave Spot some," Myles said, laughing.

"Or KJ went to sleep eating a hot dog, and Spot helped himself to it." We were both laughing. "When I went into the nursery, Kaylin was standing up, sucking on her pacifier."

"Was she crying?"

"No, just standing there. I changed her diaper, and she laid back down on her own."

"Too funny! That little girl does not like being wet," Myles said.

"Myles, from today on, I don't want to hear anything else about what Keith did or didn't do. I don't want to talk about him anymore. He's in my past. All I can say is that out of the marriage, I had KJ. He is the only good thing that came from it."

Myles was laughing. "Okay, don't be angry at me. I didn't do or say anything. What was said, Matthew said it. I don't know anything about the man, except that he might have a new girlfriend. KJ saw his daddy holding a lady's hand one Sunday at church."

"Well, good for him. He now has another lady's skirt tail to hide behind if it's true," I responded.

Myles looked at me sweetly and said, "Babe, you look good in that swimsuit. Is it new?"

"Yes, I got it a couple of weeks ago. I wanted one to cover more of my body."

"Do you miss me, my lady?"

"No, you're right here."

He laughed and replied, "Well, I miss you." He hugged me and started singing in my ear. As he was singing in one ear, mosquitoes were buzzing in the other.

"Myles, these mosquitoes are bad!"

He looked toward the burners and said, "The burners have gone out. Are you ready to go inside?"

"Yes, I am," I replied, trying to fan away the pesky bugs.

Once inside, he said, "We must do that again soon. I enjoyed spending time with you in the pool."

As we walked into our bedroom, Karson was standing in his crib. I changed and fed him, then laid him back down. Myles took his shower, and then I took mine. While showering, I felt the Spirit of the Lord come on me. I began thanking God for His presence and how good He had been to my family. By the time I got out of the shower, Myles had gathered all the children in the bed with him, and they were all asleep. I noticed Myles' Bible lying on my pillow, which let me know he had read to them.

I looked at my handsome husband and my beautiful children sleeping in my bed and was inspired to take pictures of them. I grabbed my camera and snapped a few images before getting a sheet and blanket out of the closet. That night, I slept on the couch.

I was awakened by Myles kissing me on my forehead. "Good morning, my lady. What took you so long to get out of the shower last night?"

"I spent some time with God, thanking Him for my family, my friends, and for blessing me to find LT. I'm just so grateful to Him for how good He's been to us."

"Yes, Babe, God has been good to us. That's what I told KJ last night when he came in looking for you. He said he couldn't go to sleep, so I read the Bible and talked to him—which woke up the babies. That's how they all ended up in our bed. Let's pray before I leave," he said. After prayer, Myles said, "Thanks for being such a good wife to me." He kissed me on the cheek. "Breakfast is ready. I woke up hungry this morning."

"Where are you going? You're already dressed?"

"I'm heading to the shop. This man dropped off his laptop that needed a new battery. I had to order it. It took two weeks for them to ship it to me. I told the guy he could pick up his laptop at 9:00 this morning."

I stopped him before he left. "Look at this," I said, handing him my camera. He took it and looked at the pictures I had taken of them while they slept.

He laughed at one of them. "Is this how I look when I'm asleep?! Wow, look at KJ. He sleeps with his eyes half-open. Kaylin looks like she's running, and Karson is sleeping on his knees." He continued to laugh as he looked at the kids still sleeping in our bed. "Let me get out of here. Tell KJ when I get back, we're going fishing, so be ready." He kissed me on the lips and left, still laughing.

Chapter 106

The twins were nearing the two-year-old mark, and KJ would be turning ten in a couple of months. I thought, "I'll ask Brenda if KJ's brother can come over for a sleepover on his birthday. KJ would be truly surprised if she said Brandon could come."

I had already started planning the family reunion and KJ's birthday party. Everyone I called said they would attend, including the families from South Carolina and my cousins who lived in the area. I also asked Irma to come and bring LT and her family. When I called Myles' Army buddy, Ed, to ask if they could come to the reunion, he replied, "Yes, I was just talking to Faye yesterday and told her we needed to come for a visit."

"Okay, you will be getting a letter from me in about two weeks with the date and time. I know Myles will be surprised to see you."

"I will be on the lookout for the letter. Thanks for the invite," he said before hanging up.

I then called Mrs. Riddle and Jessica. Both said they would come and bring their families. Once all the calls were made, I worked on the letter and asked for them to RSVP so that I could get a headcount of how many people were actually going to come.

I started outlining the activities. I knew Myles would take the men fishing. The younger people could swim and play basketball in the backyard. I wanted to have a singing contest, scavenger hunt, and fashion show for those ages 15 and under. I would ask them to bring one casual and one dressy outfit for the fashion show. I would provide various types of fleece material for the older ladies and show them how to make a tie blanket. That Sunday, we could all attend church together. The more I planned, the more excited I became!

When Mrs. Riddle came to clean the house the following Saturday, I left to get my hair and nails done, leaving Myles and KJ to babysit. After getting my hair done, I walked out of the salon and saw Keith dropping off a lady who had entered the salon. Keith sat in his car, looking at me. "Are you going to speak?" he asked.

"How are you, Pastor Montgomery?"

"I'm doing better now that I see you. You know you're looking good," he said, laughing.

"Thank you, that's what my husband tells me every morning when I rise." He looked at me, grinning. It disgusted me. I got into my car and pulled away, thinking, "That must be his new woman KJ told Myles about."

While out, I called Irma to see if they were home and asked if I could stop by. "Yes, you can. We're home, but LT walked to the store. He should be back by the time you get here." When I arrived, they were all outside waiting for me. LT smiled and hugged me, saying, "Aunt Lexie, it's good to see you again!" I met her husband, and she told me again how much she enjoyed herself when she visited my home. She explained to her husband that my house looked like a mansion and how she loved the backyard and sitting by the pool. Her girls told me they enjoyed playing in the pool, too.

I gave LT two pictures of his daddy: one from when Leon was around his age and another from when Leon graduated from high school. He sat on the couch, looking at the pictures. "I really do look like my daddy! Thank you, Aunt Lexie, for these pictures."

Before leaving, I reminded Irma about the reunion. I told her to expect the letter with the details. I then told her husband he was welcome to come. "I'd love to come and see this mansion of yours," he replied, smiling.

When I walked out, LT walked with me to my car. "I'm so glad you let us come to your house, Aunt Lexie. You are a pretty lady with a beautiful home."

"Thank you, LT. It just amazes me how much you look just like your daddy." I hugged him, got in the car, and closed the door.

"I like your car," he said.

"Thanks, but this one is my husband's." He smiled and waved bye. As I drove away, loving thoughts of my brother floated through my mind. I missed him so much.

Once settled back at home, Myles came into the sitting room. "I took the babies out for a stroll down to Mr. Johnson's house. KJ rode his bike, and the dog followed us. Mrs. Johnson came out and saw the babies, saying how beautiful they are and how much they look like you and me. While we were there, a man and his wife drove up, saying they had purchased the land before the Johnson's house to build their new home. We laughed when the woman mentioned the Private

Property sign. The man asked if anyone else was seen looking at the land, and Mrs. Johnson told him why that sign was put up. The man thanked her and said he was sure they would like it out here. After we all introduced ourselves, the man handed each of us his and his wife's business cards. It turns out he's a doctor, and his wife's a dentist. They have three children. He's Black and his wife's Latino. He also said he bought five acres of the land, and his brother bought the other five acres on the other side of him. When they left, Mrs. Johnson said, 'I'm glad I put that sign up there. It looks like we are going to have some nice neighbors after all!'"

"Wow, Myles! For real? He and his brother will each have five acres of land down there?"

"Yes, that's what the man said. Two houses will be going up in less than a year."

Chapter 107

One Saturday morning, Myles made breakfast before he and KJ left to help Uncle Eddie paint a room in his house. While the twins slept, I had the TV on, washed clothes, and reorganized my closet. Around 11:30, a breaking news bulletin came on the TV, saying the Pastor of New Harvest Church was found dead in his home. The reporter interviewed one of the neighbors, who said, "This is a quiet neighborhood. We have never had anything like this happen here before. A lady left the house about an hour ago, but she was one of the renters who lived in the house. Later I heard a gunshot. I called the police immediately but didn't see anyone leave after hearing that gunshot." Another neighbor who lived across the street got on camera and said, "I didn't hear a gunshot, but I saw a man in a black hoodie walking toward the church, carrying a garment bag. He had on a backpack. I don't know where the man came from, though." The reporter finished the segment, saying, "No suspect is in custody as of now. There will be an investigation."

I sat on the bed, thinking, "The Pastor of New Harvest Church? That's Keith! Oh, my God! It can't be him. I just saw him a couple of weeks ago when he dropped off that lady at the beauty salon. No, he can't be dead."

Just as I picked up my cell phone to call Myles, he called me to let me know they were leaving Uncle Eddie's house with some lasagna and garlic bread Aunt Ruby made. "KJ and I have already eaten. Guess what? Uncle Eddie said he's going to start making tamales to sell, and he needs my help," he said, laughing. I heard KJ in the background, saying, "Tell Mama that Uncle Eddie let me paint!"

I didn't know how to tell him about KJ's dad because I knew he had me on speakerphone. Karson started to cry at the same time the house phone started ringing. Looking at the caller ID, I saw it was Mrs. Riddle. Myles heard the ruckus and said, "Bye, Babe. See you in a few," he said, laughing.

I picked up Mrs. Riddle's call. "I was calling to see if you heard the news about Keith."

"Yes, ma'am. I just heard it on the news."

"Are you alright?" she asked.

"Yes, I am okay. I'll have to find a way to tell KJ when he gets home." I was sure she could hear Karson crying his eyes out.

"Call me if you need me. I'll let you go so that you can take care of the baby," she said.

I changed Karson and gave him his bottle. When the house phone rang again, it was Matthew. "Lexie, I was dropping off my twins down the street from the preacher's house, and the ambulance and police cars were there."

I cut him off and said, "Yes, I already heard what happened on the news."

"Does your son know?"

"No, he's with Myles. They went to help Myles' uncle paint. Myles called a few minutes ago and said they were on their way home. He should be pulling soon."

"Do you need me to come out there?" he asked, concerned.

"I'm okay. Myles will be here in a little while. Thanks for asking."

"If you need me, call me," he replied.

"Thank you, Matthew."

About 30 minutes later, I heard Myles coming into the house, telling KJ to clean the dog's cage. I was in my closet, hanging up clothes. "Where are you, Babe?" he called out.

"I'm in the closet, putting my clothes away. Lower your voice. Don't wake the babies."

He came up behind me, hugging me. "I put your food in the refrigerator." When he kissed me on the cheek, he felt the moisture from my tears. He turned me around, looked me in the eyes, and asked, "What's wrong? Why are you crying?"

"Myles, Keith is dead."

"What?! He's dead?!"

"Yes, the news reported his death about an hour ago. Mrs. Riddle and Matthew both called me after they saw the news."

He hugged me close. "Oh, my God. What happened?"

"The reporter said he was shot and killed in his house. Myles, how am I going to tell KJ his daddy is dead?" I started crying harder.

We heard KJ heading our way. "Myles, I can't wash the cage because Spot keeps getting in my way."

Myles quickly stepped out of the closet and replied, "Okay, I'm coming."

As he exited the room, KJ asked, "Where's Mama?"

"She's hanging clothes in her closet."

I stood there, crying and thinking, "How am I going to tell KJ about his daddy?" Myles came in less than ten minutes later and said, "Go upstairs to your son. He needs you. I told him."

I ran upstairs to my son's bedside. He was lying on his side, cradling his blanket and crying. I held him in my arms, saying, "Keith, I'm so sorry. I'm so sorry."

He hugged me back. "Mama, I won't see my daddy anymore like I won't see Pawpaw?"

"That's right, Keith. They are gone now. You won't see them anymore." We sat on his bed and cried together.

On the day of Keith's viewing, I went alone and signed the book on behalf of our family. I cried as I looked at him lying in his casket. I still found it hard to believe he was dead. I was concerned about how KJ was going to deal with his loss.

Myles took KJ to the memorial service at Keith's church. The funeral service was held at the Bishop's church. KJ went with Brenda and spent the day with Brandon, his sister, and his older brother, who came in from New Orleans for the funeral. When KJ got home, he said, "Mama, Lance was mean to Mama Brenda."

"Why was he mean to her?" I asked.

"Because he didn't want to come here but Mama Brenda made him come to daddy's funeral. Mama Brenda wants Lance to stay here with her. He told her, 'That's not my daddy. My daddy lives in New Orleans. You can't make me stay here, and my daddy isn't going to let me stay with you.' He made Mama Brenda cry. She screamed at him, 'Don't you say that to me!'"

"Your brother is just upset about his daddy dying," I replied.

"No, Mama, because he said my daddy isn't his daddy."

"Baby, Lance is just upset."

With tears falling from his eyes, KJ asked, "Mama, why did daddy have to die?" I sat there, combing Kaylin's hair, trying to think of something appropriate to say.

Myles exited the laundry room and answered for me. "KJ, death is coming to all of us. It was just your daddy's time to go."

KJ jumped up and ran to Myles in hysterics. "Myles, don't you die! Don't you die! Myles, please?"

Myles hugged him, saying, "Peanut, I'm not going anywhere."

"My Pawpaw died, and then my daddy died. I won't see them anymore," he said through his sobs. Looking at Myles' face, I could see he was near tears himself.

"KJ, I'll be here a long time," he said, trying to assure him everything will be alright. I could see the love and compassion he had for my son. It was hard to see Myles in pain, causing me to cry.

I thought about Keith's sisters and the members of his church. I wondered how Brenda was truly handling the loss.

The weekend after the funeral, Myles and KJ left for a luncheon meeting that was given by Keith's sisters, Barbara and Linda, to discuss how to distribute Keith's belonging. When they left, I sat there thinking, 'Just over 11 years ago, Keith came into my life. I was lonely, broken, and needed a friend. He was a friend to me. He made me laugh, and we had fun together. Now, he's gone. I'm sorry he's dead.' I began to cry again, thinking about the good times we shared.

When they returned home, KJ came into my room, hugged me, said he was sleepy, and went to his room. I was happy they were back. I needed that hug from him.

"KJ told me he was sleepy during our ride home," Myles said, giving me a kiss.

"How was the meeting?"

"It was nice. We ate, and one of Keith's nieces took the kids with her to another room. Brenda, the Associate Pastor who will be taking over the church, and a couple of Keith's cousins came. Barbara said the house they grew up in was left to all three of them, so they're going to sell the house and split the sale into thirds. As for Keith's portion, it will be divided among his children. They asked Brenda if she wanted anything out of the house, and she asked for a picture that was hanging over the fireplace. The cousins who were there also got what they wanted." As Myles talked, he removed his clothes and got ready for bed. "When Barbara said Keith's oldest son could have his car, Brenda said, 'No, he doesn't need a car. Give it to the church.'"

"Where was her son?" I asked.

"I didn't see him. She gave me Keith's Bible to give to KJ. It was a gift from the district and a photo of Keith, Brandon, and KJ in it."

"Where is the picture?"

"I gave it to KJ already."

"What did he say when you gave it to him?

"He said, 'Myles, I remember this picture. We took it when we were at Children's Church.' He laughed at the picture and said, 'I told daddy I look like my Mama, and he said, 'Yes, your Mama is a looker.' He asked his dad what he meant, and Keith told him, 'That means she's a beautiful lady.' He kept looking at the picture on the way home, saying, 'She is a beautiful lady.'"

"He said that?"

"Yes, he did. As soon as we got in, he took his Bible and the picture upstairs." Myles sat down on the bed, laughing. "I have to agree with Keith for once: You are a beautiful lady!"

"Thank you, Honey."

"Barbara also shared what she knew about the living situation in Keith's house with all of us. The lady who rented a room from Keith had stopped by the house to get her things from the room not long after Keith was found dead. She told the officers that Keith had a friend named Sam who was also renting a room there, but Keith had asked him to move out about four months ago. Sam refused to leave. When she came home from work two days later, Keith was in his study, screaming and arguing with Sam. Keith told Sam he had to go because he had changed his life and was focusing on the church. He wanted the Lord to be pleased with him, and it didn't look good for Sam being there, and he was getting married. Later, she saw Sam getting into his car with a suitcase and garment bag. They hadn't seen him for over two months and had started planning their wedding. She said early on the morning Keith died, Sam knocked on the door and said he wanted to talk to Keith. She left the room but could still hear them talking. Sam was saying, 'Why are you doing me like this?' to which Keith replied, 'Man, will you just please leave my house?' Sam started to cry, saying, 'You are wrong for this! Where is my stuff?' Keith told him his things were in the closet. She said they had packed up Sam's things that he left behind in his room and put them in the hallway closet, preparing to take them to the Salvation Army. Later that morning, she left the house, heading to visit her mom to talk about the wedding. She was about an hour into her drive when she heard about Keith's death on a radio broadcast. She turned around immediately and drove to the police station. When they made it back to the house, Keith was dead in his bed. Sam had removed his things from the closet and was gone."

"Wow, Myles. That's tragic."

"I know, right? Poor lady. She said she wished she would have stayed there. Maybe then, Keith wouldn't be dead. Barbara said the lady cried and that she truly loved him. After the funeral, she went to stay at her mom's house. I think Barbara said the lady's name was Kellie. Anyway, they had a warrant out for Sam. Two days later, they got a call from the Highway Patrol in Arkansas, saying they found a man dead at a roadside park. After running the license plate, they determined he was Sam Hall from Nashville, Tennessee. He was found with a gunshot wound to his head, holding a note that said he was sorry."

"Myles, you mean that man shot Keith and then himself?"

"That's what his sister said."

"Oh, my God! So, where is the lady who was going to marry Keith?"

"I guess she's still at her mom's house in Kentucky. Barbara said the lady worked for the police department here."

"I'm sorry to hear all of that. I hope KJ never hears about how his dad's lover killed him and then himself."

Myles started fluffing his pillow and then climbed into bed. I laid in his arms. "Oh, and while we were there, Matthew stopped by to give his condolences. He didn't stay long because he was heading down the street to pick up his twins. Barbara walked him to his car. The other sister didn't say anything. She cried during the whole meeting. You know, they are some nice-looking ladies."

"Yes, I saw them at their dad's funeral. They are nice-looking but very conniving and crafty."

"Why do you think that about them?" Myles asked with a puzzled look.

"Keith once told me one of his sisters said I was stuck-up and thought I was too good to sit with them at the funeral. The truth was that I ran late because I had a flat tire. I didn't bother to call Keith because I knew he was with his sisters. By the time I arrived, the service had already started. The church was crowded and had standing room only. I ended up sitting in the back after a man gave up his seat to me. When the funeral was over, I went to where Keith was. He later told me his sister asked him if he was sure I was pregnant by him. When he told me that, I reflected on how they were looking at me after the funeral. I didn't say much of anything to either of them after he told me that." Myles was laughing but didn't say anything. I knew he was thinking about the time he told me I acted stuck-up, too.

"I do know that when KJ was born, they made sure to come and see him. They even stayed at my house for a week. One day, Keith and Barbara left, taking KJ with them. They said there were going to close an account their dad had with their names on it, and it was time to take the funds out without being penalized. Linda stayed behind with me. She told me their mom had a savings account with her name on it, and when they came into town to bury their dad, she withdrew her money and closed the account. Their dad had a CD account with Keith and Barbara's names on it, so they were going to get that money and close out that account, too.

"She started asking me a bunch of questions. 'How did you and Keith meet? How long have you known him before y'all got married?' When she saw the picture of me when I was in the Air Force, she asked, 'You were in the Air Force?' I told her I was and that I won 2nd Place in a beauty contest while in Germany. She said, 'You are a beautiful lady. Why did you marry my brother?' I told her he was my friend, and I enjoyed his company. She eyed me up and down. I wanted to know why she asked me such a thing, and she simply replied, 'I just wanted to know why you married him.'

"The next day, the sister left to return to Chicago. A few days later, Keith got a letter in the mail and took it upstairs to the sitting room to read it. I heard him talking to somebody on the phone. After hanging up, he left for a meeting at the church. I saw the letter sitting on the table as I passed by the door. I picked it up, read it, and saw it was a DNA test he had done on KJ. I was so upset, I called him at the church and asked him why he got the test and when he did it. He said, "The day I left to close the bank account, my sisters said KJ didn't look like me and was too cute to be my baby.' It stung to hear him say that. I told him he was a pathetic man and that I couldn't believe he did that behind my back. As I sit here talking about it, his sisters knew he liked men. They probably thought he couldn't father a child, which was why they thought KJ wasn't his. All I can say is they are KJ's aunts. I'm sorry for their loss, but I want nothing to do with them."

"I'm sorry they said that about you, Babe."

"Myles, I feel like I need to pray. Will you pray with me?" We got on our knees, and he prayed. When he finished, I felt better, but Keith was still on my mind. I thought, "After the divorce, he got on my nerves, and we weren't best friends anymore, but he was still my son's father. I'm sorry he's dead. He was a good man, just confused." I fell asleep feeling sorry for KJ losing his daddy in such a tragic way, as well as his brother and sister. KJ had Myles, but those other kids had no one. I prayed, "Lord, please keep them and Brenda covered under your wings. I know they're hurting right now."

Chapter 108

On Saturday, we went on a family outing to the Lane Car Museum. Myles and KJ were excited to see all the beautiful cars. I took pictures of them sitting on and in cars, and KJ took pictures of the babies, Myles, and me. One of the most memorable ones I took was of the twins standing in the window with KJ holding them in the backseat of a 1955 red convertible Mustang, with Myles pretending he was driving.

At one point, we asked a man to take a photo with all of us in it. Afterward, the man told Myles, "You have a good-looking family. Y'all should be on the cover of a magazine." As Myles pushed the twins in the stroller, he thanked the man for the compliment. It was a fun day, filled with making memories to last a lifetime. After leaving the museum, we went shopping in the mall and ate in the food court.

Once home, I got the babies ready for bed. Myles went into my office for his Bible study time. He was working diligently to get caught up with his lesson before the study group returned in October. As for KJ, he went to his room.

Since leaving the mall, I noticed KJ didn't talk like he always did. Maybe the mall made him think about his daddy. As we walked through the mall, he did say his daddy took him and Brandon to the mall and told them they could get any toy they wanted. KJ chose a remote-control car, and Brandon picked out a man that transformed into a car.

When the twins fell asleep, I went up to check on KJ. He was lying across his bed, coloring in his circus coloring book. He turned, looked at me, and said, "Where is Myles? He always comes up to check on me and tell me a story about Jesus. He says Jesus loves me."

I laid on the bed beside him, kissed him on the cheek, and replied, "He's doing his Bible study homework right now."

"Oh," he said, wiping my kiss off his cheek. "Mama, is Myles going to leave us?"

"No, why would you think that?"

"When you took Kaylin to the bathroom at the museum, a lady was talking to Myles. And when we made it to the mall, that same lady was there." I was rubbing him on his back as he spoke. I could see he was beginning to cry.

"Maybe she's someone he knows, out enjoying herself like we were." He didn't respond, but I did see the tears running down his cheeks. "Are you crying?"

He didn't answer. Instead, he said, "Mama, you color this page, and I'll color this one," pointing to his coloring book.

"Okay, mine is going to be prettier than yours." He smiled—finally. We talked and colored in his book until he said he was tired.

Once downstairs, I got ready for bed. Myles had finished his Bible study and was in the exercise room. When he got into bed, he asked, "Are you asleep?"

"No, I'm not asleep."

"How is KJ? He was so quiet on our ride home."

"He's okay. He said you were talking to a lady at the car museum, and then he saw the same lady at the mall." I set up on my elbow in the bed, looking at him and waiting for an answer. "Myles, who was that lady?"

He laughed and asked, "Why are you looking at me like that?"

"I'm waiting to hear what you have to say about the lady who followed you to the mall. What's her name?"

"Babe, I told you about that lady. Her name is Chelsea. We dated before I left for Iraq."

"Chelsea, huh? That doesn't sound like a black girl's name."

"That's because she is not black. A couple of weeks ago, she came by the shop and said she made a mistake by not waiting on me."

"What did you say? Did you tell her you are a married man with three children?"

"I told her it was nice seeing her, but I was busy and to have a nice day. After that, she left."

I laid there, trying to remember if I had seen a non-black woman at the museum and mall. I asked him, "Where was Mrs. Clark when Chelsea came?" He laughed at the tone in my voice.

"She was standing there, listening to us talk. After she left, I told Mrs. Clark, 'If she comes back, don't call me.'"

"Well, the problem here is that KJ thinks you are going to leave us for her," I said accusingly.

He pulled me to him and started singing Barry White's "I'm Never Going to Give You Up," kissing me all over my face. "I can't control how she feels about me. Now, I must say I was surprised to see her today. I guess she was just as surprised to see me. All she said to me was that I hurt her feelings when she stopped by the shop because she still had feelings for me."

"Wow, she said that?"

"Yes, I told her I was sorry for her hurt feelings but that I didn't have any for her anymore. I also told her I am happily married and love my wife and family. I ended our short chat by telling her I would pray for her to find someone who loves her."

"Did you say anything to her at the mall?"

"No, I didn't say anything at all."

"Well, I'm telling you now: If I ever even think you are considering cutting out on me, I will break your arm and divorce you."

He was laughing so hard and, in a low voice, said, "I believe you will do something like that."

In a threatening, mean voice, I asked, "What did you say?"

He got out of the bed and replied, "I said I was going to check on KJ."

"That's not what you said!"

He was laughing hard as he headed out the door. I threw a pillow at him, hitting him square in the back of his head.

As the weeks passed, KJ got better concerning the loss of his daddy. Myles stepped up and filled the role of the perfect father for him and kept him busy. Myles would take KJ to the shop with him, have him do yard work, wash and clean out the cars, and make sure he cleaned up behind Spot. One day, KJ said, "Mama, Myles got me cleaning his car, but the car's never dirty!"

I laughed and replied, "You know your dad wants everything spic-and-span around here."

"Mama, you said 'your dad.'"

"Well, Keith, he's your daddy now." He looked at me with a huge grin before walking out of the room.

He came right back in and asked, "Mama, do I call him dad or daddy?"

"I think he'll like you calling him dad." He walked out with a smile larger than the one before.

Chapter 109

While the babies were asleep, Myles and KJ went to get their hair cut. I sat there, remembering the day they pranked me when I was pregnant.

I came into my bedroom, and there was a mouse on my bed by my pillow. I ran out, grabbed the broom, and ran back in, trying to hit it. I cried out for Myles to come and get it off the bed. Every time I hit it, it moved. Myles hopped out of the closet, taking pictures of me and KJ hiding by the bed. KJ laughed and yelled, "Mama, you just killed my remote-control mouse!" Myles actually fell to the floor, laughing ridiculously hard. I stood there glaring at both of them with the broom in one hand and my big belly in the other.

"Today is payback time," I thought.

I set two pieces of my luggage in the garage and let the garage door up. I then went back inside, removed some of the twins' clothes from their drawers, and placed them on the bed beside their diaper bags. KJ came into the room, asking, "Mama, why is your luggage in the garage?"

I looked at him sternly and said, "Look in the laundry room. Get that brown luggage and go pack your clothes."

"Where are we going?"

"Just go and pack your clothes," I ordered.

When Myles came into the bedroom, he was smiling. He walked over to kiss me, but I dodged his show of affection. "What's wrong with you? And why did you tell KJ to pack? Where's he going? Why is your luggage in the garage?" I didn't respond. I just kept folding the babies' clothes and putting them into their diaper bags. He walked closer to me. "What's wrong with you? Why are you packing, Lexie?" He caught my hand, keeping me from continuing to place the clothes in the bags.

I couldn't look him in the face because I was trying to keep from laughing. "Let go of my hand," I commanded. When he heard the fierceness of my voice, he snatched his hand away. I finally pulled it together, looked at him, and stated, "I'm leaving you."

"Why? What did I do?!"

"I saw you with that woman!"

"Woman? What woman? What are you talking about?"

I turned and saw KJ standing at the door. "Mama, where are we going? What do you want me to pack?"

I yelled at him and said, "Boy, just go and pack your clothes!" Myles looked shocked, hearing the tone I just used at my son.

"Is Myles coming with us?" KJ asked.

"No, I'm leaving him. Now, go and pack!" Myles came over, trying to hug me. I pushed him away. "Don't you dare touch me, you cheater! I told you if I ever caught you cheating on me, I would leave and divorce you."

When he spoke, he was near tears. "What are you talking about? I have never cheated on you. And what woman did you see me with?"

I couldn't look him in the face, so I kept folding the babies' clothes, putting them in their diaper bags. I looked out the corner of my eye and saw how sad he looked with tears in his eyes. I ran into the bathroom and locked the door. I was laughing so hard at his expression.

He knocked on the door, yelling, "Open the door! Why are you calling me a cheater? I haven't done anything to you, and you are not leaving this house with my children!" I remained in the bathroom, laughing and trying to figure out how to end the prank. I didn't want to take it too far.

When I came out of the bathroom, Myles had put all the babies' clothes back in their drawers, and the diaper bags were hanging from each baby's crib. I picked up my phone that was lying on my dresser and walked out of the bedroom into the kitchen. I found him sitting at the island, holding the babies and looking hopeless. KJ stood beside him, crying.

"I don't know why you are calling me a cheater. I have never cheated on you—and you are not taking my children out of this house. None of them."

Through his tears, KJ said, "I'm going to stay here with Myles." He held on tightly to Myles' arm. I took of picture of them and started laughing at their confused expressions.

"Do you remember the mouse prank? I told you I would get you back!" Only then did they start laughing. "KJ, please get my luggage out of the garage and put your bag back in the laundry room. Let the garage door down on your way back in." He walked out smiling as he headed to the garage.

Obviously relieved, Myles laughed as he went into the bedroom to put the twins back in their cribs. "Babe, I didn't know what to think, especially when you called me a cheater." He pushed me onto the bed playfully and added, "Oh, my God! You called me a cheater!"

"Myles, it was just a prank." We laid on the bed, laughing until we cried. "Let me show you how you and KJ were looking.

As he looked at the pictures, he saw just how sad both of them looked. "Do I need to get my phone and remind you how you looked hitting that mouse? You had your eyes closed!" When KJ came in, and we showed him the pictures, he laughed, too.

"I'm ready to eat now. What did you cook?" Myles asked.

"Nothing. I had to make my prank seem real."

"Okay, Cracker Barrel! Here we come!"

On the way, I said, "Honey, I like your haircuts. And thank you for my flowers."

We laughed at those pictures for days. I had them developed and added them to the picture wall.

Chapter 110

Myles and I had discussed moving the twins into their own bedrooms when they turned two-and-a-half, especially since we had the intercom system upstairs. We decided the suite would be used for our guests.

I started decorating Kaylin's room with a princess theme. The colors were lavender, yellow, and pink on a cream-colored wall. Her name was in bold pink letters with stars that glowed when the lights were off. Opening the closet to put the leftover decorations on the shelf, I saw a large manila envelope in the far corner. I wondered, "What is that? Did KJ put this in here?"

Taking it off the shelf, I saw Keith's name on it. "What's this doing in here? He never slept in this room," I said aloud. I opened the envelope and looked through it. There were five Archie and Veronica comic books, four Spiderman, three Batman, a picture of his parents and a couple of him and his sisters when they were younger, and two magazines with nude men in them. "Oh, my God! I'm glad I found this instead of KJ!" I whispered.

I thought about KJ telling me how one day, his daddy asked him to look in the closet in the blue bedroom to see if there were some papers on the shelf that he had left behind. I remember KJ saying, "I looked, Mama, but didn't see anything." I didn't think anything about it because I knew I had given Keith everything that was left in the room he slept in. That's why KJ didn't find it; the envelope was in the cream room, not the blue one.

There were also letters still inside their envelopes, bound by a rubber band. I noticed they were from Sam with an Arkansas return address. Within the letters, Sam told Keith how much he missed him and couldn't wait to see him again. One of the letters mentioned how he enjoyed his time when he was in town. I thought, "This was written when we were together! Keith would leave home, and I wouldn't see him for days. I had no idea where he went. Was he doing the same thing when he was married to Brenda?"

I opened the last letter. It read:

"I'm sorry about your dad. I was at his funeral and saw you with your sisters. I wish I could have been with you to hold your hand. I also saw the lady you married. Why was she sitting in the back and not with you? For one thing, she doesn't look like she is your type. I see she's pregnant. Is that your baby? Why did you marry her anyway? Was it because of her big house you always talked about when you were with me or because she's rich? I know you don't love her like you love me. I know where you live. Don't be surprised if I just show up at your house. Keith, I will always love you. Sam."

I thought, "Oh, my God! That man knew where I lived a long time ago!" The last piece of content in the manila envelope was a photo of Keith and Sam that was wrapped in a napkin. The two men were passionately embracing one another. I was disgusted and hurt simultaneously. I put everything back in the envelope and went downstairs.

Myles and KJ were outside, starting up the grill, and the babies were asleep in their cribs. Walking out on the patio, I called for Myles to come in for a minute. He entered and asked, "What's wrong?" I didn't say a word as I handed him the envelope. "What's this?" He opened it, looked inside, and asked, "Where did you get this from?"

"Out of the room I'm decorating for Kaylin. It was on the shelf in the closet. Myles, what am I going to do with this?"

"Calm down. Give KJ the comic books and pictures—except the one with the two men hugging. Since I have the grill going, I'll burn everything else."

"Wait, look at this letter Sam wrote to Keith." I pulled out the last letter.

He walked into the kitchen, sat on a stool, and started reading. Suddenly, he balled it up and said to me, "I don't want to read this mess. It's getting burned up, too. I'm just glad KJ didn't find this. Did you look and make sure there's nothing else on that shelf?"

"Yes, I did."

"Well, all this is going in the grill. Go through each comic book, page by page, and make sure there are no more of these in there," he said, holding up that last picture.

KJ came in and told Myles, "I'm going upstairs to put on some shorts. It's hot out there!"

Myles laughed and replied, "Okay, I'm on my way back outside."

After KJ changed into his shorts, he passed by me in the kitchen, saying, "I'll be ready to eat when the meat is ready!"

As I prepared the baked beans, other sides, iced tea, and a small punch bowl cake, I looked through the comic books. I had to set them aside and cover them with a kitchen towel when the twins woke up from their nap. I changed them and sat them in their hi-chairs. KJ came in with the hot dogs and hamburgers, placing them on the counter before running back outside. I took one of the hot dogs and broke it into small pieces, giving each of the twins some on the tray of their hi-chair so that they could eat.

I found more pictures of Keith and Sam hidden within the pages of the comic books. Two of them were taken inside my house. I thought, "I don't believe this! Sam has been inside my house!" When Myles came in to grab a pan to put the steaks and chicken in, I handed him the pictures. "Look, here are three more pictures. Two of them were taking in my house!"

"For real?!" He grabbed the pictures and looked at them. "Wow!"

"When did Keith have that man in my house, Myles? I can't believe this!"

"I'll burn them. Forget what you saw," Myles said, heading back to the grill.

As we ate, my mind was all over the place. I couldn't believe Keith had that man in my house, taking pictures in the theater and living room—and doing only God knows what else! I remember when he called asking about that envelope a couple of years back. I told him he had nothing else here. Sometime later, Mrs. Riddle was cleaning and found an envelope on the windowsill. I told her that must have been the one Keith called and asked about. Inside was the bracelet I saw him wearing after his dad died. I called Keith and told him to look in KJ's bookbag for the envelope when he gets there. He exhaled loudly and said, "Thank you." As I sat there thinking about that call, I imagined his reaction when he realized that it was not the envelope he was expecting.

After eating, Myles went outside to make sure the letters and picture were completely burnt and that the fire was out in the grill. KJ was sitting at the table, playing with the twins. "Keith, look what I found in Kaylin's room," I said, handing him the envelope.

He looked inside and replied, "Wow! Some more pictures of my daddy! And here's Aunt Barbara and Aunt Linda. Mama, is this my grandmama and granddaddy?"

"Yes, that's your grandfather. I never met your grandmother, but I'm sure that's her."

As Myles walked back inside, KJ excitedly said, "Look, Myles!" He showed him the pictures. "And I have some comic books, too!"

"You know, I have some comic books in the shed at Mae's house. When I was leaving for Iraq, I asked my daddy to keep them for me. Lexie, when we finish cleaning the kitchen, get the babies ready. Let's go to Mae's house so I can see if my comic books are still there. If so, KJ, we may be rich!" Myles said, laughing and rubbing KJ's head.

"Mama, can I put my pictures on the picture wall?"

"Yes, but I have to get frames for them first."

He got up from the stool and headed toward the stairs. "I'm going to show Brandon these pictures."

"Keith, let me make copies, and you can give them to him," I answered.

He went upstairs, looking at the pictures. I felt sorry for him, knowing he would never see his daddy in person again. For a fleeting moment, I found myself grateful for the pictures.

Chapter 111

As we left for Mae's house, KJ asked, "Comic books can make us rich, Myles?"

"Well, they don't make certain ones anymore, and they become collectible. People who collect comic books will pay a lot of money for the rare ones."

"Wow!" KJ replied, grinning.

We pulled up to Mae's house, and Myles and KJ went in. When they emerged, Myles was carrying a case. He got back in and said, "Derrick was getting ready to go visit his mom. He gave me the key to open the shed, and the case was sitting right where daddy and I put it. Hey, since we're already out, let's go for a ride around town."

KJ was sitting quietly in the back seat, looking through the comic books in the case. "Myles, there has to be more than 100 comic books in here!"

"Yes, I know. There should be exactly 155, if I remember correctly. Look on the inside of the lid. It should show you the exact number."

"Wow, you're right! 155 comic books!"

By the time we made it home, it was time for bed. I got the babies settled, took my shower, and climbed into bed. Myles was in the living room acting KJ's age as they went through the comic books. I could tell he was having a blast as he told KJ about them.

I laid in the bed, thinking about Keith having that Sam guy in my house. All the pieces began to fit at that moment. That's why Keith kept driving past my house all those years. He was trying to figure out how to get inside. When I was in the hospital, he came looking for that envelope but likely forgot what room he had it hidden in. All that time, I thought he was obsessed with the house when the reality was that he was trying to get in to get that envelope before any of us found it.

I was asleep when Myles came to bed. He kissed me on the neck, saying, "Wake up! You're talking in your sleep."

"No, I wasn't! What was I saying?"

"You were saying how handsome your husband is and how much you love him."

"You're making that up," I said, grinning.

He laughed and said, "KJ convinced me to let him sleep down here because he's missing his daddy."

"He said that? Poor baby. He saw those pictures that probably stirred up some memories. Myles, I want the pastor, his wife, the deacons, and their wives to come here one day and pray over our house."

"Pray over our house? Why?"

"Because Keith had that man in here doing God knows what!" He was laughing so hard and hugging me. "I'm serious. I don't want that spirit in here!"

"Lexie, that was over nine years ago. If you hadn't seen those pictures and read those letters, you wouldn't be thinking like that. We've had Bible lessons and prayers in this house since Sam was here. There is no lingering spirit within these walls."

"I still want them to come and pray. If they come to the reunion, I will ask them myself."

"Okay, Lexie, but there's no spirit here that doesn't belong." He was laughing and kissing me, saying, "I can't believe you."

Chapter 112

A couple of weeks had passed. Brenda called, telling me that Barbara had called her to let her know the house was sold and that after everything was paid off, they got $60,000.00 for the house. Brenda was going to receive Keith's $20,000.00 portion. Brenda said, "I'm giving KJ $10,000.00 of it."

"No, you have three children. KJ only gets $5,000.00."

"My oldest son, Lance, isn't Keith's son. I'll keep $5,000.00 for each of Keith's children, Brandon and Breonna. With KJ being the oldest, he gets $10,000.00."

I was surprised when she said Lance wasn't Keith's son. I thought back to when KJ told me Brenda was crying when Lance told her he didn't want to live with her. "No, Brenda, give KJ $6,000.00, and you keep the rest for your children. I thought Lance was Keith's child."

"No, I was two months pregnant when I met Keith. He knew the baby wasn't his. I fell in love with him, and he said he loved me, too. When my baby was born, I went away to college, and my mom took the baby to Chicago with her. Keith wanted to keep him, but my mom thought it was best that Lance be with her. When my mom died, Lance's father took him to New Orleans. I don't think it will be right for me to give Lance any money. He's not Keith's child. That's why I told Barbara to give Keith's car to someone in the church." She paused before continuing. "I want to ask you to forgive me for what I did to you when you were married to Keith. I shouldn't have encouraged him to take your baby. I shouldn't have come to your house and had him try to take everything from you. I'm sorry for embarrassing you at that church dinner. Lexie, I really am sorry for all that I did. Please forgive me." I heard the sadness and regret in her voice. I wondered if she would be apologetic were Keith still alive. Brenda started to cry uncontrollably, saying, "I'm so sorry! Please forgive me!"

As calmly as possible, I replied, "Brenda, it's okay. Don't put yourself through that. Everything that happened was for my good."

She started babbling, saying, "If I hadn't divorced him, he might still be alive." Those tears were really falling over there.

"Brenda, there's nothing you could have done to stop his death. I'm praying for you. I know it's hard, but God will see you through this." I got teary-eyed, hearing her cry. She was so broken over Keith's death.

Before hanging up the phone, she managed to say, "I will be mailing KJ's cashier's check tomorrow."

When Myles got home, I told him about the call with Brenda. He smiled and said, "I told you. That's what Matthew said. So, the rumors were true about the baby? Wow." He kissed me and asked, "Do you miss me?"

"Myles, go play with KJ and those comic books!" We laughed as he walked away.

Chapter 113

A few months later, they started breaking ground for one of the houses to be built by the Johnson's home. I began receiving letters and calls from those who were going to attend the reunion in three weeks and got a headcount of those who needed to book rooms at the hotel. The families and friends who lived locally called to RSVP and let me know what dish they would bring.

Mrs. Riddle called and said, "I want to bring spaghetti salad and KJ's banana pudding since it's his birthday."

"Thank you, Mrs. Riddle. KJ will love that!"

Mr. Johnson called and said, "My wife wants to bring her earthquake cake and a sour cream pound cake, and I make the best coleslaw in town—at least that's what my family tells me. Oh! My daughter will be here that same weekend. Is it alright for her to come? She has two girls, ages 13 and ten."

"Mr. Johnson, that would be wonderful! I'd love to meet your daughter and her girls," I replied.

"I told her about you and that mansion of a house y'all have."

I laughed and said, "Thank you, Mr. Johnson. I look forward to seeing you guys." When I hung up the phone, I thought, "Wow, I can't believe this! Everyone who's responded from the area wants to bring food!"

When Mrs. Hill called, she thanked us for the invite and asked, "Do you need hot dogs? I work at the meat factory, and I can bring hot dogs and buns."

"That would be wonderful, but you don't have to do that. You're our guest."

"I want to, and I'll bring chips, too," she said, laughing.

"Thank you. I'll see you in three weeks."

Later that day, Mae called and said, "We'll bring the potato salad and baked beans."

"Mae, you don't have to do that."

"I know I don't, but you have my people coming in from Myrtle Beach. Girl, those people can eat!" she said, laughing.

"Thank you, Mae." One of the babies started to cry.

"I'll let you go so you can take care of the baby. Bye."

The next day, Matthew called. "We received the invitation, and we are all coming. It will be Liz and her old man, my two boys and me, and Kathy, her husband, and their three kids. Liz told me to tell you she's bringing a large seven-layer salad, and Kathy is bringing all the fixings for a large green salad. I have a large jug that I will make the punch in once I get there, and I'll bring ice, too."

"That's wonderful, Matthew, but y'all don't have to do that."

"I know, but we want to help. You don't know how happy we've been since we reconnected with you. Plus, there will be ten of us coming. We need to do something!" he said, laughing.

"I'm getting excited to see you guys again, and Myles already has his camera ready to take pictures of everybody who walks through the door."

"Okay, we'll see you in three weeks!"

I looked down at the paper where I noted everything everyone said they were bringing, realizing they were putting together the menu for me. When Myles got home, I told him about all the calls and the growing menu. "Wow, that's awesome! Well, I have another surprise for you."

"What is it?" I asked.

"Mr. Ron and Mrs. Clark are coming! They want to bring something, too! They'll call you to see what you'd like for them to bring."

"Wow, for real?!" My excitement grew by the minute.

The Monday before the reunion, I called the hotel to have them hold eight rooms for the 24th and 25th of August. I then called the table and chair rental service to rent five long tables and 50 chairs to be delivered on the 24th. We had already planned on moving the cars out of the garage and setting up everything in there. That way, rain or shine, the food and drinks will keep well in there.

I was surprised when Irma called. "I'm bringing five watermelons—and don't you say no. People in the South love watermelons!" she said, laughing.

"Thank you, Irma. I look forward to seeing you guys."

"Me, too. I gotta run now. I'm at work."

I didn't tell Myles about his friend Ed coming and staying with us that weekend. I wanted it to be one of the biggest surprises of the event.

Uncle Eddie called and asked, "Is Myles there?"

"No, Uncle Eddie, he's not here."

"Well, tell that boy not to buy any ribs. I'm bringing my barrel grill and ribs. Ruby said to tell you she's making that lasagna KJ loves so much."

"Thank you, Uncle Eddie. I love her lasagna, too, but you don't have to bring your grill. Myles has a new grill here."

"Okay," he replied, "but I'm still bringing the ribs. I think I'll bring some burgers, too."

"Uncle Eddie, you don't have to do that."

"I know that, but I want to do it. Just let this old man do what he wants to do." We laughed.

"Okay, Uncle Eddie, I'll let Myles know. I'm sure he'll call you when he returns. Bye for now."

As I looked over the list, I thought, "The only things I have to purchase are the tablecloths, plasticware, plates, cups, and hamburger buns. I think I'll make a punch bowl cake, too. Lord, You are so good, and I thank You!" I made a note to tell Myles to get chicken and Polish sausages. I knew Uncle Eddie would come bright and early to help Myles get the grill going.

I called Brenda to ask if Brandon could spend the night the Friday before the reunion that Saturday for KJ's birthday and explained we were having his birthday party the same day. I also invited her to come. She sounded excited and surprised when she asked, "You're inviting me?"

"Yes, you are still KJ's family. You are welcome to bring his sister with you. If Brandon can come, I'll have Myles and KJ pick him up that Friday afternoon."

414

"Yes, he can come. I live on the street behind Walmart on Kellyanne Parkway. KJ knows the house. I'll bring the cashier's check with me when I come. I have it in an envelope, waiting for a stamp to mail it."

"Okay, that would be great."

"Thanks again for inviting me," she said. I heard the smile in her voice. I recall telling her she would never set foot in my house, but Keith was gone. I felt sorry for her because she was still so hurt over him getting killed.

Jessica called and said, "We're coming. It will be me, Mama, and the boys. JJ is 13, and Joshua is 11."

"I was looking forward to seeing your husband. He's not coming?" I asked.

She hesitated and replied, "We are separated, Lexie."

"Jessica, no! When did that happen?"

"A couple of months ago. My suspicions about him were correct; he was having an affair with one of the teachers he worked with."

"Oh, my God, Jessica. How did you find out?"

"I got off work early one afternoon, went by the college to surprise him, and planned on taking him to dinner before his last class started. When I approached his classroom door, I heard voices on the other side. One was a lady's, and she was laughing. I peeked through the small window on the door and saw him standing between her legs, kissing her. I thought about the note I had found in his pants pocket around that same time with a number written on it but no name. The note read:

"Meet me in our favorite place. Call me when you get here. I have a surprise waiting for you."

"Lexie, there was a heart drawn on the note. When I asked him about it, he said he had picked it up off the floor when he was walking out of his classroom one day, stuck it in his pocket, and forgot it was there. Well, last weekend, I attended a conference in Cincinnati. I got home late that Saturday afternoon and JJ was upset. He said on Friday night, during the game, he saw his daddy standing close to a white woman, talking to her, and then they left. After the game, JJ looked for his dad but couldn't find him anywhere. One of the team members offered to drop him off at home. Just when they were getting ready to leave, his dad pulled up, saying he had to run back to the college to grab some papers. His dad dropped him off at home, told him to go inside, and said he'd be back in a little while. I knew something was going on with him for about six months or more. He's been coming home late, telling me he was busy in his class or had a late meeting."

"Oh no, Jessica. Did you tell him you saw him?"

"Yes, and he lied, saying it wasn't him. That very night, I told him to leave my house. I haven't seen him in over four weeks. My mom said he stopped by a couple of days ago to pick up his clothes and talk with the boys. She also told me the Saturday I was on call at the hospital, someone called the house phone but didn't say anything when she answered. James asked her who was on the phone, and when she said she didn't know, he got on the phone, said hello, and then asked, "Why did you call me on this phone?" while feeling around in his pocket. He went into the bedroom and returned with his cell phone, telling my mom he had to run out for a minute and asking if she could take JJ to basketball practice. After she dropped him off, she was on her way home and saw James walking across the street at Hamilton and Hobson Boulevards with a blonde-headed white lady, and he was holding a little girl's hands. She didn't see where they went because the light had changed. She didn't' tell me because she said she didn't want to start anything. Lexie, the lady I saw him with in his classroom was a blonde-headed white woman. Anyway, he's out of my house. I guess he's staying with that lady now."

"I am so sorry, Jessica."

She let out a soft breath and said, "I'm not." I heard her being called over the hospital's intercom. "Lex, I gotta go and check on my patient. I'm looking forward to seeing you on the 25th."

"Okay, I can't wait to see you guys. Take care. Bye." When we hung up, I thought, "Oh, my God. I wasn't expecting to hear all that. Matthew is going to be here, and she's separated from her husband. She already told me she still has feelings for Matthew. Oh, my goodness…"

Myles and KJ were coming in from sweeping the deck around the pool when I ended the call with Jessica. I was sitting on the patio with the babies as they played in their walkers. KJ passed me, heading into the kitchen, and said, "I'm tired and hot."

Myles laughed and said, "Boy, you didn't do anything!" He sat beside me and kissed me on the forehead, singing, "It's a beautiful day in the neighborhood!"

416

"Yes, it is a beautiful day." My energy didn't match his, and he felt it.

"What's going on in that pretty little head of yours? I can see something's wrong in your face." He kissed me on the tip of my nose. "Talk to me, woman!"

I started to laugh and replied, "Jessica and her husband separated. She put him out of the house."

"Who? Your friend Dr. Jessica?"

"Yes, and it wasn't her fault."

"Lexie, didn't you tell me she still had feelings for Matthew?"

"Yes, but the separation had nothing to do with Matthew. She caught her husband with another woman."

"Leave that alone. Stay out of it. I know she's your friend, but some things just aren't your business."

I knew he was right, but I felt Jessica's pain. I changed the subject. "Myles, the men will bring the tables and chairs next Friday around 11:00."

"Good, the shop will be closed on that day. I already told Ron and Mrs. Clark we will be closed."

"You don't have to close the shop. They're just dropping the stuff off and leaving."

"I know. That's why I'm going to be here when they come."

"Myles, you are acting as if you don't trust me around men."

"It's not that I don't trust you; I don't trust them." He was looking at me, licking his lips. "Baby, you are too fine to be here with men you don't know. I need to start getting things ready for the reunion anyway." He stood, pulled me to him, and whispered sweet nothings in my ear, making me laugh. I thought, "My husband is hilarious—and jealous, too!"

I looked over just in time and shouted, "Myles, get Karson!" He had gotten out of his walker and was standing in the chair part, bouncing. Myles caught him before he fell out. "I put him in his walker because he was in the playpen bouncing around while Kaylin was asleep. I went into my office to make a call, and when I turned around to walk back out, that boy had gotten out of the playpen and was standing behind me. His clothes were wet, and he had water dripping from his head with little pieces of tissue all in his hair. I followed the tissue on the floor leading back to the bathroom and saw he had played in the toilet! The floor was soaked, and tissue was everywhere!"

Myles stood there, holding Karson and laughing his head off. Karson was grinning, too, like he knew what I was talking about. Kaylin sat in her walker, looking as if she wanted to ask, "What are y'all laughing at?" "She doesn't smile as much as Karson, but when she does, she shows one dimple in her right cheek, just like mine."

Myles was still laughing when he asked, "Was Karson eating the tissue?"

"I don't know if he did or not. All I can say is that you and KJ need to keep that bathroom door closed!" Both of us were cracking up.

Chapter 114

I was getting more and more excited as the day neared for the reunion. We were one week out from the event. The hotel rooms were booked, as well as the arrangements for those who will be staying with family and friends while they're here for the weekend. If everyone who RSVP'd came, there would be 58 guests: 30 in-town guests and 28 out-of-town guests. I had a full day planned for the first day of the reunion, starting with our out-of-town guests meeting at our house for breakfast at 9:00 a.m. It was already decided that Myles, Derrick, and Rodrick would make the meal. The families and friends in town were scheduled to arrive at 2:00 p.m.

The week flew by fast. I was anxious to go to bed on Thursday night and wake up on Friday, ready for the festivities to begin. Myles and KJ picked up Brandon, and they were going to the hotel to pick up his cousins, who had already arrived to go skating. "The skating rink trip is KJ's pre-birthday gift," Myles said. When they got home, Myles was surprised to come in and see his friend Ed and his family had arrived from Myrtle Beach.

"Oh, my God! Ed! How are you?" As Myles and Ed chatted, his wife Faye helped me finish putting the tablecloths and centerpieces on the tables.

Liz called, asking if she could bring her fiancé's sister and her husband to the reunion. I told her they were welcome to come. KJ was entertaining Liz's children and his brother Brandon. When they were tired and ready for bed, Myles and I showed the group where they would be sleeping, adding that the whole upstairs was for them and KJ.

"Oh, my goodness, Lexie! It's beautiful up here! I love it!" Faye said.

"Thank you." As we went back downstairs, the phone was ringing. It was Sharon, calling to let us know they had made it to Mae's house and that her uncle and aunts were at Uncle Eddie's. The rest of the family that came in with them were at the hotel. Myles got on the phone and asked her to tell Eric, Corey, and Davis to make sure they were at our house around 8:00 a.m. to help prepare breakfast.

Saturday was KJ's birthday and the reunion. Mae's and Sharon's families were already at our house, with the men helping Myles and Ed in the kitchen. They made a massive meal that included eggs, toast, turkey sausage and bacon, regular sausage and bacon, grits, and oatmeal. For beverages, they had orange juice, coffee, and tea. There were different kinds of cereals with milk for those who wanted them. That morning, all the guests from the hotel came over for breakfast.

After breakfast, Myles left with the men to go fishing. The ladies were left to clean the kitchen. The young people who didn't go fishing stayed behind and played basketball and went swimming in the pool.

I had purchased 20 pieces of fleece material for the ladies to make tie blankets. I showed them how to do it, and they enjoyed learning how to cut and tie their blankets.

It was around noon when Myles and the men returned from fishing, along with Ed's son, KJ, and Brandon. Uncle Eddie and Myles' other two uncles were in the backyard, grilling the meat. Myles said they had caught 30 fish and had already cleaned them. He planned to give them to Uncle Eddie to take home. He also shared with me that he and the men had practiced a song for the talent show.

Starting at around 1:30 p.m., the in-town families and friends arrived with their food. When Irma and her husband came, I told her to show her husband around. I couldn't believe the amount of food that came through the door. There was so much—more than enough to feed everyone. Faye, Sharon, and Mae arranged the food on the tables as it came in. When Kathy and her family arrived, she said, "Liz will be running late. She went to pick up her fiancé, his sister, and her husband."

"Yes, she called me last night to ask if they could come," I replied.

"Lexie, this is a beautiful place. Matthew said you had a mansion out here, and you do!"

"Kathy, it's not a mansion," I said, smiling at the expression on her face.

"Okay, it's a huge house," she replied, looking around.

"Go in, Kathy. You are welcome to look around," I said, leaving her side to greet Jessica, her two sons, and her mom. It felt so good to see her mom.

Matthew saw them coming in and came over to greet them. He hugged Jessica and her mom. "Ms. Avis, it's so good to see you."

She was looking at him, trying to recognize who he was. "Matthew? Boy, it that you?"

"Yes, ma'am."

She grabbed him and gave him another hug. "Look at you! You have some meat on your bones now. You were a skinny little thang. Boy, you look good!"

He was smiling from ear to ear. "Ms. Avis, I try to live right and eat right."

"You sure were skinny, sneaking around my house," she murmured.

"Mama!" Jessica said, surprised.

"Don't Mama me! I prayed many nights that you didn't come home pregnant, always hiding out at Mr. Harris' house." Jessica was shocked to hear her mom talk like that. She stood there with her hands over her mouth, and Matthew was laughing so hard, he was bending over. I stood there in shock at what Ms. Avis said, too.

"I gotta go and get the fashion show started," I said.

As I turned to leave, Ms. Avis asked, "Lexie, you knew what was going on, didn't you?" I just laughed, shook my head, and walked away.

Liz came in and introduced me to her fiancé and his family. "This is Raymond, his sister Tenisha, and her husband, Albert." Albert was looking at me with a funny smile on his face.

"It's nice to meet you, Raymond and Tenisha, but I already know Albert," I replied.

"When we turned on your street, Albert said he knew you and asked if you still work downtown. I told him I didn't know," Liz said.

"Yes, I'm still downtown in Human Resources." I thought to myself, "He knows where I work, and I know he remembers the day I told him to leave my house." Tenisha's face looked familiar, but I couldn't place where I'd seen her before. "Go in and have a seat, everyone. I gotta go and get the children ready for the fashion show. We'll talk later."

Myles caught me on my way upstairs. "Do you know that lady with Liz?" he asked.

"Yes, her name is Tenisha. I've seen her somewhere before, but I don't remember where."

421

"Lexie, that's the lady who put her hand on my thigh!"

I looked around until I saw her again. She was sitting, talking to Sharon. "For real, Myles? She looks different."

"She has her hair styled differently, but I got a good look at her when I took her picture when she came in."

"Do you think she remembers you?" I asked.

"She didn't act like she did."

"Well, she better not lay one hand on you up in here."

"Babe, she's with her husband."

"I know her husband from school, and he's a nutcase."

He laughed and said, "Babe, go and get the kids ready for the fashion show."

The mothers of each child in the fashion show handed me a card with their child's name and what they were wearing. As they walked in, Myles took their pictures and kept the cards afterward. All of the children looked amazing in their outfits. Twelve little ones participated in the show, and we gave each of them a $10.00 Visa Gift Card for being adorable models.

The last ones to model were the teenagers: LT, one of his sisters, Trina, Ed's son, one of Mr. Johnson's granddaughters, and Jessica's son JJ. When LT walked out, it was like I was looking at my brother Leon. He walked and talked just like my brother, and when he smiled, no one could tell me I wasn't looking at my brother's face. Seeing him brought chills to my body from head to toe. When the teen portion of the show was over, we gave each of them a $15.00 Visa Gift Card.

After the fashion show, Myles asked our pastor to bless the food. Afterward, everyone lined up to get a plate of food and found a seat. During the meal, I asked each head of the family to introduce themselves and their family and tell how they knew Myles and me. I found out Mrs. Riddle was my pastor's sister-in-law, and Mr. Riddle was Tenisha's uncle. When Albert introduced himself, he said, "I own a restaurant in Franklin, about 20 miles outside of Nashville. If you're ever out that way, be sure to stop in."

There were two lawyers, one doctor, four teachers, a high school principal, two truck drivers, and two police officers in the room that day. Myles and four others owned their own businesses. I thought, "We have some business-minded people in our families!"

After dinner, I called KJ to the front and had everyone sing "Happy Birthday" to him. We then served birthday cake and ice cream to celebrate. Myles left the backyard, and when he returned, he was riding on KJ's gift: a black dirt bike. I put KJ's black matching helmet on his head that matched his bike. He was so excited, he hugged Myles and me, saying, "Thank you, Mama! Thank you, Myles! I love my birthday gift!" Afterward, everybody started pinning money to his shirt, which was a Southern tradition.

When it was time for the talent show, Mr. Riddle, Myles' Uncle Willie, and Mr. Hill were the judges. We had 1st and 2nd Place prizes and six people participating. Before the talent show started, Myles and KJ sang "If It Doesn't Have God in It, Then Something Is Wrong with It" by Jay McGee. I listened to them sing, thinking, "I haven't heard that song in a long time. When did he have time to practice with KJ?" The duo sounded fabulous!

After their song, the men who went fishing came up and sang "Cooling Water" by Lee Williams. Ed sang Lee Williams' part of the song. They sounded so good, everyone stood and clapped their hands along with the tune.

Then, the talent show portion began. Everyone sang their song and waited on the judges to make their decisions. While waiting, Trina read a poem she had written in her English class. Since we had a free moment, Myles went and changed into his white leisure suit and white sandals. I changed into my white pantsuit and let my hair hang down my back.

When Trina finished her reading, Myles started walking toward me, singing "I Am a Living Testimony." He got emotional as he sang that song. I remembered him telling me how he almost died in Iraq, but the Lord spared his life. I looked over at Ed and saw him getting emotional, too. Myles told me that they were in heavy combat one day, and he had run out of ammo. As Ed ran to bring him more, he was shot in the leg, which was why he walked with a slight limp. During Ed's recovery, the two of them grew close, much like brothers. "I owe my life to Ed because he got shot trying to help me. I will always thank God for keeping both of us alive," Myles had told me.

While Myles was singing, Karson got away from KJ and walked up to Myles, tugging on his leg. Everyone thought that was adorable. Ending his song, Myles reached out to me and played the instrumental version of "Addicted Love" by Bebe and Cece Winans. We sang the song together.

When we finished singing, Lynn said, "That's not fair! They changed clothes and had background music!" The entire group laughed.

Myles looked at the judges and said, "No, don't judge us. We just did that for entertainment."

The judges finally announced the winners. Angie won 1st Place, and Lynn won 2nd Place. We gave both a $25.00 Visa Gift Card.

Around 6:00 p.m., the pastor spoke a word of encouragement and had everyone stand to sing "I Need You to Survive." Afterward, he closed us out with prayer. He approached me and said, "I loved the way you and Myles sound singing together. Your son has a nice singing voice, too. I want you to think about singing in the church."

I started to laugh and replied, "Okay, pastor, I'll think about it." I told his wife to pick a basket before they leave and thanked them for coming and blessing my house with prayer.

The pastor smiled and said, "Daughter, think about what I asked you." He touched me gently on the shoulder, and his wife hugged and thanked me before they left.

I watched as everybody walked around, saying their goodbyes and starting to leave. I told every head of household to take a basket off the island in the kitchen on their way out. The baskets were filled with various types of candy bars and a thank you card with our family photo on it. I also reminded the ladies to take the tie blankets they had made.

Brenda approached me and asked if KJ could go home with her to spend the night with Brandon. "Do you want to go?" I asked him.

"I guess so," he replied, looking at the floor. I could tell he didn't want to disappoint Brandon.

"Go upstairs and pack two changes of clothes and your PJs. Don't forget to pack your toothbrush," I instructed.

"Okay," he said, going upstairs slowly.

Mae came over and said, "Lexie, you look good in that pantsuit. I didn't know your hair was that long!" She gave my hair a slight pull.

"Myles doesn't want me to cut it. That's why I always wear it up."

"I now see where Kaylin gets all that hair from!" she replied.

Derrick walked over and said, "Come on, Mae. This has been a long day. You can talk to Lexie another time."

She smiled, hugged me, and said, "Bye, Lexie. We'll talk later." She picked up her basket and walked out the door behind her husband.

KJ came back downstairs holding his birthday money and whispered to Myles, "What do I do with this money?"

Myles whispered back, "Put it in your secret place." KJ headed straight into my office.

"Secret place?" I asked, confused. I didn't know anything about it.

"He knows what I mean," Myles said, laughing. KJ came out of my office, prepared to leave. He hugged Myles and me. I could still tell he didn't want to go.

By 7:00 p.m., all the in-town guests were gone, and the out-of-town guests were back at the hotel. They planned on leaving early Sunday morning. The only guests we had in our home were Ed and his family. We all got slices of watermelon and went upstairs to the theater room to watch "Black Panther" and talk about how much we enjoyed the weekend.

Ed said, "We're leaving early in the morning and plan to stop in Mount Pleasant, Georgia, to visit Faye's mother."

After the movie, we all retired to bed. It had been a long, full day.

Chapter 115

Myles and I were up at 5:00 a.m. on Sunday to see Ed and his family off and immediately returned to bed. We didn't wake up until the twins woke us up around 10:00. After Myles made breakfast, we sat at the kitchen island, eating and talking about the wonderful time we had. When we finished, he took the dog out and then went upstairs to strip the beds, put the bedding in the washer, and vacuum the whole upstairs.

"When the bedding finishes washing, put them in the dryer, fold them, and set them on the beds. When Mrs. Riddle comes, she can remake the beds," Myles instructed.

"Sorry, Honey, that's your job today."

He laughed and replied, "Babe, you go back and get some rest when you finish folding the bedding. Yesterday was a busy one for you. I will be outside, washing my car. I'll keep the babies with me."

I kissed him and said, "You're the best husband."

He kissed me back. "Happy wife, happy husband!"

On Monday morning, Myles called to let Mrs. Clark know he would be coming in after noon. The men picked up the chairs and tables, and we left for the twins' doctor's appointment at 10:30. After the doctor's visit, Myles dropped us off at home, and he went to work.

When Myles got home from work on Tuesday, I took the pictures he had taken during the reunion to Walgreen's to be developed. We wanted to get them developed so that we could put them in order to make a photo album for each family that attended the reunion. There were over 200 pictures that needed to be developed! When I came home and told Myles how many pictures he had taken, he said, "Putting each picture with the correct family is going to be a family project!" I laughed at the exasperated look he had on his face.

Wednesday morning, the twins were up before Myles left for work and wouldn't go back to sleep. I fed them breakfast, dressed them, and went outside, walking down our long driveway and back. They played on their riding toys, and I played ball with them. Once back inside the house, I gave them a snack and some cold milk. Shortly after, they went to sleep. I used that quiet time to finish some work I had to do for my job and then laid down to take a nap while the babies slept.

When the phone rang, waking me from my nap, I thought it was Myles calling. I answered without looking at the caller ID and heard Jessica on the other end. She sounded excited as she told me how much she enjoyed herself at the reunion. "Mama said it was so nice to see you and meet your husband. She said Myles looked good and was very nice."

I laughed and asked, "Ms. Avis said that?"

"Yes, she did, and we both love your house."

"Thank you. It was good to see Ms. Avis, too. She really surprised me when she reminded Matthew about how skinny he used to be. Oh, my God! And when she said she prayed you didn't get pregnant, I thought I would tinkle myself!"

"Lex, when you walked away, she said a little something about everything. I was glad when your nephew came over to talk to Matthew. I think Matthew was glad he came over, too." We were laughing so hard together at what Mama was saying. "Well, I was calling to tell you I have been talking to Matthew every day since the reunion."

"For real, Jessica?"

"Yes, as a matter of fact, the boys and I went to his house. He lives three subdivisions away from me."

"Wait a minute, Jess. Are you telling me you've been to his house?" She laughed at the tone in my voice.

"Yes, but we talked in the driveway while the boys played basketball. If he would have asked me to come inside his house, I believe I would have gone in."

"Jessica, do you think you're moving a little too fast? You don't even know if he's in a relationship. Plus, you're still married."

"No, he's not in a relationship. And I forgot to tell you I signed my divorce papers the Friday before the reunion. As a matter of fact, a messenger brought the papers to me at work, which was embarrassing because he had to wait for me to sign them."

"For real, Jessica? Wow!"

"Girl, I think James had that planned months ago by the way things happened. In the divorce papers, it stated he would pay child support, get the boys every other weekend, and we would decide together about the holidays and the summer breaks. The week before I signed the papers, he picked up the boys and took them to his house. When they got back, James Jr. said his daddy took them to a big house, and one of the rooms was decorated in pink. I thought about what Mama said when she saw him holding a little girl's hand as they crossed the street. I asked JJ, 'Where was the house?' and he said, 'It's a long way from here in Nolensville.'"

"Jessica, I'm so sorry."

She hesitated and said, "I'm not; I'm glad he's out of my life." I sat there, listening to her talk. I could tell she was getting upset the more she talked about James. "Lex, I want you to know I feel free from James now. I told you why I married him, didn't I? I believe that night at that party, he put something in my punch. I didn't drink any liquor or smoke anything, yet I ended up high and pregnant. When I had my boys, I tried to make things work between us because I knew he loved his sons, but in the back of my mind, I always believed he had done something to my drink. I carried that thought around for years, thinking, 'I didn't even like James. Why did I get pregnant by him?' Lex, he knew I was with Matthew. When I was pregnant with Joshua, we were sitting home one afternoon, talking about our school days. I said to him, 'I want to ask you something: Did you do anything to my punch that night at Sonya's party?' I told him I didn't drink or smoke, yet I was high. Lex, do you know he laughed at me and told me I'll never know?"

"No way, Jessica! He said that?"

"Yes, and he laughed about it!"

"He tricked you into marrying him, and you caught him with another woman. I know you are hurt, but please don't rush into things with Matthew."

"Lex, did you hear me say I'm glad James is out of my life? I have always loved Matthew and enjoyed his company. Catching James with that lady was a blessing. I was going to ask him for a divorce anyway but was waiting until the boys got older.

I heard Myles coming into the house. "Jessica, I gotta go. Myles just walked in. We'll talk later. Bye."

By the time Myles came into the bedroom, I was lying on the bed. He laid beside me, and I asked, "Why are you home early? It's only 2:30. Are you sick?"

"Yes, I am...for you," he replied, kissing me. "Babe, I haven't held you in my arms for six days or told you how much I love you."

"You tell me every morning and night that you love me."

He was laughing and replied, "Well, I miss you."

We were talking, chatting about our day when the phone rang. It was KJ wanting to know when we were coming to pick him up. "Myles, KJ wants to know when you are coming to get him."

"Tell him we will be there at 5:00." When I hung up, he said, "Get dressed so that y'all can go with me." As we drove to get KJ from Brenda's house, I told Myles what Jessica said. He replied, "As I was leaving the shop, I saw Matthew coming out of the bank, and we talked. He told me how much he enjoyed himself on Saturday and said he had been talking to Jessica. Lexie, he really likes her."

"Jessica said she was sure James put something in her punch and got her pregnant. She said she's glad he's out of her life and that their divorce is final."

"Oh, my God! He did that to her?!"

"That's what she thinks. When she asked him about it, he laughed."

"Wow, that's criminal," Myles replied.

Chapter 116

Driving up to Brenda's house, KJ was already standing outside with his overnight bag, waiting for us. Before we could come to a complete stop, KJ was opening the door to get in. I stopped him. "No, go and let Mama Brenda know you are leaving." He turned around, running back to the house.

Brenda came to the door, waved bye to us, and yelled, "KJ has a note for you!"

"Okay!" I yelled back.

Once settled inside the vehicle, Myles asked KJ, "How was your visit?"

"It was okay, but you took a long time to come and get me. I wanted to ride my dirt bike today."

"You can ride it for a little while when you get home," Myles said with a chuckle.

"Mama, I'm hungry. Is there any more food left? That food was good!"

While we ate dinner, KJ suddenly said, "I forgot my money!" He got up from the table and went into my office. When he returned, he announced, "I have $115.00!"

"What are you going to do with your birthday money?" I asked.

"T.S.S."

"What is T.S.S.?" I wondered.

"I gotta pay my tithes, save some, and spend some. Right, Myles?"

"Yes, that right, Peanut. I thought you forgot what we had talked about."

KJ smiled and asked, "Can I go and ride my bike now?"

"As soon as you finish your food," Myles answered.

Myles, KJ, and the twins went outside. KJ rode his bike, and the babies rode their riding toys. I cleaned the kitchen and then went outside to sit in the garage and watch them play. As I looked at them have a good time, I thought about how good of a father Myles has been to KJ. I then recalled the note Brenda said KJ had for me. I called him over and asked where the note was from Mama Brenda. He removed it from his pocket, handed it to me, and ran back to play. The note read:

"Thank you for making us a part of your family. We enjoyed ourselves at the reunion. Brenda, Brandon, and Breonna. P.S. You have a beautiful home."

I thought, "I know she will be surprised when she gets her copy of the photo album from the reunion!"

As I got the babies ready for bed, KJ came down with his blanket and asked if he could sleep downstairs with us. Myles told him he could. KJ played with the twins until he got sleepy and then went to lay down in my office. As we laid in bed, I said, "Myles, I was talking to Liz, and she said she didn't know Albert knew me. I told her I knew him from school. She said he and Tenisha have been married a little over a year. Raymond said Tenisha left home when she was 19, and no one knew where she was. Rumors were going around, saying she lived on the street and used drugs. One day, she called him and said she had cleaned up her life and was getting married in two weeks. They met Albert for the first time at their wedding. Liz told me Albert was in a car accident and had received a lot of money. That's when they moved to Franklin and opened the restaurant. Apparently, they're doing very well, and Tenisha is expecting a baby."

Myles laughed and said, "Wow, that's good to hear!"

"Although I remember him as a nutcase, maybe he has changed now that he's married." I could tell Myles was almost asleep because he wasn't saying anything except 'Umm-hmm.' "I was thinking we could drive out to visit his restaurant one day." 'Umm-hmm.' "Oh, Liz asked if she could use our house for her reception next year in June."

"What did you tell her?"

"I told her I had to talk to you. She said it would be her family, Raymond's family, and a few of their friends. In total, about 30 people."

Murmuring, he responded, "That's fine with me if it's alright with you." He kissed me goodnight and fell right to sleep.

Chapter 117

On Friday morning, KJ went to work with Myles. I got the babies dressed to take them to Mrs. Johnson's home daycare. Talking with her at the reunion, she told me she had opened a daycare center in her home. I learned she worked in the early childhood program for 20 years in the school system and that since retiring two years prior, she was home every day doing nothing, so she decided to open her own daycare. Per the state's laws, she could have up to seven children in her home at the same time. She already had three children enrolled, and a lady from her church was her assistant.

I talked to Myles about putting the twins in Mrs. Johnson's daycare. He said, "We can give her a try since she lives right up the street from us and is someone we know."

I dropped them off and prayed everything would work out. I then went to my workplace to collect some information I needed to complete before returning to work the following month. I went back home and waited for Myles to get in. After he and KJ got home, we went together to pick up the twins. Myles was so pleased with how the daycare was set up and to see how the babies were playing with the other children.

After we finished our evening routine and put the children in bed, Myles started his personal bible study time. I went on the patio and sat on the bench looking at the stars and the beautiful reflection of the moon in the swimming pool. The view made me reflect on how awesome God is. I thanked God for the wonderful reunion that He blessed us to have and for blessing everyone to arrive home safely.

My quiet time was interrupted with Myles asking when I was coming to bed. I answered him, "in a little while." During quiet times like those, I am reminded of how much I miss my mom. I looked out at the beautiful flowers she planted, thinking of how she loved them and could tell what kind of flowers they were by simply looking at them.

When I finally walked into the bedroom, Myles was already sound asleep. I kissed him on his jaw and chuckled, knowing he doesn't like going to sleep without me laying beside him.

On Saturday, Myles and KJ went bowling and said he would pick up LT along the way. Matthew and his twins were going to meet them there. "Today is the boys' day out," Myles said.

As the babies slept, I thought about my life, the bad decisions and mistakes I have made, and the hurtful words I have spoken that I can never take back. I realized we all have a past. Some are good; others, we would like to forget.

Our past is engraved in our subconscious minds. We can't change it, but if we think long enough about our past, mistakes, and hurtful words we have spoken, they will pop up their ugly heads again, leaving us to think of things we don't want to remember. The Apostle Paul says, "…forgetting the things which are behind and reaching forth unto those things which are before" (Philippians 3:13).

I realize I can't go forward and look back at the same time, so I'm giving my past to God and purposely living out my future one day at a time to please Him. God truly blessed me with a man who loves my wonderful family and me, and I'll never cease to thank Him for blessing me to find my nephew, a spitting image of my brother.